EMMA MONIQUE – PROBLEM SOLVER
THE BUNCO SQUAD

NICHOLAS HUNTLEY

This novel and its series are dedicated to you, Emma, for the value of charity.

PART I: SEPTEMBER 1983

Part 1 – Chapter 1
Harlech Police Department – Jarsdel Division
Northton, Jarsdel Island
September 1983 – 01:00

In life, there is never an easy solution to a difficult problem without there being consequences for our actions or even lack of action. The complications of one action radiate around us, and the many and many actions of others bounce around and ricochet into other injuries of the body, and soul. No less is the case in the cities of this era, notably Harlech, an echo chamber where the vices of men and women have never been more poignant than ever before, to extend onto others the consequences of our failures. In these recent times, it has taken a greater man to be able to make the hardest choices and decisions in face of what may seem like an insane game where there is no resolution to that extensive spirit of malice present. In this city, some rise by sin, and others by virtue they fall. For some good men, they rise by virtue high enough so that the fall from sin can be so severe, as that spirit of malice knows no ends and lurks from the shadows by day and streets by night.

This novel is about men who sought to defy the system and refused to become a loser or slave. Kaj Julius Anders Kejsaren was an example of this sort of man, and unfortunately, he treated the battle as any great man – seeing it as the game it seemingly was, although not for its futility. This was a dangerous game, and in this one-sided play there were no means to deceive the deceiver, but only the use of wits and will to reach the end. You could either press on with persistence to attempt to win the game or give up and become a part of the system. The road to failure has many paths, while victory is said to have but one, and it was this path you aimed for. Kaj, understood the game because we had both been involved in it, while it only dawned on me in later life, because of denial of involvement, it convinces me to this day that there is no way to win against those demons. I was not as courageous as you to want to press on, to sacrifice, and to love as you did. However, even with this love, there came obsession. Perhaps, this obsession was out of love, for after all, you hated apathy. But you could never let go, Kaj, and you thought to make all the problems of the world your own; that fault was within you and not in the stars, and that is where we start, where the problems of this city were made our own.

Take for example now, this late night as you were with your former friend, Campbell Steele, on patrol throughout the streets of southern Jarsdel Island as the rain came down hard. Kaj looked ahead of him as he stood at the side of a police cruiser, dressed in the dark blue Harlech Police Department uniform. Kaj was a young, but experienced man with cold fair skin that was nearly pale white. He was tall, at six feet and one inch tall, and muscular at around two-hundred pounds. He had light strawberry-blonde hair, or a faded ginger, that was cut short, particularly on the sides with the hair extending an inch at the top. Around his chin, he had a neatly trimmed beard that stretched up to his sideburns. His eyes were light blue. The HPD uniform consisted of dark blue tactical trousers and collared shirt that were tied together by a duty belt that carried the essentials of Kaj's equipment, including a black handgun, the SIG Sauer P220, in a leather holster, a set of handcuffs, a baton in another holster, a can of pepper spray, a flashlight and a radio transceiver. The radio transceiver attached to a microphone speaker that was clipped to Kaj's shirt, almost hidden underneath his dark blue police jacket. The jacket contained the logo of the HPD on the shoulders and 'Harlech Police' on the back. The Ford LTD Crown Victoria police cruiser was white with the word 'Harlech Police' marked on both sides of the doors in blue font. Kaj had his hands in his pocket as he looked over to his co-worker and friend at the time, Campbell, who exited from the side exit of the Jarsdel Division and made his way over to the parking lot of the division headquarters.

"You're driving," Campbell said, tossing the keys to the Crown Vic. "My head still hurts."

Kaj caught the keys into his hands, catching it with ease. He wore a golden band around his ring finger on his right hand. Campbell came around to the passenger seat of the two-person vehicle. Kaj unlocked the car and entered in with him to sit down, ignited the engine, and pull out so that they could exit the precinct.

Campbell had dark fluffy hair and fair skin. He was unshaven with a stubble around his chin, and he wore glasses with a black frame. He had brown eyes and appeared to be as young as Kaj. They wore their uniforms in a similar way, but Campbell had his microphone attached to his shirt slightly differently. Campbell sat back while Kaj drove the cruiser out from the parking lot. The time on the dashboard read five minutes past one o'clock, an hour past the halfway mark of the shift.

Jarsdel Division was a medium-sized building in the heart of Lincoln, the metropolitan center of Jarsdel Island, and was a four-story tall rectangle that occupied an entire street block from North Slade Drive to Taghman Street. From the second story to the top floor, dark tinted windows occupied the entirety of the upper half of the walls while the lower half was constructed of a red brick. At the lowest floor, the windows were more sporadic, taller, and approximately seven feet above the sidewalks. The main entrance of the precinct, as Kaj drove past it as he made his way out, was on Taghman Street and consisted of a set of stairs that went upwards to the main doors that went inside. Jarsdel Division was one of three divisions in Harlech at this time, where the others were King Division at King Island, the main headquarters for the entire force, and the latter at Cliffe Division on Cliffe Island.

Kaj drove them away from Lincoln and into their patrol district, Patrol Four, via Slade Drive as they reached Northton. The rain continued to pour down hard. The car drove towards Caledonia Road and then proceeded westbound. Kaj drove them away from Northton and into their beat, which was the entirety of Harthdam between them and the rest of their squad.

"Hotel-Two-Twenty," dispatch said over the radio.

"Hotel-Two-Twenty," a woman replied over the radio.

"Hotel-Two-Twenty, we've received reports of a burglary in progress at the Goldman Pawn Shop on Walham Way and 8th Street. Suspect is described as a male in dark clothes, seen entering through the alleyway. Code Two."

"Ten-Four, Code Two."

"Hotel Two-Twenty-two copies, we're nearby" Campbell repeated.

"Hotel Two-Twenty-two, reports of a burglary in progress at the Goldman Pawn Shop on Walham Way and 8th Street. Suspect is described as a male in black clothes, seen entering through the alleyway. Code Two."

"Ten-Four, Hotel-Two-Twenty-two enroute," Campbell replied. "Finally, something…"

Kaj proceeded to drive towards Walham Street as he turned on Caledonia Street as they entered into Harthdam.

"We're hardly nearby," Kaj remarked, "besides, if you think this'll be a call that doesn't involve another homeless man, prepare to be disappointed."

"I don't care if it is," Campbell bitterly replied, "an offense is an offense, and I'm tired of acting as this city's glorified bouncers."

Kaj made his way onto Walham Way and proceeded towards 8th Street where he pulled into the alleyway next to the pawnshop.

"Hotel Two-Twenty-three," Kaj said over his radio.

"Hotel Two-Twenty-three," dispatch replied.

"Hotel Two-Twenty-three and Hotel Two-Twenty-two on-scene Goldman Pawn Shop."

"Ten-Four."

Kaj took the keys out of the ignition and stepped out of the vehicle with Campbell. The alleyway was short in length, going out to a parking lot in the back where there was a fence with a forest behind. The rain had settled down to a drizzle, and the headlights of their cruiser provided them with lights towards a side entrance that had been left ajar. Kaj took his handgun out of his holster and into his hands.

"I'll keep an eye on the entryway," Kaj said. "Take a look around the corner to check the perimeter."

Campbell went ahead with his own handgun drawn and came around to the corner of the building. Kaj went towards the door that was left ajar and took cover against the wall. He looked down at the floor and saw a crowbar had been left behind on the wet asphalt. He then looked over to the door frame where the wall had been torn near the door frame. Campbell motioned to Kaj that all was good and then moved forward to take cover at the other side of the door.

"This is the Harlech police!" Kaj announced. "Is there anyone in here?!" He then waited for a moment, but no response came.

Kaj took out his flashlight and took it into his hands to shine the way forward. He reached his hand out to push the door back so that he could shine the light inside. The flashlight revealed a pathway with wooden floorboards and wooden walls. Kaj led the way forward and entered into the corridor. On their immediate right was a closed door, while ahead the hallway led out to a clearing with a staircase that wrapped around and another closed door. Kaj went forward to check the rest of the hallway to ensure that it was clear, while Campbell lingered back and turned on his own flashlight to check the door near the entrance. Kaj looked around and saw a clutter in the open room with various foldable tables, filing boxes, and an arrangement of different objects that were stacked around.

Kaj took position at the base of the staircase while Campbell moved forward and took cover at the second closed door. Kaj was on the other side and continued to remain positioned at the stairwell. Campbell opened the second door and shined his light in. He walked in for a moment and then came back around. Kaj took a step forward and began to walk up towards the top of the stairs.

The second floor of the pawn shop revealed an office space with several more tables and shelves that contained an assortment of different items, electronics, books, and other items kept in boxes. Kaj looked around and lowered his handgun as he realized that the area had been vacated. The second floor was messy and Kaj observed that there was no visible damage anywhere.

"Damn," Kaj remarked, putting his handgun into his holster "the suspect must have bounced already. What did you see downstairs?"

"Nothing," Campbell replied, "it was all clear."

"Nothing?"

"No display cases shattered and nothing smashed," Campbell affirmed. "It was all clear."

"That doesn't make any sense…"

"Our guy probably got scared and ran off," Campbell responded, "you saw the crowbar at the door. Whoever phoned must have spooked him."

Kaj wasn't pleased with that response and continued to look around the messy room.

"I don't know," Kaj replied, "you go to the lengths to force your way in, and then you don't even take something?"

"Yeah, because he was spooked," Campbell insisted.

"Let's go back downstairs and take a second look around."

Kaj went downstairs with his flashlight shining ahead of him. He entered into the doorway that was near the staircase and came to the front of the shop where there were various display cases. Some of the cases displayed expensive jewelry, highly marked, but as Campbell had said, the cases were intact. Kaj shined his flashlight over to the cash register and saw that it was closed and didn't appear to be tampered with. He then looked over to the front windows that were barred and didn't see any visible damage to them. Kaj came into the back room and went around to the initial room from where they had entered from.

Kaj observed that this room was a bathroom, although dirty, there were nothing out of the usual in the room. Kaj stepped out and went back to the crowbar to observe it. He turned around as Campbell approached him.

"Well, let's call it in," Campbell replied. "I don't see anyone, and I don't see anything of value that was taken. All of the display cases are good."

"We don't know that for sure," Kaj dissented. "I mean, the Person of Interest is most likely gone, but we don't know what was here before he came around, and so we don't know if anything was taken."

"All of the display cases are fine," Campbell responded. "No jewelry has been taken."

"You assume that jewelry is the only thing here that there is to take," Kaj replied. "We didn't see where the safe was, or we don't know if there was something more valuable that could have been taken. The perp could have been anyone, and we don't know what he knows that's here."

"You're being ridiculous," Campbell remarked. "Fine, let's find the safe just to make you happy, and after that, I'll calling this in to clear us."

Kaj and Campbell walked upstairs to the office space and Kaj went around to the desk. He looked at the large desktop computer, a newer Neumann computer that was all the rage these days, and around the desk, there were some drawers that were closed. Campbell shined his light beneath the desk as the pair searched for a probable safe. Kaj observed that there was an assortment of papers on the floor. Campbell stepped atop of them as he went around to another desk in the corner of the room. Kaj picked up a small notebook near the computer and opened it.

Kaj skimmed through the pages and reached one that had a list of names with a particular amount of money next to them. The amounts were high, more than a hundred dollars. He looked at each name in the notebook and then sat down the book as he looked over to Campbell as he came around to the other side of the room. Kaj walked over as Campbell moved a painting from in front of a desk to reveal a safe.

Campbell squatted down to examine the safe. Kaj shined his flashlight at it and saw that it had not been tampered with nor was it open at the moment, but shut tight.

"There you go," Campbell said, standing up. "Come on, we're done here."

"I want to keep looking around," Kaj remarked, "there has to be something…"

"Why?" Campbell questioned. "We've reached our limits, and if there even was anything stolen, it's up to Investigative Services to determine. Let's type out our preliminary reports and move on. The suspect isn't here."

"Come on, you and I both know that Investigations have better stuff to do than look into something like this."

"I don't care," Campbell replied, "it's not our problem. We came, we saw, so let's get the hell out now before we get in trouble – you know how Sergeant Allard can be."

Kaj didn't respond for a moment as he looked around. He kept a frown on his face, sighed, and then turned to leave.

"Fine, let's go."

Kaj and Campbell came back downstairs and exited the building as another police cruiser pulled up into the alleyway. Kaj closed the door behind them while Campbell looked at who arrived. Kaj turned around afterwards and looked. The door opened as the car continued to run, and a woman stepped out in a similar police uniform to the two constables, but this woman had three chevrons on her arms. Sergeant Mary Allard was an older woman, in her fifties, with wavy golden blonde hair tied in a ponytail. Kaj and Campbell looked at her as she stood at the side of her and looked towards them.

"What have you got?" Sergeant Allard asked.

"Break and enter," Kaj responded, "but no suspect and no signs of any other damages than at the door."

"What about any stolen items?"

"Nothing that we could see," Campbell answered, looking to Kaj.

"It's possible that whoever broke in was here for more than just money or jewelry," Kaj asserted, "so we can't be entirely sure if anything was stolen."

"Well, if there wasn't any evidence that something had been stolen, then all we can assume is that nothing was taken," Allard stated. "We'll cordon the entryway, inform dispatch of what we found, and once a detective arrives, you can return to your patrol."

"Yes, ma'am," Kaj replied in a bitter tone.

Sergeant Allard re-entered her vehicle while the other two went to theirs and entered. She drove ahead, turned around and exited out. Campbell fetched the police tape while Kaj sat in the driver's seat and looked ahead in a blank stare. The rain picked up again and proceeded to storm down for the rest of the night, which left Kaj discontent with the rest of his shift.

Part 1 – Chapter 2
Problem Solver Inc.
Saffron, Jarsdel Island
September 1983 – 03:00

On the other side of the island, I remembered that I didn't even think about you as I attempted to maintain a business, but I hadn't forgotten about you, and I knew that you hadn't forgotten about me either. We may have split paths, but we didn't split our passions; to help others with our skills, and I was happy to hear that you had found your niche to exert that passion and help others in a way that was healthy for you, or so it seemed at the time.

I looked out of the window of my office and down towards the streets of Chinatown from where I operated from at this time. My office and home was small, but provided my own sanctuary from what lingered out on the streets, which took me on with despair. On a night like tonight where the rain poured, it seemed certain that there was no hope for this town, or so it seemed to me at this time as it seemed as if hell was empty, and all the devils were here.

The rain poured down and down, and with the neon lights that lit the surrounding neighborhood, the sound of sirens, and the shouts and screams below at three o'clock in the morning, I couldn't sleep, especially with the anxious thoughts that lurked in my mind. I simply sat atop of the window ledge and looked out towards the streets, one foot atop of the ledge and another slumped down so that the tips of my toes touched the hardwood floor. I was still dressed in my suit that usually consisted of a blouse, skirt, and leggings. Today, that was a mixed rose and beige blouse with a tanned skirt and similar leggings. I still had my straight strawberry-blonde hair in a ponytail. My green eyes were tired, and I had light freckles on my light fair-skinned face that was almost as white as snow. I held a cigarette in my small hands and blew smoke into the crack of the window above to avoid having that foul smell whose taste I enjoyed so much in my mouth pollute the room.

I looked away and towards my messy office, where the wooden desk that I worked from had piles upon piles of paper around, including unpaid bills, my typewriter with an unfinished report, and the desk lamp. To the right of my desk was a bookshelf with various books, some picture frames, and on the left was a lower bookcase with a fishbowl and some more familiar items that I took comfort in having placed in my office which was open to the public to come and see. I had my university degree framed and positioned above, highlighting my so-called achievement in the Faculty of Education. The degree listed my name, Emma Catherine Monique, the school, Declan Walham University, and the type of degree, a Bachelor of Education. I had spent four years that I shouldn't have wasted to major in a program that I had no interest in, for a career I had no business in. In the least my time spent on my minor in theatrical studies was enjoyed, but worthless, nonetheless. On the right of this lower bookcase was a door that went to the rest of my home. Around the corner was a coat rack with my tanned coat and fedora atop. The exit into the corridor was next to the coat rack, and next to the door was a couch from where clients could sit down. There was also a chair in front of my desk from where they could sit too. I looked back outdoors and continued to take in the rest of the cigarette.

Suddenly, the telephone on my desk began to ring and I jerked my neck towards it. I looked at the phone as it rang, contemplated if I should answer as my stomach filled with the butterflies I had just vanquished with this cigarette, so I decided to plug it into the ashes of the ash tray and lurch forward to pick it up.

"Emma Monique, Problem-Solver," I greeted. "How can I help you?"

"Hello, is this the private detective?" a woman on the phone said.

"Yes," I answered, "how can I help you?"

"I believe that my husband is cheating on me," the woman said. "I've seen him with this new co-worker, and he's been spending a lot of time away from home lately. Can you help me?"

A case that involved infidelity was all too common.

"Of course, what time would be best to book an appointment so that you can tell me more about this?" I asked, opening my agenda that revealed the empty week ahead of me.

"I don't have time to meet – he's not home right now, and I don't know where he is. He said that he went out to have dinner with some friends from work, but he hasn't returned yet. I need you to find him and catch him in the act – I phoned the credit card company, and he has a room at the Bradford Hotel. I phoned and have his room number – you need to go there now!"

"What kind of evidence are you looking for with this request? Pictures?"

"I need pictures of him with that woman, in the act," the woman stated. "I can give you whatever you need to pose as me so that they can give you an access card, and then I need you to go in his room and take pictures."

I frowned as I heard this request.

"I'm sorry, but I can't impersonate you," I explained. "I can search for your husband at the hotel, and even enter and go to the room to knock on the door, but it's illegal to impersonate someone, even if I have your verbal permission, and if I'm approached by security, I'm obligated to leave as I'd be trespassing."

"Well, then go there and find him – he's in Room 510 and he's in there with that bitch – I know it," the woman explained. "I need pictures of him with her – get me pictures. You need to break-in to that room somehow, or pose as a housekeeper – anything!"

I listened to the women's slurred words and gave a deep sigh.

"I'm sorry – I can't break-in to the room, the hotel, and I can't impersonate you, no less a housekeeper. I'm afraid I'm not the right person for this job, but if you'd like I can refer you to some other private investigators who may be able to assist…"

"You stupid bitch!" the woman shouted. "Screw you!"

The woman hung up and Emma listened to the dial tone before she slipped the phone down and back into its base. I gave another sigh and turned around to look out the window. From what I understood, opportunities in the face of poverty make criminals, and I wasn't going allow myself to sink to the level of a criminal to take on clients – that wasn't why I became a private investigator. I received a case like this every so often, especially ones where clients promised grand sums, but I didn't believe that it was worth the risk or the returns. All I could do was reject what seemed wrong to me, and continue to search for a case where I didn't have to compromise my principles. The drunken woman was just another compared to the various that I had deferred to other investigators and rejected, and it kept my business smaller than small, if a business at all.

I closed my agenda and set it to the side. I attempted to clean the clutter, but instead shifted the work into several disorganized piles before I decided to turn around and close the blinds so that I could finally retire for the rest of the night. I walked around my desk and entered into the second room of the office, which was my makeshift apartment home.

The room was approximately the same size as the commercial office, but converted so that I could live next to work as after all, my work was my life, even if it wasn't much. I had my bed on the left, a mini fridge to the right near a small table with the hot plate atop and some dishes and glasses behind. In the opposite corner, there was a white basin sink where I had my toothpaste and toothbrush on one side, and a bar of soap on the other. Near my bed, there was a mess of clothes, and atop of my mattress there was a contemporary book to read, pillow, and sheets drawn back. I had a window next to my bed, but the curtains and blinds were already drawn. A small table next to me held an answering machine that was connected to the telephone in the other room. I hit the button atop of the answering machine and caused it to play.

"Emma, it's me," my mother said. "I know you're busy with work, but I wanted to know if you wanted to come over for dinner some time. We haven't seen you in some time and both myself and your father miss you. Love from both."

I sighed as I walked over to the sink and washed my hands. I looked at myself in the mirror, pulled my hair down and brought it around my neck as I looked at myself.

"Hey Emma," a female said on the answering machine, "haven't talked to you in a bit. I wanted to know if you wanted to meet for lunch sometime in Central Harlech. Take care!"

The woman on the answering machine was an old friend of mine, Riley Vickery, from high school. I had been ignoring her calls lately because I was too occupied with work, or at least, my lack of work. I sighed and turned around as I held my hands at the sink. My parents were very supportive of my business, but I knew that they wanted better for me – for me to have gone into teaching and to have found someone to marry by now, but I wasn't interested in that right now. I was invested in my work. Riley supported me too, and she had what my parents wanted for me – a fiancé and a well-paying job with the courts. I didn't need a high-paying job or a fiancé, or at least, as it seemed to me.

A high-tailed mess of fur made his way towards me as I stood with my back to the sink, bringing its coat against my legs. I looked down at my cat, a grey Maine Coon mix, Bill, who was my sole companion. I untied my hair and then reached down to scoop my cat out and into my arms. I brought him over and sat down at my bed as I looked around at the emptiness within, and contemplated if this was worth it all in the end.

Part 1 – Chapter 3
Harlech Police Department – Jarsdel Division
Northton, Jarsdel Island
September 1983 – 07:00

Kaj and Campbell returned to the division headquarters in Lincoln in the morning as daylight extended to the island city, but the sun was denied an extension of its warmth and rays below. The deep grey clouds continued to dominate the skies and bring down a non-stop torrent of rain onto the city below as her citizens made their way to work, or for some like Kaj and Campbell, made their return to their homes. Kaj and Campbell left the car in the parking lot, returned to their patrol beat headquarters where their Staff Sergeant, Kilian Rosztóczy, was making conversation with Sergeant Allard in regard to the shift alongside Sergeant Smith, while the officers in Squad Three made their arrival and prepared for morning parade (briefing).

Once Kaj was off-duty, he went downstairs to the basement level to get changed in the locker room where various other officers in the Patrol Division were getting changed, showering, and making their way out. Kaj reached his locker towards the end of the room, opened it, and took out a large duffel bag that contained his change of clothes. He removed his jacket, put it inside, and then proceeded to take off his navy-blue shirt to reveal the ballistic vest underneath and atop of the white undershirt that he wore. Kaj hung his ballistic vest inside of his locker and proceeded to take off his pants to change them for a pair of light blue jeans. Kaj put his uniform into his duffel bag and took out a flannel to button up and tuck in. Afterwards, he put on a dark brown coat and proceeded to leave the locker room so that he could return to the parking lot where his personal car was, a dark red 1980 Ford Bronco.

Kaj stepped into the vehicle, ignited the engine, and then drove out of the parking lot so that he could make his way onto the streets of Lincoln. Kaj drove onto Slade Drive and went south into Northton and then came around into Lower Northton where there were some quiet suburbs of a different assortment of sheltered one-story houses, hidden from view by hedges, bushes and trees, and tall fences. The quality of the homes was poor and run down. Kaj came around to the most southern reach of the district where the houses shifted to two-story townhouses lined side by side with small yards in the front. Kaj pulled over and parked on the curb of the street.

The houses along the street were all similar in size, but different in color, where the one that Kaj had pulled up in front of was a greyish green. The yard was approximately three meters in length by five meters, and there was a concrete path that went straight to the steps of the porch and the front door. Kaj took his duffel bag out from the back of the Bronco, brought the strap down on his shoulder, and made his way to the front of his home as he held the strap of his bag in one hand and his keys in the other. The house lights were dimmed and quiet.

Kaj opened the door and entered into the small foyer where there was a set of stairs on the immediate left that went up to the top floor, and a corridor that led forward to the rest of the ground floor. On the immediate right there was a door that led into a side room. Kaj pushed through and reached the back of the house where there was an open kitchen and living room that was littered with various kid toys. The floor from the foyer to the living room was all a dark white carpet, but the kitchen was smooth linoleum tile. The top of the kitchen counters consisted of laminate, while the refrigerator was a white rectangular box. The stove ran with a pot that simmered water and cooked oatmeal. The large-reared CRT television set played an animated television show that he was not familiar with. Light poured in from the back sliding door window, especially as the clouds cleared and sunlight was able to shine down. The sliding door went to the small patio deck at the back of their house. Kaj entered the kitchen and living room with a wide smile on his face as he saw his wife in the kitchen and son in the living room.

"Papa!" Kaj's son shouted out as he entered.

"Hey, little guy," Kaj responded with a warm smile.

Kaj's son ran towards him, which caused Kaj to lower his duffel bag and scoop his son into his arms and lift him up. Kaj's son, Elias Kejsaren, was four-years old and looked much like his father, although his hair was lighter at this time and much longer, and his skin tone was warmer like his mother's, although both had fair skin.

"What have you been up to?" Kaj asked as he held his son in his arms.

Kaj looked over to the TV as his son showed him the stuffed animal in his hands of a cartoon dog, Scooby-Doo. The living room was messy with many green army men scattered across with toy tanks and such around too.

"Ah, I see," Kaj responded with a smile. "You've been watching cartoons."

"He just woke up only a couple hours ago," Kaj's wife said. "I've been trying to keep him away from those violent TV shows, but he seems to be gravitating towards them ever since my dad got those army men for him.

"No worries," Kaj replied. "It's okay. He's a smart kid."

Kaj looked over to his wife with another warm smile. His wife, Hannah, had straight light blonde hair and warm fair skin that had an orange hue. Her eyes were blue, like her husband and son, and she had a short stature. She was half a foot shorter than Kaj. Kaj gave his wife a kiss on the lips as she stepped towards him.

"Did you catch the bad guys today, papa?" Elias asked.

Kaj smiled and replied, "Oh, not today… almost one bad person, but nothing else." He looked to his wife and continued to say, "It was a slow night, not many calls in our beat."

"Well, I'd rather you have a bit of peace sometimes," Hannah responded. "I don't want you to put yourself in too much danger."

"It's fine," Kaj casually dismissed, "we've got each other's backs out there."

"Look, papa," Elias said as he pointed at the TV screen. "Scooby-Doo! He catches the bad guys just like you!"

Kaj carried Elias over to the couch and sat down. The TV displayed the television show 'Scooby-Doo, Where Are You!' as Scooby and Shaggy ran through an abandoned fairground. Kaj watched before it shifted to a commercial break, which coincidentally advertised a computer game for the same franchise.

"Wow, it's amazing how a children's toy line is now a TV show and a computer game," Kaj remarked. "Just goes to show how little I keep up with the rest of the world these days…"

The television returned to the animated TV show before he lost focus and looked at his son. Elias was deeply focused on the TV show, eyes lost into the screen as the antagonist was caught by the detective squad, and the scam of the antagonist was brought forward and he was taken away to jail. Kaj looked over to his wife as she stepped over.

"Are you going to have anything to eat before you sleep?"

"Hm, I don't think so," Kaj replied, "I think I'm fine for now. I'm done for the week, so I'll just have a nap and then stay up for the rest of the day."

"I'll take Elias to the supermarket with me so that we can give you some peace for the rest of the morning," Hannah said as she reached the kitchen and continued to stir the pot of oatmeal. "Are you sure you don't want anything before you go to bed?"

"No, I'm fine," Kaj insisted with a smile. "I'm just happy to be back home."

"Okay," Hannah replied. "Eli, come and have your breakfast. Leave papa alone so that he can get some rest. He's very tired."

"I want to stay with papa!" Elias complained.

"Eli, you've got to have your breakfast. Your papa is tired and need to rest."

"Don't worry, little guy," Kaj assured him. "I'll be right back, but papa has been up all night keeping the city safe for everyone and I need to sleep to recharge. Are you going to keep mommy safe for me while I'm gone for a few more hours?"

Elias nodded his head as Kaj sat him down at their dining table in front of the kitchen.

"Alright, I'll see you later, little man," Kaj remarked, pointing at him as he returned to the hall. "See you later."

Kaj picked up his duffel bag and came down the hall. He secured the lock on their front door and then came around to the top of the stairs to reach the small corridor that went back to Elias's bedroom immediately ahead of him, or the master bedroom towards the rear.

Kaj's home was small, but it wasn't the size of the home that mattered, because all that mattered were the people inside who made a place a home. For Kaj, and the earnings he brought to support his family, a home of this size was enough to give them both shelter and security. Kaj took his duffel bag and came into the master bedroom where he sat the duffel bag down in the corner.

The sheets of the bed were pulled back, but the blinds and curtains were still pulled in to cover the windows. The master bedroom had dark curtains to cast out any source of light, creating a void within the bedroom so that Kaj could sleep with ease. The queen-sized bed on the left was simple, nothing spectacular, and it immediately faced an elongated dresser with various shelves for both him and his wife. Around the corner there was a desk that Hannah used with a mirror, and around the other side there was a small closet with a door that went into the master bathroom, a small bathroom with a kitchen counter, shower, and toilet.

Kaj used the bathroom quickly and then exited to remove his coat and hang it on a hook on the back of the door. Kaj then came around to the dresser to get a pair of pajama pants out until he stopped to look at the pictures atop of the dresser. Kaj's favorite picture, taken four years ago, was of Kaj sat with his newborn son at Queen Victoria Hospital's maternity ward. The smile on Kaj's face was wide as he held Elias as he was a couple hours fresh from the womb. The picture had been taken not by Kaj's parents however, but Hannah's parents, or his in-laws. Kaj smiled at the picture and then looked over to the door of the master bedroom as he heard the creak of the floorboards and his wife appear.

"How was work?" Hannah asked again as they had some privacy from their son.

Hannah walked over and put her arms around Kaj's side. She gave him another kiss, this time on the cheek.

"Slow," Kaj confessed with a sigh, "but that's just how it is. Just another day of keeping this cities' homeless population in check…"

"You do your part," Hannah remarked, "and not every day is going to be like that. You've been with the force for six years…"

"Yeah..." Kaj replied as he held the picture, "and I like it a lot. I don't want anything else, because what I do... is good, in its own way. I couldn't be happier anywhere else... although sometimes I do wish that I could do a little more."

"You'll have those days too."

Kaj sighed, sat the picture down and then turned to his wife.

"This is the third time I've seen you looking at that picture," Hannah remarked. "If you want us to try for another, we can..."

"No," Kaj denied, "although I want to, and I really would like a daughter, we don't have the money for that... it's ridiculous how underpaid I am. I mean, I've been with the HPD for six years and after the third year, that's as much as I'll rake in. It's no wonder we're so short-staffed..."

Hannah didn't respond. She let go of her husband and Kaj calmed down as he raised a smile at her. Kaj put a hand on the pendant of her gold necklace, which held a small nugget of gold that Kaj had gifted her.

"I wish I could provide a little bit more for you and Eli, and also that daughter of ours... Grazyna."

"Someday you will," Hannah replied, "but for now, enough is enough."

Kaj sighed and responded, "I'm going to take a shower now and get some sleep. Do you need anything from the bedroom?"

"No, have a good sleep," Hannah said as she kissed her husband once more. "I'll see you later."

"Okay," Kaj replied, "also," he said before she left, "be careful with Elias and those violent shows. I mean, I know he's in this phase of army stuff, but I just wanted to know if we're both on the same page about it all."

"It's what he likes," Hannah simply replied. "I don't like it, but I don't want to upset him."

"Right... okay."

Hannah parted from Kaj and left so that he could rest from his twelve-hour shift. Kaj closed the door behind her and then returned to the bathroom so that he could take a shower. Once Kaj was finished, he exited the bathroom in his pajama bottoms and a grey t-shirt. He sat down in his bed and put his hands to his face, removing them and looking at the end table next to him where there was a picture of a woman. Kaj looked at her and the child in her arms, who appeared similar to Elias, but was not him. The picture was old, and the woman had golden blonde hair, warm tanned skin with hazel eyes. Her name was Grazyna, and she was Kaj's mother who had passed a few years before Elias was born and Kaj was married. He had no photos of his father, although he was still alive.

Alas, Kaj was a father himself and a husband, and learning from his father, he acted in an opposite manner as a man who was always present for both his wife and his son. Kaj looked up to the ceiling for a moment as he was quiet in his own thoughts, which I assume was in reflection to his past – a past he had left behind, a hardship he had learned from, and errors he hoped to never repeat. Kaj was his own man, and this was his home.

Several days later, I sat in my office as I finished the report for an investigation from the last week. I had recently completed an investigation into a motor vehicle accident for a client who believed that she was not being treated fairly by her insurance agency. The work was tedious and simple, but it provided with a minimum amount for me to get through to another week. Even then, I was late on this report, and it was a poor reflection on my business that I couldn't have put in more effort into something that was my lifeline. I didn't believe cases like this one to have been example in which I made a difference towards others, especially since it seemed as if there was foul play from both parties, my client, and the insurance agency involved. However, when it came to business, I had to defend the client, even if I believed that she was wrong, it was my duty as a vendor to provide the service that I promised for the cash return.

I stopped writing as I looked to the side. I blew some smoke and tapped my cigarette into the ash tray. I didn't like it, but it was the way of the world with business, and I had to oblige. Sometimes I would receive a case that I'd be interested in, but seldom as most of the cases were typical, trivial: thefts, tracking, and trial preparation. The most exhilarating case that I had my hands on was a case of identity theft, where a man had stolen the credit card and social insurance number of an elderly gentlemen. The case sent me on a chase throughout town in search of the suspect who I was able to catch in the act as he went out to Radloff, north of Harlech, where I was able to have local police apprehend the suspect. It was these small cases that I enjoyed to work on that helped ordinary people in this city, because I didn't want anything more than to make a smile on those around me with investigations that the police deemed too complicated or trivial to work on. Those cases left us private eyes to work on. However, all of that was rare to come by, but I had to be patient. I continued to write as I typed out the rest of the report and finished my cigarette.

Once I finished the report, I put together the entirety of the file and looked through it to ensure that it was all in order. I took time with my cases, not that I had time to lose – I had all the time in the world, and so I preferred to hand in something that was well done than rushed, no less if I was past the promised deadline. The client could be understandable at times, especially those that were unfamiliar with private investigators, while others were persistent and could be rude – these sorts demanded their deposits and refused to pay, but I never pursued a client to foot the bill. I simply let them off on their own, because I didn't impose onto others.

Suddenly, I heard a knock on the door as I finished proofreading the report. I was surprised to hear the sound at this time, although sometimes I would hear from a neighbor in the area, a friendly man in his late thirties who ran an accountant office nearby, but sometimes too friendly that I understood what his motives were, and that the hello was an attempt for more than just friendly chat. I understood it all too well, and so I couldn't think anything else when I saw him. His behavior repulsed me to think that men could think so low, but that was the way there were sometimes, not all of them, but most, especially men like him that seemed to run this act like it was some sort of con art. Perhaps, it was my experience to have met that one person who never expected that from me.

I looked towards the door ahead of me as the knock was heard again, and I hesitated to stand up from my desk and answer the door. The knocks were different than those from my neighbor, almost rhythmic and like a chime – they were polite. I decided to stand up and make my way around, but before I did, I made sure to put on my high heels as they were rested nearby. I walked over to the door and opened it to see who was on the other side, and sure enough, it was not my neighbor, but an elderly gentleman with a rectangular jawline and firm, thickish dark grey eyebrows over his blue eyes. He was of fair skin and had a wrinkled forehead that came up to his dark grey hair that was combed back and short. At the sides of his hair, it was whiter than the rest of his hair. He was clean-shaven and wore a dark grey plaid suit with a black vest and tie underneath with a white dress shirt. Overtop his suit he wore a black coat and in his right hand he had a briefcase with him while on his left he had a brimmed hat. The man had a straight and firm back, good posture, and appeared dignified as he stood in front of me.

"Apologies, madam" the man said in an English accent, "but I take it that you are Emma Monique, am I right?"

"Yes," I answered.

"Apologies again then, my dear," the man said with a chuckle, "but I wasn't so certain as to whether I should have phoned and made an appointment. My name is Patrick Harrington, attorney-at-law, and a client of mine had sent me to pursue your assistance with a serious matter. Did you mind if we had a moment to chat, or would I need to make an appointment? I hope that I'm not interrupting any of your work..."

"No, not at all," I politely responded. "Please, come in... sit down."

"Oh, thank you," Mr. Harrington said as he walked into my office. "I had a difficult time searching for your office, and it doesn't help that in this mess of Chinatown it is so very difficult to find parking."

I walked and offered Mr. Harrington a seat in the chair before his desk. He sat down and plopped his briefcase atop of his lap.

"Can I get you some coffee, or tea?" I offered.

"Oh, a cup please, yes," Mr. Harrington replied. "Yes, please."

I quickly opened the door into my apartment and went over to set the kettle on. I looked around for a clean mug to serve the tea in, and found the nicest one, a plain white mug that was barely nicked or chipped. I picked up the kettle, filled it with water, turned it on and then returned to the office to sit down.

"Thank you, my dear," Mr. Harrington said as he made himself comfortable. "I really am sorry for this timing, so I'll keep this brief, but your services were recommended to me, so I had to seek you out."

"Really? How can I be of service?" I asked, suspicious that I'd be recommended to someone.

"Well, it is quite a peculiar thing really," Mr. Harrington remarked, "you see, my client who I represent has had issues with his business because of what has been suspected to be the works of a 'hacker.' You see, I'm not too familiar with the details of such a thing as I hope you are, but my client's organization runs in tune with this newfangled computer system that interconnects all of the computers into what is called a 'network' by our systems manager. This network runs throughout the organization and should have been limited to those within the organization, or so we thought when one day there had been a breach from outside. According to our systems manager, a pseudonymous hacker had made his entry into the network, establishing himself within the network with this ominous handle, that is, the name that a person, or user in this network uses."

"What was the name?" I asked.

"Piato," Mr. Harrington answered.

"Piato?" I questioned, "interesting…"

"Yes, it is, and so when this handle was discovered in the user logs, our systems manager deleted it, but after a couple of days, we had another log in, but this time from a user of a person who had not been in the office for a couple of months. The account had been inactive you see, and somehow, someone had been able to access onto the network through this user. We believe these two incidents to be related, especially since it appears that this user had access to a collection of files that included confidential data that belonged to my client and is believed to have been accessed, and possibly stolen from my client's databases."

"One second," I remarked as I left to collect that tea.

I left the room and went to the kettle. I poured the tea into the cup with the tea bag and then returned the cup to Mr. Harrington. I rushed out with the cup in my hands, but I was negligent of the door behind me as Bill ran out the door.

"Darn, I'm sorry, he jumped out," I said, looking down at the floor as my cat got into the room and going over to grab him.

"No, that's quite alright," Mr. Harrington replied as he looked over to him. "What a precious boy you have there."

"Thank you," I remarked. "Did you want some cream or sugar with that?"

"Oh, I'm fine just black, if you'll please. I need to watch my intake of those two," Mr. Harrington remarked, causing me to leave and drop Bill off onto my bed.

I returned to the office and stopped as I looked at what Mr. Harrington had laid on the front of my desk in two neat piles.

"Now," Mr. Harrington said as he pointed to two stacks of banknotes with his cup while I went over to sit down at my desk. "The task is simple and straightforward: my client wishes for you to investigate this intrusion and find out what information was taken from his database, and if possible, to retrieve this information and assess the extent of the data leak. My client fears that if this information were to find itself on the black market, it could be a vital concern as he believes that the hackers were politically-minded. In return, I've been told to offer this precious sum, in advanced, to secure your expertise in this matter."

I looked at the money with discomfort.

"H-how much is that?" I asked.

"Four-thousand dollars," Mr. Harrington responded, "to start, of course. I know you have your hourly rates and all that, and my client is prepared to reimburse all costs, but he was firm that it shall be twenty percent at the start to secure your services, and then the rest at the end of the investigation, in cash.

"Twenty thousand?" I questioned with further unease.

I hadn't even made that amount as a sum of my entire career.

"I…"

"Is that enough?" Mr. Harrington asked. "if not, I could see about a bit more…"

"No, it *is* enough," I replied, in shock, "but… I… I don't believe that I can accept that, or this case for that matter. I mean, I'm familiar with the very basics of computer works since I studied it in university…"

"Ah, good!"

"… but I can't accept this sort of money, or this case, because… I don't think that I am the type of person that you are looking for with a case like this. I… I handle smaller cases, such as those that have to do with insurance fraud or thefts. What you're presenting to me now… it needs a lot more attention, a professional firm with a lot more private investigators at their disposal. Here, it's just me and me alone, and I don't think that I can handle a case this big."

"Well," Mr. Harrington responded as he sat back with his cup of tea, "my client believes that you are the best of the best when it comes to private investigators. In addition, given that you have a somewhat idea of these computation machines and that there are few in your field who do understand these sorts of things, I believe that you truly are the man – or woman I should say, for this job. My client's concerns were quickly dismissed by the Harlech Police Department," he said as he took a sip, "and even they have yet to keep up with this new science in computers and such, but at any rate…."

Mr. Harrington rummaged through his briefcase and produced a thick folder.

"I have here all that you should need to become familiar and up to speed with what my client's concerns are…" Mr. Harrington remarked, setting it on the desk as he set his cup of tea on the other side. "I also have some more papers here for you… just a moment."

I remained silent as I looked at the money, the thick folder, and then back at Mr. Harrington.

"Who is your client? Just out of curiosity?" I asked as I looked back at the folder.

Mr. Harrington looked towards me.

"I'm afraid that my client's identity is something that I will not be able to reveal to you, and it should offer no impact to the result of your investigation, but for security concerns, due to the nature of what is at stake, my client would prefer if him and his organization are not named during this investigation to protect the secrets that could be exposed. You'll find in most of these documents for there to be redactions here and there."

"Okay…." I quietly replied.

"Here we are," Mr. Harrington said as he put down another folder. "All of this should be what you need – emails, documentation on the intrusion, and some logs too. If you need anything, you can of course reach out to me whenever – I can provide my business card, but that will of course be dependent on whether or not you decide to take on this case."

I looked at the folders, the money, and then Mr. Harrington. I had no idea who this man was other than the fact that he was a lawyer who seemingly represented a very wealthy client, most likely an industrialist as I'd never expect anyone from the public sector to reach out a low life like me. I wasn't sure who this client could have been for me to have been recommended to take this case, but I had met several people in my time as a private investigator and it could have been anyone who I had impacted in a positive manner to now be met with this opportunity.

I didn't know what implications this investigation would have, but this man, Mr. Harrington, did say that there were possibly politically-minded groups involved and possible information taken from the client. What was stolen? Weaponry of some kind? Banking information? I didn't have any clue, but it seemed interesting, especially since I really was slightly familiar with computer science. I pulled the folder my way and set my hands on it – I looked over to Mr. Harrington and then skimmed through what was inside, and none of it seemed too complicated for me to understand.

Once I had finished skimming through the contents, I looked at Mr. Harrington again and said, "I'll review this information you have for me and assess whether I can commit to this investigation. I don't want to give an answer for something that I cannot promise to resolve, so I'll reach out to you tomorrow morning with a definite answer."

"Excellent," Mr. Harrington responded, taking out a notepad and pen. "If you decide to take on this investigation, please do not hesitate to simply jump on board because time is of the essence and the more we wait, the more likely this classified information lands in the hands of dangerous criminals in our world. Here," he said, writing on the notepad with his pen, "you'll want to speak with my client's systems manager who works from this address."

I set the file aside and then took the note. I looked at the information and my eyes widened as I recognized the name.

"Paul Schmidt?" I asked. "I know him. We went to high school together and graduated in the same year. He was a good friend of mine."

"Well, it should be well that your paths cross once more for this important moment," Mr. Harrington said as he stood up and sat the cup of tea down. "Mr. Schmidt should be able to get you to speed with what has been happening, and he will also be available to assist you with any technical details that I have not yet provided. If you have any other questions, please feel free to reach out to me, and I will be in touch as well."

I stood up as Mr. Harrington appeared as if he was about to leave.

"Oh, and before I forget, there should be another man that you meet, but you will have to find him elsewhere as he works all around. Here…"

Mr. Harrington set the money aside and opened his briefcase atop of my desk. He took a note and passed it to me.

"He is a former colleague of my client who is owed a favor or two, and he'll be instructed to provide you with relevant information," Mr. Harrington remarked. "You'll need to reach out to him in order to set up a meeting of some sort. At any rate, I do hope that you decide to take on this investigation, although I do trust that you will make that right decision if my client has had anything to say about you, it is that you were the right woman for the job."

"Thank you…" I replied.

Mr. Harrington put on his hat and said, "Take care now," before he left out the door.

I glanced down and noticed that Mr. Harrington had left the money behind, as if he really did expect for me to take the case, and it unsettled me that so much money had been left behind on my desk for a case that I was so uncertain of. I sat back down and leaned back.

"With that much money, I could pay my rent for the rest of the next couple months..." I whispered to myself before I picked up the files again, "but I'm one person. I can't do all of this on my own..."

I looked at the contact information for my friend Paul, and with hesitation, I pondered if I would allow myself to be dragged into such a wide investigation, but I knew that the answer was obvious. I needed to review the files and speak with Paul to get his insight into what he believed to be going on. However, before I met with Paul, I wondered if perhaps I should rendezvous with this informant that Mr. Harrington had told me about because he may have information that could be useful before I met with Paul. I decided that I would think through my decision carefully because I had never been put in a position like this one, and I wasn't entirely confident that I could be of assistance. I also thought about who this client could have been, because whoever it was, he had confidence in me, and perhaps that was confidence I needed to share so that I could take on what was obviously a case of a lifetime.

The next day, Kaj was on patrol with Campbell throughout Harthdam in the early morning of the end of the week when the rain had stopped, but the clouds remained in a patchwork of light grey. The two were in the southern part of Harthdam, also known as South Harthdam, where crime was worse on the island, and the development seemed to have stopped and reversed. This part of the district was in decline and decay, and it was the prime location for all the island's homeless, unemployed, and for criminal gangs to thrive in recent years. However, South Harthdam was nothing in comparison to the worst neighborhood, Keswick, on the north island known as King Island as that district was the haven for scum, criminals, and worse, who preyed on the weak, the homeless, and the vulnerable, and recent years had attracted the attention of drug vendors and addicts. There was no hope for Keswick, but at least there was a bleak promise yet for old South Harthdam.

"Did you hear that the police commissioner resigned?" Campbell said to Kaj as he drove through the city centre.

"No," Kaj replied.

"Apparently he was caught out on allegations of embezzling money from the department and so he was forced to resign," Campbell explained. "I read about this morning in the paper – how come we haven't heard anything about it from within the department?"

Kaj shrugged and said, "I don't really care about what goes on above our heads."

"You should," Campbell replied.

"Why? I'm sure there's a lot more that goes on above our heads, so why should I care about it when I can't do anything about it? I'm just a patrolman looking to earn my miserable salary from month to month so that I can feed my family. I don't give a damn about something that I can't change."

"I've never complained about how much we earn. I think we earn enough."

"Maybe you think that," Kaj deflected, "but at the same time, you don't have a wife and kid to support. All you do is go home, play computer games, and get drunk."

"Why would I want anything more?"

"You do whatever you want with your life," Kaj remarked. "So who's the commissioner now?"

"The deputy commissioner," Campbell responded, "Newton Mackenzie. He's the acting commissioner until they find someone else. Apparently he's one of the oldest members of the police force; around since the 1940s. I heard from my brother that he's great and could have been commissioner a long time ago, but refused the role."

"Wait a minute…" Kaj replied. "isn't your brother pretty up there with Investigations? Did he tell you about the embezzlement scandal?"

"No," Campbell answered, "I told you I read about it in the paper. He's just told me about Mackenzie before."

"So how come he hasn't told you about what happened to the former commissioner?"

Campbell shrugged and replied, "We don't really talk."

"So, you don't talk to your parents *or* your brother?"

Campbell didn't reply.

"Sorry," Kaj said as he continued to drive. "I know what it's like… especially with the older brother."

"I thought your older brother was dead."

"Yeah, but before he died, we seldom spoke – it was tumultuous, which made the experience all the more harder. As for my parents, you know my mom is dead too, but my dad isn't. We haven't spoken to each other in years."

"Hotel Two-Twenty," dispatch said over the radio.

"Hotel Two-Twenty," Sergeant Allard replied.

"Hotel Two-Twenty, Delta Five-Two is requesting patrol officers to attend for a shooting at Harthdam Way and 19th Street. Requesting assistance for an evidence search. Code Two."

"Ten-Four, evidence search at Harthdam Way and 19th Street," Sergeant Allard repeated. "Hotel-Twenty-two?"

"Hotel Twenty-two," Campbell replied via his radio mic.

"Hotel Twenty-two, can you and Hotel Twenty-three attend the evidence search at Harthdam Way and 19th Street?

"Copy, evidence search, enroute," Campbell responded. "What a waste of our time... Isn't that for criminalistics to do?"

"Typically, yes," Kaj replied, "except when they're overloaded."

"So what if they're overloaded?" Campbell complained.

"Come on, let's just get this over with – it'll take only a couple minutes."

Kaj drove their patrol cruiser through South Harthdam to reach the location of the shooting at Harthdam Way and 19th Street. Once they arrived, Kaj pulled over at a curb and parked the car. He turned off the engine and then got out of the cruiser while Campbell announced their arrival to dispatch to mark them on scene. Kaj looked around Harthdam Way where there were various shops and small businesses around, but the street was mostly quiet as it was still early morning.

Campbell walked towards the entrance of an alleyway between 19th Street and 18th Street where there were some barriers and a police line where there were two other members from their squad who were posted at the entrance of the alleyway. Kaj and Campbell had heard about the shooting in this area during their morning parade as it had occurred during the night shift, and these two members in his squad were the unlucky two that had relieved the other officers from the night shift as Investigations continued to review the crime scene. Campbell walked over to the officers, Constable Leiffsen, who was a young female, same age as Kaj and Campbell, with golden blonde hair tied in a bun and tanned fair skin, and Constable Arciaga, who was likewise the same age as the two, a young Filipino male with neatly trimmed black hair and dark skin.

"Hey," Kaj greeted, "what's going on?"

"Oh, you know, just another shooting. Detective Pearson is the officer in charge and was looking for help with searching for evidence," Constable Leiffsen said. "You should ask him what exactly he wants you to do. We're just here providing access and waiting for the coroner to show up"

"Sure thing," Kaj replied, looking over to Campbell who was stood at attention so much that it caused his back to arch and chest to puff out.

Campbell and Kaj walked into the crime scene.

"There's no need to be standing like a complete idiot when you're around her," Kaj said in a hush to Campbell as they walked in. "You're not in the army anymore."

"I served for five years, show a little respect."

"I served as well, but neither of us saw any combat, so get over it," Kaj snapped. "You're behaving worse than my three-year old with this military phase he's going through thanks to my father-in-law."

"Good, at least he'll push himself somewhere better than policing."

Kaj glared back at Campbell and replied, "So he can die in some war-torn country for a less than noble cause? No thanks. The sooner my kid is over with this stuff, the better..."

Kaj and Campbell reached the crime scene where there was a corpse on the alleyway floor, lifeless, but remnant of former life. Kaj looked at the man with a displeasing glance, eyeing before him what used to be a human being. The appearance of a corpse always hit differently, for me at least, I could see the life that was missing from once an animated body that was now nothing more than a disunion of tissues and cells, starting its decay. In case you, the reader, have had the privilege to never see a corpse before, a corpse didn't look like a human being at all. In fact, they looked like a wax figure, and I suppose both of them had as much life in one as the other, aside from the microflora inside that now eating at the remains. Kaj and Campbell looked down at the body and then over to Detective Pearson as he appeared.

"You two my backup?" Detective Pearson asked.

Detective Eric Pearson was a middle-aged man with short dark hair in a buzzcut and a thick moustache across his upper lip. He had dark eyes and a tall nose. He held a plain expression on his face and spoke in a deep tone with a Yorkshire accent.

"Yes, sir," Kaj replied. "Constable *Kejsaren* and Constable Steele."

"Good," Detective Pearson responded. "We had a shooting at approximately 0550 hours, and the victim is this low-life with an extensive criminal record. I have just about all that I need, and I'm almost done here, but support services has been short-staffed this morning and so I'm going to need you two to collect any evidence you see and turn it in to the criminalistics lab at King Island."

"Do you have any idea who did the shooting?" Kaj asked out of curiosity.

"No idea," Detective Pearson responded, "I'm only getting started, but from what I've been able to gather, it's most likely gang-related. The coroner has been running a bit late as well, but should be around to pick up the body so be mindful of that. I'll be around for another few and then I'll be off, so I'll see you lads then."

Detective Pearson walked off as he held a notebook in his hands and continued to take notes. Kaj looked at him and then continued to look down at the body.

"Doesn't it seem like there's a shooting every week at this point?" Campbell asked.

"Yeah, but luckily nobody innocent is getting hurt," Kaj remarked as he looked at the corpse of the man in front of them.

The body of the victim was that of a stocky middle-aged male with cold light brown skin, greasy long black hair that was combed back and ran up to his neck, and thick black eyebrows. He was clean shaven and had dark eyes that looked upwards to the sky above. The male wore a white suit with a pink dress shirt without a tie and the top buttons poking out. The victim had a gunshot wound on the right-side of his abdomen, just below the chest, which was where his right hand had come to rest as it must have been applying pressure to the wound as the victim lay on the ground. The other hand and arm was at the left side, parallel to the torso. The victim also wore white shoes that matched the suit.

Kaj studied the corpse and then looked around the crime scene at where markers had been placed with the evidence that had already been discovered, such as a few bullet cases, a streak of blood, a bloodied knife nearby, and of course the body of the deceased. Kaj put on some leather gloves so that he could handle the evidence around him and then went to retrieve some plastic evidence bags from their cruiser so that they could start to collect the evidence.

By the time that Kaj returned with the evidence bags, the detective had disappeared as did most of the support crew that had been around, which left only Kaj and Campbell at the crime scene and the Leiffsen and Arciega at the very beginning of the alleyway. Campbell proceeded to drop the bullets into a bag while Kaj went to retrieve the knife. Kaj picked up the knife and put it into the sealable bag before he looked at where the bullets were and then the streak of blood, which was before the knife, but after the body and corpse. He thought for a moment and then picked up the knife, which was near a dumpster. Kaj put the knife into the bag and then carried it over to give it to Campbell.

"Well, this has been a waste of time," Campbell repeated. "At least we can get out of here."

"Not so fast," Kaj responded. "Let's make sure we've got all of it, huh? Take this stuff back to the car and I'll take a look around."

"Sure."

Kaj looked as Campbell walked off before he went over to the corpse and looked down at the victim. Kaj took a step closer and began to examine the corpse, starting with the face, and then reaching down to the torso where the gunshot wound was. He picked up each hand, examined them, and then set the right hand down so that it was on the side like the left, and then began to open each sleeve of the blazer to look inside. He felt around for a wallet of some kind, but couldn't feel it anywhere. Kaj examined the gunshot wound and then stood up as he left the body alone. Kaj looked down towards the end of the alleyway, which led to a three-way intersection where there were police barriers on either side. Kaj proceeded to walk towards the intersection as he went to the dumpster at the corner, stopped, and then dropped down to look beneath the dumpster where he saw a thick-sized wallet hidden underneath. Kaj reached in to retrieve the wallet before he stopped moving as he heard some mutters come from around the corner. Kaj looked ahead of him and then quietly stood up so that he could come around to the corner while he held the wallet in his hands.

Kaj listened carefully and could hear the voice of Detective Pearson, so he peaked around the corner and saw the detective with his back turned towards him as he was speaking with another unknown person who wore a trench coat and brimmed hat. Kaj couldn't see the face of the person that the detective spoke with as he was stood directly in front of this person. He also couldn't hear the voice of this person as they spoke quietly and the detective's car, which was right beside him with the engine running, muffled out this person's voice. Kaj saw the detective pass a folder to the person in the trench coat.

"You should have all that you need here," Detective Pearson said. "All that the police department has is in these files."

Kaj took a step back and breathed quietly as he continued to listen for further chatter, but it was quiet for brief moment, perhaps as the other person spoke. Kaj wasn't entirely certain.

"If you need anything else, you have my number," Detective Pearson remarked.

Kaj heard the footsteps of the detective, which prompted him to move silently away and then turn around in anticipation for the detective to return, but he didn't. Instead, Kaj heard the detective's car door shut and then for the car to roll off as he left the crime scene. Kaj peaked back around the corner to see if he could see the person that he had been talking to, but the stranger was gone before he could get a proper look. Kaj came back around to the rest of the crime scene as he held the wallet of the victim.

Campbell returned and saw Kaj looking through the wallet. Kaj read the driver's license of the victim where the name identified him as Eldon Hearne, with an address at Shai Street in Chinatown. Kaj looked at the rear pouch to see if there was any money, which there wasn't, and then he looked to see if there were any credit cards, which there were. Kaj also managed to find a business card with the victim's name on it, providing his job title as General Manager with Neumann

Developments & Computer Repair Shop at 13th Street in Harthdam. Campbell looked at what Kaj was looking at and then looked at him.

"You see? I found this gem underneath the dumpster, which was totally overlooked by the detective," Kaj remarked. "I now have his name, residence, and place of work."

"Detective probably already knew all of that," Campbell replied. "He said that this guy had a record, so he must have been well-known to Investigations."

"I hope for his sake that he does know," Kaj said, putting the wallet with all its items into an evidence bag. "Otherwise, he won't find this to review for a couple of days when it might be too late. He'll probably make his way to the victim's residence if he has any sort of initiative. The thing is that I know this guy – or at least, I knew him from when I was in high school. Even back then he was a low-life scum, so I suppose not much has changed. I swear that if he was killed, it was probably because he rubbed the wrong person the wrong way. I bet you that if we go to his work, we can find some sort of hint or clue. A majority of murders are done by someone with some sort of connection to the victim, and the detective won't be there any time soon. If we let whoever shot this man wait for the detective to come around, he'll have left town before he could have known it."

"Are you crazy? You're going to get us in trouble with the sergeant."

"What did we come here to do? We were requested to attend for an evidence search, so as far as I'm concerned, this is a continuation of that request, but at a different location. Come on, we're done here, and it won't hurt to pay this place a visit."

"Alright, but if the sergeant asks what we're doing, you're explaining all of this to her and I'm saying that I couldn't stop you."

"Sounds like a fair deal."

Part 1 – Chapter 6
13th and Higgins Street
Harthdam, Jarsdel Island
September 1983 – 09:00

Kaj and Campbell left the crime scene and drove to the address of the computer repair shop, which was nearby on the other side of South Harthdam.

"I don't know what you expect to find at this shop," Campbell said. "I'm telling you, this guy was shot dead because he had some sort of gang affiliation; maybe some unpaid debt or competitive drug dealing."

"No," Kaj denied. "Eldon was scum, but he wasn't a drug dealer. From what I remember, he was a professional thief and a fraudster. If I had to guess too, I'd say he rubbed some wrong people the wrong way. To be honest, I'm surprised he's made it this far, but after all, he was sneaky – he could evade police for who knows who long, but I guess even legends die."

"Legend?"

"Well, not so much of a legend…" Kaj replied.

"How did you say you knew him? You said he went to your high school?"

"No," Kaj denied, "I said I knew him from when I was in high school – when I was sixteen."

"And? How did you meet him?"

"I don't really want to talk about that right now. I didn't like him and couldn't care less that he's dead, but I am interested to know how he died, or who it was that killed him."

"Alright."

Kaj drove to the front of the computer repair shop at 13th Street and Higgins Street. He parked the car in front of the shop, turned off the engine, and then came around to the sidewalk to look towards the two-story building where the computer repair shop was on the ground floor with a barred display window that showed the inside of the shop. Kaj stepped towards the entrance, pushed the door open causing the ring of a bell to announce their entry, and then looked around the entry room of the shop.

The shop consisted of a grey carpet with industrial shelves in the middle, holding various computers of different makes and models, but the majority of which were this new make of computer that had been released in the last year, the Neumann Machine. The Neumann Machine was a large computer with a disc drive beneath a thick monitor almost as big as a CRT television, but with a smaller screen. At the disc drive, the logo of the brand, Neumann, was marked in chrome cursive letters. In the year since their release, they had become one of the most popular personal computers in North America and Europe, and they were quickly becoming popular for use in the workspace due to their simple operating system that anyone could comprehend. For this reason, they marketed themselves as an invention for the 'New Man.' Along with computers, there were also computer parts littered around on the shelves. At the rear of the shop there was a display case that contained further parts behind a lockable case. The display case was also where the cash register was, and behind there was a countertop with various other computers, and then a doorway in the midst that went into a back room with various other shelves, and also a staircase in between that went to the second floor.

Kaj and Campbell entered and approached the cash register where a store associate appeared upon their announcement by the bell that they had arrived. The store associate wore everyday clothes, a salmon-colored t-shirt and cargo pants. He was a slim person with fair skin and light brown hair. He had a narrow face and was bucktoothed to a degree as the front of his teeth could be seen through his plain expression. It didn't help that his upper lips were curled. Kaj and Campbell stood together in front of him, and he looked at them without any intrigue.

"Hey," Kaj greeted, "I'm Constable Kejsaren and this is my partner, Constable Steele. We're investigating a case that involves your manager, Mr. Hearne, and we're wondering if we can speak with the supervisor in charge for a few questions."

"Mr. Hearne is in charge here..." the man replied with a lisp. "I don't know who else you'd want to talk to..."

"Do you have any sort of assistant manager, or any other team lead?" Kaj asked.

"Hm... maybe..." the store associate said. "One second..."

The store associate left and went upstairs. Kaj glanced over to Campbell who simply kept his hands at the sides of his duty belt as he looked down and waited. A couple seconds passed by until it was a minute, and then finally the store associate returned, alone, and approached Kaj and Campbell.

"Nobody upstairs is really in charge of the store..."

"What about Mr. Hearne's boss? Who does he report to?" Kaj questioned.

"Nobody," the store associate answered. "This is a franchise, and Mr. Hearne runs stuff around here with a license from the Neumann Corporation."

"Interesting... What about you? Can I ask you some questions about your boss?"

"Hm, I don't think I should..."

Kaj sighed and lowered his expression to less of a friendly one and more of a bored one.

"Look," Kaj said, putting his hands on the display case, "I know Mr. Hearne has had his run-ins with the law, but he isn't in trouble. In fact, this matter concerns his welfare. I only want to ask a couple of questions about him for his own safety."

"Okay..."

Kaj took out his notebook and held a steel pen in his hand.

"Can I start with your name?"

"Sheldon, sir," the store associate answered. "Sheldon Jones."

Kaj wrote the person's name down, and then asked, "What's your birthday?"

"January 31st, 1959."

"How long have you known Mr. Hearne?"

"Since last year," Sheldon answered. "I started in May last year."

Kaj wrote down this detail and asked, "When was the last time that you saw your boss?"

"Last evening, at around 5 PM when I left," Sheldon replied in an anxious tone. "Are these questions going to take long? I have a lot of work to do."

"Shouldn't take more than a couple of minutes," Kaj responded in a calm tone. "How has business been?"

"Busy," Sheldon answered. "We've had a lot of computers turned in for repair, and I have a lot of work to do with the other techs."

Kaj wrote down this detail and then looked back at the sales associate.

"What do you do here?"

"I'm a technician and I also run sales downstairs," Sheldon replied.

"Where did you study?"

"CIT."

"When you saw Mr. Hearne yesterday, did he say anything about where he was going or what he was doing after work?"

"No..." Sheldon replied in a dismissive tone.

Kaj raised an eyebrow as he looked at the tech.

"We know that wherever Mr. Hearne went after work, it resulted in him getting into some trouble with some people," Kaj stated. "We need to know where he went so that we can know what happened to him."

"What? Is he okay?"

"Answer the question," Kaj requested.

"Eldon said that he had some business to attend to with some old friends," Sheldon clarified. "That's all I know."

Kaj wrote this detail down and then asked, "What friends?"

"Old friends," Sheldon simply said. "He didn't say anything more – I don't know who it was, or where he went."

"Do you know anyone that might have wanted to hurt or harm your boss?" Kaj asked.

"No," Sheldon plainly responded, "I don't. Should I be worried?"

"No," Kaj replied as he closed his notebook. "You may have a detective attend later today, or this week, but that's all the questions I can think of right now. Do you mind if we look around?"

"Only if you tell me what's happened to my boss."

Kaj looked at Campbell and then looked at the tech as he replied, "I'm afraid I don't have the authority to tell you what happened – a detective will be around for that, but we just want to look around so that we can the Person of Interest behind all of this. Does Mr. Hearne have an office here?"

"Yeah, it's upstairs…"

"Thanks," Kaj replied, "we'll only be a moment. If we have any more questions, we'll come find you."

Campbell and Kaj came around the countertop desk and followed the tech up the set of stairs to the top floor where there were various desks and tables with computers lined around. At the back of the room from the right of the stairs there was a room with a closed door. The tech opened the door and allowed them to enter. Campbell and Kaj stepped in and looked around.

The office was small and messy, and there were lots of papers scattered atop of the desk, which had its own Neumann Machine, but an older model. Behind the desk there were two filing cabinets, one that had contained two wide drawers and another that had three wide drawers with a printer atop. To the left, there was a foldable table with various storage file boxes. The floor consisted of the same carpet as the rest of the store below. There was a foldable chair in front of the desk and then a simple black office chair behind the desk.

The technician stood at the doorway while Kaj and Campbell stood inside the office. Kaj turned to the tech.

"We'll take a moment as we look around for any clues," Kaj said. "I don't want to keep you waiting for us."

"Okay…"

The tech left and Campbell went to the door and closed it. He then turned to Kaj.

"We shouldn't have come here," Campbell whispered. "We're out of our depth."

"We're not doing anything wrong," Kaj argued. "We're just doing our due diligence – it's not like there's anything else going on."

"What? You think that nerd killed this guy?"

"No," Kaj responded. "I don't know who, but we're slowly starting to piece together what possibly happened. I'm going to look around to see if I can find anything else that might be of value. Just stay at the door because I don't want that guy to come back and see what we're doing."

Campbell opened the door and stood underneath the doorframe so that he was both in the office and within the vicinity of the rest of the staff. Kaj proceeded to shuffle through all of the papers, looking at bills, invoices, and other technical documents that didn't mean anything to him.

"Did you see how many computers they had around here? I was thinking about getting the newer one, but I think I just changed my mind. You don't usually hear about stuff like this," Campbell remarked. "I wonder what's wrong with all of them."

Kaj paused for a moment as he looked at Campbell, didn't respond, and then continued to shuffle through all of the papers.

"No agenda," Kaj remarked, "I suppose it was optimistic to believe that someone like Eldon Hearne was organized."

"You were optimistic to think that coming here would offer any sort of revelation," Campbell bitterly whispered to him. "Hurry up."

Kaj continued to rummage through all of the papers, going around to the top of the filing cabinet where there were some more invoices. Kaj found a newspaper underneath some of the invoices and dug it out to see that it had been folded to show a specific article from the *The Harlech Herald*, also known as *The Herald*, which was a national newspaper company. He read the title of the article, which said, 'Latest Neumann Machines struck with computer virus,' and he skimmed through the short excerpt that explained a trend with the latest model of Neumann Machine computers that had become infected with a common computer virus that was circulating around the Internet. Kaj lowered the newspaper and then continued to look around, checking the shelves in the filing cabinet, but only seeing various folders with more invoices, and then looking through the shelves of the desk, but not finding anything of significance.

Kaj finally returned to where Campbell was and said, "Alright, I don't think there's anything of value here."

"Told you."

Kaj and Campbell exited the room and went to the top of the stairs.

"We're all done here. If we have any more questions, we'll be in touch," Kaj said, waving to the tech.

The tech didn't respond and the two quickly went downstairs to the ground floor of the shop where they quickly left and returned outside.

"I told you that was a waste of our time," Campbell said to Kaj from outside. "Let's not include that in our report – we didn't find anything related to the murder here, and if sergeant or that detective finds out that we were snooping around the murder victim's place of work, we're both going to get disciplined."

"We can't lie in our report," Kaj responded.

"So, you want us to get in trouble?"

"No," Kaj denied, "but it doesn't mean we have to include that we went to the repair shop. Let's just say that we picked up the evidence, found a wallet, and that we returned the items to criminalistics. I avoided telling the guy that his boss was murdered, so hopefully that's enough to avoid comprising the actual case if that detective ever chooses to visit this place." Kaj paused for a moment as he looked to the side. "I still want to visit this dude's place of residence, and if possible, do a search with dispatch for any prior addresses."

"You're nuts, man."

Kaj glared at him and then brought a hand to his mic.

"Hotel-Two-Two-Three," Kaj said over the radio.

"Hotel-Two-Two-Three, need an address check on a male suspect, last name Hotel-Echo-Alpha-Romeo-Echo. First name, Echo-Lima-Delta-Oscar-November. Birthdate: August 11th, 1950."

"Ten-Four, Hotel-Two-Twenty-three. Please stand-by for Ten-Twenty-nine," dispatch responded.

Kaj and Campbell waited a brief moment.

"Hotel-Two-Twenty-three," dispatch replied. "Last known address for suspect, last name Hotel-Echo-Alpha-Romeo-Echo, and first name Echo-Lima-Delta-Oscar-November, is 15868 Bennett Street, Unit #3, in Keswick District."

"Ten-Four," Kaj responded before looking over to Campbell. "Come on, both Chinatown and Keswick are on the way. We're going to have to ask Allard for permission to leave the island anyways to return this evidence, so may as well make the most of it."

"Whatever, dude," Campbell replied. "Just hurry up so we can make it to lunch."

Campbell and Kaj entered the police cruiser and began to drive towards Caledonia Street so that they could leave Harthdam and head towards Chinatown. Kaj drove into the heart of Northton and then turned left onto Bering Street, going into Lincoln and then around the roundabout at the city center to come out onto Shai Street and head north towards Shai Street. Campbell and Kaj stopped in front of 52 Shai Street, which was a brownstone townhouse lined up at the outskirts of the district.

Kaj drove past the house as there were various vehicles parked on the curb and not enough space for him to park, so he turned right on Lim Street, drove around and then came back onto Shai Street to simply stop the vehicle in front of the house. Kaj exited the vehicle, followed by Campbell as they went to the front steps of the house.

"What do you expect to find exactly?" Campbell questioned.

"Anything," Kaj responded, "maybe he has a wife, or a girlfriend with him. If there's nobody home, we won't bother."

Kaj knocked on the front door and waited for someone to come around. A couple minutes passed, and there was no response. Kaj knocked again and waited, but again, there was no response.

"Nobody home," Kaj simply said. "Come on, let's head over to King Island and see this other address in Keswick. After that, we'll head to the precinct and drop off the evidence."

Campbell didn't respond, but followed Kaj back to the car. They entered and drove off, driving to the end of Shai Street and turning left onto Burnes Drive. From Burnes Drive, Kaj drove west towards the highway, merging on and driving over the Henley River.

"Hotel-Two-Twenty-two," Campbell said over the radio.

"Hotel-Two-Twenty-two?" dispatch replied.

"Requesting permission from Hotel-Two-Twenty to leave Jarsdel Division to deliver evidence to King Division."

"Ten-Four, Hotel-Two-Twenty-three. Hotel-Two-Twenty?"

"Hotel-Two-Twenty here. Hotel-Two-Twenty-three is okay to leave to deliver that evidence, but make it quick."

"Ten-Four, Hotel-Two-Twenty-two, do you copy?"

"Copy," Campbell responded as Kaj brought them off the highway and onto Bailey Drive.

Kaj drove away from the precinct and up north into Keswick. The shift in atmosphere was quick as they became surrounded by rundown structures, the mirage of drug addicts lurking on the sidewalks, hunched over, and others tweaking out. Kaj continued to drive until he reached Stuart Street where he turned left onto West Stuart Street and then right onto Bennett Street. Kaj saw the previous address, 15868 Bennett Street, which was across from the street with Mackenzie Street. Kaj drove onto Mackenzie Street and then drove the car around in a U-turn to stop at the side of the building where he parked.

"Come on," Kaj said as he opened the door, "let's see if we have any luck with this place."

"Luck?"

Kaj and Campbell reached a brick apartment building and came around to the front of the building where they entered through into the lobby. Kaj stopped at the mailboxes where there were individual names listed for each unit, and he read the tenant's name for Unit #3, which was a person by then name of 'E. Hearne.' Kaj pointed out the detail to Campbell, and the two then looked around the ground floor where there was a staircase in the center that went up to the rest of the building, and there were three other units on the ground floor. Kaj and Campbell walked over to Unit #3 on the right, and approached the door, knocking and waiting for a response.

Kaj waited with a tight fist in his right hand, and when there was no response, he knocked again, which prompted the door to finally open as an elderly women stood before them on the other side. Kaj looked at the woman who had long dark grey and wrinkled light brown skin. Her eyes were barely kept open as she squinted back at them, looking upwards, and she held a cane in her hand. She wore clothes that were too big for her, as she was small and frail, and just about five feet tall. Kaj looked at the woman and leaned over as he was about to talk.

"Excuse me, ma'am, does Eldon Hearne live here?"

"What?" the woman replied in a foreign accent. "Eladon?"

"Eldon," Kaj enunciated. "Does he live here?"

"Who are you?"

"We're with the police, ma'am. We're looking for Eldon Hearne."

"Police, go away," the woman said, flicking her wrist at them. "Bad police."

The woman closed the door of them. Kaj looked at Campbell, who was apathetic at the outcome and began to leave. Kaj followed him and the two regrouped in the cruiser.

"Alright, take us to the precinct," Campbell said, opening his notebook.

"That must have been his mother," Kaj instead replied. "Dammit…"

"We're going to be lucky if we don't get in trouble now," Campbell stated. "You've gone way too far out of our boundaries."

"We showed a little initiative," Kaj deflected, "but unfortunately, it didn't turn up much. I'm going to include the addresses in my report, but I'm not going to write down that we went to these places or what we found at them."

"We didn't find anything related to the murder."

"Exactly, and between that old woman and the store associate, I don't think we have to worry about it any of it coming around to the detective. It's not like we gave our names or anything…"

"Whatever, man," Campbell remarked. "Let's just get out of here."

"Alright…" Kaj said, "I'm sorry I took us this far."

"Shut up – let's just go."

Kaj ignited the engine and drove off from Mackenzie Street, driving onto Bennett Street and making his way back onto Stuart Street so that he could return to Bailey Drive and go to the King Division precinct. He held a contemplative look on his face as he drove, unsatisfied by his efforts, despite the efforts made, but sometimes, even when you hope to put in that extra effort, there isn't a guarantee on a payout, and that was the risk he took, and sure enough, seemingly, there didn't appear to have been a payout to this risk. Kaj continued to review the details in his head as he drove, and Campbell's silence enabled that effort as Kaj put the pieces together in an attempt to find a new idea based on intuition, but for now at least, Kaj had done all that he could to solve the murder of Eldon Hearne.

Late morning, I sat in the back of a taxicab that drove through Caledonia Street, entering into Northton as we slowly made our way through the late morning traffic. I took off my fedora and sat it beside me as I looked through documents in a folder that contained police reports related to criminal activities that were being organized and reported on the Internet. These crimes, dubbed 'cyber crimes' by the investigators within the General Investigations section, highlighted an assortment of criminal activities, from chat groups that talked about 'hacking' into websites to access private information, to chat groups that talked about ideas for scams to exploit everyday people for basic private information, including credit card information. I looked through each of the papers, seeing that the response by the Harlech Police Department had been minimal and these activities were a novel phenomenon for these investigators who had very little insight or knowledge into the technical details of computers, and due to lack of insight, lacked any resolution into these unresolved cases.

I closed the folder and opened another, which contained specific details by an investigator with Administrative Vice, into online activities of anarchists. The people that were mentioned in these chat logs did not use their real name, and there was a citation by an investigator that the identities of these people were impossible to guess as they all used pseudonyms for their usernames, or handles. A user that was of note within these chat groups was a person that went by the pseudonym 'Piato,' the Person of Interest in the case that was presented to me by Mr. Harrington. I looked through the assessment by the detective with Ad Vice, and he believed that this user was not a ringleader of a wider anarchist group that called themselves 'V' for an unknown reason. Piato was a source of inspiration and who was 'looked up to' by the other users. Piato spoke a lot about 'the people's revolution,' or the 'revolution in the future,' and occasionally stated that he had 'connections' in certain places and that he 'knew stuff' that he couldn't share. The details of these connections and information was vague and uncertain. However, more than anything, Piato spoke about revenge, revenge against the capitalists, and revenge against the authorities that oppressed them. The overall assessment by the detective was that these activities were small groups of people that posed no threat to public safety or national security, especially since they had no ties to the Soviet Union, the KGB, and if anything, spoke poorly of the Second World. I closed the folder once I read through the last of this information, and then looked out the window as we arrived at the intersection with South Slade Drive, thinking about this information.

The taxicab came around onto Slade Drive and then drove northwards into Lincoln. The car drove around and through Jarsdel Park, whose trees at this time had started to fade from their greenish sheen, and into the warm colors of autumn. The cab came out to head towards Chinatown on Shai Street, but then made a left turn on Urhan Street to proceed halfway where it stopped in front of a forty-story neo-gothic skyscraper known as Calypso Tower. Calypso Tower was home to various businesses within, the most famous of which was the office for *The Harlech Herald* newspaper, their sister publication, *The Dornoch Chronicles*, and their owners, Sutherland Publishing.

I put together all the folders into a pouch and brought the straps to my shoulders as I exited out of the cab. I walked across the sidewalk and up the steps of the building to enter into the lobby where there was a security officer at the front desk of the building who greeted me as I entered. I looked at him and went over to the desk, putting my hands atop of the counter as I looked at him. He was an older male with fair skin and a bald head.

"How can I help you?" he asked.

"I'm here to meet with the computer system manager – Paul Schmidt. He told me that he'd meet me here."

"Feel free to have a seat then," the officer replied.

I walked over to a bench in the lobby and went to sit down. I briefly looked around the interior lobby of Calypso Tower, which had a warm glow with the golden marble tiles, dark oak wood panels, crème colored wallpaper against the walls, and gold-colored lamps with crème white shades hanging from the ceiling. I looked at the time on my watch and noticed that I was early, so I waited for five minutes until I heard the chime of the elevator open. I walked over to the corridor from the lobby that went to the elevators and met with my old friend, Paul Schmidt.

Paul looked at me with a smile as I met him. He raised his hand up to wave and then brought both hands to his side. I looked at him and could barely recognize him from when I had last seen him nearly ten years ago. He appeared older than I remembered, and his hair had become a lot longer and beard a lot bushier. Paul had dark blonde hair that was unkempt and curved at the ends. He had a thick beard around his chin that was trimmed, but thick and the same color as his hair. He had blue eyes that looked at me with recognition as nearly the same person I was ten years ago, and before those eyes were a pair of gold-colored eyeglasses. Paul had light fair skin, warmer than mine, but light. He was dressed in a brown blazer with a brown sweater vest and green collared shirt underneath. Paul also wore brown trousers, shoes, and around his neck, he had a lanyard with an ID that displayed his photo and first name.

"Hello," Paul greeted to Emma.

I smiled back to him and replied, "Hello, fancy meeting you here. It's been a while."

"A long time, really. How have you been?"

"I've been okay," I replied. "How about you?"

"It's been steady," Paul responded. "Sorry I seemed rushed on the phone, but it was a bad time to call. I'm free now for you to come down and we can talk about this problem that our client has been having."

Paul stepped back and pressed a button to call an elevator to go down. An elevator car door opened and Paul offered for me to step in before him. I walked in and Paul followed. He selected the basement level and the elevator took us down to the depths of the tower, opening and bringing us out to a corridor that was less fancy than the upstairs lobby. The walls and floor were composed of concrete, and there was piping on the walls and panels above us that contained various cables that ran through the ceiling. Paul walked me down the corridor so that we could go to his workspace.

"So, what have you been doing since university?" Paul questioned.

"Oh, I've been doing a bit of work. I was a teacher's assistant for a bit, and then I got bored of that and started my own business for this private investigation services. I like it a lot, but business can be slow sometimes."

"Wow, that sounds really interesting," Paul remarked. "I suppose I should have seen something like that coming though. You and Kaj were always the ones with keen eyes."

My ear twitched as I heard that name, which I hadn't heard for a long time.

"Have you heard from Kaj?" Paul asked me.

My face sunk and I looked down as we walked.

"No," I simply replied, "I haven't. I haven't seen him since the end of high school. What about you?"

"We sometimes chat and meet for lunch," Paul replied. "Last time I saw him was a couple of months ago."

"How is he?"

"He's okay. He's married, to Hannah Summer if you remember her, and they have a kid together. He's been with the Harlech Police Department for a couple of years now, and he likes it a lot."

I simply nodded with a quiet smile on my face. We entered a period of silence for a moment before we turned a corner and I took a deep breath in.

"So, what about you? You're a system manager now? That's impressive," I remarked. "Who do you work for?"

"My own company," Paul replied. "but contracted for the same client – I've been told that I can't really disclose who that is to you though…"

"Really? I suppose that's understandable… annoying, but understandable. A lot of my clients try to conceal their identities, but a lot of them never pull it off because I find out eventually. I'm assuming that you're the one that recommended me to them though?" "Me?" Paul questioned as he arrived at a set of double doors. "No. I had no idea that you were in this line of work, but they told me that they would hire a private investigator to help out with these issues. To be honest, I never expected that you'd be the one, but I'm happy you are. You're just the person we need to help with all this."

Paul took his lanyard off which had two sets of keys on it. He opened the door to his workspace with one of the keys and opened the door for me to enter. I walked through and entered into a room with various unfamiliar machines that were lined against the walls, providing an open space in the center of the room where there were various more machines, desks with computer terminals, filing cabinets, and carts that contained various reel cases. The room was bright and the floor wasn't marble tile, but it was a particular board tiles that created a raised floor for wires and other electrical components below. The room also had a suspended ceiling above us that had standard white lights. Paul stopped in the center of the room and looked around.

"Here is where I work," Paul remarked. "In this room, we control an entire network for our client's business as well as some other businesses in the building."

"Including The Herald?" I questioned.

"Sorry," Paul remarked in a sheepish tone, "can't say. However, I can give you a better understanding of what I've done so far. Several weeks ago, we had a hacker infiltrate our network in the building by dialing in from outside somewhere. I've reviewed records for the last months, and I don't think that this person entered through a traditional method that most people have used to hack into computer systems."

"What are the traditional methods?" I asked.

"Well, when an operating system is developed, the developers typically leave behind a 'backdoor' that allows them to enter into a system without any provided credentials so that they can run tests and such. Typically, this is basically done by a 'Guest' handle and password. However, I understood that backdoor method when I developed the network for our client, so I terminated that option. The secondary method is by simply attempting to log-in with someone else's handle, but in order to create his own account, Piato, our hacker would have had to have hacked into a super-user account so that he could have made his own account and even into a super-user. The only accounts that are super-users belong to me and some of the other technicians I work with, and I've reviewed login records, and none of us, except for myself on occasion, have logged in from outside of the building. In my opinion, I believe there could be some sort of other, more intricate backdoor method that was implemented into these types of computers that we're using, these Neumann Machines, which I've been suspicious about ever since I started to put together this system."

"Yeah, that's close to what I was told in the report the client gave to me," I replied, crossing my arms. "What makes you think that there's a backdoor?"

"I wrote that report," Paul responded, "and at first I thought that this wasn't a backdoor mechanism, but instead a flaw until I dug deeper into the development process. Do you remember Glenn? Glenn Bertrand?"

"Yeah," I replied.

"Glenn was a developer associated with the development of the latest Neumann Machine that our system is designed on. I tried to confirm if he was actually associated with the development, but his name isn't listed as an engineer that worked on the latest machine, which I thought was weird because I heard from Kieran who is still good friends with Glenn that he was working closely with them to develop a new operating system and computer. Coincidentally, Glenn is listed neither on the operating system patent nor on the computer model patent."

"Strange…"

"Yes," Paul affirmed, "so I tried to phone him to get his input about these issues we were having and to see if he knew about any backdoor, but he wouldn't tell me anything; almost as if he wasn't allowed to talk about it. As soon as I started to talk about the Neumann Machines, he shut me out. We were never that close to be fair, but it was a strange shift in his tone. I can understand company confidentiality and such, but the questions I started to ask didn't even relate to the machines itself, but our system, which he dismissed as a technical fault on our side."

"Jeez," Emma replied.

"Anyways, if there is some sort of intricate backdoor, only someone within the Neumann development group would know about it, so if this hacker did enter through that, he would have had to have been with that group, which I think is a little farfetched. I haven't terminated the account that this Piato has been entering with and kept the channel open so that I can monitor his activities, which our client hasn't been too happy about, but understood the necessity to monitor what they are doing. Ever since our initial breach, most of our confidential documents have now been encrypted or cut-off from the main system so there should be no way to access them, but our friend Piato doesn't know about that. Let me take you to my workstation and show you what I have right now."

"Okay."

Paul walked me in deeper into the lab and took me to the back of the room where there were various machines lined in aisles with a computer terminal in the midst of them. I looked through the aisles as we reached the final one and saw that some of the raised floors had been exposed with wires pulled out as if there was some sort of maintenance going on. Paul took me to the terminal at the end of the room where there was another square hole in the floor nearby. The cables that came out of this whole were attached to the computer and to a printer on the same desk. Paul walked over pointed at the open tile in the raised floor.

"Right now, I've been able to discover which telephone line our hacker is able to enter through, and I've connected a wire from the modem line to this printer to record every keystroke that comes in by the hacker. It was a dubious process, but I was able to figure out which of the fifty or so telephone lines it was by the fact that his connection is so slow. I initially thought that that it was possible that he was coming in from another country until I was able to get the phone number that he dialed in with. Here."

Paul picked up a sticky note on his desk and gave it to me. I looked at the phone number and noticed that it was a local number.

"Wow," I remarked, "that was easy. You've practically done all the work then."

"Not yet," Paul replied with a light laugh. "I don't know who this phone number is for within the entire city, or even the service provider, but I guess that's where you come in. You'll have to find out who this belongs to and what service provider they use. Once you find out an address, you'll be able to investigate who our hacker is."

"I don't think that'll be too much of an issue. I'll review phonebooks to get an address and property owner."

"Our client wants to terminate the hackers connection to the computer network by the end of the week because they don't want to keep their documents restricted for too long since some people need access to them to work. However, we should have all that we need from this connection I've kept open now that we have this phone number, so all we need is to verify the address and the identity of this hacker. I'll continue to keep it open just in case."

"Thanks, Paul," I remarked. "This'll really help with the investigation – I appreciate it."

"No problem. To be honest it was kind of fun," Paul replied. "It felt like a puzzle of my own – I mean, a lot of what I do has its own puzzles, but this one felt unique. I can see why you and Kaj were always into these sorts of things. It felt a lot like a game…"

"Yeah… a game…"

"Do you need anything else from me, or is that all you'll need?"

"I think this'll all I'll need from now. I'm glad you were able to explain it all to me, and I'm glad you'll keep that connection open for now. I'll run an address check and drive to the place to scope it out. I'll be in touch."

"Sounds good," Paul responded with a smile as I stepped back with eagerness. "It was nice seeing you again. I'll see you later – good luck."

"Thanks!"

Part 1 – Chapter 8
Harlech Police Department – Jarsdel Division
Northton, Jarsdel Island
September 1983 – 11:00

Kaj and Campbell returned from King Island after they had dropped off the evidence to criminalistics at the main precinct. The drive from the precinct and along the highway going towards the south of the island was quiet. Was Kaj thinking about the murder case still? It's quite possible, because he was never someone that could let go of something so quickly, and I believe that even at this point in his life, he wouldn't allow something from the past get by him, no less than the murder of Eldon Hearne. At this point however, Campbell was well annoyed with Kaj, and as it almost reached the halfway point of their shift, Kaj pulled out at Lincoln Drive and began to drive them back to their own headquarters so that they could have their lunch break.

"Hotel-Two-Twenty," dispatch announced over the radio.

"Hotel-Two-Twenty," Sergeant Allard responded.

"Hotel-Two-Twenty, received a report of a disturbance at the Neontronic Arcade inside of the Harthdam Mall at West Boundary Drive and Caledonia Street. See the caller, the owner of the arcade, who has reported several teenagers that have engaged in a verbal dispute with the owner and refused to leave."

"Ten-Four, disturbance at Harthdam Mall," Sergeant Allard replied. "Hotel-Two-Twenty-two?"

"Oh no," Campbell complained before he pressed the button on his mic. "Hotel-Two-Twenty-two."

"Hotel-Two-Twenty-two, can you and Hotel-Two-Twenty-three check out the disturbance at the Neontronic Arcade at Harthdam Mall?"

"Ten-Four, we're enroute," Campbell begrudgingly responded. "She knows we wasted more time than we should have with that evidence collection. She's getting back at us for it with this BS."

"Calm down," Kaj replied. "We just reported that we were back in-service, and who knows if the others are busy or not. For all we know, Alex and J.P. could still be at the murder because SMC haven't been able to takeover."

Kaj drove to the end of Lincoln Drive, came into Jarsdel Park, and then drove onto the roundabout to exit onto Bering Street to drive towards East Boundary Drive and make their way towards Harthdam Mall. The drive from Lincoln to Harthdam was longwinded since there were various intersections and it was the midday traffic. Within twenty minutes, the pair arrived at the parking lot of the mall, pulled up at the curb at the entrance of the mall, and then exited out to make their way inside. Kaj eyed the front doors of the mall, which led to the main corridor where there were various advertisements for the stores inside: Eaton's, Simpsons, and a Chamberlain's - the major department stores and also a Lourens Supermarket, an Aptheker Drugstore, and a Millennium Electronics store – other major retailers. The rest of the mall consisted of the minor retail stores, clothing stores, gift shops, and other assortment of specialty retailers. Kaj and Campbell walked in, immediately catching the eyes of other people as they made their way through the shopping centre on the late Saturday morning.

The pair stopped at a directory to locate the arcade and then proceeded to make their way to the back of the mall where they reached a corridor that had a lengthy venue with the entire façade open and exposed to reveal the mass of amusement arcade games that were available to play. The walls of the arcade had a dark blue to an almost black color with dots that resembled stars to give the impression that the walls reflected outer space, but divided into squares where the perimeters of each square were a glowing neon pink. The floor design was a carpet that had designs of stars, comets, and planets. The light tone in the arcade was dark and there was a smell of sweat all around.

Kaj and Campbell overheard the sound of some bickers from the other side of the façade where there was a group of teenagers confronting a security guard. Upon sight of Kaj, half of the kids left, leaving two behind, two fair-skinned teenagers, one with medium length blonde hair in an oversized flannel, and another with short dark hair. They both appeared to be either fifteen or sixteen years old. Kaj and Campbell approached them.

"Why don't you go and find our caller and ask them what happened," Kaj suggested to Campbell. "I'll handle these kids."

"Roger," Campbell replied, breaking off from Kaj to enter into the arcade.

Kaj sighed as he approached the two kids and the security officer.

"You here about these kids?" the officer asked.

"Yes, sir," Kaj responded. "My partner's just gone in to talk to the store manager or supervisor – why don't you go and join him? I can take over from here."

The security officer backed off and entered the store. Kaj looked at the kids and put his hands on the side of his hips.

"Get out of here," the blonde-haired kid said to Kaj. "The owner of this store is a total gyp man. They completely conned me."

"I don't know about that," Kaj responded, "but I've been told that you've been causing a disturbance and they've asked you to leave."

"No way," the blonde-haired kid argued. "I wanted my money back because I was scammed – that Bunco game, there's no way to win. He scammed me, refused to admit it, and now he's called you guys because he's such a coward, man. I want my money back."

Kaj sighed and replied, "What makes you think that it's a scam?"

"You can't win the game, dude," the blonde-haired kid exclaimed. "No matter how many times I tried, the game always scores more than me. It's rigged, and that SHILL KNOWS IT."

"Alright, that's enough," Kaj responded. "Look, I know you're upset, but here's the deal, kid. You lost your money and I don't see any way of you getting it back, at least right here and right now – you've been asked to leave, but since you refused to leave, we've been called to make sure you leave. I'm sorry, but I'm going to have to ask you both to leave.

"I want my money!"

Kaj looked at the kid and shifted his tone, "You're not going to get it," he said in a stern voice. "This is private property, and you've been asked to leave. If you don't leave, I'll place the two of you under arrest for mischief. Am I clear?"

The blonde-haired kid looked at Kaj with a deep frown. Kaj looked at his tanned cheeks to see that they were deeply red. For a moment, it seemed like he wouldn't leave – he was so effusive and assured of himself being in the right, but it was not Kaj's place to care, but to enforce the law. The dark-haired kid pulled at his friend's sleeve.

"Come on, Gary," the dark-haired kid said. "Let's get out of here…"

Gary looked at his friend with a deep frown, and after a brief moment of hesitation, the two backed off and left. Kaj watched them off and then turned around as Campbell approached him.

"What do you have?" Kaj asked.

"The owner says that the blonde kid was upset that he lost at one of the games, wanted his money back, but that wasn't policy and refused. Apparently the blonde-haired kid cracked the glass on the game he was playing at, which was when he decided to call security. Security got them out, but the blonde kid refused to leave until he got his money back, which was when we were called. The owner didn't want to press charges for the damages since he's had worse."

"That was nice of him," Kaj responded. "Where's the owner now?"

"In the back office," Campbell replied.

"Let him know that the kids left, and if they return to let us know," Kaj remarked. "I'm going to go and check this game out – the damages, I mean."

Campbell walked off and Kaj entered into the arcade. He looked around, seemingly lost at all of the bright consoles around him until his eyes spotted the light blue rectangular machine in the corner with the cracked screen. The top of the screen displayed the name of the game, 'Bunco!' in a bright orange font above the LED screen that showed three digits, alternating on the screen from one to nine, occasionally stopped all in a complete series, for example, all ones, or all threes before flashing and displaying the words 'BUNCO' underneath. Below where the words spelt out 'BUNCO' there was a two-column grid where the player would hit the red button in front to generate their series of three numbers, which would be added to provide their score for that round, while the computer would do the same in an attempt to receive their own score. Kaj read the instructions on the base of the machine near the button where it said that the more coins that were inserted, the more rounds and higher the payout could be in a successful attempt to beat the computer in producing a high score – with a minimum of three rounds per game up to a maximum of eight. Kaj read the instructions once more before his eyes wandered over to the logo of the manufacturer of this game at the top corner of the base, which was the same reflective logo of the Neumann Machine computers at the repair shop in chrome cursive font, 'Neumann.' Campbell walked back as Kaj frowned and looked at the logo.

"Alright, we're all done," Campbell said. "I've got all the info for our report – let's get out of here."

"Do you know where the phrase 'bunco' comes from? It used to be this game that was played with the intent to scam people," Kaj explained. "There's no way this game wasn't designed without an intent to scam people out of money, or coins at that matter. How is this game even here – it's borderline gambling…"

"Who cares?" Campbell replied. "I'm hungry, let's leave."

Kaj and Campbell walked out of the arcade and made their exit out of the mall.

"Hotel-Two-Twenty-two," Campbell said over the radio.

"Hotel-Two-Twenty-two," dispatch replied.

"Hotel-Two-Twenty-two, you can mark us clear from the disturbance at Harthdam Mall."

"Ten-Four."

Kaj opened the car and entered in to sit down so that they could return back onto the road and make their way to the police headquarters. Campbell entered and sat down as Kaj turned on the engine. He shifted gears, but stopped as he looked ahead and saw the blonde-haired boy, Gary, glance at him as he was with his friends at a fountain in front of the mall at the corner. Kaj looked at him for a brief moment before he refocused on driving out.

Kaj and Campbell were quiet as Kaj drove them quickly from the mall and back all the way to Lincoln to pull into the parking lot. Campbell pushed the door open and left the car without a moment of hesitation as he was ready to go on break, but Kaj remained in the car seat, both hands at the steering wheel, looking ahead of him as he was in deep thought. Campbell looked back at him as turned around to look at his partner. Kaj noticed his glance, opened his door and put a foot out to stand up and then turn around to look over to his partner.

"Hey, why don't you go on ahead," Kaj said. "I think I'm going to go and eat out somewhere. I'll be back in a few."

"Sure thing," Campbell responded before he turned around and continued on.

Kaj watched him for a few more seconds and then slipped down back into the car to turn on the engine again, pull out, and then return onto the road. He drove into Harthdam via Boundary Drive, turned right onto Caledonia Street, and then turned left onto 13th Street where he drove a short distance, passed Higgins Street, and then pulled over in front of the computer repair shop. Kaj glanced over to the shop, paused for a moment, and then left the car to walk back over to where he was two or three hours ago into the shift.

Sheldon Jones looked up from the counter as the bell announced Kaj's arrival into the store. He walked over and took his notebook out. He clicked his pen and looked at the technician. Sheldon appeared startled and intimidated by Kaj's appearance again.

"Sorry to bother you, but I had a few more questions about your boss," Kaj stated. "Do you have time for one or two questions?"

"Sure…"

"What kind of a business did Eldon primarily run here?" Kaj asked.

"What? This is a computer repair shop… we repair computers…"

"All kinds of computers? I see a lot of Neumann Machines around here, but I know there are a different variety, i.e. Apple, IBM."

"Well, Neumann is the most popular brand in these parts," Sheldon answered, "so of course we receive a lot of Neumann Machines."

"Earlier you said that Eldon owned this store as a franchise – in other words, it's licensed to work on behalf of the Neumann company, and I suppose to repair their computers."

"Yes," Sheldon confirmed, "we're also licensed to sell Neumann Machines."

"As technicians, I suppose you'd all be familiar with Neumann Machines, wouldn't you? I've heard there to be a lot of issues with Neumann Machines, especially with computer viruses. What's your take on that?"

"It's just a flaw with the latest operating system – an easy fix, otherwise, there's nothing wrong with the craftsmanship of the Neumann Machine."

"Interesting…" Kaj replied, "you know, I heard that our police department was thinking of getting Neumann Machines for us too…"

"Look man, I have a lot of work still to do, so if you have anything related to Eldon, please ask. I have to get back to work."

"I'm sorry," Kaj apologized. "Do you happen to have a list of staff that work here? I'd like to know more about Eldon's contacts around here if you wouldn't mind, and if possible, his contacts with the Neumann company."

"Okay…"

Sheldon left and went upstairs, leaving Kaj alone for a moment, which provided him with time to write in his notebook. He jotted down some notes, closed his notebook and then glanced to the side as he looked at some of the computers before Sheldon returned with a folder. Sheldon placed the folder on the counter and pushed it towards Kaj.

"Here are all of Eldon's business contacts," Sheldon stated.

Kaj opened the folder and looked at the short list of people on the single sheet of paper in the folder attached by a paperclip. The sheet included his entire staff including Sheldon Jones who was listed as a technician. Kaj eyes the list and then looked up at Sheldon.

"Who isn't here today on this list?" Kaj asked.

"Earnest and Melvin aren't in today," Sheldon stated.

Kaj looked over to Sheldon once more and asked, "In your experience, do customers usually return once they have their computers repaired here?"

"No," Sheldon quickly replied. "We usually never see them again because we do such a fine job."

"Hm…" Kaj responded. "Can I have a copy of this?"

"Sure," Sheldon replied.

Kaj flipped the sheet up as he noticed a sticky note attached to the folder on the other side. He read the sticky note, which said 'Any problems, contact Glenn Bertrand' with a phone number listed. Kaj unpeeled the sticky note and placed it on the front of the sheet.

"Do you know who Glenn Bertrand is? How come he isn't listed on the staff roster?"

"Glenn doesn't work here," Sheldon replied. "To be honest, I don't really know who he is," he said as he looked at the sticky note. "I never call him."

Kaj surrendered the folder to Sheldon who went upstairs to make a copy of the sheet. He then returned and gave Kaj the copy, which included the sticky note on top with Glenn Bertrand's name and his phone number underneath. Kaj thanked Sheldon and then left with both hands on the photocopy of the roster, eyes on Glenn's name, and a concentrative frown on his face as he looked at the sticky note with a brim hope. He folded the paper and put it in his jacket, but held a gleam of hope in his eyes as he returned to his patrol car, sat down, and proceeded to return to the division headquarters to act on this lead. Kaj would not back down now.

Part 1 – Chapter 9
Problem Solver Inc.
Saffron, Jarsdel Island
September 1983 – 11:30

I returned to my office in Chinatown after I met with Paul so that I could locate the address associated with the telephone number that Paul had provided with me. When it came to locating addresses, it was only a matter of a phonebook, but with so many people, nearly a million, living amongst Harlech, to find this seven-digit chain would be time consuming to say the least. The phonebook listed nearly every resident in the Greater Harlech region, which in addition to the City of Harlech, included the District of New Harlech, District of Walham Valley, and University Endowment Lands. Both New Harlech and Walham Valley, despite having district in their names, were municipalities of their own, entirely separate from the city with their own bylaws, jurisdictions, and other utilities. The university lands, where the University of Harlech was located, was on land owned through the federal government, but governed through the university board and informally considered to be a part of the city.

Unfortunately, residents and their phone numbers were not listed in alphabetical order rather than in numerical order. Nonetheless, I considered the phonebook to be a treasured tool for the private investigator because it was my database for everyone in the city, at least, those that paid the telecom companies for their own landline.

I ran through the entire phonebook using a system that I had developed for this sort of task. I would run through each column searching for the final digit in the string of numbers, which in this case was a seven. If I could find a number with a seven, I'd look at the next digit and see if it was the second-last number, which in this case was a seven too. The entire process took me less than twenty minutes to run through half of the alphabet when I found the exact phone number that Paul had provided me, which listed the landline to belong to Ms. Beatrice Swanson at 3234 Sussex Street. Based on my geographical knowledge of the city, this possibly placed the residence in Attlewood on Cliffe Island since streets on this part of the city were named after place names from the British Isles. I jotted down the name and address, and closed the phonebook to open a map booklet that contained detail maps of Greater Harlech, as well as the neighboring towns nearby, such as Lennox, Douglas, Radloff, and Vollmer. I searched through the section on Attlewood, which posted approximate addresses along the street lines, and found the approximate location of the residence on Sussex Street, near Perth Street.

With all this information collected, now I had to develop a plan so that I could scout and learn more about this residence, Beatrice Swanson, and the possible location of this infamous Piato. I wrote all of these details into my notebook, a neat two inch by three-inch leather notebook, which I stashed in my jacket. I called a taxicab, left my office and returned to the streets, putting my hat on as I stepped outside as well as a pair of dark brown leather gloves to cover my hands. The clouds above had darkened and it started to rain again. The taxi arrived and I stepped in, gave the address to the driver, and then waited in the car as we drove from Chinatown, onto the highway, and then went southbound to Cliffe Island. The drive into Attlewood and then into the suburbs took approximately twenty minutes.

Once we were in the suburbs, I looked around at the houses, searching for the address. I saw 3222, 3224, and so on as we went further down the street at a slow pace.

"Do you know which house it is?" the cab driver asked.

"No," I replied. "I'm not familiar with the house – it should be around here."

I continued to peek out towards the houses around us.

"Ah, there it is," the cab driver stated, pointing ahead. "3234 Sussex Street."

I looked ahead and saw the two-story, green-painted house ahead. The houses in this area were small and cute, two-story homes that must have been constructed in the last thirty years or so because they were older than most architecture, but not as old as the oldest that dated to the colonization of the island almost a hundred years ago. However, all of the homes were pretty and well-maintained, unlike the homes in some of the other suburban districts from Harthdam and Jarsdel. Attlewood was considered to be a bit upper class, especially the southmost reaches and the neighborhoods closer to the university where the wealthier people in the city lived. Besides the stores and venues on Thames Street, Queen Boulevard, Slinfold Street, and Southeast Marshall Drive, the rest of Attlewood and Southton consisted of suburban neighborhoods. 3234 Sussex Street was one of these homes, with its green-painted panel exterior walls, dark shingled roof, and white front door with an oval translucent window and white-framed windows. The front garden was enclosed by a medium-length white picket fence with a bounty of shrubs and flowers inside. I didn't expect this sort of place to be the hideaway for an anarchist, no less because of the appearance of the house, but also due to the fact that we were in a wealthier neighborhood.

The taxi came to a halt near the green home, where I paid the driver and then stepped out. The rain had settled down to a light drizzle, which didn't bother. I preferred to work in the rain, especially when I needed to do some reconnaissance about a property. I watched the taxi drive off and then I looked around at the neighborhood. Most of the homes were similar to the target house, but none of them had a garden as well-maintained and enclosed as 3234 Sussex Street. The front yards were small, approximately five meters by eight meters. The street was narrow because of the various cars that were parked on the curb, which created a single lane in the centre. This parking situation was typical for Harlech's suburbs. At either side from the road there was a paved sidewalk with a strip of green in between, and occasionally along this strip of grass there was an oak tree planted with its warm autumn leaves decorating the street ahead. I moved away from the road and onto the sidewalk as I looked behind and ahead of me.

I retrieved a disposable camera from my jacket, scrolled the film ready, and then shot a picture of the target's home from the west side. I hid the camera in my coat and then walked forward, passing the house while keeping my eyes to the side as I kept my face forward so that I could catch a glance of the home. I walked ahead until I was approximately three meters from the corner of the property so that I could take another picture from the east face. I then put the camera away and began to look around as I considered a ploy to approach the home and see if I could enter inside.

The most dangerous aspect of private investigation was putting yourself out there in the field, no less the location where you suspected the target to function from. If there was any reason for my target to believe that I was a private investigator, or even a police detective, I could jeopardize the entire case and also draw attention from law enforcement onto me. In this case, I was more worried about the former rather than the latter, but it still concerned me to not draw too close. At the same time, I had to push myself into dangerous locations and places sometimes in order to extract information that would otherwise not be readily available. If I hoped to succeed, it had to be done. I learned that the hard way. Luckily, I had a minor in theatrical studies, and a passion for theatrics that would allow me to put on a smile and get the job done – it was now time to get creative.

I approached the picket gate at the front of the property, opened it, and then made my way forward to the house. I walked down the path, up the steps, and came up to the front door. I took off my hat as I came under the cover and stepped onto the mat. I then pressed the doorbell and waited for a response. Within a few seconds, the door opened and I looked at the other side as a frail elderly woman opened the door and peeked out towards me. As soon as she caught a glimpse of me, she opened the door wider and looked at me with curious eyes. The woman, who I assumed to be Beatrice Swanson, appeared as if she was in her seventies with wrinkled fair skin and snow-white short, curled hair. She wore a light blue dress and held a hand at her mouth.

"Yes?" the woman asked.

"Hi," I said in a friendly tone, "sorry to bother you, but I was just in the neighborhood when my car broke down. I have no way to get ahold of my husband, so I was wondering if it'd be alright to use your telephone."

I would never allow anyone into my own home to use a telephone, not because I knew the benefits of this old trick, but because I could never trust anyone who I didn't know personally into my place of residence. However, this old lady was born from a different time period, possibly at the start of the century, when Harlech was a safer place to live in and there was more trust between citizens. Did I consider it to be unethical to deceive this old lady with these theatrics? Perhaps fifteen years ago. The woman lowered her hand from her mouth and ushered me in.

"Oh, alright," the old woman replied. "Come on in – the telephone is just in the kitchen."

I entered and stepped onto the tiled floor of the foyer, which was very small and connected to a living room on the left and dining room on the right. The foyer had a set of stairs on the right that went up to the second floor. From where I stood, I could see the kitchen in the back through the archway door at the rear of the foyer as well as the rear of the dining room. I eyed around at the foyer some more, looking at some picture frames that had some colored photographs of some blonde-haired children. I assumed these must be the grandchildren, which meant that there was possibly a son or daughter that this old woman had, but I couldn't see any pictures related in this corridor. I could only see a black and white wedding picture on a table parallel to the staircase. Once I had a glance at the foyer, I caught a glance around the rest of the ground floor as much as I could, took my shoes off, and then continued into the kitchen where the old woman led me to.

"You must be cold," the old woman stated. "Can I get you any coffee or tea?"

"No, I'm alright," I replied. "Sorry, I didn't get to introduce myself. My name is Catherine. I'm so sorry to have to intrude on your home at this awkward time, ma'am."

"Oh, don't apologize, my dear," the old lady responded. "You can call me Betty."

I smiled as I confirmed her identity – Beatrice Swanson. Beatrice turned on the kettle regardless and then walked over to a kitchen counter where there was a rotary phone.

"You aren't making a long distance call, are you?" Beatrice asked.

"No," I denied. "Local. My husband and I live in Harthdam. He should be at work right now. He's a technician in Lincoln."

"Alright then, go ahead."

I approached the telephone and thought for a moment how I would approach this. My principal rule when it came to these sorts of gambits was that I would never leave a trace of myself, including genetic samples in case anything were to backfire against me. I didn't know who my client was after all. I picked up the telephone with my gloved hand and began to dial – I knew exactly who to phone. I dialed for Paul and waited for him to respond.

"Hello?" Paul answered.

"Hey, it's me," I replied. "My car broke down and I need you to come pick me up."

"Who is this?"

"I'm at 3234 Sussex Drive at the moment – I was on my way to check that thing you wanted me to check."

"Emma?"

"Yes, I'm sorry that I couldn't reach you, but I'm here and everything seems to be fine. I'll find out a bit more and get back to you, but in the meantime, could you please pick me up?"

"I can't really leave right now."

"Oh, that's okay. Okay. I'll wait for you here and we can call a tow truck later. Thanks. Love you. Bye."

I hung up the phone and then looked over to Betty as she prepared a pot of tea.

"Were you able to get ahold of your husband?" Beatrice asked.

"Yes," I replied. "He'll be on his way. Thank you so much. I've just had such a manic day today – lots of work. I'm a school teacher and it's September..."

"No worries, so your husband will come around to pick you up?"

"Yes," I replied. "He should be a couple of minutes."

"Would you like to wait here? It's pouring right now – please, enjoy a cup of tea."

An opportunity... I thought.

"You're very kind," I replied. "If you wouldn't mind, I can stay here and wait for him."

"Have a seat then. The tea will be ready soon."

I walked over to the round table at the corner of the kitchen. I caught a glimpse of the back garden which was small. I sat down and attempted to look around for more details into the life of Beatrice, but as I looked around the kitchen, I couldn't see much except for more photos of her grandchildren on the refrigerator.

"Are these your grandchildren? I asked. They're both very beautiful."

"Yes," Beatrice replied. "My son's children. Do you have any children?"

"No, not yet," I responded. "My husband and I have talked about it, but I'm not brave enough to go through all that. What does your son do?"

"He's a lawyer," Beatrice replied. "He works for this big firm downtown."

"Really... How many children do you have?"

"Only two," Beatrice responded. "Both sons. The other one is an architect – he lives in London."

"Wow," I replied. "Impressive."

"Yes."

I looked around as I noticed that it seemed like we were alone.

"Sorry, but what about your husband?" I asked.

"He's passed on."

"I'm so sorry."

"No need. It was three years ago, lung cancer, but we all go someday..."

"Yes..."

"All I have left is this home..." Beatrice said as she poured the tea and brought a cup over.

"It's a beautiful home," I remarked.

"Too big for me to be honest, but I haven't the resilience to move out. The pension is hardly enough to pay for it all, no less the bills."

"I'm so sorry to hear that – I can understand. My husband and I are homeowners and all the bills at once between the telephone, gas, and electricity can overwhelm us sometimes. Have you had any issues with the telephone bills? Sometimes I have issues with my service provider."

"As a matter of fact, I have," Beatrice stated, walking over to the telephone where there were some envelopes. "You see, every month, it seems as if I'm paying for more time than I use. I hardly ever make a phone call, but for some reason, I'm charged for calls that go out to other provinces and countries. I've attempted to phone Polaris about it, but the customer service line is no help."

Beatrice handed me the bill and as I looked at it, I now understood the situation more clearly. There was no way that this elderly retiree, in the midst of the suburbs of Attlewood with two children, one of which was a lawyer and another of which was an architect in the United Kingdom could have been the home of Piato. However, there was a link, and within me, even as I deceived this old woman to extract information from her, I was annoyed that there was someone out there financially exploiting her. Beatrice shook her head as she stood down, pushed the bill over to me, and then grabbed her tea.

"Maybe you can make more sense of this than I can. I certainly can't understand it, and my son is no help. He insists I made those phone calls."

I looked at the bill and noticed that there were overcharges for long distance calls placed that put the monthly bill into over a hundred dollars owed. The bill displayed various phone numbers that were called using the landline. The bill also displayed the landline here to be the same phone number as the one that Paul had showed me and which I used to trace to this location. I looked at the area codes and noticed a variety of the area codes from all over the world, many of which I didn't recognize. I lowered the bill and then pressed it over to Beatrice.

"What do you think this could be?"

"It seems to me like someone is dialing into your phone line," I honestly stated. "If I were you, I'd address that to your service provider, Polaris, because that's a serious issue that they should look into."

I looked to the side as I took a mental note of this information.

"Well, your husband is a technician, isn't he? Do you think he could look into this?"

"Not him, but I think I could work something out," I replied, opening my coat and retrieving my notebook. "I'll make a note and get back to you. In the meantime, I think that my husband might be here now. I'm going to leave because I just remembered I left the car unlocked – thank you so much for your hospitality, I really do appreciate it, and the least I can do to return the favor is have the police look into this issue for you."

"Thank you very much, my dear," Beatrice replied as I stood up and put my hat on. "I appreciate that. That'd be very kind of you."

"No problem, miss," I replied with a smile. "Thank you and I'll be in touch."

I left the kitchen and went back to the foyer. I put my shoes on and then opened the door to leave the house. I walked down the path, opened the gate, and then spun around to make my way towards Thames Street so that I could call a taxi and return to my apartment office.

Based on my limited knowledge of computers, I now understood that the hacker had dialed into Beatrice's landline to bounce off her line and connect with Paul's computers at Calypso Tower – I should never have underestimated Piato and expected this outcome. However, I was not at a dead end because I wasn't sure how I could trace the phone number that Piato had used to dial into Beatrice's line, or even if I were able to find out, if that would be the initial line, because they could connect from another line, and then another, to reach his targets. From what I understood from Beatrice's phone bill, however, was that Calypso Tower was not the only target that Piato had when he was targeting since it seemed like he was connecting to computers across North America and Europe. All of these details opened more questions, such as from where Piato was connecting from since he could be connecting from anywhere in Western

Civilization, or what he was doing connecting to all these different computers across the West, and why he was doing it. Before I could answer any of these questions, I had to find out more about these Neumann Computers and the supposed back door that Paul hypothesized about, but to do that, I would need to locate Glenn Bertrand.

Kaj typed at one of the computers in the office that belonged to the Harthdam Beat at the Jarsdel Division headquarters. The office was small and contained three cubicles with computers for officers to work from. At the side, there was a private office from where their staff sergeant worked from, and another room with equipment and radios. Kaj looked through the database as he searched Glenn Bertrand's name, but he did not produce any information related to criminal charges or warrants for his arrest. Kaj logged off the computer and then stood up – Campbell sat behind him and had put his head down as they continued on their lunch break.

Kaj passed Staff Sergeant Rosztóczy's office, who was out at the moment for a meeting, and went to where there were a bunch of books piled up, including phonebooks. He began to search through to find the B section and then scouted through to locate Glenn Bertrand, locating his address to be in Chinatown – 523-310 Manangan Street. Kaj noted the address on the sticky note and then looked up above where there was a large poster map of all of Jarsdel, eyeing the top of the map where Chinatown was and then looked at Manangan Street, which was behind Burnes Drive. Kaj stepped back and went over to the cubicle behind where Sergeant Allard was on the computer and eating lunch.

Kaj turned around to face her as he poked over the cubicle and said, "I'm going out on a patrol. Campbell still has reports to finish – we'll be split up for an hour and a half to an hour, just so you know."

"Are you done all your reports?" Sergeant Allard questioned.

"Yes, ma'am. I am."

"Alright then."

Kaj left the office and came into the corridor that went towards the elevators. He took the elevator down and went to the parking lot to return to his police cruiser. He entered and sat down, opened his notebook and took the sticky note to place on the dashboard before he started the engine. Kaj drove out of the parking lot and came onto Taghman Street.

From Taghman Street, Kaj went left on Slade Drive and then north towards Chinatown. The rain had picked up across the city, but there was little traffic at the current hour. Kaj drove past Frontier Street and made his way towards the waterfront of Chinatown, just before Burnes Drive, and turned left onto Manangan Street as he started to search for Glenn Betrand's apartment. There were various apartment buildings along the road. Kaj passed Hudson Street, James Street, and then Beaufort Street as he began to come to the end of Manangan Street. However, he started to notice that he was getting closer to the street address. At the corner of Vancouver Street and Manangan Street, Kaj found 523 Manangan Street in a quieter part of Chinatown.

Kaj parked on the side, exited, and then looked around. The neighborhood was standard, cars parked on the side and sidewalks with trees on the side. 523 Manangan Street was a four-story apartment building with wide balconies for the tenants. The exterior surface of the complex appeared to consist of a mixture of red brick and stucco. There were plenty of shrubs in the front yard that covered the ground floors of the building and there was a path that went to the front doors. Kaj walked towards the entrance and noticed that there was an intercom with a nine digit panel to either call a unit or enter a code.

Kaj brought a hand to his mic and said, "Hotel-Two-Two-Three."

"Hotel-Two-Two-Three," dispatch replied.

"I need an access code for an apartment building at 523 Manangan Street," Kaj stated.

"Ten-Four, access code for apartment building at 523 Manangan Street. Hotel-Two-Two-Three, please stand-by."

Kaj waited for less than a minute. He looked at the list of tenants near the intercom as he waited, confirming that Glenn Bertrand was on the third floor, Unit #310.

"Hotel-Two-Two-Three, access code for 523 Manangan Street is One-Seven-Zero-One."

"Ten-Four," Kaj replied, bringing a hand to the access code panel.

Kaj put the master code in and then heard the front door click. He quickly went over and opened the door, entering the building and going over to a set of stairs at the back of the entrance that took him all the way to the third floor. Kaj looked left and right as he arrived at the top of the stairs, attempting to see which way went to Unit #310. There was a distinct scent amongst the apartment; that scent of other people's homes all crowded amongst one building. Kaj walked left and came to the end of the hallway where he found T-intersection with Unit #310 on the left.

Kaj approached, looking at the peephole at the door and bringing his fist up to knock hard. He then waited a moment, but there was no response. Kaj brought his fist up again, knocked and then cleared his throat.

"Harlech Police, open up," Kaj asserted.

Kaj waited another moment until he heard the hatch on the other side open, and then the door slowly pull back. Kaj looked in and saw the darkness on the other side and the reflection of some glasses hit back at him as someone poked their head out to see who was on the other side.

"Harlech Police," Kaj stated. "Glenn?"

"Yes?" Glenn questioned from the other side in a nasally voice.

"Glenn, open up. I need to talk to you – it's me, Kaj Kejsaren. We went to high school together – you're not in trouble."

"Kejsaren?" Glenn questioned next, adjusting his glasses as he looked. "I would have never have predicted this outcome – that you would have become a police constable. What do you need from me? If I am the subject of an investigation, you'll have to return with a warrant."

"Do I look like I'm here to investigate you? If I was here looking to arrest you, I'd be here with a lot more members. I'm not a detective. I'm just a patrol officer whose come across your name on a roster. Let me in, I just want to chat and ask some questions."

"What questions?"

"About computers," Kaj stated. "Neumann Machines. Your name was on a list of people to contact in case of any issues with them, so here I am with some questions related to that."

"Where did you receive my information from?"

"From Eldon Hearne," Kaj remarked.

"Oh, that dimwit," Glenn cursed. "I told him not to pass my name on like that. Very well, come in if you must."

Glenn closed the door, slid the chain off, and then opened the door again to reveal himself on the other side. Kaj looked at him and could somewhat recognize the boy that had been at the same high school as him. Glenn had pale fair skin to the point that he appeared malnourished. He was slender and tall, and had a slight hunch to his back. He had messy light brown hair and thick glasses with light brown eyes on the other side. He wore a collared shirt with a star pattern on it, tucked into light brown pants that were pulled up. Glenn turned to the side and extended his hand out for Kaj to walk in.

Kaj walked in and went down the corridor, passing the kitchen and seeing the state of it where there were various unwashed dishes and takeout containers littered around. He continued on and entered the living room where the workstation was towards the back, near the balcony with various tables and computers set up. There were lots of boxes stacked around with machine parts, and others with various folders and papers. Kaj looked around and then over to Glenn who passed him.

"You live alone?" Kaj asked.

"Yes."

"I would have thought that you would have married Abigail – I remember you were both very close."

"Abigail's demands were too much of a cost for the benefits that she provided. In the end, I chose to value my work and it has been a reward. She has also been rewarded – she is now a professor at the University of Harlech with their political science department. She has specialized in feminist studies as you can imagine."

"Good for her," Kaj responded without much interest. "And you?"

"I am a developer for computer software, operating systems, and hardware. I own my own company. My work has been important in the development of various computer models and operation systems that are in use at this time, such as the Neumann Machine, which you said was the topic of discussion."

"Yes," Kaj replied, looking over to the dining table in the corner nearby. "Let's sit down."

Kaj took out his notebook as he went to sit down with Glenn, opposite from each other at the square dining table. Kaj reviewed his notebook and then looked over to Glenn who sat hunched with his hands together, atop of the table.

"Today, I came across your name while I was investigating a matter related to Eldon Hearne, who is the manager of a computer repair shop in Harthdam. Your name was on a sticky note in a roster which said that if there were any troubles, you should be the primary contact for those issues."

"Yes."

"What issues would that be related to?"

"Any issue. I am a developer with Neumann Corporation, and I was a part of the development team of the latest Neumann Machine, specifically, the operating system associated with those computers. Of course you'd find my name around for issues related to the computer, especially when it was in its early stages given that I am a part of the team of scientists that developed it."

"Really? I didn't think that it was a common practice for repair shops to contact developers for issues related to devices. Shouldn't they know what they're fixing? Isn't it all common knowledge?"

"The workings of these computers are a lot more complex than you can imagine, Kejsaren."

"How so?"

"I cannot disclose the technical details with you," Glenn expressed, releasing his hands and sitting back. "All of that is classified information."

"Really? Well, how about this... Eldon Hearne was found murdered this morning, and if I remember anything about Eldon

Hearne, it was that he was a con artist that lived to deceive people. Between that, his association with Neumann Company, and now your name appearing on a roster of people for him and his people to contact for assistance with these machines, I'd say that there's a lot more than you're not telling me, Glenn. What is going on with these computers? Who did Eldon piss off to get himself killed?"

"Shouting at me is not going to get you anywhere, Kejsaren. We're not in high school anymore. You cannot bully me into submission as you once did – you're a peace officer, and I will not be intimidated."

Kaj stood up and pushed the table back. Glenn jumped and pointed towards the exit.

"Get out!" Glenn demanded. "I demand that you leave."

Kaj pushed the table aside and approached Glenn who cowered in the corner. Kaj grabbed him by his shirt when there was a sudden knock on the front door. Kaj froze and looked back. The two went quiet and then the knock was heard again.

"Who is that?" Kaj questioned. "Were you expecting someone else?"

Glenn shook his head with confusion. Kaj grabbed him by the arm and took him with him to the front door of the apartment. Kaj looked into the peephole, but could not see who was on the other side as his sight was blocked by the hat of the person on the other end. Kaj put a hand on his handgun and then took Glenn over to the door.

"Answer it," Kaj demanded, stepping back. "Tell them to go away."

Glenn went over and looked into the peephole while Kaj stepped back, took out his firearm, and readied it as he knelt down and took cover by the kitchen.

"Wh-who is it?" Glenn asked.

Kaj could hear some murmuring from the other side and couldn't catch a word that the other person said. Glenn turned around to look at Kaj as his body tremored violently.

"I- I'm afraid that you'll have to come back some other time... I'm... I'm busy at the moment," Glenn said, speaking as if he was about to cry with a shaky voice.

Kaj could hear some more murmurs.

"No, I am all okay," Glenn stated. "Please – do not think that I am in any sort of danger."

Kaj rolled his eyes. He then frowned as he saw Glenn put a hand on the doorknob. Suddenly, and expectingly, Glenn opened the door and attempted to rush out, but the person on the other side pushed both of them back. Kaj immediately picked himself up and pointed his handgun towards the person that had forced themselves in, but was stunned by the fact that she had immediately snuck in and disappeared into the bedroom at the side.

"Harlech Police!" Kaj shouted, aiming his gun towards the bedroom door. "Put your hands up and come out!"

Kaj moved and pressed a knee down on Glenn's shoulder to prevent him from moving. He looked towards the bedroom door and watched as the person slowly moved out with their hands up. Kaj continued to aim the gun until he lowered it with stun as he saw who the person was.

I looked at Kaj with a bit of sadness in my eyes, recognizing him as the same person that I had last seen so long ago in high school. Even with the changes that had come across him in the last fifteen or so years, he was the same boy that I had known once upon a time.

"Emma…" Kaj remarked with astonish. "What- what the heck are you doing here?"

"I should be asking you the same," I replied, lowering her hands and bringing them to her hips. "I'm here on official business as a matter of fact – I've been recruited by the Harlech Police Department to assist with a murder case, which is believed to be related to some anarchist activities on the Internet that led to the theft of some important documents from my hired client."

"You were recruited by HPD? What?"

"Unrelated to my own business really, but at the same time, believed to be related by the detective – Detective Pearson, who informed me that he believed the murder victim to be connected to the group I was investigating for my client."

"Detective Pearson recruited you? Wait – you were the person in the alleyway, weren't you? He met with you at the murder scene?"

"You were there?"

"Yes, and I'm here because I've been looking into the murder of Eldon Hearne, that scumbag – I'm sure you remember him."

"Of course," I responded. "The moment that I knew he was related to all this, I knew that there was something serious going on."

"You bet there is," Kaj stated. "You wouldn't believe what that idiot got himself into – he owns a computer repair shop where he manages a team of technicians that are licensed to repair Neumann Machines. Funny enough, a lot of Neumann Machines have had a lot of faults and vulnerability to a computer virus, almost as if there was something inherently wrong with them, and of all people, this idiot here is associated with Neumann as a developer."

"Yes, he is," I confirmed, "and I came here to ask him some questions about that. My client had a lot of valuable and confidential data stolen from him. The system manager for the computer database believed there to be something inherently wrong with the computers they use, Neumann Machines, since there was a way for a hacker known as 'Piato' to walk into the system without even being able to hack in through traditional methods. If it wasn't for the fact that him and Glenn weren't a part of the same implications, fifteen years ago, I wouldn't have come here now to ask him some questions. I could never dismiss a coincidence like that."

"Me too."

"Unfortunately, based on what you're telling me about Eldon, I think that there could be something even more than what you expected."

"I'd say, because while I'm chasing a murderer and you're chasing anarchists for what could be a very related case, I think I now have an idea on how Eldon could have risked his life."

"I'm not entirely sure, but I was intrigued to know that Eldon was murdered and that Detective Pearson believed it to be tied to the anarchist group that I was going to be investigating. From what you've told me, I think that we can form a link with these Neumann Machines now to get an idea on what is really going on. You wouldn't believe it, Kaj, but it's eerily similar to what happened fifteen years ago, especially with that name, Neumann." I then paused for a moment as I looked at him closely, remembering myself of the boy that I had used to know, and as much as I recognized him, I forgot what that boy looked like and was unfamiliar with this man who had taken his place. "Do you remember?"

"I do, and I know exactly what you mean…"

PART II: SEPTEMBER 1968

St. Augustine of Hippo Regional Secondary School
Harthdam, Jarsdel Island
September 1968 – 08:00 hours

The difference between now and then was only fifteen years, and I remembered that at the start of it, we weren't even friends even though we had known each other since kindergarten. Even though we weren't so different, we were both in the same clique in that clique-ridden school, and all it took was that single event for us to recognize each other.

St. Augustine of Hippo Secondary was a modest-sized two-story school, on a large plot of land in the midst of those developing suburbs of what was once a rural part of Harlech, Harthdam, and what is now one of the most crime-ridden districts in all of the region. St. Augustine sat behind Harbor Avenue in North Harthdam, at the other end of a parking lot that made it seem like a strip mall. To its left from the avenue street was St. Monica Parish and behind it was St. Monica Elementary School, where the youngsters transitioned to St. Augustine. To the right was the football field surrounded by the oval running track. Behind the school was the dirt field by the scrapyard.

St. Augustine of Hippo Secondary was a divided school, between the six cliques that had themselves divided the area of the school into their own nihilistic domains. From the garages, the Outsiders lurked by the mechanic shops in their world of sorrows and emotion. As if they were inspired by the late-fifties and the subculture of Greasers, their signature was in their leather jackets that they wore over their uniforms, and their darkened, greasy hair, which combined to give the dirtied and tattered look they wished to present. Their leader, Knox Gareth, was a tough Iberian-looking Welshman with brown-hair, brown eyes, and dark fair skin. He was rumored to be an orphan, adopted only by two loving Catholics who he was indifferent too, which made him a loner even at home.

From within the school on the west-side, the library was the less than silent den of the Nerds which was the cave that they could expand their knowledge, but sadly, form their delusions of the world. They were frail and slim, but glass cannons, never weak with the intelligence they claimed to possess and sometimes show through their execution of calculated strikes. However, they were still cowards. They were led by Glenn Bertrand, a genius even then whose superior intellect had won him the loyalty of those below him, coming from a home of devout Catholics too, they were also cold-calculating scientists.

On the second floor, above school administration at the center of the school was the parlor, or student council room, where the wealthiest students met who were known as the Preppies, named for the way that they behaved. Despite the fact that all students wore the same clothes, they had their own way to make themselves look rich, fashionable, and cool. Their leader was the son of Reinhardt Thiessen, the founder and owner of Thiessen automobiles in Austria remnant from the Old Germany, Jan Thiessen, who was tall and handsome with dark blonde hair, fair, but tanned skin, and bright blue eyes.

At the rear of the east wing was the drama room that connected with the stage, which itself was connected and yet also divided from the gym, and from here the Thespians presented themselves. They behaved like protégé Hollywood actors and actresses, with chests and heads held up higher than the Preppies, breathy voices, and outgoing personalities. They were led by a red-headed, tall and lanky boy named Robin O'Connor with skin as white as snow. He was flamboyant, overly outgoing, and immensely dramatic, but skilled in the art of theater. Robin was surprisingly not raised by actors, but only by his faithful mother who supported all that her son aimed for.

From the gym and to the grassy field, there were the hard-headed brutes, the Jocks, who spent the majority of their time in the weight room if not the football field. They were athletic, fit, and muscular men, and their women were likewise athletic and fit, as well as beautiful and slim. However, their physical appearance and abilities were the extent of their prowess, because in mind they were fools. Lance Stützle, the son of the renowned and eccentric German American film director, Ezekiel Stützle, led the Jock clique like the popular champion that he was. His charm echoed across the halls and won the hearts of the many girls at the school with his fine white smile, light and short blonde hair, and radiant green eyes.

Lastly, there were also those that had no clique, even if there were some sort of affinity towards these five groups, and that was where Kaj and I, and our own friends, found ourselves; close, but far, brought together by our characters that objected to a conformity they could have given into. We had no home in the school but the halls we walked. We were not outsiders, however, but ironically, for being abnormal, we were in fact as normal as an adolescent could be, or so it seemed in a world of conformities.

I looked ahead to St. Augustine Secondary School as I stood on the sidewalk of Harbor Avenue in Harthdam. There was a minor breeze that caused my hair to blow to the right, but a warmness back that way from the sunshine that cancelled out the cold morning air. I wore the school uniform as it was meant to be worn; my crimson red sweater without any modifications, no scarf, my sleeves rolled down, and the top buttons of the collar of my blouse together. My strawberry-blonde hair was behind me and loose, and at the top of her head was a black felt beret. My kilt was just above my knees, socks pulled up, and black flats shined and clean. My height was the same even then, but I was youthful and energetic. My skin was very light and my cheeks rosy. I looked back to the school ahead of me. My name was then, just as it is now, Emma Catherine Monique.

Again, St. Augustine of Hippo Secondary was a school that was two-stories tall, the walls consisting of horizontal panels in white for three feet and then red for another three feet, interchanging so there were three pairs up to the roof. To the right, above the gym exit, there was a large Christian cross. Directly towards Harbor Avenue to the entrance and exit to the parking lot there was a concrete block on four pillars above a bed of yellow flowers, reading on the side 'St. Augustine High School,' and on the front face the address, '13354.' The property was divided from the street sidewalk by a low fence consisting of cylindrical concrete pillars spread across the grass with two eight feet long metal poles horizontally stretched across each pillar. Behind the fences, on the side of the school, there were maple trees spread across. Westbound on Harbor Avenue there was another entrance into the parking lot in front of St. Monica Parish, a newly constructed one-story church joint with the elementary school that continued vertically across the left-side of the property. Eastbound, on the opposite side of the property, the school field was surrounded by a chain-link fence in the leftmost corner where was a sign on pillars with the mascot of the school, a muscular warhorse, the St. Augustinian Hippos (where Hippos is the Ancient Greek word for horse, or in collective, for calvary). At the opposite corner was a tall scoreboard. The track and field was accessible from the school by a set of stairs next to another set of wider and steeper steps that acted as the stands for spectators. Behind the field, north, were two tennis courts, and behind them were some newly constructed two-story homes at the street parallel to Harbor Avenue due north, Oben Street.

On the opposite-side from Harbor Avenue there was a dense forest with offshoot roads spread generously, going towards hidden properties within. Behind the parish and elementary school, there were some homes on 13th Street where across, the forested land continued. On the other side, opposite longest side of the field at 12th Street where the land was elevated, there was a mixture of continued forest as well as a farm further north before the suburbs past Oben Street.

I walked into the school through the main pedestrian walkway in the middle of the parking lot, stepping through to where there were a few cars parked around. I wasn't alone as I went across. There were other students, some that were younger than me and some that were older than me. The boys wore grey trousers and black shoes in contrast to us girls who wore grey plaid kilts and black dress shoes. I crossed the one-hundred yards of concrete and reached the shelter that led to the main entrance doors. I pushed through the doors and entered the main lobby, which consisted of a fresco tiled floor that was designed into a cross. Across from the entrance there was an open window that looked into the main office on the other side. There was a set of double doors on the right that walked in, and the school secretary who sat behind the window at her desk. I walked to the right and went down the hallway. The tiles were white, the walls above the lockers and around were a faint beige, and the school lockers were tall and maroon-colored.

At the end of the corridor, at a junction that went left and right, directly ahead of me was the school cafeteria that was two-stories tall with sunroof windows in the ceiling and bright lamps in between both of which shined light down from above. The lunch tables inside consisted of polished oak wood. At each table, students were sat down, divided into their own cliques. I turned right and then left to enter through a stairwell on my right that brought me up to the second floor. From the hallway on the second floor, there were windows that looked down into the cafeteria with benches on the other side of the window for students to sit down and look down from above. I turned right and went around to the opposite-side of the east wing where I stopped before Room 206 and the Drama Room at the end of the corridor.

I opened my locker, second from the left-most door into Room 206 when I looked to my left and saw a familiar face come to rest her side on the locker to the right of me. The girl had medium-brown hair tied in a ponytail, light tanned fair skin, and soft blue eyes. Her cheeks were smooth and round as she smiled at me. She was taller than me by close to four inches. Her arms were wrapped around her textbook before her. At her index finger was a topaz encrusted gold ring and at her ear lobes were matching topaz earrings. Her name was Riley Nouna Vickery and she was my best friend. I looked to her with a smile as I rummaged through my locker.

"How was your weekend?" Riley asked in a joyful tone.

I hesitated to respond as I continued to rummage through my book bag and locker. Finally, I responded and said, "I worked at my mom's shop – both Saturday and Sunday, because my dad was away on a business trip."

"Oh…" Riley responded, "I'm sorry to hear."

"It's alright," I replied. "In English, we're going to start our unit on Hamlet, so I was looking forward to be back ever since Friday."

I looked past Riley and towards a boy nearby. The boy was significantly taller than both of us, under six feet though. He had curled dark brown hair and fair skin. He was stocky, but neither slim nor wide. He wore his uniform with the sleeves of his black sweater rolled up and a flat cap at the top of his head. His name was Jamie Donovan. I smiled as I saw him.

Jamie stopped as he was about to pass and smiled at me.

"Hey!" Jamie greeted in a breathy and polite manner. "We missed you on Saturday!"

My cheeks reddened.

"What were you doing that was more important than the festival?!"

"Oh..." I hesitated to respond, "nothing..."

"Nothing? So nothing was more important than the festival?" Jamie quickly questioned.

"No..."

Riley raised an eyebrow and then turned to face Jamie.

"She was with me!" Riley interjected. "I needed her to help me babysit – I'm sorry!"

Jamie was stunned at Riley's response.

"No worries," Jamie energetically replied. "Am I going to see you later today at rehearsal?"

"Yes, of course," I confirmed. "I won't miss that."

"Great!"

Jamie left and I let out a breath of air. Riley looked at me.

"You didn't have to lie for me," I stated.

"Of course I did," Riley replied. "You were choking – what was I supposed to do? You said, 'Nothing' and that was the most socially awkward I think I could ever stand to see. Now that I've done you a favor, you need to tell me what that was all about and why Jamie Donovan was talking to you. He's in Grade Twelve."

My cheeks flushed as she mentioned the age difference. I looked to Riley with slight annoyance and looked back into my locker as if I was lost.

"I was supposed to be at the fair yesterday, but couldn't because I was stuck doing inventory with my mom."

"Oh..." Riley replied, lowering her smile, "I'm sorry, but cheer up – the fair closes at the end of the month."

"What?" I questioned. "No, not that fair. I meant the Shakespeare Summer Festival in Southton. Last night was the closing night to mark the end of summer, but I couldn't go because I was stuck with my mom."

"Oh, that's right!" Riley replied, lowering her smile, "I'm so sorry, I completely forgot that you've been doing that. I thought it was over."

Emma sighed.

"No, I thought that you were talking about the Neumann Fair in Northton, not the one at Driftwood Beach."

"No..."

"Have you been to the Neumann Fair? I hear that it's all the rage right now – we should go, or..."

I looked at Riley again as I raised an eyebrow.

"Or, perhaps you would like to go with someone else? I mean, it is a couple's destination, and..."

"And?" I questioned in a dull tone.

"Well, maybe you'd prefer to go with Jamie?"

My eyes widened and I looked back at Riley with disapproval. I closed her locker door and began to make my way towards the door going into Room 206.

"No," I denied, turning back around. "Never. I like him, but not..."

I paused. Riley's smile returned.

"Okay, you hold onto that thought. I'll see you at lunch!" Riley said with a laugh as we parted ways. "Bye!"

I shook my head and entered into homeroom. At the end of attendance and at the sound of the bell, I walked out of Room 206 and then went downstairs again, exiting outdoors. I walked around the perimeter of the main building, around the gym at the end of the east wing and to a set of stairs at the annex behind where a set of doors led into the trophy room on the ground floor. Above, I reached a classroom where I had my English class, Room 213, and this room was different from the rest of the classrooms. For a start, there was carpet, and even the desks were different, a lot smaller, and made of plain wood rather than plywood.

From the classroom entrance, I looked in and went to sit down at my seat at the back of the room where I waited for the class to start. At the end of the room, there was a nook behind the teacher's desk and then a door that went to the classroom on the opposite-side, Room 214, and another door on the left that went into a storage room. Several more students arrived and entered until there was about twenty in total. We were a small school and this was the maximum size that classes got to. From the left of the classroom, appearing from the storage room, a woman in a light-green and white long-sleeved dress stepped out and came to the front of the classroom. She had thick, but short ash blonde hair and very light fair skin. Around her neck was a golden amulet with an emerald in the midst that mirrored the color of her eyes. Across her face was a bright, youthful smile, and she was known by us as Ms. Christopher.

"Good morning, everyone," Ms. Christopher greeted to the class as they quieted down. "Today, we embark on a new adventure as we start our primary module of the school year focused on an important book."

I looked to Ms. Christopher with a wide smile.

"As per school curriculum, I've been required to teach you on this piece which lectures on topics of prejudice and revenge..." Ms. Christopher continued to say, going back into her book to pick up a book, "and the futility of both."

Ms. Christopher returned and presented the cover of the book to class. Emma's smile dropped as she saw the title of the novel, *'Negro'* with the cover depicting a shaven sub-Saharan African female. The class murmured.

"Now, I know that it isn't Hamlet, and I know a lot of you expected us to start our unit on Hamlet as I said last week, but this recent best seller was ordered by the diocese in order to comply with the new curriculum that takes into consideration certain events that are occurring south of the border that we must, as a society, consider here as well."

"Why in the hell should we consider that left-wing nonsense here?" a boy questioned.

I looked over to the boy, Tyler Hughes. He had short light-brown hair, fair skin, and dark blue eyes. He didn't wear the school sweater, but instead only wore the short-sleeved shirt. He had a slim, but athletic figure. He was of course associated with the Jock clique. He was the best friend of Lance Stützle's younger brother, Elias Stützle. My eyes flashed over to Tyler, or 'Tye' as he was referred to by his friends. I looked back over to Ms. Christopher afterwards who frowned at him.

"Now, Tyler, I know that perhaps this change may upset you and others, but I'm afraid that it is within the curriculum now. Shakespeare is simply out of the syllabus for this year. Since you've kindly spoken your opinion, why don't you come and stand up to help me distribute the books so that we can get started…"

"We don't even have more than one black kid at this school, so why should we have to pick up the buck for what's an American cross rather than our own?" Tyler spoke up as he stood up. "Honestly?"

"Not another word from you," Ms. Christopher demanded. "Now come here and help me distribute the books."

Tyler walked down the aisle to assist Ms. Christopher with passing out the books. Ms. Christopher faced the class as he handed them out.

"I'm sorry for his abrupt change, but it really does come from the department rather than my own control," Ms. Christopher apologized, "but either way, it's important to have an open perspective to all sorts of stories for what they have to offer. I've read the novel, and I can say that there is certainly a perspective that can be told from the story of Malia. *Negro* is a historical novel told from her perspective from the days she lived in Africa to the days that she was kidnapped by a rival tribe, sold into slavery, and taken across the Atlantic to become a slave for a Jewish merchant in New England. It is a well-written book, and from what I understand, a real-life experience, so please give it a chance."

I looked over to Tyler who held a grumpy look on his face as he tossed a book over to me and it slid across my desk. I looked at the cover and then over to Tyler who promptly left. I then looked back down at the novel with disapproval, bringing my right hand to the side of my cheek as I looked to the side, eyes lost in a thought as I sighed.

Part 2 – Chapter 12
St. Augustine of Hippo Regional Secondary School
Harthdam, Jarsdel Island
September 1968 – 14:30 hours

Kaj looked down at his physics notebook with pencil in hand, working on an algebraic equation in silence at a two-person desk that was behind many more similar tables. On his left was Paul Schmidt, who like Kaj, was without his facial hair and instead held a youthful appearance that displayed life and energy. Kaj especially, whose reddish-blonde hair was cut short at the sides, had soft fair skin in the same hue as when he was older. His eyes blue and bright, and cheeks soft and round without the mask of his beard. At this age, Paul Schmidt had the same golden blonde hair, but it was a lot lighter, but still curled and at medium length. Before his own blue eyes, which were lighter than Kaj's, was a pair of black-framed eyeglasses. Both Kaj and Paul wore their uniforms normally, with the crimson red sweater, and as males, wore the grey trousers that went down to their ankles, paired with black socks and shoes. Around Paul's wrist was a new fashion at the time, a digital watch. Around Kaj's wrist in contrast was a standard, traditional silver analog watch. Aside from these differences, Kaj would keep the sleeves of his sweater raised to expose his forearms, the light blonde hairs on his arm, especially with the late summer heat on this afternoon. Both Kaj and Paul were slim at this time, but Kaj was more athletic looking, a natural athlete, but unaffiliated with the Jocks where Paul had some connections with the Nerds, but didn't spend much time with them. Most of his time was spent with Kaj, because they were both good friends and preferred each other's quiet company that talked about a variety of interests that they shared in common rather than one.

The bell went off to signal the end of the day and the P.A. screeched to spew out the end of day announcement as students in the laboratory classroom stood up from their stools and began to put their books away. These classrooms located at the west wing of the school were large and spacious, consisting of various counter-top tables with stools on one side and a sink on the other. At the front was a long counter-top desk from where the teacher stood and taught from, with a stool at the side to rest. Paul and Kaj's physics teacher was a quiet man who slowly marked quizzes with a pen in one hand and a fist at his jaw with the other. Mr. McKeown was a young Irish man with cool medium fair skin and curly brown hair. He wore a plaid collared shirt with the sleeves rolled up and was deep in thought as he marked. Kaj closed his notebook and put it and his physics textbook into his backpack before he looked over to Paul as he put his own stuff away into his backpack. Once they were ready, the pair of them walked out of the classroom and into the west wing corridor, which led down and shot off into the library on the right towards the end, or into the center of the building from the left halfway. Kaj stopped at his locker nearby and waved goodbye to Paul.

"I'll see you tomorrow in history," Kaj remarked.

"Yeah, I'll see you then," Paul replied, going off down to the other end of the corridor where his locker was.

Kaj unlocked his locker and then proceeded to shift books from his backpack and locker. He was then startled by the loud slap of a palm onto his back as someone approached from behind. Kaj turned around and saw the sight of a husky-looking student, Zachary Nicholson.

"Jeez, Zach, you startled me," Kaj complained as he closed his locker.

Zach gave off his foolish laugh. Kaj looked at him with a friendly face. Zachary was shorter than him, where Kaj was approximately six feet at this time, Zach was at least five feet and eight inches. Zach was rounder at the waist. He was not of fair skin, but brown as he was a member of the indigenous population, specifically the R'alagah people, and thus an Amerindian. Zach was somewhat of an outsider, although not a member of that clique, but he had good relations and an affinity towards them. Zach's loyalties lied in Kaj however, who was his best friend and valued more than the Outsiders. Although Zach was considered foreign to the students, being the only Amerindian in the entire school, it was his foreignness that caught the appeal of the Outsiders who took him in as a brother. He also held a noble reputation with the other males in the other cliques, aside from the Thespians and Preppies who were too snobbish for the likes of him. Zach wore a denim jacket overtop his uniform and a baseball cap that covered his medium length dark hair. He had round cheeks and black eyes, and he was jovial and fun with others; somewhat of a comedian who loved to fool around and laugh. Zach also had an obsession with cameras, always having a film camera with him to take pictures of whatever curiosities caught his eye.

Kaj and Zach began to walk down the hall together.

"Do you want to come over to try and sneak into the construction site for the amusement park being built in Northton?" Zach questioned. "It's behind the carnival that's going on right now. I know a way through the rollercoaster that connects them. I want to take some pictures atop of the scaffolding – it could be a great shot."

"Sorry, but I have to walk Katelyn home and then I've got to do some homework for chemistry that's due tomorrow," Kaj apologized.

"Chemistry? I thought you were in physics…"

"I'm in chemistry, biology and physics," Kaj remarked. "I'm doing all three because I can, and I want to keep my options open for whatever I could want to do in the future."

"All I want to do is take pictures."

"Yeah, I know that," Kaj said with a laugh as they made their way to the foyer, "but I… I don't really know what I want to do. I don't have much time left to decide, and I'm expected to apply for university next year. Not to mention, my mom wants me to work towards some sort of professional career, like a doctor or a lawyer, so that I can be successful, like my dad…"

"Listen, what's the point of worrying so much? If you don't know what you want to do, it's because you haven't found your passion. If you keep going the direction you're in, you'll be expected to make a decision, and that could be a decision for something that you don't like. You have to simply let yourself follow your passion, what you like to do, and then do that for a living – that's what I want to do. You don't have to worry to be like your dad, or surpass him…"

Kaj and Zach walked into the foyer. They paused for a moment.

"Maybe you've got the right idea," Kaj remarked. "Maybe I don't have to go to school when I'm done here. I mean, my grades are okay, but probably not good enough for the University of Harlech. I... I just want to do something that helps others out, a lot of people. Right now I help people out at the community center as a lifeguard, and I like it, but I want to do more than just that. At the same time, I know this guy who I work with who recently graduated from the University of Harlech with a major in psychology, and he's still working with us. What was the point of all that time and money if he's where I am now?"

"I don't envy you, buddy," Zach stated. "You seem like you've got some tough decisions to make, but I think you should just relax, and it'll come to you."

"I wish I could be as carefree as you," Kaj affirmed with a sigh, "But man, Grade Eleven has its ups and downs. I don't like looking to the future like this – it makes me anxious."

Kaj gave off another sigh and then looked out to the windows of the doors of the main entrance to look underneath the shelter where there was a female student with auburn hair tied in a bun. She had her arms rested around her textbooks to her chest. She didn't wear a sweater, but instead wore a short-sleeved blouse and kilt that was up to her waist. Her skin was fair and there was a ruddiness to her cheeks. Around her neck, she wore a silver necklace with a purple sapphire pendant. Kaj smiled as he looked over to her, speaking to the girl in front of her who had dark brown hair and blue eyes. She had fair skin too and was about the same height as Kaj. They were with a male who had tanned fair skin and sandy blonde hair that was at a short length. He had a Nordic nose that was pointed outwards and was small. He had soft and round cheeks that were exposed with his bright smile. His eyes were dark blue, and he didn't wear the school sweater, but instead wore the short-sleeved shirt with sleeves slightly rolled up. He was approximately six feet tall, close to the same height as Kaj. Kaj recognized the boy as Elias Stützle, the girl with dark brown hair as his girlfriend, Meghan Walker, and the other girl with auburn as his own, Katelyn Falkes.

"Anyways, I'll see you tomorrow in history," Kaj remarked to Zachary, raising his hand to signal goodbye as he turned to the exit. "I got to go."

Kaj pushed the door open and looked over to Katelyn who spotted him. She smiled brightly as she saw him and left the others to walk towards Kaj quickly. Kaj opened his arms up wide, as wide as his smile on his face as he rushed over to pick up his girlfriend by the waist and spin her around as they embraced. The pair of them held each other tightly, but Kaj soon let her down to the ground while they continued to hold each other's hands.

"How was your day?" Kaj questioned. "I didn't get to see you at all today!"

"I'm sorry," Katelyn apologized, "but my day was good! It's not fair that we don't share any other class aside from religion."

"And even then, Mr. Gosling has us sit in separate parts of the room," Kaj pouted.

Katelyn embraced Kaj once more and she brought a hand to his chest.

"They can't separate our love," Katelyn said.

Kaj parted Kaylen from him and they continued to hold hands.

"Nothing can come between us," Kaj added. "Nothing."

"Katelyn!" Meghan chimed.

Kaj looked over to Meghan who waved over to her. Elias continued to stand beside her.

"Oh, I have to go now though," Katelyn said to Kaj.

"You don't want me to walk you home?" Kaj questioned, lowering his smile slightly.

"No, Meghan and I are going over to that fair over in Northton," Katelyn announced. "The Neumann Fairground."

"Isn't that a little dangerous?" Kaj questioned. "I mean, it's in *Northton* of all places, and I heard that there's a lot of crime around there, especially near the carnival."

"No, it'll be fine," Katlyn assured him. "It'll be during the daytime and there are thousands of people there... surely nothing bad can happen with so many people around, right?"

Kaj didn't immediately respond.

"Right, well, if your parents are okay with it, then I guess I am too…."

"They are," Katelyn answered. "Don't you see? It's perfectly safe. You have nothing to worry about," she remarked, bringing a hand to Kaj's cheek. "I don't need my knight to escort me or anything this time. I'll talk to you later, if not, I'll see you tomorrow. Okay?"

"Okay."

Katelyn proceeded to walk away from Kaj as she continued to stand where he was with a somewhat flat expression, uncertain to what exactly his girlfriend was going into with her best friend. He looked over to Meghan as she kissed Elias on the mouth with a quick peck, and then the two girls joined arms and began to walk across the parking lot together. Elias gave a quick glance over to Kaj and then promptly left. Katelyn and Meghan disappeared from Kaj's sight soon enough, so he began to walk across the parking lot in the opposite direction so that he could make his own way home.

Kaj arrived at the sidewalk and began to walk down the street, going towards 13th Street with St. Monica Parish and then passing the church to come to the 13th Street and Harbor Avenue intersection. On the opposite end of Harbor Avenue, there were more trees while there were houses on the northern end of 13th Street. Once the intersection light turned red, Kaj crossed 13th Street and continued westward towards 14th Street and then 15th Street. On his left and right there were a lot more houses, newly built and two stories tall. The houses were hidden behind tall shrubs that were at least three years tall. The sidewalk pavement was narrow, and the road was wide, two lanes on each direction, or four lanes in total. On the opposite side on Harbor Avenue, trees continued to cover the southern end with a gulley and power line before the road. Kaj continued to walk down for four hundred meters until he reached the deepest end of the neighborhood at 16th Street. Kaj turned onto 16th Street and walked north.

The sidewalk continued north on the east side of the road, which stretched up and down, but with only one lane for each direction, or two lanes in total. The houses continued on the east side, but on the west side there was a forest with an offshoot road that composed Westbrook Crescent. Kaj crossed the street, walking on the right side of the entrance into Westbrook Crescent as there was no sidewalk. He then continued forward into the depths of this block where there were one-story homes on fairly-sized plots of land, large enough for a sizeable front yard, driveway and backyard behind. Kaj turned left at a T-intersection, and came around the block until he was on the other side, reaching the inner northwest corner where there was a rancher home with a lengthy driveway that ran up to the house. The front yard was at least forty feet by sixty feet, while the driveway was forty feet by sixteen feet.

Kaj came all the way around to the driveway so that he could walk up and come around the side of the house. The exterior of the house consisted of white horizontal wooden panels, and the roof was composed of dark grey shingles. The house had a chimney at the centre that consisted of white brick. At the top of the driveway, on the left, there was a white front door, while on the right there was a white wooden garage door with a handle at the bottom. The garage existed as a sort of annex as it was lower than the rest of the house and seemingly attached to the building. In front of the garage shutter door was a dark red 1965 Hiawatha Huron, a common American-made sedan. Kaj entered around via a path at the right-side that came to a door into a corridor behind the garage, and from there he inserted his key, opened the door, and then disappeared at the side – this was Kaj's family home at 1260 Westbrook Crescent.

St. Augustine of Hippo Regional Secondary School
Harthdam, Jarsdel Island
September 1968 – 15:30 hours

I opened my locker at the end of the school day. The school halls had quieted down as more than ninety percent of the student population had fled home. I rearranged the items in my small bookbag and then picked up my beret that rested on a hook inside. I put it atop my head and then closed the door, bringing my backpack, and then walking down the corridor to a set of double doors that entered into the drama room. I then went to a solid door at the right-side and entered through to reach the top of a staircase that went down to the back of the stage. I looked around from the top of the stairs and towards the other stagehands that were together, separated from the main cast of what would be the school play, which coincidentally composed the core of the Thespian clique.

Jamie looked over to me as I came down the set of stairs and joined him. I looked at him. He had removed his sweater and was not wearing his hat, which exposed his curled dark hair. He smiled.

"Hey!" Jamie enthusiastically greeted as he parted from the others in the main cast.

"Hey," I responded in a calm and quiet tone.

"How was your day?"

"It was quite a day really," I replied. "I've honestly just been looking forward to this more than anything."

"I'm sorry you had an exhausting day," Jamie apologized. "Hopefully this will be more fun."

"Attention everyone!" a high-pitched male shouted out.

Emma looked over to see Robin O'Connor step forward with Mr. Whitaker, the Head of the English Department and the director of the school play. Robin was dressed in a black sweater like Jamie was because these sweaters were worn by the senior class to depict their seniority. His sleeves were rolled up and had one arm at his hip. His red hair was medium length and that distinct shade of fiery orange-red that was known as ginger. He was approximately six feet and three inches tall with fair skin like snow. He also had freckles across his face and green eyes. Mr. Whitaker was only six feet tall with fair skin and dark auburn hair that was balding at the top. He had a goatee and was dressed in beige dress pants, a white collared shirt with a cross pattern, and a scarf around his neck. He was in his late forties with crow's feet at the sides of his eyes. He was also slim.

"Your attention please, ladies and gentlemen!" Mr. Whitaker spoke in a coarse and deep voice in contrast to Robin's. "We have less than three months to the Christmas performance, so we need to work hard, hard, hard, and quickly, quickly, quickly if we expect to perform at all!"

I stood next to Jamie as our attention turned to Mr. Whitaker. The performers and volunteers formed a circle with him.

"Okay, my main cast: Robin is here; Cassandra?" Mr. Whitaker called out.

"Here!"

I looked over to Cassandra Bates, another senior student who was second only to Robin in her performances even though she could capture the hearts of both women, and men. She had soft and straight black hair, fair skin like my own, and dark green eyes like a cat. She was an undistinguishable beauty. My eyes returned to Mr. Whitaker.

"Jamie?"

"Here."

"Graham?"

"Here, sir."

"Raymond?"

"Here."

Graham Tarrant was a junior in my class with fair skin and brown hair. Raymond Moreno was a Dravidian student, raised locally among the small community of people from India that was settled in South Harthdam. I believe his parents settled from Goa, a former Portuguese colony. He had of course brown skin, and dark hair and eyes. Mr. Whitaker quickly went through the supporting cast and then looked about.

"Okay!" Mr. Whitaker remarked, looking about. "I've got my supporting cast, and I see I also have a few volunteers. Perfect!"

Mr. Whitaker's eyes met with me as he looked across the circle.

"Alright," Mr. Whitaker said in a firm tone, attention turning to the rest of the students. "Today, our cast will begin a cold reading of our script for *La Bella et la Bête!*"

Mr. Whitaker took his clipboard and brought it underneath his armpit so that he could unroll a French movie poster and present it to the group.

"For those of you that have had siblings in my French class, or are in my French class, you will know that this is a French *mise en scene* that I show based on the story of the same title. Right here, three months from now, we are going to recreate that exact story as a live performance, and it will be *magnificent!*"

I looked back over to Jamie who went to join the other cast members as they went with Mr. Whitaker upstairs to the drama room. I played my part as a volunteer under the supervision of Mrs. MacAllister, who I assisted with the preparation of the set. Although I enjoyed plays and theatrics, I didn't have the talent to be a part of the performance. I knew my place, and it was with the volunteers creating props, the backgrounds, and the costumes. When we were closer to the performance, I also put a hand in with Riley to help with makeup. Today, I sat down at the front of the stage on a foldable chair putting together snowflakes on a fishing wire, which was when I began to overhear an interesting conversation from nearby. My ears twitched as I picked up on the gossip as I caught the word 'robbery' in the mix. I turned slightly to face the two girls who sat on similar chairs nearby, sharing the intrigue.

"My daddy told me that they wanted to keep it quiet, so that nobody knew that it happened at the school. He said that it would upset other parents," a girl with blonde hair said in a black sweater, "but he told me there was nothing to worry about."

"It doesn't worry me," the other student in a red sweater replied. "Although, who could imagine such a thing? Thieves at our school?"

"Keep quiet," the blonde-haired girl spoke with a hush.

"Do you know what was stolen?"

"They said that it was a bunch of dumb old books... from the bookroom in the annex," the blonde-haired girl said. "That's also why they didn't want anything said, because there was hardly anything stolen. My daddy thinks that it could have been a student at the school playing a mean joke, but the police are investigating..."

"Really? A student? Oh my gosh! Who? What grade?"

"How am I supposed to know?" the blonde-haired girl said with a shrug. "They're investigating it!"

My attention turned towards the gym doors at the opposite end of the gym. There, I saw Lance Stützle and Brock Marshall enter into the gym, dressed in their gym strip as if they were still in class, which consisted of a grey t-shirt with the school logo on it and black shorts. Where Lance had blonde hair, blue eyes, and warm fair skin that was tanned like his younger brother, his second-in-command and best friend, Brock, had black hair, blue eyes, and fair skin like mine.

"Hey!" Head's up!" Brock shouted out.

I watched as a football spiraled towards us from the others side of the gym. The girls shrieked while I ducked my head to the side. The football landed between us like a missile, bouncing upwards and then making its way towards the end of the stage near the background where it rested. The boys laughed as they walked along the side of the gym. I looked back at them with a frown and then over to the two girls as they composed themselves as they had fallen off their chairs in their fright.

"What's all the noise!" a strict voice shouted from above.

I turned my head and looked up towards the catwalk above the stage background. Cassandra stood at the very centre and looked down onto them as she rested both hands on the railings, appearing like the matriarch she was. She had an unimpressed glare on her face. Cassandra's attention was noticeably not on the distress of us, but on the boyish laughter from Lance and Brock. She quickly came around the end of the catwalk, down the stairs, took the football, and then swung it back towards the boys. She missed by a longshot, but the statement was well made as the boys attempted to go to the corridor on the left that went towards the locker rooms. I watched as Cassandra stood with her hands at her hips, looking over to the Jocks angrily.

"Hey!" Cassandra shouted out. "What do you think you're doing here causing a disturbance?! We have this space reserved from four to six!"

"Go and cry about it somewhere else!" Lance responded. "See if anyone else cares, drama queen."

The boys left into the corridor and disappeared, leaving Cassandra with her cheeks reddened and silent. She spun around and glared over to the two volunteers who had composed themselves. She tilted her chin upwards slightly.

"And you two, you better put in more effort into my dress than you are into that pile of snow," Cassandra criticized as she looked at the blanket of snow that they had been sowing together. "If I am to play the role of *Belle*, then I expect to look *beautiful!*"

The girls were quiet. Cassandra walked past them and disappeared into the backstage. I finished up tying the last bits of snowflakes to the wire and then put all of my work into a small cardboard box to bring with me to the shelves at the backstage as it became late. I would have to finish my work another time. Most of the volunteers and cast had left by now, but not Jamie who waited for me outside of the drama room near my locker.

I looked at him as I exited and attempted to pass him as I made my way out.

"Hey," Jamie greeted.

"*Salut!*" I responded, stopping, and spinning around to talk to him. "See you tomorrow!"

I spun back around and attempted to walk off, but Jamie caught up and walked with me as I made my way to the exit.

"Sorry, I didn't get a chance to talk as much as I wanted since Mr. Whitaker had us held up going over the script for the cold reading. I had a lot more lines than I thought I would have."

"You *are* Belle's father. Haven't you seen the movie? It's okay anyways," I assured him. "I was really busy getting some of the props ready anyways. We were a little shorthanded than I thought we'd be."

"Yeah, I can definitely see that," Jamie responded. "The volunteers really pull a lot of weight around on the set. We're really thankful for that."

I didn't respond as I reached the staircase and continued down with him.

"You know," Jamie said, "although we appreciate your contributions as a volunteer, you should have really auditioned for the main cast. It would have been really fun to have you onboard."

I shook my head at the idea and replied, "I don't act."

"You'd be good at it," Jamie replied with confidence. "You should have even played a good Belle."

I looked back at him with uncertainty and responded, "I could never unseat Cassandra with that leading role. I'm nothing like her."

"You're right, you're not. You're nice, and sweet, and..."

I glanced over to Jamie as we continued to walk.

"... I mean, as far as Cassandra goes, she'll be gone next year, and as far as Mr. Whitaker and Mrs. MacAllister are concerned, they'll both need a new female lead for the play they do next year..."

"No way," I denied. "I can think of half a dozen girls in sophomore and junior year that are much more qualified than I am. When Cassandra leaves, a new one will turn up. I'm not up for it. It's too late for me. Whitaker and MacAllister will probably decide on one of the females in the supporting cast to start to prepare her this year, and they'll have her be their female lead. That's the way it was with Robin when he made his debut in his sophomore year as Peter Pan. I appreciate the enthusiasm from you, but I'm content to be just another stagehand."

"Well, suit yourself," Jamie replied as we reached the lobby. "I just thought I'd express that thought and desire. Anyways, I really did miss you last weekend because there was something that I wanted to ask you. Do you maybe want to go with me to the carnival in Northton this next weekend? I have tickets for two, and... I'd actually like to take you."

My face went flush. I took a step back as my stomach twisted and turned.

"I- I don't know about that," I remarked. "I'm not – well, I don't think I'd have time for that right now."

"Right, sorry. I forgot," Jamie responded, "you're really busy with a lot of stuff. I mean, you have work, the play, and..."

"... ballet and gymnastics," I quickly added to the list. "I'm sorry..."

"No need," Jamie assured me.

I took a sidestep without another word and then left. I didn't look back as I made my exeunt from the building and off into the evening so that I could return to my own home as the sun set.

Part 2 – Chapter 14
St. Augustine of Hippo Regional Secondary School
Harthdam, Jarsdel Island
September 1968 – 08:00 hours

Kaj arrived at St. Augustine the next morning and went to the west wing where his locker was along with Katelynn's nearby. Kaj caught a glance of her on her own, approached her, and held a wide smile on his face as he was assured of her safety.

"Good morning, my beautiful princess!" Kaj joyfully greeted. "How are you?"

Katelyn straightened up and looked at Kaj with a dismal appearance. She closed her locker, put her bookbag around her, and then looked upon her boyfriend with sadness. Kaj immediately detected the emotion within her and lowered his smile for a frown.

"What's wrong? What happened? Is everything okay?"

"Oh Kaj..." Katelyn remarked, turning to the side. "No, it's not..."

"What do you mean? Tell me what happened," Kaj insisted.

Katelyn took a deep breath and then turned back to face Kaj.

"Yesterday, while at the fairground... Meghan and I... we went and saw a psychic, and she predicted our futures. She told me that I'd live a long and happy life with you, where we'd have lots of children, but that there were some bad spirits in our way and that they were going to try to drive us apart. She told me that the evil spirits had latched onto the necklace that you gave me, because it symbolized our love, and that the necklace itself didn't belong to me, but to a local lady which was why the spirits were targeting us – I didn't know if it was true or not – but I didn't want it to drive us apart. The woman gave me a traditional Romani silk bag and told me to put the necklace inside, and then told me to take it to a specific gravestone at cemetery nearby to give the necklace back to the original owner, which was the only way that the curse could be broken. The psychic told Meghan a similar thing, but with a bracelet that she had, and so we went to the cemetery to leave the items behind. I'm sorry, Kaj... I know you gave me that necklace, but I didn't think that it was worth it to have it tear us apart…"

Kaj was stunned at the story that his girlfriend had given him. He hesitated to say another word and then he swallowed his abated breath.

"Kate… I… I appreciate your intentions, but I really don't think that any of that was true. Evil spirits? A curse?"

"I know," Katelyn confessed, "but by the time I realized, it was too late. I told my father about what happened, and he was furious at me. He called Meghan's father to let him know about it. He then went to the cemetery to retrieve our stuff, but someone took it from where I placed it by then. The woman… she just seemed so believable because she knew about us, our relationship, or at least she seemed to have glimpse of it, and she knew that the necklace was given to me by you. She knew that I really love you, and that I want to be with you for the rest of my life, and I was scared so much that I… I…"

Katelyn proceeded to cry as she stuttered to produce coherent words. Kaj embraced her and held onto her as he held a worrisome look on his face.

"Oh Kaj," Katelyn said, "I'm so sorry. I shouldn't have fallen for that dubious trick. I should have been smarter, but she tricked me. She tricked me into giving away the necklace that you gave me, and I'm so sorry…"

"Hey, take it easy," Kaj replied in a soft voice. "The important thing is that both you and Meghan are safe. I'm sorry you were both scammed, but you're safe now."

"I'm sorry that I let her deceive me…"

"It's okay…"

"I… I wish there was something that we could do to get it back… but it's gone, Kaj. I don't know where it went, but it's gone."

Kaj looked ahead as he continued to comfort his girlfriend.

"It has to be somewhere," Kaj stated.

"Huh?"

Kaj and Katelyn parted. He held onto her by her waist and looked at her.

"The necklace," Kaj repeated, "it has to be somewhere, or with someone, and I bet that this someone is probably related, or associated with the psychic."

"What do you mean?"

"I'm going to find out who stole your necklace," Kaj stated, letting go of Katelyn with his left hand while he used the right to guide her away. "Come on, let's go and talk somewhere else. I want you tell me all that you can about what happened when you went to the fair."

Kaj took Katelyn to the cafeteria, towards the corner where they usually sat near their friends. The cafeteria was quiet at this hour as it was still early into the morning. Kaj sat across from Katelyn, holding her hands as she stretched them out towards him.

"Tell me what happened from the very start," Kaj requested.

"Kaj..."

"Please," Kaj insisted. "I want to hear all of it so that I can figure out who stole the necklace. I *will* get it back for you, Kate."

Katelyn sighed and she sniffled for a moment.

"Meghan and I went to this machine near all of the games," Katelyn explained. "It was a psychic machine – you know, the ones with the puppet fortuneteller inside that moves around and talks – I can't remember what his name was. Meghan and I put a coin in for the machine and it started to move and speak, saying that there was a special energy within us and that were destined for something special but that we needed to make the right choices or else we would be doomed. The machine then printed out a ticket, the size of a card, and it said that we were being referred to seek our special assistance in order to know what we needed to do. So, we took the card and went to find the psychic at the fair. I can't remember her name – Madame... I don't remember. Anyways, we gave her the card and said that we had been referred to her, so she agreed to do our reading, free of charge, and then she started with me. She asked me to stretch a hand out, and then she started to read my palm, and once she said that she had a sense for me, she put her hands around her crystal ball and began to say these weird things about me... She knew that I had a boyfriend, you..."

"Hold on, did she say that I was your boyfriend, or just that you had a boyfriend?"

"She said that I had a boyfriend, and that he was a caring man who loved me a lot…"

"Okay…"

"She said that I loved him too, but that I was anxious of losing you. She told me that as long as I kept my chin up and stayed with you, we'd be happy forever. She envisioned a bright future for us both, with lots of children, a farmhouse, and even a dog. However, then she began to convulse almost… She told me that she felt some spirits were attempting to prevent my happiness, and it was all because of that necklace which she said belonged to someone else – Iris… I can't remember the last name. She told me that the necklace belonged to her, and that she was buried nearby, and that if I didn't take the necklace, put it in this special silk bag that she would give me, then I would become cursed and all my fortunes would reverse. I was stunned. Before she even did Meghan's fortune, she felt a same energy from the fact that we were close friends, which Meghan was extremely upset about. We almost had a fight over it, but then we agreed that we'd both go to the cemetery for the sake of our relationships, which we did…."

Kaj listened and allowed Katelyn to finish. He then paused for a moment, possibly to review the story in his head and generate more questions.

"At any point did the lady ask you any personal questions when she was delivering your fortune?" Kaj questioned.

"No," Katelyn denied after a brief pause of thought. "I didn't tell her a thing about me."

"But did you agree at all when she suggested certain points, such as that you had a boyfriend?"

"Yes, I did…"

"Did you reveal any personal information to her?"

"No…"

"Anything at all, such as where you live, who you are, or where you go to school?"

"No."

"What about the necklace? Did you tell her who gave it to you?"

"No..."

"Did you agree when she asked if it was yours or not that it was not originally yours?"

"Yes..."

"And you said that your dad went to check the gravestones afterwards, but he couldn't find the bag with the necklace in it?"

"That's right," Katelyn confirmed. "I took him to the exact grave that I put it at – the one for that dead woman. I forgot her full name, but I knew what grave it was."

"What about Meghan's lost item? You said she lost the bracelet that she was wearing?"

"Yes," Katelyn responded. "Elias gave her that bracelet for their anniversary."

"I suppose that's gone too?"

"Yes," Katelyn sadly confirmed.

"Okay..." Kaj replied. "I think I have a sense of what happened last night – I'm going to have to think about it some more, and maybe do a bit of research into scams because from what it sounds like, I think that the scam basically involved you releasing your items out of fear of being cursed, and that the items were then picked up possibly. I'm not entirely sure. If they were picked up by the same person that ran the scam, then they must still be at the fair. I'll do some research at lunch, and then after school I'm going to go and find out where your necklace is so that I can get it back."

Katelyn didn't respond to Kaj's promise. Instead, Meghan arrived with the same gloomy expression on her face. Kaj let go of his girlfriend's hands as she arrived and they looked at her.

"Hey," Katelyn said to her friend.

"I'm sorry about what happened last night," Kaj instead said, eyeing Elias on approach with his best friend, Tyler. "I'll let you girls be and catch you later."

Kaj stood up and picked up his backpack. He looked over to Katelyn as Meghan sat down together.

"Is there anything else that I should know about yesterday?" Kaj questioned before he left.

"No."

"Okay," Kaj responded. "I'll see you later."

Kaj left and disappeared back to his locker. He exchanged the books in his backpack for those in his locker so that he could get ready for the day. He then went upstairs and met with Zachary in the hallways that overlooked the cafeteria where he looked down to see his girlfriend with Meghan, Elias, and Tyler. Kaj sat down from nearby and looked over at his friend who was fiddling with his camera.

"Hey…" Kaj greeted.

"What's going on with you and Katelyn?"

"Oh, nothing much," Kaj responded.

Kaj explained to Zachary a basic rundown of the situation from what he had gathered from Katelyn. Kaj knew exactly what was stolen, including Meghan's bracelet, which was a thin gold chain with various charms attached – it had been gifted to her by her boyfriend, Elias.

"What are you going to do?" Zachary questioned.

"What am I going to do? I'm going to go after the crooks that stole their stuff of course! I'm not going to let them get away with stealing my girlfriend's necklace – that necklace was special – I gave it to her, and besides that, it also belonged to my grandmother."

"Seems like a lot of effort for some fancy metals."

Kaj scoffed at that remark and replied, "It's more than just some fancy metals, although I see your point, but you have to understand that those metals have sentimental values. Kate is heartbroken that she lost the necklace, and although it was my grandmother's, my interest in getting it back is to right the wrong and get my girlfriend's necklace back more than to please me. Imagine if someone stole your camera – you'd rip their arms off."

"Hehe," Zach responded in his foolish laugh, "I would."

"You see," Kaj replied. "I'm completely justified to be angry and want to get back at these people by looking into this – I will find out who stole their jewelry and I'm going to get it back."

"If you say so," Zach responded as the bell went off for homeroom. "I'll see you later."

"Okay," Kaj said to him, looking down to his girlfriend as she separated from Elias and Tyler and then left with Meghan for homeroom. "I'll catch you later…"

Part 2 – Chapter 15
St. Augustine of Hippo Regional Secondary School
Harthdam, Jarsdel Island
September 1968 – 12:00 hours

I was in the school library at lunch, reviewing newspapers so that I could find out more information about recent thefts across the entire city. The school library, located in the west wing of the school, was large and two stories tall. On the ground floor, the library mostly consisted of corridors and aisles of books with the checkout desk on the right from the entrance from where students could sign-out books with the librarian, Ms. Mayhew. At the far reaches, there were some desks for students to study from and review books on their own. On the second floor, accessible either from the staircase at the centre or from the upstairs west wring corridor, there were a few aisles where the fictional books were, and there were also more spaces to privately study at. However, the main caveat was the group space where there were larger tables from where groups convened, studied together, and also played board and card games together – and this feature was where the Nerd clique primarily met with each other. I attempted to avoid the second floor as much as possible because of the dominant presence of the Nerds, situating myself on the ground floor, especially the nooks and corners from where I could hide.

Today, I was at the northern corner of the school library, at the far reaches where there were wide tables with shelves underneath from where the school kept research magazines in archive. Nearby, there were also shelves that contained stacks upon stacks of newspapers, with the most recent prints from the last year closest on a table, awaiting to be sorted. The notable newspapers in Harlech were much the same as fifteen years later. *The Herald* was the dominating newspaper for nationwide coverage that almost everyone read, especially since it had been around for a long time and thus it had a firm reputation as a credible and unbiased newspaper. *The Herald* also had its sister newspaper, a tabloid known as *The Dornoch Chronicles*. There were also other newspapers that were read nationwide, such as

The National Focus (a broadsheet) and *The Toronto Spectator* (a tabloid), although it had recently rebranded itself as simply *The Spectator*. However, there were then the local newspapers which aimed at local news, and these were *The Colony* (a broadsheet) and *The Island Sentinel* (a tabloid). Today, I reviewed the local newspapers for information that could aid me, so there I was going through the copies of *The Colony* and *The Sentinel* for more information about this supposed theft from the school.

I looked through each copy of both *The Colony* and *The Sentinel* thoroughly for the last two weeks, but I couldn't find much about any sort of robbery, which led me to believe that it had been effectively unreported.

Riley looked at me from nearby where she was studying for her own courses. She observed me as I surrounded myself upon piles and piles of newspapers, sheets spread out around. If I was any other person, Riley would have believed that I was crazy, but as I looked through the last one and confirmed there was no further information related to the theft from the school, I started to put away all the newspapers and then sit back down. Both my hands and my surroundings wreaked of printer ink. I laid back and looked up to the ceiling as I thought for a moment.

"So?" Riley questioned, breaking my concentration.

I looked back over to her and sighed.

"I've got nothing," I concluded. "Well, that's disappointing, but I guess it was a longshot."

"What if you look further back?"

"No," I denied, not itching to stretch this any further, "I'm not too crazed to look into this anymore than I have. I'll have to let it rest – I've got homework to do before I leave for gymnastics practice after school."

"I thought you had ballet today?"

"Ballet is tomorrow. Monday and Thursday, I help with the school play. Tuesday and Friday, I have gymnastics practice."

"What a complicated schedule – why do you complicate your life so much? All I have to worry about is babysitting from time to time –

not that I do that voluntarily, but because my mother forces me to. If she isn't forcing me to do that, I have to babysit my own siblings! Why couldn't I be an only-child like you…"

I sighed and thought for another moment.

"I wish I had a sibling – at least a brother so then I wasn't the one that had to help my parents with their shop," I moped as I rested my head down onto the table ahead. "A sister would be too complicated."

"Hey," Riley suddenly said, looking at all my newspapers, "you checked *The Sentinel* and *The Colony*, but you didn't check the community paper – you know, the one that we all get for free… *The Jarsdel Journal.*"

I immediately straightened up and remarked, "Of course! How could I have been so obtuse?!"

I stood up and went back to the shelves, looking around for copies of *The Jarsdel Journal*, which wasn't a daily newspaper, but was released on Wednesday and Fridays. It was also a slim paper that contained at most twenty pages in total. Unfortunately, I couldn't find any copies of *The Jarsdel Journal* near where I was, so I went around to the other side to continue my search. I saw Elias Stützle on the other side, which caused me to feel awkward, so I briefly searched, but only saw more copies of the standard broadsheets and tabloids. I came back around, brought my hands to my hips, and thought for a moment before I turned to Riley.

"I can't find them," I stated, "but come to think about it, I don't think that the school receives *The Jarsdel Journal*. I may have to wait until I'm back home to check if we have any copies left. Darn…"

I turned my glance to the side as I saw someone that I didn't expect to see, other than Elias who I wasn't sure why he was nearby – the last place anyone would expect a Jock like him to be was the library. No less, Kaj, who was now here and who I knew little about since I never spoke with him, rarely shared any classes with him, and all I thought about him was that he was a quiet boy who was in a relationship with Katelyn Falkes, who also I also did not speak much with. Riley on the other hand lived near Kaj and the two had been friends once upon a time, and Riley was on good terms with Kaj's girlfriend. Riley was more social than Kaj and I combined, and her reputation was in her ability to converse and chat with anyone anywhere. Riley's eyes met Kaj as I looked at him and then turned back around. I walked back over to the table where I was working and saw him approach closer, reviewing the stacks of newspapers on the shelf near us. Riley continued to track him. I turned my glance away and pretended like I didn't notice him, as I usually did towards someone who I wasn't familiar with.

"Hi Kaj," Riley greeted with a smile.

"Oh, hey," Kaj responded, looking over to her.

"How are you?"

"I'm okay," Kaj replied. "How about you?"

"I'm good, thanks for asking," Riley said. "How's your mother? Is she doing okay?"

"Oh… she's alright…"

"What're you up to?" Riley questioned. "Are you doing a project of some sort? Is it that project for Mr. Robertson's class?"

"No," Kaj replied, "I'm just trying to find *The Sentinel* or *The Colonist* to reference some stuff."

"Well, as a matter of fact, Emma has all of those from the last two weeks," Riley replied.

"Oh, does she?" Kaj questioned.

I turned my glance towards Kaj and stood up. I looked at Kaj and observed his appearance – I hadn't even realized how different he appeared since we were in close quarters like this – he was a different person almost from when I remembered him. His hair for example was a lot darker than the light blonde shade of strawberry blonde that it used to be. We had a similar hair color, and I remember that it was a running joke in elementary school that some people thought that we were siblings… Kaj held a book in one of his arms, and I noticed that it didn't look like a textbook. The title of the book read, 'Bunco – Modern Scams, Tricks, and Con Artistry in the 20th Century.' I looked back at Kaj as he looked at my table and all the newspapers.

"Are you using them for something?"

"Sorry, no. I don't need them anymore – you can have a look at them if you'd like," I said, moving away with my book bag in hand.

I moved over to stand next to Riley, hoping that she would stand up and leave with me. However, instead, she continued to sit where she was, leg raised over her knee, twirling a strand of her hair she talked to her old friend. I faced away from her and placed my book bag atop of another nearby table so that I could fix my stuff while I listened to their conversation.

"What kind of information are you looking to reference?" Riley asked. "Emma and I were looking through all of them just now so maybe we can help save you some time."

"Oh, it's just some stuff related to the Neumann Fairgrounds," Kaj stated. "I saw something in the news related to a recent amount of thefts near the fair, and I wanted to find the article."

"Is that because of what happened to Katelyn yesterday?" Riley pondered.

"Sort of…" Kaj confirmed.

I turned around and looked over to Riley. I was intrigued – another theft?

"What happened to Katelyn?" I quietly asked Riley.

Riley turned to face me as she put both feet on the ground.

"Well, I only heard the rumors, but apparently they both got robbed at the fair yesterday – pretty horrible if you ask me," Riley stated, "but maybe Kaj knows more about what really happened – Kaj? What happened to Katelyn and Meghan?"

Kaj turned his eyes towards us as he sheepishly looked at the newspapers I had laid out.

"Kate and Meg didn't really get robbed," Kaj clarified, "but they did get scammed out of some jewelry, and I've been looking into it a bit."

"How did they get scammed?" Riley asked.

I turned to the side again as I became uninterested – a part of me had hoped that what happened to Katelyn Falkes and Meghan Walker would somehow be related to my case, but it wasn't.

"It was a sort of an elaborate trick, but from what I've been able to read, apparently it was an old one that's common amongst gypsies in Europe where a fortune teller presents a problem to a person that is deemed the 'mark' in the scam. The fortuneteller firstly gains the trust of a person by giving them a promising fortune, and also by doing a cold reading to reveal some personal details about the person to build up the credibility of the fortune teller. Once there is trust and a promising fortune is provided, the fortuneteller states that there is a problem but that he can provide a solution… at a cost. From what I've read, this used to be in the form of money, but with Kate and Meg, they had to pay with their jewelry. The fortune teller told them to leave their items in a nearby cemetery, and when they later came back, the items were gone – stolen essentially."

"How awful," Riley remarked. "I would never believe in any of that stuff, along with zodiac signs and horoscopes. Mr. Gosling told us that all of that stuff was demonic and evil…"

"Yeah…" Kaj replied.

"You know, I read a study that said the reason why some people steal is because of adverse social conditions in which the subjects held little to no control over. For example, bad parents, or a bad upbringing, or any other event in their life that preceded the act of larceny. Interestingly, and I brought this up to Mr. Gosling after class once, but religious upbringing played no role in whether a person resorted to larceny or not."

"Interesting…"

"I found it was *very* interesting, but I have hard time thinking what psychological motive would cause someone to steal a bunch of books from the school…"

My head turned up as I heard Riley expose what I was researching. Kaj and I both looked at Riley.

"What?" Kaj questioned.

Riley turned to me and then over to Kaj as she realized she had spilt the gossip.

"Oh sorry, but you didn't hear?" Riley questioned. "Apparently, a bunch of books were stolen from the school – that's what Emma was looking into at least, or what she had heard."

Kaj glanced over to me. I continued to put stuff back into my backpack as I avoided eye contact with him.

"So what are you going to do about your case of theft? Did Katelyn call the police?" Riley asked, looking back over to Kaj while I listened.

"Right now I'm just trying to understand it a bit more," Kaj responded, looking at the newspapers again. "I don't think that calling the police would do much… as of yet, so after school I'm going to go to the fairgrounds and see if I can find the fortuneteller and this machine that they visited yesterday."

"Oh… well, be safe," Riley stated, looking over to me as I finished to pack up and put my book bag around me. "I heard that the fairs weren't the safest place, so don't do anything that could get you hurt. I'll see you later, Kaj. Best of luck!"

Riley stood up and I led her away from where we were hanging out. I looked to my right and down the aisle behind the shelf we were near and saw Elias once more – I wondered if he heard what Riley and Kaj were talking about. Kaj continued to look at all the newspapers I had laid out when he collected the ones from the last week since the fair had started and then took them with him back over to a study table that he and Paul were at. Paul look over as Kaj slammed the newspapers down.

"Do you really think you'll be able to go through all of those in the last thirty minutes of lunch?" Paul remarked.

"No," Kaj replied, "but I'll try my best. I know that there must be something in here – I think I remember reading about it last Friday or Thursday…"

Kaj began to look through the newspapers, starting with the last Friday edition, where he saw that I had circled the heading for a case of theft in Harthdam, but which was unrelated to either of our situations. Kaj glanced at it and then continued to look through the rest of the newspaper as he skimmed the headings. Kaj looked at the Thursday edition, and then looked at where I had circled the word 'robbery' in another heading related to a robbery in Keswick. Kaj was able to go through each newspaper a lot easier because I had highlighted these key words for him to key in on. Soon, he was able to find the news article that he had seen.

The headline read, 'Pickpockets on the rise in South Northton,' and unfortunately, after Kaj read the article from the beginning to the end, it didn't suggest anything related to the fortune teller and her scams, but made a broad reference to a recent trend since the start of the month that was announced by the Harlech Police Department in which police reports related to thefts, specifically pickpocketing near the Neumann Fairground, had been on the uptick ever since the start of the month, which was when the carnival began on September 2nd – Labor Day.

Kaj took notes of the article in a notebook, cited which newspaper he extracted this information from (*The Colonist*) and wrote the date of that paper for future reference. He then continued to read through the rest of the newspapers in hopes of a reference to the fortune teller, but couldn't find one. By the end of the lunch period, Kaj was able to skim through all of the newspapers he had brought, but there wasn't any further information for him to jot down, so he was only left with an idea that there were crimes possibly related to the presence of the carnival in South Northton.

"I wish I had a bit more time to do some research," Kaj said to Paul, "but I'll have to come back and do some more tomorrow. I'm definitely going to visit this place after school today – do you want to come? Zach already said he was busy…"

"Sorry, but I have to study for a math test tomorrow," Paul remarked. "I guess you're really serious about all of this?"

"Of course," Kaj replied as he put his stuff away and stacked the newspapers. "I'm not going to rest until I have Kate's necklace back."

"Understandable," Paul acknowledged. "If you ask me, there has to be some sort of logical conclusion to these thefts, but I'm sure you're already aware of that. From a book that I read, larceny is said to be the most common form of crime next to fraud. In Harlech, I believe that over seventy percent of crimes are related to larceny and break and enters. However, that's what's reported. The bright side is that almost three-quarters of all crimes in Harlech are said to be solved and lead to criminal charges."

"Thanks," Kaj responded. "Let's hope that this one can make the three-quarters then."

At the end of the day, Kaj carried his persistence onwards as he intended to visit the Neumann Fairground at the other side of the island in South Northton. After all, Kaj was a persistent person, and I don't believe that there was anything in the world that could have stopped him. There was another person that felt the same, but perhaps for differing reasons, and that was Elias Stützle who observed Kaj from afar as he met with his girlfriend in the parking lot.

"Please Kaj, be careful and phone as soon as you return from the carnival," Katelyn insisted. "I want to make sure that you're safe – don't do anything reckless."

"Relax, princess," Kaj replied. "It's me you're talking to."

Katelyn brought a hand to Kaj's cheeks and then heard a shout from afar of her name. The couple looked over to the parking lot where a blue 1965 Armstrong Hoosier sedan was parked with an older male in jeans, a tucked in shirt, and slicked back greyish-dark hair was waving over to Katelyn. She gave a quick peck on the cheek to her boyfriend and then quickly left. Katelyn waved her hand over to Kaj before she entered the car and then disappeared from the parking lot.

Kaj watched her off, sighed, and then proceeded to walk towards the sidewalk so that he could proceed to Northton from the school. There was at least a ten to fifteen kilometer difference between his current location and where he needed to be, so there was no time to lose. However, as Kaj stepped onto the sidewalk, he was suddenly met with the shout of his own name from afar. Kaj turned around and saw Elias approximately ten meters from him. He frowned as he looked at him.

Elias wore a letterman jacket overtop his uniform that was commonly worn by members of the Jock clique, signifying their membership among the athletics department with the school and their status as an athlete. The jacket was crimson at the torso and had dark white sleeves. On the right side of the front of the jacket, the letter A was displayed to signify St. Augustine of Hippo Secondary, and at the left side, Elias' name was written in a cursive font. At the back of the jacket, the school team logo was displayed for the Augustinian Hippos. Meanwhile, Kaj wore a simple black rain coat overtop his uniform sweater. The clouds were slightly grey at the moment since it had been raining earlier in the day, but as these two met at the end of that brief storm throughout the day, the sun had started to shine a bit. Elias approached Kaj who looked at him with a bit of surprise.

"You're going to the Neumann Fairground?" Elias asked.

"Yeah, what about it?"

"You're going to go try and get your girlfriend's necklace back?"

"Yeah."

"I want to come with you. They stole the bracelet that I gave Meghan, and I want it back – they can't get away with it."

"I don't intend for them to get away with it..."

"What do you intend to do?"

"I'm just going to go over and snoop around," Kaj explained. "I need to learn more about who these people are before I do anything else."

"So can I come with you then?"

"If you want," Kaj remarked, "but I'm taking the bus."

"No problem."

Elias approached Kaj and the pair started to walk together. Despite the fact that Elias and Kaj's girlfriends were both best friends, the pair of them seldom spoke to each other. This fact wasn't entirely because of their cliques though, because both Katelyn and Meghan were not affiliated with any clique, although it could be said for Katelyn that she had some affiliation, if not an affinity to the Jocks, she was never really one of them. Meghan on the other hand had an affiliation to the Thespian clique. In my opinion, the fact that Kaj and Elias never spoke to each other was because they never had a chance to, but this rare instance would not be the start of a friendship, but a brief and awkward collaboration out of mutual interests. Elias and Kaj walked together, quietly, crossing Harbor Avenue, and continuing southbound on foot via 12th Street to reach Walham Way.

From Walham Way, the pair continued across the major street, crossed Rostill Avenue, then Hoogeveen Avenue, and then Holwill Avenue through the southern suburbs of North Harthdam to reach Caledonia Street that crossed through the middle of the district. From Caledonia Street, Kaj and Elias rode a bus that went from Harthdam to Northton, and then another that went along Riverside Drive at the southeast corner of the island to reach the large plot of land where Neumann Fairgrounds existed.

Kaj viewed the fairground from the bus window and noticed that there was a construction site next to it, which Zachary had described to him yesterday and visited himself. The entire property was divided between the active fairgrounds and the construction zone for a future, new and improved amusement park. The entirety of these land once composed the site of an amusement park that was known as Joyland, but had been shut down at the end of the last decade due to health and safety concerns. Since then, the remains of Joyland existed, and some other attractions that could not be seen from the outside. Half of these were locked away, that half a part of the construction site and another half rented out and incorporated into the travelling fairground. On the side of the fairground, the Ferris wheel could be seen for example, while on the side of the construction site, the wooden rollercoaster was out of commission. Kaj viewed and saw there to be a lot more activity and life on the side of the Neumann Fairground, including a large red and white tent that was hosted in the center back.

Elias and Kaj crossed the street and reached the gates of the fairground, which consisted of kiosks with turnstile gates. The kiosks were empty. There was a small crowd of people in front of the entrance, mostly teenagers who had just left school. People entered and exited the fairgrounds as they pleased. Elias and Kaj approached and entered through. On the other side, the site of tents, concession stands, and an assortment of attractions could be seen. As the pair walked through the carnival, it became apparent that payment was done through the exchange of tickets that could be used to access the attractions. Kaj walked through with Elias as they searched for the fortune teller tent and after their walkthrough, Kaj was able to see attractions such as the carousel, a chair swing ride, a Scrambler, and a tunnel of love. The rides that were sheltered and appeared old and rundown, such as the Ferris wheel, carousel, swing ride, and tunnel were noticeably remnant of Joyland. Even a few of the carnival games appeared as if they were a part of the old amusement park, which suggested that all that was new that was brought to the fairground was the concessions stands, tent games, and the large circular tent at the back where the freak show was advertised to be. Elias and Kaj soon arrived at a sheltered building with an open façade that contained a variety of electro-mechanical games – like an arcade, but instead of computerized video games, there were intricate devices, such as shooter games, Skee-Ball, basketball, and the fortuneteller machine that Katelyn had described.

Kaj pointed out the device to Elias. "That's the machine they said told them to consult a fortuneteller," Kaj remarked. "Let's go and see if it gives us the same card."

Elias and Kaj approached the device, which read Mystic Marvin. They read the instructions on the wooden base of the machine. The base was carved out of a fine oak wood that was polished. Above the base, inside of a glass case, there was an animatronic of a fair-skinned male with a dark beard and a turban atop of his head. In front of the animatronic was a lavender crystal ball. The machine did not accept tickets, but instead quarters. Most of the other machines in the arcade accepted nickels instead. Kaj saw what payment the machine received and then looked to Elias.

"Do you have any quarters?"

"Yeah, I think so…"

Elias rummaged through his jacket and then took off his backpack to find some loose change. He took out a quarter and inserted it into the machine. The animatronic inside the case sprung to life and started to move its hands around the crystal ball.

"So, you have come to me for my insight?" the animatronic spoke. "Yes, I sense your troubles and dreadful fright."

Kaj observed as the animatronic waved his hands around the crystal ball, which itself lit up and flashed. The eyes of the animatronic moved left and right, and even blinked as if it were a real person.

"Let me glimpse into my crystal ball here," the animatronic said, "and see what problems come your way this year."

The animatronic closed its eyes as it continued to wave its hands around its crystal ball. It then opened its eyes and stopped.

"Look now, below, I have seen your future," the animatronic said as a ticket printed out from below, "act now, and the fabric of fate will require a suture."

Kaj ripped the card out from where it printed and read the fortune, 'Always remember to watch your back wherever you are.'

"What the heck is that supposed to mean?" Kaj questioned, looking at the fortune.

"What?" Elias asked, looking at the fortune.

"Kate and Meghan got a card that said they needed to see the fortuneteller – how come we didn't get that card?"

"Maybe it's one in a few," Elias suggested.

"Give me another quarter," Kaj requested.

Elias took a quarter from his pocket and gave it to Kaj, who put the quarter in. The animatronic repeated its ritual verbatim and then another card printed out. Elias took the card and read it aloud.

"The future will bring about a great amount of change," Elias read out.

Kaj took the card from his hand and read it. He then frowned.

"Do you have another quarter?"

"No," Elias responded. "How about we just find this fortuneteller? I don't see why we need the card to go and see her?"

"I wanted to see if we'd get the same card..." Kaj replied, disappointed in the results, "but sure, let's go and see her anyways."

Elias and Kaj left the arcade and returned outdoors to look around for the fortuneteller tent. Kaj was soon able to sight a small purple tent that had a sign on the front that read, 'Ellerada the Enchanted' and below it described, 'Receive your fortune and learn what awaits you in the near future: $5' with a list of other services, such as palm readings, tarot card readings, and natal chart readings for five dollars. Elias and Kaj entered into the tent where it was dim and their surroundings lit by candles. In front of them was a short table with two cushions before them, and then a larger cushion behind the crystal ball placed on the middle of the table. The table was decorated with a red table runner that was stretched horizontally. On the left and right of the crystal ball, which rested on a red velvet pillow, there were gold-colored candle holders with white candles lit. Behind the table, there were stacks of large books around the work area for the psychic. Elias and Kaj noticed that there was nobody around, which prompted them to stand awkwardly.

"Hello?" Kaj shouted out.

Suddenly, the tent flap opened on the other side and a short woman in a flamboyant dress with a turban wrapped around her head approach them. She appeared to be elderly, in her fifties or so, with greying dark hair poking out from around her headdress.

"Ah, I thought I felt your presence," the woman spoke in a foreign accent. "Please, sit down – I am pleased that you have decided to visit me. Together, we can see what it is that ails your heart... Let me tell you your fortune."

Elias approached Kaj and whispered into his ear.

"Why don't we just ask her about the bracelet and necklace? I'm not paying five dollars for her to scam us."

Kaj looked back at Elias and then over to Ellerada.

"We're here to learn about our future," Kaj stated.

"Take a seat, take seat," Ellerada encouraged as she did the same and sat down at her cushion. "So I can read your future, I must ask for ten dollars please."

"The sign outside said five," Elias pointed out.

"You are two, two is ten dollars," Ellerada clarified.

Kaj took out a leather wallet from his jacket and put down ten dollars, sliding it over to Ellerada, and prompting her to take the money and place it within her clothes. Kaj went to sit down, which prompted Elias to do the same. They watched as she closed her eyes, tilted her head up, and took a deep breath in. Kaj attempted to study her carefully as he observed her.

"Yes," Ellerada said as she looked back over to them and opened her eyes. "I am sensing your energies, yes. You are both troubled, yes – frustrated and confused with nowhere else to turn. I feel… a deep conflict within you both, but that is not why you are here. I feel… ooh, yes… I feel it is a pain in your heart," she expressed, bringing her hands to her chest as she looked back at them, "a man in your lives that has caused you pain… and now you are here."

Kaj raised an eyebrow as she looked at him.

"Yes, your energies are intertwined – you are one the same. There is a trauma, and I feel the trauma that you have held back that is strong, but… that is not why you are here. It is, however, what will lead your futures – a near future that is close, but a far one that is apart, and… I feel heartbreak from one of you at that point, a great amount of sadness to come."

Ellerada closed her eyes and went quiet for a moment. Kaj and Elias both looked at each other. She soon opened her eyes.

"It is difficult," Ellerada stated, "it is too similar and I cannot differentiate between each of you – there is too much interference from the other side and I cannot pickup on the signals."

"Is that all?" Kaj questioned. "What does any of that mean? Can we fix it?"

"No," Ellerada denied, "you can only prepare for the future – for what fate has in store, you cannot change it. You can only play your part. I'm sorry, but that is all – I do not want to look anymore, it is too dark. We are done."

Kaj looked at her with disappointment as she stood up to have them leave.

"What a load of shit," Elias interjected, standing up, "neither of us are here because of any pain like that – we're here because you stole from our girlfriends yesterday. You told them to bury their jewelry in a cemetery so you could take it off them! We want their stuff back!"

Ellerada brought hand to her chest in insult. She pointed a finger towards the exit.

"Out, both of you! Out! I will not have such insults in my tent! Begone before I put a curse on you both! I will wipe this arrogance from your mouths! Begone!"

"Tell us where my girlfriend's bracelet is!" Elias shouted.

Ellerada began to chant in an unknown language – possibly Romani, but it could have been any foreign language, if a language at all. Kaj pulled at Elias' arm to get him to leave with him. The pair then left as they saw that Ellerada would be uncooperative with them. Ellerada fluttered her hands at them as they left, but Elias was hot with anger, pushing Kaj as they exited.

"What the hell was all that about?" Elias questioned. "You paid ten dollars for her to tell us a crock of shit that has nothing to do with anything? What a waste of time and money…"

"She didn't ask us to ditch any of our items to change our future…" Kaj noted. "All she did was tell us that our fate was sealed…"

"What fate? There's no such thing as fate. All of it was a lie…"

"I know it was a lie," Kaj replied, "but I was looking to see if she'd try to con us like she did with Kate and Meg, but she didn't. I… I must have missed something – this is all wrong. If she's a scammer, then why didn't she scam us? She was supposed to tell us that we could repair our future, or that we were cursed and she could alleviate that from us, but she didn't…"

"She scammed ten dollars off of you… seems like a good profit."

"I'm going to go back to the psychic machine… maybe there's something more to it."

"Yeah, go ahead," Elias replied, putting his hands in his jacket pocket. "I'm out of here, Kaj, this was a waste of time. I would have expected a little more from you – Meghan's bracelet and your girl's necklace is probably long gone by now. There's no way to get it back…"

Kaj frowned at Elias.

"Fine," Kaj replied, "leave. I don't know why you bothered to come with me in the first place."

Elias and Kaj split paths. Kaj held an annoying glance on his face as though he was frustrated with more than just the fact that the con had not gone as he had expected. Kaj returned to the arcade and the machine with the animatronic. He looked at it and studied it more closely now that Elias was gone, paying attention to the details. He put a hand at the coin slot, observing the shape and size of the slot. He looked around and to the other coin slots, seeing them to be a particular shape for the coin they accepted, where this one was supposed to accept quarters and the others accept nickels. Kaj then looked at the animatronic, but didn't see any significant details to note in his mind. He looked around and noticed that the arcade was relatively quiet compared to the rest of the fair and unsupervised, so he began to inch around the back of the machine to see the rear. Kaj held a focused look on his face as he studied the hatch at the rear. In front of the hatch was a sticker with a column that listed names and dates for routine maintenance checks. Kaj looked at the names and recognized one of them as a student, Glenn Bertrand, with a checkup several weeks ago during the summer. He then noticed someone come around to the arcade, which prompted him to exit from out of the back to avoid suspicion. Kaj looked back at the machine, took a sidestep, and then proceeded to leave as he found his next lead.

I brushed my hair in the mirror of the locker room in the gym as I finished gymnastics practice and I was all alone. I had just finished putting on my uniform and I was just about ready to leave, but with each stroke of my brush, I became more and more pensive of the stolen books. *What books were stolen?* was the question that was at the top of my mind, and after the fact that Ms. Christopher had seemingly forced us to comply and read *Negro*, although I was just about finished reading the novel, my heart was lost on how she could have betrayed us, the same way that Claudius had betrayed King Hamlet, to read a book on the hot topic of racial prejudice at a time of racial tension in the United States instead of a seamless classic. Of course, although I did not know it for sure, I could not for a second believe that the two instances were not a coincidence – it would have been foolish and unintuitive of me to not believe it, so I had to see her and ask her myself.

I left the locker room and took my gym bag with me to the exit at the end of the gym that led out to the parking lot. From there, I came around and went upstairs to Room 213 where Ms. Christopher's classroom was. I knocked on the door in hopes that she was inside. The door into the classroom had a square window on the upper half, but it was covered with a curtain that didn't allow me to look in. I knocked again, but there was no response. I wouldn't allow this to stop me, because I was angry. I knocked harder, and when there was no response again, I put my hand on the doorknob and turned it. The door was unlocked.

I entered into the darkened classroom and looked around. Ms. Christopher was nowhere in sight. I stepped forward and felt an eerie loneliness in the fact that the classroom was so empty. If the door was unlocked, I dreaded to believe that such a simple fault could have been the cause of the tragic thefts, no less, the embarrassment on the school that would cause them to want to avoid any press coverage of the matter. I attempted not to concentrate on that fact too much as I went over to Ms. Christopher's desk where copies of *Negro* were piled up. I came around to the desk and then peeked into the bookroom. The door was wide open and the room on the other side was dark. I then looked at the door that went to Room 214, Mr. Power's classroom, before I took in a deep breath.

Without a doubt, I was alone. I looked at Ms. Christopher's desk and observed that her papers were neatly piled on one side on the right, stationary organized on the left, and the copies of *Negro* on the far left. On the far right there was a picture frame of Ms. Christopher and an unknown man – I wasn't sure if this man was her husband, but I didn't recognize him and the two appeared to be shaking hands as if Ms. Christopher had received an award from him. He was an older man with dark greyish-black hair slicked back and he wore a suit with a dark blue tie. He had cold fair skin and dark eyes. I put my hand over the papers on Ms. Christopher's desk and picked up the sheet that was neatly folded, reading it as a letter addressed to Ms. Christopher from Mr. Whitaker, and it read 'Dear Agatha, My deepest regret for the incident that occurred over the weekend, but as discussed during the staff meeting, the archdiocese would like to move forward with having your class adopt this contemporary novel '*Negro*' by Lars van den Berg, which has received high appraise from most English Studies academics. Although I have not yet finished the book, it has been given approval from the archdiocese, so please see to it that your class studies this novel in lieu of your unit on *Hamlet*. Kindest regards, Ryan.' I folded the letter and put it back where I had found it.

I looked away from Ms. Christopher's desk and began to examine the door behind us. I was anxious to touch it less there was a person on the other side, such as Ms. Christopher – I was already putting myself in danger by being in this room alone. I observed the door frame and didn't see any signs of forced entry, such as scratches from a crowbar or any damage to the doorknob. I moved on and entered into the bookroom, switching the light on to look at all the books inside.

The school had a bounty of various books, including textbooks, poetry books, and novels. I recognized a few of the poetry books from the last two years. The textbooks were familiar too. At the side of the door was a manifesto on a clipboard with all the books that were taken out by teachers and distributed to classes for them to be read this year so far. I looked at the top and saw *Negro* was out with a total of sixty-one copies for our entire grade. Below, there were other novels that I knew about, but did not recognize to be ones that were typically studied in the school curriculum, such as *The Children of Spartakus*, and *The Nurse's Tale*. I noticed that these had been signed-out for the ninth and tenth grade classes respectively. Last year in English class I remember that we had read *Little Women* by Louisa May Alcott, and then in ninth grade, we read *Dracula* by Bram Stoker. I noticed both of these novels to be missing from the stock. Additionally, I also noticed that the Shakespeare books that we had read in the last two years, *The Merchant of Venice* and *The Taming of The Shrew* were also missing in addition to the copies of *Hamlet*. In fact, I didn't see any Shakespeare work in here, nor any of the novels from the past. Instead I saw a bunch of brand new books that included these trendy new novels I had never heard about. I looked around with disarray and slowly made my way out in shock.

I came around to the back of Ms. Christopher's desk and thought for a moment. I thought that I should leave, but as I held those exact thoughts, I turned to the classroom door as it opened and Ms. Christopher stepped inside.

"Emma?" Ms. Christopher questioned as she looked over to me.

I stuttered as I looked at her from behind her desk.

"Emma, what are you doing here all alone?" Ms. Christopher asked as she moved in.

Ms. Christopher wore a similar dress to the one that she wore yesterday, but this one was all black. She held a folder in her hands, hugging it close to her chest with both arms. She walked over to where I was as I froze up.

"Emma? Did you hear me?"

"I'm sorry," I confessed. "I- I wanted to find you and the classroom door was open, so I entered thinking you were inside…"

Ms. Christopher tilted her head slightly with a look of disbelief, but also understanding.

"What can I help you with then?" Ms. Christopher asked.

"I wanted to know more about why we had to drop *Hamlet* from the curriculum," I stated. "I thought it was a strange last-minute decision after you promised it to us last week."

"Come out from behind there and I'll explain," Ms. Christopher replied, ushering me to come out from behind her desk.

I stepped out and we switched spots so that I was in front of her desk. Ms. Christopher put the folder down at the center of her desk and then put her hands together, palm over palm.

"Unfortunately, I overstepped my bounds when it came to the curriculum – I didn't realize that the archdiocese had made the sudden change for this year, but I was reminded by Mr. Whitaker of what was expected from me and complied. I'm really sorry that I misled you and the other students into believing that we'd be studying Shakespeare, but in my opinion," she said with a sigh, "a break from Shakespeare could be good for us. You study it every year in your other English classes, and there's no stopping you from going out and reading *Hamlet* yourself."

I paused for a moment as I processed her response. I couldn't believe that she would lie to me like that, but I shouldn't have been surprised because she had done it yesterday to all of us. She was compelled to deliver this falsified truth – this official response, as if she was a politician, but she was no politician – she was my English teacher and my favorite one at that.

"I've already read *Hamlet*," I pointed out, "but I was excited to take it apart with you and the rest of the class… that's something that you really miss out on. I understand that you have to give this explanation to me since you're not allowed to talk about what really happened, but I heard the truth and I know that the copies of *Hamlet* were stolen from the bookroom."

Ms. Christopher's eyes lit up as I mentioned the thefts. I saw her move her tongue around her mouth as she swallowed her breath and then took in a deep breath in.

"I don't know what you're talking about, Emma," Ms. Christopher defended.

"There's a letter on your desk that says it all," I remarked. "Mr. Whitaker says that the copies of *Negro* were bought to replace the copies of *Hamlet* that were stolen. Pretty convenient to have a trendy new novel like that ready to replace the stolen readings."

Ms. Christopher frowned and lowered her hands, bringing them to her side.

"I'm very disappointed that you'd come around and read the mail on my desk, Emma," Ms. Christopher instead said. "I would have expected a higher level of integrity from you."

"Integrity?" I questioned, my face red. "You lied to all of us – why?"

Ms. Christopher took in another deep breath and replied, "I'm sorry, but that's a discussion that I wasn't privy to. You have to understand that anywhere you are in life there will be moments in which certain pieces of information won't be readily available to you with the position or rank you hold at a job. I'm only a teacher, a new teacher at that, and I haven't been teaching very long. From what I understand, the exact reasoning is not even privy to Mr. Whitaker, but was a part of a higher discussion between the school administration and the archdiocese. Although you believe that I have lied, the truth of the matter is that yes, the books were stolen, but the archdiocese truly believed that this was a good opportunity for us to transition to this material that was set out by the academic experts they consulted with. They believed that with recent racial tensions in the United States, the continued discrimination against and segregation of African Americans in the United States, and the cross-national history of slavery, it would be a beneficial opportunity for us to reflect and sympathize with this cause."

"So, it was a social justice effort on their part?" I remarked.

Ms. Christopher didn't respond as she looked at me with another look of disbelief.

"I heard that the theft was reported to the police – have they been able to identify who stole the books?"

"The police do not update me with information related to the case, but I have not heard any news from Mr. Whitaker. As far as I know, there have been no suspects or leads," Ms. Christopher responded in a firm tone. "Who told you about the thefts?"

"I heard from someone who has connections with the police," I replied. "They said that police didn't know who it was too. You don't have any idea of who could have stolen the books?"

"Well, it must have been someone who didn't like *Hamlet*, that's for sure," Ms. Christopher replied, "but just as I told the police, I have no idea who that could have been."

"Are you in the least a little concerned that something like this happened – in your own classroom?"

"Of course I am, and to be honest, I'm not happy about the transition either," Ms. Christopher replied. "I've read *Negro* and you will come to see that the craftsmanship behind the novel was subpar to what we could have offered to us through *Hamlet*. Although the story was based on real-life experiences, from what I understand, the ending was fictional in order to deliver a message of hope, especially to activists apart of the ongoing civil rights movement, which denigrates the memory of the woman who this book is based upon."

"How do you think whoever broken in got in? When I came inside, the door to the classroom was wide open? Do you usually leave the door unlocked?"

"Of course not," Ms. Christopher replied, "but police did seem to treat this as a case of break and enter, although nothing was broken, they didn't see any signs of forced entry from any of the entryways."

Ms. Christopher sighed again.

"What's your interest in what happened Emma? I know you're upset about what happened with the loss of *Hamlet* from the school curriculum, but you seem to be asking a lot of questions. You aren't writing an article on this for the school newspaper, are you?"

"No," I denied, "I'm not a part of the newspaper club. I… I'm just curious as to what happened, because I did hope that we would read *Hamlet* and I was suspicious of the circumstances that led to us having to read *Negro*."

"You're very intuitive to believe that there was something more than it seemed," Ms. Christopher acknowledged. "I'm impressed. Do you have any more questions?"

"No, that was all that I wanted to ask…"

Despite the fact that Ms. Christopher had lied to be, I understood why she had lied to me, as much as it annoyed me given that she's a teacher, not a politician. I also knew that she was not lying to me now that I had asserted that I understood what was going on and we were on the same level. I didn't want to ask though why there was a bunch of other books, such as *Children of Spartakus* or *The Nurse's Tale*, because I didn't think that she could provide an answer. Instead, I looked at her and she gave me an empathetic smile.

"I'm really sorry Emma, but this is just the way that it's going to be. We have to simply live with these changes, as we live in changing times – I certainly know that I wouldn't have been happy with these changes when I was your age… but there's nothing that we can do."

I nodded to her and then started to leave the classroom. I felt her eyes watch me until I was out of the room. I took in a deep sigh as I exited the room and then looked out across the parking lot from atop of the staircase. At this point, I knew for certain that something more was going on, but I didn't know how to proceed – I still had to review copies of *The Jarsdel Journal* and now that I had confirmed with Ms. Christopher that there was a break and enter, I wanted to also inquire with the Harlech Police Department about details if I could… I would probably have to see if that was even possible, but I knew for certain as this all became a lot more interesting, and that was that I was going to get to the bottom of this mystery.

Kaj sat in his English class with Ms. Christopher at the end of the morning during third period, listening to her speak about the beginning of *Negro*, which Kaj had little to no interest in. Instead, his mind wandered and thought about Ellerada and the Mystic Marvin device. The experience confused him because it was not what he expected to have occurred, and that was a typical outcome in the investigation field, but instead of attempting to work around these details, all one had to do was expand their vision. Unfortunately, that wasn't what Kaj was doing at this time. Instead, his mind was buzzing around details without drawing connections. I wouldn't be surprised if it had never left his mind as soon as he returned home from the fairground and stayed with him throughout the night. Kaj looked out the window to his right as it poured with rain, and then he looked straight forward as the bell signaled the end of class and he returned back to reality. Kaj stood up, began to pack up his stuff, and then left the room to come to the main building.

Kaj went to his locker to transfer his books for his physics textbook and notebook. He then closed his locker and began walk down the corridor in the west wing, reaching the library entrance. He then went upstairs, but it was too early into the lunch period to find any of the Nerds in their domain. Instead, he came around to the east wing and sat down with Zach at the benches in front of the windows that looked down the cafeteria. Zach ate his lunch while he joked around with some of the other younger boys that sat around the benches. Kaj held a serious glance and didn't laugh once – there was anxiety within him, and that anxiety didn't allow him to even eat.

Instead, Kaj looked down to the ground floor of the cafeteria and around at the tables where the cliques sat around. He could see the Jocks, the Preppies, the Thespians, and even the unaffiliated where his girlfriend was with Meghan and Riley. Kaj's eyes met with the Nerds at their table, and there he saw a few of them, including Abigail Olga Meier, Glenn's second-in-command, who had auburn hair tied in a bun with feminine black glasses around her brown eyes. She had fair, almost pale skin, a hooked nose, and was taller than most women her age at almost six feet tall. Abigail was in Kaj's class. She was sat with Kieran Alto Palate, Glenn's best friend and also a good friend of Paul. Kieran was average height with cold fair skin, medium-length wavy brown hair, and brown eyes. Among them was Arnold Watts, a peer in my grade who had wavy blonde hair and light blue eyes; Herbert Hecht, a student in tenth grade with light brown hair and blue eyes; and Joss Chan, the son of Chinese parents who fled from Guangzhouwan and came to Canada when the Japanese occupied the city and kicked the French out. At the center of the table, Glenn Bertrand sat with his peers as they discussed whatever technical nonsense that they discussed when they came together. Glenn appeared similar to how he did fifteen years later, except of course, he held his youth then. I remember the only association I had with them was through Kieran, who was friends with Paul and on good terms with me. He was an old friend from elementary school. Otherwise, the rest of them rarely spoke to anyone outside of their clique as far as I could recall. Kaj had no association with them whatsoever aside from the fact that Paul was friends with Kieran – Kaj in fact held a cold shoulder towards Kieran and the rest of the Nerds. I remember that when it came to the time that students began to associate with cliques, which was around the end of ninth grade and start of tenth grade, Paul almost landed himself with them, but it was Kaj's athleticism and their friendship that set him apart. If it wasn't for the fact that Kaj's athleticism was not a ritual part of his life, and he was not friends with Paul, I'm sure he would have landed himself with the Jocks, but that's a story for another time. At this moment, Kaj studied the Nerds and decided to allow his anxiety to control him.

Kaj suddenly left Zach on his own, who was too engaged with the other kids to even notice that Kaj had left, and made his way downstairs to confront the Nerds at their table. Kaj approached the table from the corner where Kieran and Abigail were sitting on opposing sides, Abigail next to Glenn. The group turned their stares towards Kaj who stood at the head of the table – each of them calculating what the threat level was in this stranger at their table. Kaj looked at them with a firm face, displaying the tension within him as he held closed fists in each other. Glenn stared back at Kaj with unfamiliarity.

"State your business," Glenn questioned in his nasally voice.

"I need to talk to you," Kaj replied.

"I have no recollection of who you are," Glenn responded. "Why would I offer my precious time to you?"

"His name is *Kai*," Kieran explained. "He's in my grade. He's not a threat."

"Kai? What a peculiar name – is that Danish? I believe there was a story where that name came from."

"It's Swedish."

"Not in origin."

"Your name was on the back of a machine at the Neumann Fairground – Mystic Marvin – you did maintenance for them over the summer? I need to know what the details are of that machine."

Glenn looked at Kaj for a moment and then replied, "I have no recollection of what you are describing. I did not work at a fairground over the summer…"

"Kaj, get lost," Kieran warned.

"No," Kaj denied, "I saw your name – you signed-off on the machine for a routine checkup a couple weeks ago. You expect me to believe that was another Glenn Bertrand?"

"By my calculations, the probability that there is another Glenn Bertrand in Harlech is one-hundred percent," Glenn replied in a patronizing manner. "Please, follow the advice of your cohort and 'get lost.'"

"You're in on it then, aren't you?" Kaj accused. "You're a part of the thefts – you know where my girlfriend's necklace is?"

Glenn frowned deeper at Kaj as he accused him in front of his friends.

"Glenn, what is he talking about?" Abigail asked.

"He is saying nothing of use," Glenn affirmed to her.

"What's your stake in that con, Bertrand?" a firm voice stated from behind.

Kaj turned and saw that the voice was from Lance Stützle, Elias' older brother.

"Is it true what Kaj is saying?" Lance asked.

"The proper syntax is 'Is what Kaj is saying true?'" Glenn corrected.

"Don't play mind games with me, four-eyes," Lance refuted. "My little brother's girlfriend had a valuable bracelet stolen, and her friend had a sapphire necklace stolen. If you're a part of what had happened, I swear to you – I'll break your pencil neck."

"You do not threaten me, monkey man," Glenn barked back.

Kaj noticed that a lot more members of the Jock clique, including Elias, had walked over to where Kaj was, supporting him, but this support was not what Kaj needed right now. The Nerds started to stand up and back away, which caused the Jocks to confront them as they began to bicker. Kaj had become lost in this conflict. Suddenly, Lance pointed over to Kaj and a Jock pushed him forward.

"Say it again, what did this Nerd do to my brother's girlfriend?" Lance asked Kaj.

"I…"

"He said that Glenn's name was at the back of that psychic machine," Elias explained instead. "He's a part of it!"

"You son of a bitch…" Lance remarked to Glenn as he was about to punch him.

Glenn ducked like a coward and the two cliques came into conflict with each other. Kaj noticed Glenn escape through the back as they started to push and shove, and soon Kaj's ears cringed at the sound of a whistle to break up the fight. Glenn ran out of the cafeteria and Kaj went after him. He came into the southern corridor outside of the cafeteria, noticed Kaj was behind him, and then immediately went down the corridor and out of the building through the side door. Glenn ducked as Tyler was about to tackle him and then went on the run.

Kaj gave chase and pushed through the fire door and came outside where the rain had stopped, but deep grey clouds continued to cover the skies. Glenn ran eastbound, towards the track. Kaj ran after him. Glenn came around the corner of the annex and went down towards the gravel field behind the school. Kaj nearly caught up to him, but slipped on some mud between the concrete and gravel. He landed on the grass at the side, but quickly recovered to continue chasing him as he went over to the scrapyard. He went around the mechanic garages and Kaj managed to corner him at a fence near the school buses. Kaj took slow steps towards him, causing Glenn to step back and put himself against the fence.

Glenn made a last attempt to go around Kaj, but Kaj lunged towards him and tackled him onto the ground. Kaj then began to hold Glenn down.

"Get off me!" Glenn complained.

"Answer my questions!"

"No!"

Kaj felt a rage within him as Glenn refused to cooperate. Kaj continued to press him into the ground.

"Answer me!" Kaj shouted.

"I can't breathe!"

"Tell me about Mystic Marvin! If you don't tell me, I'm going to take you straight to Lance for him to knock some sense into you. How about that?"

"Please, no... I don't even work for the fairground," Glenn remarked. "I- I'll tell you what I know, but please get off of me..."

Kaj released some pressure, but continued to hold physical control of Glenn. Glenn coughed and wheezed.

"I- I need my Analgizer..." Glenn complained, reaching around his neck.

Kaj saw him pull off what appeared to look like a marker to him, but was in fact a single-use inhaler to relieve asthma. Glenn coughed and Kaj began to release more pressure as he started to worry that he was being too harsh on him. Kaj finally let total control of him and helped him onto his feet as he continued to cough.

Glenn sat down in the corner and Kaj got him to breathe. Once he was calm, Kaj decided to ask again.

"What do you know about Mystic Marvin?" Kaj questioned.

"Mystic Marvin – I made him," Glenn stated. "He's mine."

"My girlfriend said that when she and her friend used the machine and it told them to see a fortuneteller. The fortuneteller then scammed them into giving up their jewelry – you see how bad that is, right?"

"I- I didn't intend to give him Mystic Marvin so that he could scam people…" Glenn affirmed. "He was supposed to be just a game – like the rest of them there."

"How does the machine work?"

"How else? You put a coin in, and a card pops out."

"When I went there yesterday, I didn't get any card that told me to see the psychic, so why did my girlfriend get one when she visited?"

"By my prediction, it would have been because she was given a token to insert into the machine rather than a standard coin."

"A token?"

"The machine accepts standard currency, twenty-five cents, but also special tokens that could be inserted into the machine. The specific size and grooves on the coin would cause it to roll into the machine and trigger a different reaction from the robot. The end result would be a different card, such as the one that your girlfriend received. I know no other details of the card other than that – I assumed that the feature would have been used to provide specific prizes in a controlled manner."

"How do people get that token?"

"I do not know. You should ask your girlfriend how she got the token."

"Okay, but who did you design this machine for? Ellerada? You told me that you made it for a dude."

"The name of my contact was a Romani man, but I do not believe that he used his actual first name with me, as is typical with Romani people. The name that he provided me was 'Elroy.'"

"Elroy…" Kaj repeated. "Where can I find him?"

"Most likely, at the fairground," Glenn responded. "If you have any more questions, you should ask him. I do not know anything else."

"Okay…" Kaj replied, "so how come your name is on the back?"

"Since the machine is my design, I'm required to visit when it breaks down to fix it. As per legislation, I'm required to sign-off my name on the back and the date that I performed maintenance to protect myself from any liability."

"Okay…" Kaj responded, "alright, if you say that's everything that you know, then I'll believe you, but if I find out you're more involved in this than you let on, I swear that I'll tell Lance you're involved and then you won't be happy."

Glenn frowned and stood up.

"So be it," Glenn replied, "but for now, tell him to back off."

"Fine…"

Glenn walked off with a limp. Kaj watched him disappear and then thought for a moment as he stared at the ground. Kaj made his approach to the main building from the opposite-side that Glenn had walked off on, arriving underneath the shelter as it started to rain again. Now that Kaj understood the details of Mystic Marvin, it was time to speak with Katelyn again to get the whole details of her experiences at the fairground, because evidently, something was amiss.

I had heard about the scuffle in the cafeteria during lunch period from Riley, but I had no idea of the breadth of it nor that Kaj was involved. I had no idea what he was working on at the time, and I didn't care because I was too focused on my own project. I was in the library, attempting to sift through the collection of newspapers so that I could find some copies of *The Jarsdel Journal*, but I couldn't find anything. I didn't have any copies at home either of course, but luckily, I was able to find some at the dance studio breakroom going back a couple of weeks, so I collected all of those and brought them with me. I sat atop of my bed at home, sifting through all the outdated copies of *The Jarsdel Journal* in search of some sort of relevant information that I could connect to the break and enter at St. Augustine of Hippo Secondary.

I sat cross-legged on my bed with its white quilt stretched across the single bed in our family home. My bedroom was small in comparison to other girls that I knew, such as Riley, but at the same time, Riley lived in a spacious two-story country home in North Harthdam, while I lived on the hills of East Harthdam. We lived in a one-story rancher near the highway, although our home did have a crawlspace below, that was hardly another level. My bedroom was at the side of the house facing north. I had a single window that looked out towards the gravel driveway next to us and also near the gate to the backyard. My bed was opposite, near the door on its right, backed up on the same wall with a small nook where the door met the hallway. From the door, on the left, there was a small dark wooden dresser with three shelves. A mirror was situated above on the wall. Behind the dresser, there was a dark wooden bookshelf with a few books, some stuffed animals, and a couple of picture frames. In front of the bookshelf, there was an armchair, and then on the perpendicular wall where the window was, in front of the window, there was a desk with a glass surface atop with a wooden chair behind. Atop of the armchair, one of the two cats in the house, a male Persian with grey fur named Marius, was sleeping atop. Our other cat, a Maine coon with soft white fur, Yvette, was most likely with my parents. The gap between the desk and the bed was tight enough for the chair to fit in, measuring the same length as the chair. On the other perpendicular wall, there was a closet in the wall. On both sides of my bed there were circular end tables with lamps atop. On the table closest to the exit there was an analog clock. Next to the closet, which only measured two-thirds of the wall, there was a painting that depicted Miranda from *The Tempest*, on the island beach. She was beautifully dressed in the painting with a dark green dress, bare feet, and luscious reddish hair. I liked the painting a lot.

At the moment, it was late and both my parents had retired to their bedroom. Behind the westward wall was a bathroom, and behind the bathroom was their bedroom where I could hear my father's snores through the hallway. I attempted to sit quietly, looking through each of the newspapers with a pen in hand and a highlighter within reaches so that I could circle and highlight important and possibly relevant information. I read through each copy, eyes on the headlines, and scanned through each article like a computer searching through mounds of data. When my eyes finally met a possible match for what I was looking for, I stopped to reach the article, only to continue as I went through article to article.

The quality of work in *The Jarsdel Journal* was about the same as the mainstream media, but of course there was less activity on this singular island than there was on the other two, or even the entire region. I had heard from my parents that crime was still a problem in the city, or at least, on the rise since the start of the decade. However, in my opinion, it never compared to the tide that would come in the future. I reviewed the newspapers from the last week in search of some sort of mention of the incident at St. Augustine of Hippo, but came short as I didn't find a single mention of our school. I didn't like that.

I sat on my bed, frustrated with the results of my search, and decided that I had to broaden my scopes. If I was to believe that there was some sort of conspiracy attached to these missing copies of *Hamlet*, then surely our school couldn't have been the only one. In the least, other Catholic high schools in the region should have been impacted if the letter on Ms. Christopher's desk suggested a policy change within the archdiocese. What about the other schools? St. Augustine of Hippo Secondary was the only Catholic high school on Jarsdel Island and in Harlech, but there were at least two other Catholic high schools in the archdiocese, St. Thomas More in New Harlech and St. Frances de Sales in Lennox. I didn't have the resources on hand to research these schools, but my suspicion was deep that they must have been affected by these policy changes. I didn't know what else to do except hold a strange feeling, because it didn't seem right.

If the archdiocese wanted to exercise policy changes on the entire archdiocese, why wouldn't they simply change the policy? Why would they make the effort to have their own books stolen in order to justify a policy change? I wasn't one to understand politics, so perhaps it was something that I had missed from an administrative and political angle. I didn't want to believe that this was something larger than it was – I wanted to believe that this was small, confined, and unique to St. Augustine of Hippo, rather than the entire archdiocese. From what I understood from reading the mainstream news though, there were no similar reports out of the other islands, at least from their general viewpoint. However, the decision for us to read *Negro* and other contemporary novels came from top-down. Perhaps, the relationship of this situation was cause and effect, the novels at our school were stolen, and simply put, the archdiocese saw an opportunity to bring about changes to our curriculum.

I went over to my dresser and picked up the rest of the copies of *The Jarsdel Journal* so that I could sneak out to the garage and dispose of them, but before I could, I looked at the cover. The question came to my head again, and I thought about whether this situation was unique to the archdiocese or not. The evidence that I had suggested that this was unique to the Catholic schools and not a change to simply all high schools. I didn't have any evidence to suggest that this was affecting other high schools… but at the same time, I didn't have any evidence to suggest that this was not affecting other high school. I took the newspapers and brought them onto my bed so that I could review them.

I looked through each newspaper, starting with the earliest one from August over six weeks ago, which was published on a Sunday. I broadened the keywords on my mind as I started to read the headlines from page to page, and as I turned to the seventh page, my eyes focused on the headline for an article that said, 'Suspected vandalism at Spencer E. Lincoln Secondary School.' I read through the article and it explained that a side entrance door window had been smashed with a rock and it was suspected that a Person of Interest could have gained entry into the school over the weekend, but there were no details into whether something had been taken. The Harlech Police Department were not contacted, but when the school was contacted for a comment, they denied that it had been a break and enter attempt and brushed it off as vandalism. I recalled that Spencer E. Lincoln was a high school in the southern area of Lincoln near the suburbs. Once I finished reading the article, I paused for a moment to reflect on this information – I also wondered, for my reference, how journalists caught wind of information like this because it would be beneficial if I knew their secrets, but that was a secondary issue at this moment.

I stood up and went to my desk to pick up a pair of scissors. I took the scissors and started to cut the article out of the newspaper. The incident at Spencer E. Lincoln sounded eerily similar to what had occurred at St. Augustine of Hippo. I cut out the article and laid it out on my desk, and then I continued to search through the rest of the newspaper as I sat down on my bed. I reached the end and didn't find anything else. I folded the newspaper, sat it down on my chair, and then picked up the following one, the Friday edition, and I scanned through it.

I didn't find any relevant information. I picked up another Wednesday edition and read through it. A part of me hoped that I would be lucky again with some sort of mention of any of the schools on the island, but as I reached the end, I was disappointed. Nothing. I looked through the newspaper again with hope that I had missed something, but I hadn't. I put the newspaper aside and then read the next one. The Friday edition from five weeks ago didn't mention anything related. Neither did the Wednesday edition from four weeks ago nor the Friday edition from that same week. I picked up the Wednesday edition from three weeks ago, read through it, and reached the fifth page when I came to a headline that said, 'Break and Enter at Vanessa Lacson Secondary School.' Bingo - unlike the article from the high school in Lincoln or the incident at St. Augustine of Hippo, this incident was crisp and clear. I read through the article and it described an incident over the weekend in which a window had been smashed open and a door into the school had been broken into by force. The incident was investigated by the Harlech Police Department and they assessed that nothing of value had been taken. I recalled that Vanessa Lacson Secondary School was a high school in Chinatown. I paused for another moment to reflect on this information. It was a curious situation, but now I had probable evidence to suggest that the archdiocese was not alone and that this was an island-wide issue. I would still have to confirm and do some research to ensure that St. Thomas More and St. Frances de Sales was not affected, or in the least, didn't have any break and enters, but now I had doubt as I leaned on this other of the two theories, Jarsdel Island versus the Harlech Archdiocese, but still, I only had one or two unconfirmed cases in the public schools. I reached for another copy of *The Jarsdel Journal* and sighed as I dreaded to believe that this was an issue that could possibly affect the entire region, nudging onto my anxieties around a wider issue rather than a smaller one, no less because it would be impossible for me to prove.

I realized that there was a gap between the incident at Vanessa Lacson, the incident at Lincoln, and the incident at St. Augustine of Hippo by about three weeks in total. I made a note of this pattern and then continued to review the rest of the newspapers. I reached for the Friday edition from three weeks ago and didn't find any relevant information. I read the next Wednesday edition and closed in on the fourth page where the headline read, 'Vandalism at John Brindley Secondary School,' which was a school nearby in East Harthdam. I read through the article and it explained that a side entrance at the school had been smashed with a rock alongside a window. The school commented that the vandalism was believed to be related to a prank by the graduating class that had gone wrong, and that it was being investigated internally by the school. The Harlech Police Department were not involved. The fact that the incident occurred a week after the incident at Vanessa Lacson disproved my three week theory and now gave me a sporadic pattern that I couldn't work with.

I cut out the article and then continued with the next edition, which again, didn't have any relevant information. The Friday editions were useless to me. I moved on to the Wednesday edition from a week ago and read through it, and on the third page, I had a headline that read 'Break and Enter at North Harthdam Secondary School,' and I looked through it and it explained that a side entrance displayed signs of break and enter at the high school, which was discovered on Monday morning and was assumed to have been caused over the weekend. The Harlech Police Department attended to collect evidence – the conclusion of the investigation had not been released to the public. Both the police and the school district refused to comment on the incident. I cut out this article and then I was done. I had already read the Friday edition and the Wednesday edition, and both of them didn't have any relevant information.

In sum, I had four articles that reported similar incidents as that had occurred at St. Augustine of Hippo. The only pattern in each of them was that they had occurred over the weekend and suggested a break and enter via an entrance or window to gain entry into the school, possibly to access the books if I'm to believe that all of these are the same. I had to believe that this was all connected – I couldn't believe that all of this wasn't a coincidence, but at the same time, I was hesitant to believe in anything that didn't have any sort of evidence attached to it. I laid out the four articles and began to wonder about the other schools on the island.

I left my room and stepped into the corridor, and then I proceeded down with careful steps to the den on the left and entered into the home office. The den was small, smaller than my bedroom, and it consisted of a loveseat directly ahead in front of a window, a desk on the left with various bookkeeping booklets on the side, a desk lamp, and a magnifying glass attached, and then bookshelves all around elsewhere with various books. I went to my dad's desk, opened a drawer and took out a map of Harlech that we had along with some others from the province and country. I took the map with me, opened it, and then cut out Jarsdel Island so that I could place it on my desk with the articles. I frowned as I looked down, went back out into the corridor, but went directly left and down a separate corridor that went to the garage. I stepped down onto the cold concrete and came around to the left where there were shelves with an assortment of clutter to retrieve a corkboard. I then brought the corkboard and used it to attach the map to the center, and then the articles at the side with some thumbtacks.

I went to my closet, opened it, and pulled out a basket with yarn in it so that I could pull some red yarn out. I took some more thumbtacks and started to put them down at the location of each school on the island, including the ones that were seemingly not hit by any sort of suspected vandalism or break and enter. I then took the yarn, tied it around the thumbtacks at the top of the articles and then connected the piece of string to the location of the school. On Jarsdel Island, there were eight high schools, including St. Augustine of Hippo Secondary (seven within control of the public school district): Vanessa Lacson Secondary School, Spencer E. Lincoln Secondary School, John Brindley Secondary School, and North Harthdam Secondary School had all been hit alongside St. Augustine of Hippo Secondary School. At this point, I didn't have any evidence to suggest that Queen Charlotte Secondary School (in Port Burnes), Riverside Secondary School (in Lower Northton), or South Harthdam Secondary School had been hit as they didn't have any associated articles in *The Jarsdel Journal*, but at the same time, they could have been hit earlier and been mentioned in newspapers that I didn't have access to anymore. In the last six weeks, four schools had a similar incident occur in which a Person of Interest had gained access, and in that time, there was a two week gap in which no incidents seemingly took place – had I not known about St. Augustine of Hippo being robbed, I would have had a gap this week too, so there were two possibilities within that two week gap: there were no thefts or there were thefts that went unreported. I now needed to confirm if any of these schools had been hit, and if so, which ones, because if that theory held, it could mean that there was a school on the island that had yet to be hit – provided that the start of all this was six weeks ago and not seven weeks ago. If possible, I needed to find a copy of *The Jarsdel Journal* from seven weeks ago, a Wednesday edition, which I could possibly retrieve from the publishing company somehow.

I made a list of all the tasks that I needed to complete tomorrow and then set it into my bookbag so that I would remember tomorrow. The time was nearly the start of the next day, so I decided to retire and go to bed. As I closed my eyes, I felt all these possibilities and questions stir in my mind, followed with an anxiety over chasing a certain theory when so many other possibilities existed, and how I hated to waste my time only to be wrong. However, I was certain now that there was something more going on as I found out that St. Augustine was not alone – other schools had similar robberies, so this problem was in the least island-wide. Tomorrow, I'd try to find out if this was an archdiocese problem too, and if so, I'd have to expand into King Island and Cliffe Island, and possibly even Lennox and New Harlech. For now though, I had to get a copy of *The Jarsdel Journal* from seven weeks ago, and also communicate with the other schools somehow in a way so that I could extract information, perhaps with the assumption that I knew about what had happened – I was excited to see my project move forward with potential for results.

Part 2 – Chapter 20
St. Augustine of Hippo Regional Secondary School
Harthdam, Jarsdel Island
September 1968 – 08:30 hours

The next day, I continued to follow-up with this investigation into the missing copies of *Hamlet* as I made a note of the phone numbers and addresses of the schools that I had to contact. I also took note of the phone number and address for the office that publishes *The Jarsdel Journal*, which unfortunately was located all the way in Lincoln. I wrote all this information on a loose piece of lined paper and then made my way to each class, awaiting lunch hour and plotting in the meantime how I would approach the schools.

At the start of lunch, I left home economics and went straight to the payphone that was at the side of the school in the alleyway that separated us from St. Monica. I reached the payphone, inserted a dime, and then began to dial the office for Queen Charlotte Secondary School. I waited for a moment until someone answered, thinking carefully of how I was going to approach this situation.

"Queen Charlotte Secondary, how can I help you?" a woman answered.

"Hello, this is Catherine Bard with the Harlech School District – sorry, my records are a little outdated. Who is the department head for your English Department?"

"That would be Mr. Aris," the woman replied. "Would you like to speak with him?"

"Yes, please," I responded in a polite tone.

"Please hold."

The woman cut out and I waited for a moment.

"Hello?"

"Hi, Mr. Aris? Catherine Bard with the Harlech School District. I'm sorry, but I don't think we've talked before, but I wanted to ask you some questions related to the disappearance of several books following the break and enter that happened a couple of weeks ago."

"Of course," Mr. Aris replied.

"Remind me, when did this robbery occur? We've had a few incidents across the school district, and I don't want to mix up yours with the others."

"I can't remember. It was sometime before school started again. I remember I came into the bookroom on the 26th and noticed all of the novels were gone."

"Right… and you've received the replacements. Right?"

"Yes, of course. We received them within the week so that we were ready for the school year. From the feedback I've received from teachers, the students have been receptive of the new content."

"Good, good… Alright, thank you, Mr. Aris. My office will be in touch if we have any more questions. Take care."

I immediately hung up and took a deep exhale. I wasn't sure how I managed to pull that off, but I did. I liked it – it felt fun, like a game. I took a moment to breathe before I continued and dialed the office for South Harthdam Secondary School. I waited for a moment and then someone answered.

"Hello?" a lady asked in a rushed tone.

"Hi, Catherine Bard with the Harlech School District. Could I speak with the English department head? Apologies, but my records are a bit outdated, but-"

"What is this about?" the woman asked, interrupting me.

"It's related to an incident that occurred at the school several weeks ago," I explained. "Would I be able to speak with the department head?"

"Department head… you'll want to speak with Ellis Graham. Please hold."

I waited for a moment – the tone of the woman was brash and made me nervous.

"Hello?"

"Hi, is this Ellis Graham? Catherine Bard with the Harlech School District. I wanted to speak with you regarding the break and enter that had occurred at the school a couple of weeks ago?"

"What? Break and enter? I'm sorry, I don't understand what you mean? Who are you?"

"Catherine Bard," I repeated, increasingly nervous. "Do you not recall the break and enter that happened in which various books were stolen from the bookstores?"

"No, I don't. I don't know what you're talking about. I think you must be confused. You say you're with the school district?"

"Yes... I'm sorry, but is this... is this North Harthdam?" I questioned in an attempt to obscure myself as ignorant.

"This is South Harthdam – you have the wrong school."

"Sorry..."

The teacher hung up before I could finish apologizing. He was incredibly rude – I put the telephone back and waited for a moment before I decided to phone the last school – Riverside Secondary School, who I hoped would be a lot friendlier than the last one. I inserted another dime, dialed the number, and then waited for someone to answer.

"Hello?" a woman answered.

"Hi, this is Catherine Bard with the Harlech School District. I wanted to get in touch with the department head for the English department if possible. I'm afraid I don't have his name..."

"Ms. Patricia Keel would be the department head. Would you like me to transfer you to her?"

"Yes, please," I replied.

"One moment..."

I waited for a brief moment.

"Hello?"

"Hi, Patricia? This is Catherine with the Harlech School District – I wanted to get in touch related to the break and enter that occurred at the end of the summer break. Would you have a moment to chat?"

"Yes, what about the thefts?"

"I just had some details that I wanted to flesh out with you – do you remember when the thefts occurred?"

"I'm fairly certain it was on Friday evening because I came in on Saturday morning and found all of the books missing. I phoned the principal, and he told me to phone the police, and here we are yet without those books."

"What date was that? August 17th?"

"Yes."

"Have you received the replacement material?"

"Yes, we received that before the school year started."

"What is your feedback on that material?"

"Oh, I haven't had much within my own classes – I'd have to ask around and get back to you."

"No worries," I responded.

"I'm sorry, but you're with school district, right? Are you working with Edgar?"

I froze as I was thrown this curveball by the teacher.

"Edgar? Yes, why?"

"I thought that he was handling the missing books... has there been any recent developments?"

"No," I responded, "I only wanted to reach out to confirm the details – anyways, that's all the questions I have. If I have any other questions, I'll be reaching out. Take care."

I quickly hung up before she could question my identity any more. I took in a deep breath and then processed what I had learned. Both Riverside and Queen Charlotte had been hit by the book thief, while South Harthdam had not been hit, but was most likely next. I didn't need to visit *The Jarsdel Journal* office anymore. I had the confirmation that I needed, and now I had to do what was right: call the police.

I looked at the piece of paper in my hands with all of the phone numbers and homed in on one at the bottom, which was the non-emergency phone number for the Harlech Police Department. I dialed and then waited to speak with an operator.

"Harlech Police Department, how can I address your call?"

"Hi, I need to forward some important information to the police," I stated. "I've been looking into a series of thefts that have occurred across Jarsdel Island and from what I've gathered, there's been a pattern of thefts occurring every week at each high school and I believe I know which high school is next and going to be hit this weekend."

The operator didn't immediately respond.

"Sorry, but who am I speaking with?"

"My name is Emma Monique," I responded. "I'm a student at St. Augustine of Hippo Secondary and I want to share some information that I've gathered. I think that there is going to be an attempted break and enter, and some thefts of some books this weekend at South Harthdam Secondary School. Last weekend there were some thefts from my school, St. Augustine of Hippo, and a bunch of books were stolen. I've researching similar incidents across other high schools on the island, and I believe that South Harthdam Secondary School is next…"

"Okay…" the operator replied, "one moment, please."

I waited for a moment and attempted to articulate the important points related to the thefts in my head – I should have taken notes instead of calling the police straight away."

"Hello, Harlech Police Department, this is Lieutenant Jordan Game, Watch Commander for Jarsdel Island."

"Hello, my name is Emma Monique," I stated in a panicked voice, "I believe that there is going to be another break and enter, and a theft this weekend at South Harthdam Secondary School."

"What makes you believe that?" Lieutenant Game questioned.

I attempted to explain my findings, starting from what happened at St. Augustine, the fact that it was a confirmed theft, and then my findings in the newspapers that were related. I believe that I gave him a basic understanding of what I had been led to believe.

"I see…" Lieutenant Game responded, "and you say that these were books that were stolen – or at least, you believe that books were stolen from the other schools."

"Yes."

"Okay…" Lieutenant Game replied, "well, I'll have to check the details of those police reports for those incidents that you mentioned and see what we can do from my end. Thank you for taking the time to give us this insight and we'll look into it."

"Wait…"

The Watch Commander hung up on me before I could offer to share my sources. I heard the dial tone and thought that I had been abandoned. I didn't believe him to have taken me seriously, and as a fifteen-year-old girl who had just been brushed aside, I wasn't going to let that get me down. I would never let that moment bring me down, because it was the moment that I learned a lot about the authorities in this city, the Harlech Police Department mainly, and would be the start of a bitter relationship with them that alienated me from them, unlike Kaj.

I didn't believe that the Harlech Police Department would act on this information that I had provided them. I didn't understand at the time, probably because I was too frustrated. In hindsight, what I understood to be the most important thing in the world right now was nothing more than a couple of books that could possibly be stolen on an anthill of evidence that I had provided them. Even then, in my eyes, a potential crime was a potential crime, and the police should have treated this warning for the face value that a crime could be committed this Friday evening. I now took it upon myself to see it through that there was a witness to these crimes, and I wanted to see it happen myself because if that wasn't evidence, then I wasn't sure what was. However, I knew that before I went and chased this criminal, or group of criminals, I would need some sort of transport, and permission.

I returned to my locker as the early details of a plan began to organize in my head. Riley met with me as I thought to myself.

"Oh, there you are," Riley said. "I was looking for you."

I didn't respond. She looked at me.

"Is everything alright?"

I explained the details that I had gathered and my conclusion so far with the stolen books – that almost every high school on the island aside from South Harthdam Secondary School had been hit, the Harlech Police Department brushed off my concerns, and that I wanted to catch the thief red-handed as he most likely hit South Harthdam this Friday or Saturday.

"You should ask Kaj for some help," Riley suggested. "You know, he's pretty smart and he could give you more than a ride, but also a hand in all of this – I think I know where we can find him."

Riley was about to walk off before I grabbed her wrist.

"No, please, not him," I pleaded. "Why would he help us?"

Riley turned around and looked at me with surprise.

"Why not? He's an old friend. He'd surely help us."

I shook my head at her, doubting her and what she believed in Kaj.

"Well, then who else do you think would have a car and be willing to drive you to South Harthdam late at night? I don't have a car, and neither do any of our other friends. Kaj is the only one, and face it, when you ask your dad for permission, he's the only one that he'd trust for you to spend time with that late other than me."

Riley turned forward again and walked off. I lowered my head as I processed her point. She was right – my father knew Kaj and he would trust him to be alone with me because he'd know that I would be safe with him. I walked with her as we went around to the opposite-side of the east wing and met with Kaj at the bench where he sat with Zachary.

I looked over to them as they were in the middle of conversation, stopping as they looked at us. I glanced at them with a shy face and then turned away while Riley acted as my ambassador.

"Want to hear a joke?" Zachary asked as he finished to laugh.

"What is it?" Riley questioned.

"What did Karl Marx think when he found out a burglar broke into his home?"

"What?"

"He never really considered the theft of all his property…"

"Amusing," Riley replied with a shrewd smile. "Kaj," she said, turning to him, "Emma has a favor to ask from you."

"From me?" Kaj questioned.

"Emma?" Riley asked, looking at me.

I froze as I looked at him and then looked aside. I felt Kaj's eyes look at me. Riley rolled her eyes and then sighed.

"Emma needs your help with the stolen books she's been looking for. She's managed to narrow down the next location that her thief will strike to be South Harthdam Secondary School, and she wants to catch the thief in the act, but for that, she'll need someone to drive her and do a stakeout with her."

"A stakeout?" Kaj questioned. "Hm, I don't know... I mean, I'm working Friday night and I've been busy looking for Kate's necklace still."

"That's alright," I suddenly responded, "thanks anyways."

I quickly left, which caught Riley by surprise. She looked at me as I left and then faced back to Zachary and Kaj.

"Sorry about her," Riley apologized. "I don't know what's wrong with her – thanks for listening at least, Kaj. I'll see you later – best of luck with your own mystery."

Kaj watched Riley off as she went after me. He then looked back to Zachary and then down to the cafeteria where Kate was with Meghan.

"Well, that was weird," Zachary remarked.

"No, that's just Emma and Riley," Kaj replied. "Emma has always been a quiet one..."

"You're still looking for your girlfriend's necklace?" Zachary asked.

"Yeah," Kaj answered, "and I have the next step in all of it, but I have to ask Kate about some more details when I get the chance. I haven't been able to talk to her about it because I don't want to burden her too much with all of this – she's starting to get annoyed whenever I bring up what happened."

"Hmph, as if it wasn't her jewelry that was stolen."

Kaj ignored Zachary's point. The two friends continued to sit together for the rest of lunch period. Afterwards, they walked together downstairs so that they could go to history class with Mr. Robertson. Mr. Robertson had a bald head and slim body. He wore a tan dress shirt with a brown striped tie, and wore dark brown pants. In addition to teaching history class, he was also a band teacher and the school vice-principal. Kaj thought about his own mystery with the necklace again as he looked out the window and imagined his next steps. Likewise, I was elsewhere in the school in French class, drawing ideas in my mind with the next steps for this stakeout, and we were both frustrated where I lacked transport and Kaj lacked support from his girlfriend to carry on. Kaj's attention came back towards the end of the class as Abigail Meier stepped forward to deliver her presentation.

"My family's history this century is a dark one," Abigail stated, "because we were stuck in the middle of the deadliest clash in all of human history, the German invasion of the Soviet Union. Although my father's family escaped to Canada from Germany at the rise of Nazism, my mother's family was not so lucky since they had been stuck in the Ukraine. When the German invasion began in June 1941, my parents were captured because of their Jewish faith and heritage and sent to a concentration camp in Poland. My mother, her siblings, and her parents suffered in that camp, and only her, her brother, and her sister survived long enough to be liberated because their mother and father, my grandmother and grandfather, had died from typhus before we could be liberated. Towards the end of the war, the Germans moved us from Poland back into Germany, where we were liberated by American troops.

"At the end of the war, my mother and her siblings were shocked to have survived for so many years in the camps and each took the lesson of the camps in different ways. Her older sister, for example, could never forgive the German population for what had happened to their kin and their parents, so she entered into politics and became involved in anti-fascism activism so that the horrors that she and others had experienced could never happen again. Her younger brother however was angrier than her for what had happened and vowed vengeance. He involved himself in a plot with some other liberated Jews to poison up to six million German civilians by tampering their water supply to avenge the approximately six million Jews that had died by the German's hands. However, before that plot could come to fruition, he and his accomplices were caught by the authorities, arrested, and imprisoned once more for their own crimes. Although their parents were dead, my mother saw the situation differently and held no hatred towards the German populace, but instead, she was so sickened by the loss of life from everywhere that she decided to leave

Europe and start a new life in North America, and so she chose Harlech. However, that wasn't enough.

"Although she wanted to forget what had happened, her mind was scarred and she was scared to relive those events as she looked upon humanity with fear – fear for their vices and wickedness, which had led to the war that had led to so much loss of life. Eventually, her trauma and fear had made her sick, so sick that she reached the point where she felt that enough was enough, so one night, she ran from the synagogue and found herself on the steps of a church, a Catholic church, and she joined the congregation and felt uplifted by their hope for the future, where despite the sins of humanity, there was hope in a community of believers. In Hebrew, the term hope comes from the word that closely means 'to endure,' and it was the endurance of this community of believers that made my mother become in love with their hope in humanity. My mother converted to Catholicism and had my father convert too. We are a family of Catholic Jews, lucky to be a part of the new nation of believers, and who look forward with endurance to the pains of humanity, to the better and brighter future we walk towards together. I hope that their story can enlighten your heart, as their experiences have enlightened theirs to come to the one true faith. Thank you."

"Thank you, Abigail," Mr. Robertson thanked as he stood up from his desk, "a very positive message out of a very dark time in history. Let's be sure that that hope means a future where history does not repeat itself."

Kaj watched as Abigail returned to her desk. He then looked out the window and listened to Mr. Robertson's final remarks before the P.A. screeched and Principal Donnelly delivered the end of the day announcements. Kaj left the classroom as soon as he could, ignoring both Zachary and Paul, and going to his girlfriend's locker in the west wing where he met her.

"Hey, Kate," Kaj greeted, rushing over.

"Kaj," she replied, "what's wrong?"

"Nothing," Kaj responded, "but listen, I need to ask you something – I know you don't want to hear anything more about the necklaces ever since what happened in the cafeteria, but I really think that I need to know some more details about what happened with you and Meghan so that I can continue my search for who stole the necklace and bracelet."

"Kaj…"

"Please, I just need to ask a few more questions about what happened."

"Kaj, how do you seriously intend to get the necklace back if you were to find out who stole them? My father already looked into it; he's a detective, and the cops that went with him to the fairground asked the fortuneteller and even looked around the tent, but they didn't find anything anywhere. We just have to accept that it's gone…"

"They didn't look hard enough," Kaj insisted, "but I have. Listen, I'm starting to understand how their scam works, but I need to know about what happened before you and Meghan visited Mystic Marvin. What attractions did you visit? Did you receive a prize from one of them and was it a coin?"

"We didn't visit any attraction before we went to the fortuneteller machine," Katelyn replied. "All we did when we arrived was look around, and then they gave us that coin to try out that machine."

"Who gave you the coin? Tell me about the coin," Kaj pleaded.

"When Meghan and I arrived, this boy approached us. His name was Elroy and he noticed that we looked different because of our uniforms. He started to make conversation with us, and we said that we weren't sure what ride or attraction we wanted to see, so he recommended that we see the fortuneteller. We weren't too keen to spend money on an arcade machine, so he gave us the coin and said that it was on the house. He then left and so we went to the machine, and you know the rest…"

"What did the coin look like?"

"What does that matter?"

"Please, tell me," Kaj insisted. "What did the coin look like?

"It was just a coin, Kaj. A stupid plastic green coin about this big," Kate said, holding her index finger to her thumb to create a circle around the size of a dollar coin. "All it said was that it was to be redeemed at the fortuneteller machine."

Kaj listened and took mental note as he grew quiet. Kate continued to rummage through her locker.

"What about this Elroy person?" Kaj questioned. "Why didn't you tell me about him? These are some pretty important details that you missed telling me…"

Kate looked back at Kaj with an annoyed glance.

"How am I supposed to know it's relevant or that you'd want to know about it?" Kate questioned. "Elroy was nice to us. He was foreign. He had brownish skin and dark hair. He was taller than me, but shorter than you. He was slim and wore a leather coat like the Outsiders, but brown with a white shirt and ripped jeans. His hair was brushed back and long. I think he's older than us, probably eighteen or nineteen."

"You said that he asked questions about you guys – what did you say to him?"

"Simple questions," Kate answered. "He wanted to get to know us, and he saw our uniform, so he asked us what school we went to, what grade we were in, whether we were local, and also some other questions, like if we had boyfriends, and stuff. I told him that I had a boyfriend, in case you were wondering. He didn't care. I think he was a part of the staff, because it really felt like he was trying to sell us into the rides since we had just been wandering around."

"Of course he was a part of the staff," Kaj replied. "He was extracting information from you so that he could tell Ellerada all about you so that she could give you a plausible reading that would make you trust her. Ellerada didn't need to ask about you to know you when she had someone out there extracting information for her."

Kate didn't reply. Kaj thought for a moment as he scratched the back of his head.

"We need to go back – I need you to identify this Elroy person for me so that I can investigate him some more."

"You're not a detective, Kaj," Katelyn responded. "What is any of this going to do? It's not going to get the necklace back and you know it."

"Please, we have to at least try," Kaj insisted. "I know you may have lost hope, but I haven't yet, so please, let's at least try and in the least understand what happened?"

Katelyn looked back at me, rolled her eyes, and then closed her locker.

"Fine," Katelyn replied, "but you're going to have to wait for me to finish with the sowing club – afterwards, we'll go back to that amusement park so that I can point out that boy for you."

"Thank you," Kaj responded with a sigh of relief. "I'll be right here waiting for you – don't you worry.

PART III: SEPTEMBER 1968

Part 3 – Chapter 21
St. Augustine of Hippo Regional Secondary School
Harthdam, Jarsdel Island
September 1968 – 15:30 hours

At the end of the day, I went to the drama room to join the Thespians and volunteers for another rehearsal session for the school play. As much as I was disappointed by the fact that Kaj was unavailable to help me, or that the police had ignored my concerns, I was able to live with it because it wasn't the end of the world for me. I had a bit of peace in the fact that I had gotten so far with this mystery to deduce that the next school to be hit with the same thief would be South Harthdam. Perhaps the phone conversation that I had with their department head would cross his mind once it did happen, and perhaps they would phone the police and the police lieutenant will mention that they had received a warning beforehand. I had done my part, and now it was time to be patient; the rest was not my concern, and as much as I cared, this moment was the end of the mystery for me.

Today, Mr. Whitaker had the performers run through the play again, but on stage and without any motions. All they did was stand on stage when required to as part of the scene and read their parts. I enjoyed being able to listen to them speak and talk because between that and the fact that my hands were at work with the props, I was able to find peace of mind away from the issue with *Hamlet* and simply focus on something else. I remember that as I worked, I was calm and complacent with the situation, even thinking that perhaps this change from *Hamlet* to *Negro* would be okay. After all, even if I were to discover the missing copies of *Hamlet*, we were already too invested in *Negro* to change back to it and the changes to the curriculum were unfortunately done and I didn't see them being reversed at all. As Mr. Whitaker had once said, quoting Shakespeare, the robbed that smiles steals something from the thief, and I was smiling to have uncovered the truth that now set me free.

I watched the Thespians as they performed, and of course, Robin played the leading role of the princely beast, Prince Ardent, while

Cassandra played the leading role of the humble beauty, Belle. Mr. Whitaker would occasionally pause the cast as they performed, highlighting certain wants and expectations that he desired from the play, such as what certain props he would like, scenery, or other technical aspects that seemed very idealistic. I sat next to Ms. MacAllister and two students who held sketch pads, one that drew the clothes and another that drew the scene. Ms. MacAllister had a clipboard and took notes with a copy of the script. Mr. Whitaker was a harsh director and he held very high expectations out of his cast. I watched him as he scolded both Robin and Cassandra, and I was astonished that they could take such verbal abuse and not walk-off, but perhaps they were used to it, knew that he was right, and knew that they could do better.

I didn't understand since I thought that the efforts they were putting in were enough, but like a coach, Mr. Whitaker continued to push them. He was a perfectionist. I simply continued to watch, paying attention at times when Jamie would be present to read his lines with a nervous voice, stopping on occasion at the sound of Mr. Whitaker's whistle and criticism, and then continuing on. Jamie held the secondary role in the play as Belle's father, and between his tall and stocky appearance, a bit of makeup and perhaps a wig, he'd pass off as her father on stage. The other two boys in the Thespian clique, Graham and Raymond, played the tertiary roles of Ludovic, Belle's brutish brother, and his brutish friend, Avenant, respectively. Both of whom were more or less the antagonists of this play. There were a few other cast members who played the supporting roles, and these students weren't necessarily in the Thespian clique, but I could see their membership applications in the works, figuratively, as they were all young students in ninth grade who had at most an early concept of the clique system at our school. Among them were two girls who would play the roles of Belle's younger sisters, Adelaide and Felicie, and a boy who would play the role of an usurer. The entire play was aimed to take less than two hours in total, and with Mr. Whitaker's constant pauses, an hour had passed and we weren't even halfway.

I watched Jamie on stage as he read out the scene in which he arrives at the Beast's castle after becoming lost. Mr. Whitaker narrated the parts that were meant to be animated.

"Belle's father awakens from where he had drunk from the goblet and begins to wander through the castle," Mr. Whitaker said. "He reaches a corridor and stops to look around."

"Hello there!" Jamie acted.

"We'll need to record that as an audio recording somehow and play it back to act out the echo of his voice in the castle," Mr. Whitaker stated, looking over to Ms. MacAllister. "Once more for the rest of your two lines as Belle's father continues forward."

"Hello there!" Jamie repeated.

"Hello there echoes," Mr. Whitaker said, "he continues to walk forward."

"Hello there!" Jamie said once more.

"Belle's father comes to the end of the corridor and goes down some steps to reach a rose garden. He remembers that he was supposed to collect a rose for his daughter, and he sees that these roses are particularly beautiful. Make a note – we are going to need lots and lots of roses, preferably fresh roses."

"Got it," Ms. MacAllister replied.

"Now, Jamie, you approach the roses, and you look around to ensure that nobody is watching. You then bring your hand to your mouth for one last shout of the words…"

"Hello there!" Jamie shouted out, actually bringing his hand to his mouth.

"You look around as nobody responds and then bring a hand to the rose bush to pluck one out. As you bring the rose towards you, suddenly the Beast emerges from a curtain of leaves."

"Hello there!" Robin shouted outwards.

"The Beast approaches, and you, Jamie, are horrified by his appearance which is like a werewolf. Artists – take note of the Beast's appearance on the script, I want that verbatim for Robin's costume. As the Beast speaks, there is a serious wind that blows the bushes – we're going to need fans for that. Robin…"

"So, my dear sir, you steal my roses," Robin said. "My roses which are the most precious things in the whole world to me. You are most unfortunate since you could have taken anything but my roses. The penalty for such a simple theft is death."

"Jamie, you come down to your knees," Mr. Whitaker read aloud, "and you plead…"

"My Lord, I did not know. I did not think I would offend anyone by plucking a rose for my daughter. She asked for one."

"One does not call me 'my Lord,' one calls me 'Beast,' and I don't like compliments. No, don't try to understand. You have fifteen minutes in which to prepare yourself for your death."

"Good," Mr. Whitaker remarked.

"My Lord," Jamie pleaded.

"Alright, Robin, you're angry – try to be angry," Mr. Whitaker said.

"Again!" Robin shouted. "The Beast orders you to be silent! You stole my rose, and you shall die! Unless… unless one of your daughters… how many do you have?"

"Three."

"Unless one of your daughters agrees to pay the penalty and take your place…"

"But…"

"Don't argue! Take advantage of the one chance that I have given you, and if your daughters refuse to die instead of you, swear that you'll return in three days' time. Swear it!"

"I swear… but I don't know my way through the forest…"

"You'll find a white horse in my stables. His name is 'Magnificent.' Just whisper his name in his ear, 'Go where I am going, Magnificent, go,' and he will lead you back home, but if your daughters are too cowardly to mount him, then he will take you back to me. Now leave!"

"Good. The Beast leaves and then Belle's father runs off and goes to find the horse. A beautiful white stallion awaits him and he mounts him and sets off. End of scene."

Mr. Whitaker flipped the page on the script and then looked over to the cast.

"Okay, Robin, take a breather – I need Jamie, Cassandra, Graham, Ray, and my Adelaide and Felicie."

"Mr. Whitaker?" Ms. MacAllister interrupted. "It's four o'clock."

"Hm?" Mr. Whitaker questioned, looking at his watch. "Damn, so it is. Okay, that's a wrap for today, folks. We'll carry on next week with this continued rehearsal starting with this scene at the Belle family home. Cast – please remember to go through your lines and start to memorize them. Everyone, dismissed."

I put together the props that I had worked on, which mostly consisted of the snowflakes and put them in a cardboard box as I started to pack up. The other student volunteers from earlier in the week from whom I had heard about the break-in initially weren't here. I picked up the box and began to carry it with me to the backstage when Jamie followed me.

"Need a hand?" Jamie offered.

"No, I'm good," I replied, putting the box on its shelf.

I attempted to leave towards the stairs, but Jamie followed me and walked with me.

"So, what did you think of my acting?"

"It was good," I simply replied. "I mean, the plot is a bit questionable, but the overall narrative is pretty good and you work well with it."

"Questionable?"

"The ending of the play doesn't make much sense to me," I remarked as we reached the drama room. "I mean, the moment between Belle and Beast are touching, but the fate of Ludovic and Avenant is questionable. Sure, they're punished for their greed in trying to steal from the Beast's riches, but it seems out of place almost. I feel like a direct conflict between the Beast and the antagonists would have been more dramatic and exhilarating, but that's just me."

"Right..." Jamie simply responded. "You really have a way with stories, don't you."

I shrugged as we left the drama room and went to my locker.

"Say, are you doing anything this Friday evening?" Jamie asked.

My heart plummeted as I knew what he wanted from me. I opened my locker and then looked back at him.

"Yes," I replied, "I… I mean, it's complicated to explain, but I am busy."

"Doing what? I'm all for a complicated explanation."

I sighed and then looked towards him. I explained to him that I had heard about the stolen copies of *Hamlet* from the bookroom, and how I had investigated to learn that more than just that was stolen and that what was stolen was quickly replaced with contemporary novels that promote social justice themes. I then explained that I had been able to deduce that these thefts had been systematic throughout the entire island and affected a high school each week up to now except South Harthdam. I then explained that I intended to catch the thief in the act and take pictures of him to provide evidence to the police. I also explained that the police had ignored my warning, which was why I had now taken it upon myself to do this task.

"Wow, that's quite a lot," Jamie replied. "I'm impressed that you've managed to put all of that together on your own. You're like a detective."

I blushed as he said that. I took out my backpack from my locker and then closed it. I looked at Jamie as he looked down at me.

"Are you going to do that all alone? South Harthdam isn't the nicest place to be at dark."

"Yes," I replied.

"If you want, I could join you – I'm not doing anything and I'm quite intrigued at all you've done so far so I'd be happy to get involved. I could drive us, unless you already have that sorted out."

My eyes widened for a brief moment and my nose flared. A part of me didn't want to spend time with him and give him this opportunity, but the part of me that really wanted to have some sort of transport and means to properly chase this thief told me to accept.

"Okay," I replied, "that would actually be really helpful. I could use some help and I don't have a ride down there."

"What? How were you going to do all this without a car?"

I didn't respond.

"Anyways, I'm happy to help," Jamie said. "What time do you think would be best?"

"I wanted to go after sundown, so around seven thirty," I responded. "I don't know what time they'll try and steal from the school, so just you're aware, I intend to wait for hours until something happens."

"No problem," Jamie replied. "I'm all for a stakeout. I'll pick you up from your place at around half past seven. Where do you live again?"

"I'm at East Harthdam, 543 Gaul Street. It's at the end past Brindley Street."

"Great, I won't forget it. Can I walk you out?"

"Sure," I responded, starting to walk with him to the school entrance.

I turned to Jamie once we were outside.

"I'll see you tomorrow," I said to him in a timid tone, waving to him.

"Yeah, I'll see you tomorrow at school, if not, I'll catch you at your place at around seven. See you!"

I watched Jamie walk off and then I went the opposite direction so that I could make my way towards Caledonia Street. From what I understood, Jamie lived in Attlewood. I wasn't entirely sure what commute he had to take to get from here to Attlewood, but I didn't want to spend another moment with him because I know had sold myself to be with him for the whole evening, possibly the night as well, all so I could prove a point. Just like that, I was back on the case and I was exhilarated.

Part 3 – Chapter 22
St. Augustine of Hippo Regional Secondary School
Harthdam, Jarsdel Island
September 1968 – 16:15 hours

Kaj met with Katelyn at around a quarter past four o'clock so that they could walk together from St. Augustine of Hippo Secondary and go towards the Neumann Fairground. I recall that there was something beautiful about the love between Kaj and Kate, which made me regret that the two didn't stay together to the very end. Kaj and Kate were star-crossed lovers that had been together since the start of high school when the two were pushed together by their respective friends, where Meghan had teased Kate with her emotions towards Kaj and likewise, Zach, in his typical jokingly manner, teased Kaj towards Kate. The average romantic relationship begins with a high of euphoria as the love blooms between the lovers, and then usually slows down as the relationship sets in and the couple becomes habituated towards each other. Kaj and Kate had hit their euphoric highs in ninth grade, and with time, the two had become established with one another that they were like a married couple. They would argue, bicker, and she would nag him and he wouldn't listen, and there would be tough times, but there would also still be hints of fresh love, hugging and kissing, and signs of an everlasting adoration for each other that would spring most when kept apart. In other words, no matter what came between them, they persevered and continued to love each other – and love each other they did. If you were to ask anyone at St. Augustine about the relationship between Kaj and Kate, they would have said that this love would have no end.

Despite the anxieties that Katelyn felt when she had lost the necklace on Monday and her desire to move on, she understood her boyfriend's own need to solve the issue rather than avoid it, because she knew Kaj. She understood that Kaj had a habit with becoming obsessed with his problems and that he also held a persistence to never let down. This deadly combination made him relentless to solve the problems he faced, and this applied to the loss of her necklace. Katelyn understood this habit about Kaj, just as he understood when yesterday Kate attempted to get him to stop looking into the necklace any further after a fight broke out between the Jocks and the Nerds. Katelyn had heard from Meghan that Elias had found himself in trouble after the fight had broken out, and hearing about the violence, Kaj knew that he was not in a position to inquire into this Elroy person or the coin for the Mystic Marvin machine. Kaj knew that Katelyn was emotional at that time, angry at Kaj and Elias, but that these emotions would come to pass with time. She attempted to get him to stop, but he wouldn't and she knew that. She was annoyed at his obsession, but it would come to pass and all she could do was enable and support him, because she cared about him and his desire to correct the err against her. Katelyn had the power to stop him definitively, but she wouldn't use it unless she knew that he was in danger. At the same time, she was anxious to use such powers, because with such obsession, she wasn't entirely confident that if Kaj were to choose between her and his obsession that she would choose him – that would be an answer she would later come to learn at the end of their relationship. Nonetheless, as far as Katelyn was concerned now, she was in this mess with Kaj even if she didn't want to be, and she didn't want to be. She wanted to go home and forget about her own err, but she couldn't. She had to continue to support Kaj until he either reached a conclusion, or became bored with the mystery.

Hand-in-hand the two travelled towards Caledonia Street and took the same buses that took them to the fairground. The evening was setting in as the clouds turned to a reddish-orange hue, but there was still ample light out for them to travel together into Northton. Kate embraced Kaj's arm as they sat together on the bus. She wore a wool coat that kept her warm and masked most of her uniform. Kaj wore his same raincoat from Tuesday in case it would start to rain. Kate held onto her bookbag, a plaid satchel, like a purse and the two stuck together for the entire ride until it was time for them to get up and hop off.

Kaj eyed the fairgrounds from across Riverside Drive as they arrived and then he took Katelyn's hand and began to walk with her to the crosswalk. They crossed Riverside Drive and made it to the front gates of the amusement park, entering through and then stopping to look around. There was a modest-sized crowd of people in the fairground at this time, slightly more people than there were on Tuesday. Katelyn pivoted around and put herself in front of Kaj as he looked around. Kaj looked down at her.

"Kaj, maybe this is a bad idea," Katelyn warned. "I mean, this person, Elroy, probably remembers me and after the ruckus that my father caused with the police, they would likely not like it that we're here, or perhaps would know why it is that we're here."

"Please, I just need you to identify this person so that I can get a glimpse of him. I know it's not the safest place for us to be, but you're with me and I won't let you be alone for even a second. Come on, let's walk around – I'll be looking for him too based on the description you gave me. Brown skin, dark eyes, and black hair, right?"

Kaj took Katelyn's hand, and the couple began to walk through the fairgrounds. Katelyn held onto Kaj's arm tightly as they roamed throughout. Kaj kept a sharp eye out for a person that matched the description that Katelyn had provided, while Kate only gave a brief glance around the park as they walked.

The couple walked down an aisle in which there were a lot of carnival games on the left, followed by concession stands on the right. At the end of the aisle, the purple tent that belonged to Ellerada could be seen and it appeared as if she was in service, which told Kaj that Elroy could not be far. The couple continued to walk around and came to the middle of the amusement park where the fences blocked off the condemned and abandoned segments.

Kaj stopped and looked around a large crowd of people around them as they were near the Tunnel of Love and the Ferris wheel behind them. They looked around all the people and nobody even remotely matched the description that Kate had provided. It wouldn't have been difficult to spot a man that looked like Elroy was described. Kaj could see some South Asians and East Asians, but they were plainly and noticeably fairgoers rather than con artists.

Despite the fact that Kaj had not seen this person, Elroy, in person yet, he had a vision of him in his mind. He was looking for a sneaky and sly person with the slicked back black hair that Katelyn had described, but he simply wasn't around as he had hoped.

"See him?" Kaj asked.

"No…"

"We'll walk around once more," Kaj encouraged.

Katelyn and Kaj continued to walk around so that they covered the entire inner perimeter. Afterwards, they walked the aisles again, passing Ellerada's tent and then the arcade tent. Once they had covered the entire fairground, they came back to the Tunnel of Love and Ferris wheel.

"Hmph," Kaj expressed, "I refuse to believe that he's vanished or wouldn't be around, poaching more innocent people."

"What if he recognizes me and the fact that I'm with you? If I were him, I would be hiding right now."

"Hmph," Kaj expressed again, turning around. "I want to get a better look – let's ride the Ferris wheel and blend in a bit. Maybe if we disappear from the public crowd, he'll pop out to continue his work."

"You'll need to buy tickets before we ride…"

"Let's go buy some tickets then."

Kaj took Kate to the ticket stand so that they could get the least amount of tickets possible. A fair bunch for five dollars. He then took Kate back to the Ferris wheel and they redeemed six tickets, three for each person, and then stepped in line for the Ferris wheel. The Ferris wheel was tall and approximately fifty feet in length. Kate continued to hold onto Kaj as she watched the attraction slowly roll around while they waited in the queue. Kaj continued to look around the park as they waited. He still couldn't see Elroy around. Kate pulled at Kaj's arm once it was their turn to step forward. Kaj took Kate into their compartment and they stepped in.

Kate continued to hold onto Kaj as they sat down. The attendant closed the gate and stepped away from the compartment as they started to lift upwards. Each compartment began to slowly fill as they were lifted up into the sky, providing them with sights on the massive crowd around them. Kaj squinted as he looked out towards the people, searching for Elroy, but not seeing him. Kate then let out a sigh as she tightened her squeeze on Kaj's left arm.

"This isn't what I had in mind when I thought about us coming here," Kate said. "I mean, I didn't have any intentions on returning after what happened with me and Meg, but still…"

Kaj turned to face Kate who held a somber look on her face. He frowned and brought a hand to her cheek.

"A crooked place like this is not worth our time together – I'd prefer to make memories anywhere else with you."

Kate gave a simple smile back at Kaj who lowered his hand and placed it on his right knee.

"We're definitely making memories now – I don't think I could ever forget a moment like this week where that necklace was stolen… even as much as I want to forget what happened. I'm just… so sorry that I lost your grandma's necklace."

"Hey, it's not your fault," Kaj expressed. "You were manipulated by a bunch of low lives. I will find where they've taken your necklace and I will get it back."

"Oh Kaj, how can you make such bold promises like that to me? I really wish that you wouldn't sometimes."

"I intend to deliver on those bold promises – those thieves have no idea who they decided to mess with. I want the whole world to know that if you ever get into the path of Kaj Kejsaren or his loved ones, then there is hell to pay."

Katelyn smiled. She kissed Kaj on the cheek and then he went back to looking out to the fairground, but they were now too high up and in an awkward position to see anything. Katelyn sighed and inched away from Kaj.

"Kaj, can I ask you something?"

"What is it?"

"If I asked you to stop looking for this necklace, would you stop?"

"What? Why would you ask me something like that?"

"For no reason other than to just stop – would you respect my wishes if I wanted you to stop?"

"Are you asking me?"

"Pretend as if I were."

Kaj looked back at Katelyn and hesitated for a moment.

"I mean, I…" Kaj sighed and then replied, "yes. If you ask me to stop, I will respect that, Kate. I love you and I would understand when you tell me to stop, it's time for me to stop."

Kate gave a warm smile. "Thank you."

The Ferris wheel began to cycle once every compartment was ready. The machine went by slowly, down and then up again. The compartments shook and swung in place, delivering a thrilling sensation that they weren't as secure as one would think them to be as if they could swing too much or drop suddenly.

Kaj kept his eye out as they came down, looking around the group of people. However, Elroy could not be seen. The Ferris wheel came down to the bottom and then began to rise again. Kaj looked out and scanned the population, but again, he couldn't see Elroy. The compartment slowly rose to the top and Katelyn brushed her head into Kaj's arm. Kaj released his arm and brought it around so that he could hold his girlfriend. She held onto his chest now and they looked out towards the scenery. Suddenly, Kaj's eyes met with the sight of a shadowy figure lurking between two tents.

The man that Kaj saw had the same appearance that was in his mind, with the greasy dark hair and the light brown skin tone. He almost stood up from the compartment as they started to come down, but that caused it to violently shake back and forth. Kaj sat back down and Kate held onto him again.

"That's him! I know it – that's got be him, over there," Kaj said, pointing over to where the person he thought to be Elroy was.

"I can't see," Kate remarked, attempting to move herself up slowly.

Kate came down again and waited for the compartment to simply come down. She glanced at the person before they disappeared.

"Well?" Kaj asked.

"I think that's him," she simply said.

"I need to get off," Kaj declared, forcing Kate off him and going towards the exit.

"Kaj, no, the ride is still going," Kate complained.

The compartment began to tip upwards for another cycle. Kate pulled Kaj back and they sat down again. The compartment rolled back and forth once more. Kaj held both hands on his lap in tightened fists. Kate could sense the determination and anger within him; to go after the person that had manipulated and wronged his girlfriend.

"Kaj, what are you going do when we stop?" Kate questioned. "Chase him?"

"Yes," Kaj replied. "I want that necklace back…"

"What if he doesn't have it? They're going to call the police and you're going to get in trouble with them. This isn't the right thing to do."

Kaj tightened his fists harder. He didn't reply to her.

"Kaj, please no more," Kate requested. "I don't want to you to get yourself in trouble over something so trivial – I know what that necklace meant to you, and it meant a lot to me too, but when I gave it up because I believed the fortune lady when she said it was cursed, I did so because I valued our love more than the necklace. It's just a necklace."

"He's probably lurking around, trying to wrong more people and steal more stuff," Kaj replied. "He can't get away with that – he has to be stopped."

"You're not the right person for that… you're not the police."

"Well, the police aren't doing anything!" Kaj complained.

"Kaj, calm down," Kate warned. "When we get off, please don't do anything stupid. Please don't leave me on my own here."

Kaj heard these words and released his fists. He let out a sharp, heated breath from his nostrils and settled down a bit. The ride came to a halt and each compartment ahead of them began to empty out as the ride was over. Kate held onto her boyfriend, but not out of comfort anymore, but restraint. Kaj had settled down more by the time that they were next to be released.

The couple exited off the ride and stepped down the metal platform to return to the concrete surface of the fairgrounds. Kaj looked around and then looked at Kate.

"Can I at least get a better look at him?" Kaj requested. "I promise I won't do anything stupid."

Kate nodded and the couple began to walk in the direction that they had seen him. Kaj looked over to the alleyway between two tents in which he had seen Elroy, but he was gone.

"Dammit..." Kaj muttered.

Kaj and Kate walked to the end and came up to the outer fence that faced the sidewalk and Riverside Drive.

"Kaj, just take me home, please," Kate requested. "I don't want to be here anymore and this isn't good for you. You're getting angry and I don't like seeing you like this."

Kaj looked at Kate and hesitated to respond for a moment.

"Kaj?"

"Okay," Kaj responded. "Let me walk you home."

The couple began to walk towards the exit of the fairgrounds while Kaj continued to keep his eye out for Elroy. His eyes caught sight of him again within the crowd of people, near the concession stands, leaning against the structure with his arms crossed. Elroy's dark eyes met with Kaj's blue ones. Elroy was clean-shaven and had long black hair that was pulled back. He also had thick dark eyebrows. He wore a brown cargo jacket, grey dress shirt and dark pants. He appeared to be just about the age that Kate said he was, between eighteen to nineteen years old. Kaj looked away from him and guided Kate towards the exit. He let go so that she could pass through the turnstile, and then passed through himself, and then rejoined her as they came to the sidewalk. The couple proceeded back towards the bus stop and waited at the bench, while Kaj looked across the street and towards the carnival.

A displeasure stirred within Kaj at the sight of his enemy, and although he didn't voice to Katelyn his intentions, he plotted to return and continue this investigation so that he could recover the necklace once and for all.

I kept my eye on the street in front of the family home for when I anticipated Jamie would arrive. My stomach was filled with dread at the thought of spending time with him, not because I didn't like him. I did like spending time with him, and we shared certain passions for literature, theatre and Shakespeare plays, but any intimacy that was more than just between friends felt like a road that I was not ready for. The emotions that I felt when around him made me too anxious. I had never had a boyfriend before, and as much as I liked Jamie, it wasn't enough to make me change my mind. Perhaps tonight I could start to feel more comfortable around him outside of being friends. I saw a car pull up to the curb of the front yard – it was a blue Lawrence Bateau, an American-made car from the last decade as they were only made from 1951-54. Once I saw the car, I stood up from the pink couch in front of the large window that looked out to the garden, went down to the end of the living room, and then entered into the foyer. I took my coat from the coat rack, a brown rain coat, and also picked up the film camera that I had left on the table nearby. I put on my coat, brought the camera sling around, and then stepped out and closed the door behind me.

My parents had left for the evening to have dinner and spend some time together. I didn't tell them about Jamie, or the fact that I would be out for almost the entire night. My intentions were to see what happens, even if it took all night, because that's what Jamie had promised me, and then return home late to go back to my room. My parents wouldn't be happy with me if they knew the truth, but to witness and confirm my suspicions had become my priority and I was in too deep to back out now – I had to instead venture forward.

The sun was down, but there was still a bit of twilight out in the night as the skies slowly dimmed and nightfall came down. I arrived at the passenger seat door, opened it, and entered in. Jamie had the radio quietly on and there was an indistinct odor – I couldn't put my nose on what it was though. I looked over to him with a timid smile.

"Hi," I greeted.

"Hey," Jamie said in a warm tone. "Are you ready for our night out?"

I didn't like that he had to call it that.

"Yeah, I'm ready for our stakeout," I replied. "Thanks again for helping me with this – I really appreciate it."

"No problem," Jamie responded.

Jamie pulled out of the curb and made a three-point turn to head back towards Gaul and Brindley Street. He turned onto Brindley and went down to Caledonia Street.

"So, tell me what's your obsession with these books?" Jamie wondered.

"I'm not obsessed," I corrected, "I'm interested in the mystery and I want to know what happened. We were supposed to read *Hamlet* in English class, but since all of the books were stolen, we're now reading *Negro* which I just finished reading a couple minutes ago."

"How was it?"

"I noticed a few plot holes, which was annoying because it's supposed to be based on a true story. Overall, it was pretty gruesome – can I spoil it for you?"

"Sure."

"The main character, Malia, was born and grew up in this village in Central Africa with her parents where she was raised as a Muslim. One day, a rival tribe raids their village and capture her so that they can sell her into slavery. She's brought across the Atlantic by a merchant who brings several more who are all sold into slavery. Malia is sold to another merchant, who is friends with the merchant who sold the slaves in the first place. There is some weird understanding between Malia and her master because she is Muslim and he's Jewish, and so he makes the effort to have her educated somewhat and treat her 'normal' despite the fact that he holds her as a slave. Eventually, he goes off and tries to rape her, but she escapes and finds herself in the midst of the American Revolution where she helps the British in exchange for her freedom. The rest of the novel details her life as a freed woman who returns to Africa, but doesn't feel the same anymore, so she spends the rest of her life in British North America advocating against slavery. It was a really bizarre novel and I'm going to have to look through some parts again to catch wind of its themes."

"Yeah, sounds interesting somewhat though," Jamie replied.

"Not as good as *Hamlet*, but I suppose it is what it is. I think slavery in general was a key theme of the novel, not just literal slavery, but also bondage to a system and state, because it talked about her time as a freed woman in the British Empire as no different than her time as a literal slave," I remarked, pausing for a moment. "I don't know. It was very confusing and made me uncomfortable at times. What book is Mr. Whitaker going to have you guys read?"

"We were supposed to read *Cymbeline* apparently, but then Mr. Whitaker made a sudden change and instead we're going to read something else. I can't remember what…"

"*Cymbeline*… that's a good one, but a little hard to understand."

"Hm… you talking about the British Empire made me recall that the novel we're going to read is something to do about that, or at least, decolonization of the British Empire… it talks about some of the bad stuff that the British used to do in its empires… something do with a famine in India or something."

"Really…? Interesting…"

"Yeah, but we're not going to read that until later on in the semester. Right now, we're just doing some short stories."

"Better than *Negro* if you ask me. Anyways, as I was saying, all of the copies of *Hamlet* were stolen, and I've been following that ever since. I mean, this person did steal one of my most favorite plays in all time. How could I not forgive that?"

Jamie shrugged and replied, "I can see your travesty, but we were really bound by the limits of that school curriculum to explore old ideas. Mr. Whitaker told us that we can read Shakespeare and the classical novels in our own time, but that he'd prefer to use school time to explore these more contemporary novels and the issues they discuss since they're relevant to us now. Don't get me wrong, he was empathetic and annoyed at the change, because I don't know if you know him, but he really has a passion for classics."

"Yeah, I had him as a teacher for ninth grade."

"So you should understand how choked he must be about all this, but he made a valid point and we can take that with us and try to understand these different stories rather than the ones we're familiar with, because these are related to current events that should get us to think critically about those social issues."

I crossed my arms and looked out the window. I didn't agree. I wanted to read about *Hamlet* and not about the tale of Malia.

"So, who do you think stole all the books from the school?"

"Same person who's been stealing all the books from elsewhere on the island."

"Who do you think that is? You said that this was happening every week, and that these thefts were followed up with changes to school curriculums…"

"I don't know who exactly," I replied, "and as far as the changes of curriculum go, I don't know what the deal is with that exactly – so far, I've only seen that happen at St. Augustine, but I suspect it's happening elsewhere too."

"Do you think there's some sort of conspiracy going on?"

"I don't know."

Jamie didn't continue to pester that topic anymore as we both became quiet. I noticed that we were close to where South Harthdam Secondary School was located as we turned onto 8th Street. The lights appeared to still be on in the school. Jamie drove south and passed Jacobs Avenue when I saw the large structure that housed the school. Jamie drove past a short offshoot road with a cul-de-sac at the end that led to the front entrance and instead turned left onto Gray Avenue.

South Harthdam Secondary School had its own football field on Gray Avenue with a track course around the perimeter similarly to St. Augustine of Hippo. The school structure was approximately three-stories tall, each floor stacked neatly, and the shape of the building was elongated like a long rectangle from the end of the offshoot road, to house the many high school students in South Harthdam. From Gray

Avenue, the road provided access to the parking lot that was at the east end of the field. Behind the school, there was a small forest that covered the rest of the land up to Jacobs Avenue. Overall, South Harthdam Secondary School was about the same size as St. Augustine of Hippo.

"Where should I park the car?" Jamie asked.

"Drive into the parking lot," I requested. "I want to look around the perimeter of the school to get an idea of its entrances."

Jamie drove into the parking lot and parked the car near a path that ran on the perimeter of the school and side of the field. He turned off the car and looked at me.

"What now?"

"Wait here," I suggested, leaving the camera behind. "I'll be right back."

I went out and began to look around my surroundings. As far as I was concerned, I was alone and there was nobody else around. We were in the midst of a suburban neighborhood. Across the street on both 8th Street and Gray Avenue there were two-story houses. I began to walk towards the path and look at where the most likely place would be for the thief to enter from. At the end of the school, there was a wide annex, which I presumed to be either an auditorium or a gym. This annex had two double sets of doors with no handles to enter through the outside. I continued down and reached a set of double doors in the middle of the main structure and these doors did have handles and could provide egress into the building. I walked to the end and came around to the main entrance, which was a double set of two double doors to walk into the main foyer. On the north side of the off-shoot road, there was a large two-story house with a sign on the front that said, 'South Harthdam Secondary School,' so I suspected that the two-story house was a part of the overall campus. Behind the house and to the side, all along the north side, there were a bounty of trees that formed a forest. I began to walk around to see if there was any sort of entrance, but it didn't seem like there were any that walked into the forest. I went back around to the parking lot and gym to get a better look around the other side. On the opposite-side, there was in fact a door that walked into the main structure with a small patio with tables. A tall chain-link fence separated this section from the forest beyond and concrete paths connected with the patio to the parking lot. I walked back around to the parking lot and re-entered the vehicle.

"So?"

"If the thief is going to strike, he's going to enter from the north side entrance," I concluded, "which is awkward since it's really out of view, but there is only one way in and it's from this parking lot. I think it would be best if we parked the car on the street, preferably away from a street lamp so that we're out of sight, but have visibility to the parking lot and could see if anyone attempts to enter."

"What about the main entrance?"

"No," I denied, "that's not within this thief's method of operating."

"Oh…"

Jamie started the car and drove it around onto Gray Avenue. He drove towards the end and made a three-point turn before he reached Boundary Drive and then came back around to park the car on the southern side of the avenue with enough visibility for me to see whoever comes into the parking lot and enough cover to blend into the shadows as the sun set. Jamie turned off the car and we now sat back, in silence, awaiting the potential strike on the school.

"So, now we wait?"

"Yup, now we wait," I replied with a sigh. "It's going to be a long time, so I hope you brought something to do."

"I was kind of hoping that we'd just chat," Jamie responded.

"We can do that too," I replied, "it does pass time."

"I have to say, this isn't what I expected from you," Jamie confessed. "I mean, I understood that you had a passion for Shakespeare, but I didn't realize that you were also passionate about mysteries like this… or adventurous."

I looked at him and then looked back out towards the school as I kept watch for activity.

"I've never done this before," I confessed. "I mean, I think I've always looked at mysteries as a problem meant to be solved, but small ones and I liked to solve them. I never liked big problems because they always seemed too large for me, and in a way I suppose, I could never believe a large problem to be something for someone as small as me to solve, but this one… it's slowly grown and grown, and now here I am. I still think it's within my hands to manage, but I don't think that I'm… obsessed, because I know that I can stop, and I was prepared to stop up until you volunteered to help me out. To be honest, if you hadn't volunteered, I would have quit and that would have maybe been it, so thanks for helping me."

"No problem… like I said, I'm happy to help and support you. It's exciting to be involved, so I'm looking forward to seeing how this turns out."

I sighed and then began to ready the camera.

"Sorry if I offended you by saying that you were obsessed with this case – I believe you when you say you don't look at this with madness, because you're not someone who I think would become mad… Instead, you seem really responsible, and I like that about you, Emma. You seem to know that this is within your duty, and you're willing to see it through by the way that you feel obligated to complete this task. You promise to deliver, and that's a good quality to have."

"Thanks…" I replied, blushing, "I'm only willing to see this out as long as it doesn't become too enlarged. If this gets any bigger than it is, then I'm going to have to call it quits. I… I don't want to invest any more than I have now into this…"

"I'm glad you understand your limits."

Jamie and I set in and began to talk more with each other. We were usually like this a lot at the Shakespeare festival, and I was glad that we could return to this sort of chatter that didn't involve any flirting or romance – that's what I feared when I agreed to let him help me. However, even then, I feared the turn, and as it became later into the night, I thought that he would become hungrier to make that turn, but I didn't want to disappoint him, or lie to him, but I also didn't want to compromise my support on this mission. He then had to say the words to me after close to two hours of us just talking as friends.

"I like you a lot, Emma. Ever since we started to chat at the festival, I really started to like the sort of person that you are. You're pretty too, I don't want to leave that out."

I froze. I didn't immediately respond as my eyes looked to the school. I didn't know what to say to these words. Instead, I looked down slightly as I attempted to conjugate and put words together to make some sort of sentence to reply to that.

"I understand if you don't like me though…"

"No," I denied, "I do like you, Jamie, but… it's hard to explain…"

"What? You don't have a boyfriend, do you?"

"No…" I replied, "but at the same time," I said, looking towards the school once more, "oh my goodness, I think that's him."

I watched as I saw a short grey sedan, a 1958 Hiawatha Seneca, pulled into the parking lot and parked near the annex. The Hiawatha Seneca was another American-made car that was notably produced in the Great Lakes region, including provinces in both the U.S. and Canada. This vehicle was known for its rectangular shape and being low to the ground compared to other vehicles. I saw the car engine shut off and then someone emerged from within. I couldn't see what he looked like exactly, but he wore a grey coat, trousers, and a flat cap that concealed his hair. From what I could see, he appeared to have fair skin and be average height. I thought that the coat that he wore could have been too big for him since I couldn't see his hands although from the end of one sleeve, he must have had a hand holding onto a satchel that he carried with him. I watched as he walked from the car and went towards the exit, looking around suspiciously as he disappeared to the back of the school.

"What are you going to do?" Jamie asked me.

"I'm going to get pictures," I replied, opening the door and taking the camera with me. "Stay here."

"What?"

I left Jamie in the car and began to sneak to the other side of the street and then go down the sidewalk to reach the parking lot. The parking lot was well lit, and I didn't want him to see me approach if he peaked around the corner, so I went around on the grass and stayed in the darkness of the night. So much time had passed since we had arrived, the school was now dark inside and it seemed like a prime time to perform a heist. I approached some bushes on the outskirts of the property that could provide me with some cover. I caught eye of the thief from where I positioned myself. I observed him for a moment as I got a somewhat closer look, but there was still close to fifty feet between us. From what I could see, he appeared to be young and clean-shaven with ears that plopped out a bit. I believed that he could have most likely had short dark hair based on as much as I could see from him. I raised the camera so that I could grab a picture of him in the act. I snapped a picture and then hid back into the bushes as I knew the sound could trigger him to react. I wasn't sure what he was doing, but it seemed like he was attempting to break into the door somehow by some method. I left the thief on his own as I continued to observe him from where I was, studying him and his careful mannerisms.

I looked to my side and felt a gentle wind pick, causing the leaves to rustle. I proceeded to move through the darkness of the bushes so that I could come around and take cover behind a tree. I wanted to get a better look at him. I approached with caution as he worked, and I shortened our distance to about ten feet. However, all I could see now was the back of him, which didn't give me much of a view.

Suddenly, a stream of headlights poked towards the grass through the space that led to where we were. The lights alarmed me that it could have been the police. I was shocked and stayed put. I looked over to see the thief's reaction and he had moved from the door and taken cover around the corner of the annex. I heard him mutter some words and then began to look around for a way out. The thief went back westward to the chain-link fence and threw his bag onto the other side. He then began to climb up and hop over to get down. He then proceeded down the side of the building and through the forest. I wasn't going to pursue him on foot. Once I was sure he was a decent distance away, I dashed back into some bushes and tried to see who had intruded on us. The stream of headlights didn't come from a police car, but from the Lawrence Bateau – it was Jamie.

I rushed through the bushes, came over to the car, entered and then sat down.

"What the heck?" I questioned in an annoyed tone. "You startled him."

"Sorry, but I wasn't sure what you wanted me to do," Jamie complained. "Where is he?"

"You spooked him," I answered. "Pull back – I want to see what he does now. Maybe we can at least follow him back to someplace."

Jamie pulled around and returned to Gray Avenue. He then proceeded towards Boundary Drive before turning around and driving back to the school.

"Turn off your headlights," Emma requested.

Jamie turned off the headlights and then pulled over. I saw that the Hiawatha Seneca was still there, so I hoped that perhaps our disappearance would cause him to return. Within a few seconds, the thief emerged from the shadows at the side of the school and returned to the vehicle. He opened the trunk and dropped the satchel inside, and then closed it before he went to the driver's seat. I watched him as he drove out of the parking lot and turned right onto Gray Avenue. He passed us, which prompted me to look in the rear view mirror to track him.

"Follow him," I directed, causing Jamie to quickly ignite the engine and pull out.

Jamie made a quick three-point turn and began to pursue the person from a fair distance. The car ahead stopped at Boundary Drive and waited for the lights to turn. I hoped that the thief didn't recognize the Lawrence Bateau too closely so that we could approach from the behind. Jamie slowed down and stopped behind the car as we both now waited for the green light to turn left.

Once the light turned green, Jamie followed and we made our way along Boundary Drive, through the rest of Harthdam, past the Caledonia Street intersection, and then past the Walham Way intersection to make our way towards Upper Northton and Lincoln. We stopped at Boundary Drive and Slade Drive, and Jamie stayed behind the vehicle directly, which made me anxious. Once the light turned green, Jamie continued to follow and we made it to Bering Street where there was a heavier flow of traffic.

The thief went left and stopped to wait for the light to change again. We then turned onto Bering Street and continued into Lincoln. Both cars passed through the island center, approaching the roundabout around Jarsdel Park, and then going around. Jamie kept back at this point and exited onto Shai Street, going north towards Chinatown. The thief changed into the right lane and signaled to turn right onto Riverside Drive. He then changed lanes to stop at the intersection with University Hill Drive where he signaled to turn left.

Jamie was too slow to join him and went right past him. I tensed the muscle on my lower lip as I frowned deeply. The thief had slipped into University Hill where Declan Walham University was located.

"Shoot," Jamie claimed. "I'll reach around the other intersection."

Jamie drove faster and sped along to the next intersection. University Hill Drive looped around and exited onto Riverside Drive again. Jamie signaled to turn right and then waited for traffic to clear. He then sped forward and then came around onto a lane on the left that connected with the path that the thief had gone on. He then sped forward and turned right again to continue his pursuit. I felt as if he was gone as we were the only ones that went along the lane. We then approached an intersection and my mind grew anxious at the thought that he could have turned right and disappeared, but Jamie continued forward on the main drive and approached the top of the university. Jamie slowed down and I squinted ahead to notice that a car could be seen, turning right at the intersection ahead.

Jamie sped up again, reached the intersection, and then continued forward as we were now a fair distance away from the vehicle. I recognized the vehicle as the Hiawatha Seneca – the same one that was at South Harthdam Secondary. Although I was still annoyed at Jamie, he had somewhat redeemed himself as he caught up with the suspect. Jamie slowed down again as the thief turned onto another intersection and then into a parking lot near some residences.

"Should I pull in behind him?"

"No," I denied, "just slow down so I can see where he parks."

Jamie slowed down and passed the car as it parked in front of the residence. The car shut off, but the person didn't immediately exit from the car. After a few seconds, the thief finally exited and began to approach one of the units on the ground floor directly ahead of the parking lot. I made a mental note of the unit number, Unit #9. Jamie passed through and then continued forward as we moved away from the residence.

I thought for a moment and then looked forward as we started to reach University Hill Drive.

"Do you want me to go around again?" Jamie asked.

"No…" I replied, thinking for a moment. "How about we go somewhere quiet? Like a park – I need to think for a moment."

"Okay…" Jamie replied.

Jamie drove us from University Hill back onto Riverside Drive and then came down the island on the east coast. We passed several intersections and then finally arrived at one where we turned left to enter a parking lot that faced the Walham River. Jamie parked the car and then looked at me.

"So?"

My mind froze for a moment and then I looked over to him. I was still frustrated with his reckless decision to bring the car into the parking lot and scare the thief out of his work. I knew that Jamie didn't receive high marks in classes, but even then, I thought he had a lot more common sense than that. I sighed and then looked ahead towards the river.

"Obviously, the thief is a university student," I remarked. "I've deduced that as much by the fact that he lives in some dorms at Declan Walham University. I have the car model, make, and license plate, but he didn't actually steal anything, so the picture that I have is useless."

"I'm sorry…"

"No, it's okay." Of course, it was not okay.

"What do you want to do now?" Jamie questioned.

I looked at the time on the dashboard of the car and it was close to ten o'clock at night. I didn't want to spend another second more with him. I was annoyed at him.

"I think – I think I need to go home," I remarked. "To be honest, I never told my parents that I would out for this long, so I need to be sure I get home on time. I also need to think this over and see what my next step is."

"Oh, okay…"

Jamie ignited the engine and went back onto the road again. He drove me back home and didn't say a word, which I preferred since I needed the quiet to think about the mystery a bit more. Once Jamie arrived at the family home, he looked over to me. Jamie appeared apologetic. He turned off the radio as I grabbed my camera and put a hand on the car door. Jamie then turned off the car.

"I'm really sorry about what I did, I didn't mean to and just wanted to be helpful. I'm sorry if I messed things up in your plans for tonight."

"No need to apologize," I responded, looking to him and letting go of the camera. "I was able to get at least some useful information, so it's not the end of the world."

"Right… are you sure you don't want to spend a bit more time together?"

Yes, I'm sure.

"As I said, I need to get home before my parents get mad. I'll see you at school next week…"

Without a moment of hesitation, I opened the door and closed it. I then began to walk back to the house as I took my set of keys from my jacket and then turned around to wave goodbye. Jamie ignited the engine once more and then drove off. I thought at this moment, give what happened, that any hopes or dreams between us for a relationship were shattered. I didn't like to say it to him, but he was quite incompetent in his performance, and that bothered me a lot. Was I being picky towards him? Perhaps. I simply didn't see any possibility for a relationship between us anymore.

I entered the house and closed the door behind me. It was dark, so I turned on a light and turned right to walk down the corridor, pass the den, and go towards the bedrooms. I looked to the left at the end of the corridor to notice the door to my parent's bedroom was open and it was dark inside, which told me that my parents weren't home. I then went into my bedroom, turned on the light, and saw Marius sleeping atop of my bed. I went over to the map on my desk and looked at it as I sat down. I let out a sigh and attempted to not think about Jamie anymore.

I now had the location of the suspect, which was not my precedented outcome of this stakeout. I suppose my repulsion towards Jamie was not an expected outcome either, but once I have a taste in my mouth, it's hard to get it out and these emotions were now how I felt about him. I had a bit of optimism in the least, but that was now gone. I hoped that we could remain as friends, but a part of me did not believe that would be possible. I could at least avoid any future anxieties around him. I could now also focus on this mystery with the books – I believed my next steps would be to visit the residence and learn more about the thief.

Kaj stood in the locker room of the North Harthdam Community Centre and looked at himself at the end of his shift. He wore a red tank top and short white swimming shorts. The locker room was quiet as it was after hours and he was the only male on shift. He began to undress himself and put on some normal clothes, tan trousers and blue dress shirt. He then put on his raincoat, brought his satchel with him, and exited the locker room to step out into the darkness of the Friday evening. Kaj stepped towards the parking lot that emptied out onto 13th Street and found his mom's car where he parked it, the red 1965 Hiawatha Huron. Kaj opened the trunk and put his satchel in, but before he closed the trunk, he put his keys in his jacket pocket and his wallet in the pocket in his trousers. He then he came around to unlock the front door and enter in. Kaj sat down and looked ahead as he waited for a moment.

The night was quiet and there was a quarter moon out. The time read ten minutes to ten o'clock on Kaj's watch. He ignited the engine and began to pull out of the parking lot. He then drove onto 13th Street and went forward towards Walham Way. He stopped at the red light on the intersection and faced forward. Kaj's home was a short distance from Walham Way, but he wasn't going to go home. Instead, he turned right onto Walham Way and began to drive down with the minor evening traffic. The night was just beginning and there was work to be done.

Kaj drove to the end of Walham Way, which merged with Harthdam Way and then came up to the intersection at the bend of Boundary Drive, connecting with Burnes Drive. Kaj continued forward, driving onto Boundary Drive and going eastbound and under the highway. He stopped at the intersection with Slade Drive and took a right again. He then went south into Northton, crossing Caledonia Street and reaching Lower Northton until he was at the T-intersection with Riverside Drive. Kaj drove left onto Riverside Drive and carried on for a short distance to reach the fairgrounds.

Neumann Fairgrounds was brightly lit and alive with a large crowd of people around. Of course, the fairground was open late on a Friday night. Kaj drove past and came around to turn left onto Reeth Street. He then went and turned left onto the large parking lot where there were a fair amount of vehicles parked behind the park, by the entrance of what formally was the Riverside Aquarium & Petting Zoo. The aquarium and entire structure, much like Joyland, had been condemned and sealed behind a tall chain-link fence. Kaj parked the car, put his keys back in his jacket pocket, and then came around to the sidewalk. He walked around to the front entrance where there was a minor crowd of people, mostly young people, talking and hanging out in groups. Kaj approached the entrance, but stopped to read a sign that said that the fairground was set to close at the end of the month, which meant that this weekend would be its last in Harlech before it moved on. Additionally, the hours of operation tonight were until eleven o'clock, which provided Kaj with an hour to investigate the property, at least, while they continued to operate. Kaj entered through the turnstile and then stopped to look around some more. Neumann Fairgrounds appeared the same as it had yesterday, aside from the additional people, additional concession stands and carnival games available, and busyness with queues of people at each attraction.

Kaj looked around and at all the people. His eyes scanned from left and right because he was searching for none other than this person named Elroy so that he could carry on his work. Surely, on a night like tonight, Elroy would be lurking around somewhere, seeking to exploit the vulnerable for their worth. Kaj proceeded to walk around the fairgrounds, appearing casual and a part of the scene, although he was alone and most people were either in pairs or groups. He kept close to the eastward side of the carnival where there were lots of games, moving his eyes to the shadows and corners in anticipation of Elroy leaning against a pole or choosing his prey. Kaj looked around the area for him and then moved on to the middle section where the large tent was at the head and then smaller tents with concessions, the fortuneteller tent, and then some food tents could be seen.

Kaj eyed some white tents behind the large red and white carnival tent where the main show was set in, but these were behind a tall chain-link fence that also blocked off the condemned section of the fairground. He continued down the main aisle, kept a close eye on Ellerada's tent, and then continued down to the end, but he didn't see Elroy anywhere in sight. Kaj came back to the main entrance of the park and then moved on to the westward section where the rest of the attractions were. Kaj eyed the aisles of the tents from the middle section, especially the aisle where he had seen Elroy yesterday, but he couldn't see him, so he slowly made his way around then came back to the main tent.

A poster on a sign displayed an advertisement for the main show that the Neumann Fairgrounds hosted in the main tent. The event was the freak show and led by the ringleader, a man named Hammond Neumann, and it portrayed a variety of so-called freaks, humans with deformities who had no other life than to be gawked at. Unfortunately, the show had ended already for the night, but was set to play out tomorrow again. The curtains at the front of the tent were rolled down to prevent any entry. Another poster displayed an advertisement for the fairground itself, bragging that it hailed across the country on their cross-country tour through Canada, while a footnote at the bottom read 'Copyright © Hamon Neumann – 231 Whidbey Street, Seattle, Washington.'

Kaj took a step back away from the signs and bumped into someone behind him. He looked at who it was, and it was none other than Elroy. Kaj looked at him with a deep frown. Elroy was slightly shorter than him, but distinctly older in appearance. Kaj took a step back away from Elroy as they continued to look at each other.

Suddenly, Elroy left and walked off towards the eastward portion of the campground. Kaj watched where he went and then decided to follow him. Elroy blended into the crowds of people on the east section and so Kaj attempted to track him from afar. Elroy went to the other side of the fairground and then walked into an alley between two structures where it was dark enough for him to lurk.

Kaj kept an eye on him from afar, but couldn't stay put without appearing suspicious to others and possibly being seen by Elroy. Instead, Kaj took a mental note of where Elroy was and then came around to the other side where he looked at the many games and began to pretend to watch some people play ring toss. Kaj kept the corner of his eye to his left in case Elroy moved.

Suddenly, Elroy moved and walked into the aisle of the middle section. He walked forward and began to approach a pair of girls who were on their own near a tent. Kaj kept his distance and then began to walk forward so that he could be a little closer. He then began to look at another game, balloons and darts, and so he stopped there to watch a couple of boys play while Elroy chatted with the girls. Elroy had dropped the dark and concentrated look on his face and immediately switched to a façade of approachability and charisma as he chatted with the girls, laughing and smiling. He chatted with them for several minutes until they began to leave. He pointed them towards the arcade tent and then watched them leave. Elroy moved away and returned to an alleyway in the darkness where he disappeared into.

"Hey man, do you want a turn?" an attendant said to Kaj.

Kaj turned to him as he resumed attention at the game, but ignored him as he went to follow and see where Elroy had gone. Elroy had gone past the dark alleyway and to the other side. Kaj pursued and saw him in the westward section, navigating through the crowd and then coming around to the north. Kaj followed and then stopped as he saw Elroy disappear into the purple tent through an entrance around the side. He walked over to the tent and attempted to listen for voices within, but he couldn't hear anything. Kaj turned to face the Scrambler nearby and then waited for any voices if they came up.

Suddenly, Kaj began to hear a faint mutter of voices, but they didn't speak English. They possibly spoke Romani or some other Indo-European language. Once Elroy was finished speaking with presumably Ellerada, he left the tent and disappeared into the park once more. Kaj looked over to him and thought for a moment as he held his hands on the railing. He now understood the scam that the two were running together, where Elroy operated in the field to scope targets and gather information, while Ellerada remained in the tent to propose the hoax in the minds of the marks, both working together to con others out of their goods. Kaj tightened his hands on the railing, gripping hard as he grew frustrated at what had possibly been going on for weeks, perhaps even months and not just in Harlech, but across the country, perhaps even in the United States too. Kaj began to walk away, going the opposite direction from Elroy and walking into the middle section of the fairground to make his way down to the arcade.

Kaj entered the arcade and went straight towards the pair of females, both slightly older than him by two or three years.

"Whatever you two do, do not visit Ellerada the fortuneteller and do not believe anything she says! She and that boy that spoke to you are trying to scam you out of your money and jewelry, so stay away!" Kaj proclaimed.

The girls were speechless to Kaj's warning. Kaj looked around and then quickly left. He went down the aisle and came to the entrance into the fairgrounds. He exited out and then began to walk off back to the parking lot. Kaj opened his jacket pocket to retrieve the keys, but as he did so, he brushed a hand into his right pocket on his trousers to feel that something was amiss. Kaj put a hand into the pocket and suddenly realized that his wallet wasn't there anymore. Kaj looked around and then looked back at the fairground.

"Dammit, that son of a bitch!" Kaj remarked at Elroy.

Kaj brought a pair of fists down atop of the Huron and then looked around as thought about what to do next. Kaj took his keys and decided to drive off and visit the cemetery nearby.

Riverside Cemetery was a large graveyard on Bering Street, approximately a block away from the fairground and across the street from Riverside Secondary School in the suburbs of Lower Northton. Kaj pulled over in front of Riverside Secondary School, retrieved a flashlight from the trunk of the car, locked it, and then jaywalked across the street to enter into the cemetery. Riverside Cemetery contained an enormous amount of tombstones across the entire property, which stretched approximately an entire two city blocks.

Kaj opened the iron gate that led into the cemetery. He then walked down the center path as it was nearly eleven o'clock and shined his light from tombstone to tombstone so that he could look for items that may have been left behind by the helpless victims to Ellerada and Elroy's scheme. Within fifteen minutes, Kaj found a grave that had a silk-like bag in front of it, similar to what Kate had told him about, so he went over and picked it up. Kaj opened the bag and saw that there was a silver necklace inside.

Suddenly, Kaj looked down and over to the front gate of the cemetery where the gates opened and two people entered with their own flashlights pointing beams of light around. Kaj turned off his flashlight and put the silk bag down so that he could go and take cover behind a large tombstone. The pair walked slowly and went down the path, but knew which graves to go to as they went to the one near Kaj almost immediately, picked up the silk bag, and then carried on deeper into the cemetery. Kaj came around to the other side of the tombstone to watch where the figures went and saw them approach two more tombstones deeper within the cemetery before they started to leave. Once they passed Kaj, he started to silently follow them from behind, keeping to the grass to avoid the gravel path. They exited out of the cemetery through the iron gate and then went to the car parked on the curb of the street. Kaj looked from afar as they entered the car and then drove off.

Kaj sprinted out of the cemetery, went across the street and then kept an eye on the car in the rear-view mirror as he started it and then spun around to drive after them. The car went down Bering Street and made its way towards Riverside Drive, but turned left as it was about to reach the intersection to enter into a lane behind an equestrian centre on Reeth Street. The lane was between the equestrian centre and a small arena on Riverside Drive and Bering Street. Both venues were behind the amusement park and had tall, but slim walls that created the concrete lane ahead. Kaj pulled over onto Bering Street, parked the car, and then got out so that he could see where the car went towards. Kaj then sprinted across the road, flashlight in hand, and went down the lane as he pursued the car down the dark lane.

Kaj saw some large trucks parked in the lane, possibly tied to the fairgrounds. He ran faster and saw a chain-link fence at the end. He then saw the lights of the car turn off up ahead, so he hid behind a dumpster and saw them exit. Both figures went down the rest of the lane to reach a gate that went into the back of the amusement park where there were some white tents plotted around. The chain-link fence ahead was tall and had barbed wire atop of it. Kaj saw the two figures approach a gate to the side that they simply pushed through to get through.

Elroy was one of the two figures, while the other one was unrecognizable and unseeable to him. Kaj saw them enter into the back section of the amusement park and then wander out of sight, so he continued forward and went towards the fence to look in. The back section had a similar appearance to the rest of the fairgrounds, except there were no attractions, no games, and no concessions, but instead several different tents, mostly all white, scattered around. Elroy split off from the other figure and entered into a tent with the sacks in hand.

Kaj eyed the tent while the other mysterious figure waited outside for Elroy. Elroy then appeared again and walked with the other elsewhere. Kaj eyed which tent Elroy had entered, which presumably was the tent where all of the loot was stored, so he pushed through the gate, kept low, and dashed for the tent to enter through.

Kaj entered into the tent and looked around, realizing that this tent wasn't a storage tent, but a personal tent with a table, cot, and other personal belongings around. The tent was darker on the inside than he anticipated, as if there was a different lining on the inside. The tent was homely almost, with a carpet stretched out for most of the floor. The table next to the cot had a mirror and there was a picture frame, a candle, and a booklet atop. The cot had various blankets of different thickness on top with lots of pillows. Nearby, there was a padded chest with boxes on top. Kaj stepped towards the table where the sacks were placed on top of and found his wallet on the table. Kaj picked up his wallet, looked inside to see if everything was there, but noticed that a ten dollar bill was missing. He put the wallet into his other jacket pocket so that it was nice and secure, and then looked around so that he could possibly find other sacks like the ones that Elroy had just brought in. There weren't many spaces to search around. Kaj searched thoroughly. Kaj noticed that this tent connected to another room past a set of curtains, but he didn't venture forward out of fear of what could be on the other side.

Kaj came back to the table and picked up the booklet. The booklet was on top of several sheets of paper, letters, and torn envelopes. Kaj opened the booklet and saw that there were lists of transactions in the booklet, similar to a bank registry, but it was a personal registry that listed amounts received and given. Kaj looked down the list to the most recent transactions where a fair sum was received last Wednesday from a man named 'S. Goldman.' After that entry, a share of that sum appeared to have been immediately given to the ringleader, 'H. Neumann.' Kaj saw that most of the transactions in the booklet were similar in nature, but added up to almost ten thousand dollars in total. Kaj put the booklet down and then began to go through the mail. He picked up a piece of paper, which appeared to be a receipt from Goldman's Pawn Shop in Harthdam. The receipt listed various items sold last Wednesday, including a sapphire necklace and a silver diamond bracelet. Kaj frowned at the receipt, but made note of the address so that he could follow-up on it later. At the top of the receipt, it stated that the items were sold from a person named 'Eldon Hearne,' similar to Elroy. Kaj put the receipt down and then picked up the next item in the pile, which was a pamphlet for an anarchist essay 'Law and Authority' by Pyotr Kropotkin. He put that down and the picked up a letter, opened it and read the top that said, 'Dear Eldon,' but before Kaj could read it, he looked over and saw Elroy step in.

"Hey, what are you doing with my stuff?" Elroy complained.

Kaj turned to face Eldon, frowned at him, and found him cornered and ready for a fight. Kaj raised his fists as Eldon approached him. Eldon raised his own fists and quickly snatched Kaj over and threw him onto the ground. Kaj kicked back and then quickly stood up again, but before he could exit, the other person that Eldon had been with, who was much larger, entered in and grabbed Kaj. The man had light fair skin, a round face and bald head, and wore a denim jacket with dark trousers. Kaj tossed and turned as he was captured within the large man's arms.

"Let go of me," Kaj complained.

"Wait," Eldon told the large man as he was about to take him out of the tent, "I want to know what this sneaky fox was doing in my tent."

"Me the sneaky fox? You stole from me, you weasel – I just came to get what you had taken from me."

"You take from him?" the big guy asked in an Eastern European accent.

"No," Eldon lied.

"You stole my wallet!"

"Igor, get rid of him – I'll tell Hammond and make sure he's banned from the fairgrounds for the rest of his life. Stay out or we'll call the police!"

"I should be calling the police on you," Kaj remarked. "You're nothing but a con artist, you and Ellerada."

Eldon's eyes flashed. He ignored Kaj's accusation otherwise.

"Get him out of here!" Eldon simply said.

Igor took Kaj and dropped him off by the gate, pushing him forward.

"Go on, and stay out! You are banned from the fair – never come back!" Igor threatened.

Kaj looked at him and then over to where he saw Eldon in front of his tent, arms crossed. Kaj turned around and looked forward. He felt his wallet in his coat and knew that Katelyn's necklace and Meghan's bracelet was nowhere to be seen inside the fairground, so it was pointless to break-in again. He needed to instead visit the pawnshop where the items could be found. However, within Kaj's eyes and tightened fists as he walked down the lane back to the Hiawatha Huron, was a desire for a delicate revenge – to expose the con artists in their act, but in order to do so, he would require evidence to present to the police. Kaj looked behind him once more, saw that Igor and

Eldon were gone, and then crossed the street to return to his car with certainty that he would be back again at least once more to tie up loose ends.

Early next morning, Kaj went to Goldman's Pawn Shop on Walham Way before he went to work to see if they had Katelyn's necklace and Meghan's bracelet. However, they were closed, so he decided to return after the end of his shift at the community center. Kaj exited the community center and started to walk home. He still partially wore his uniform, wearing a white short-sleeved shirt instead that had the word 'Lifeguard' on the left crest. The rest of his clothes were everyday clothing, dark trousers and his rain jacket. Kaj reached Walham Way and walked northeast until he saw the pawn shop just before they were about to close for the day. He entered and met with the shopkeeper, a middle-aged man with brown hair, cold fairish skin, and a hooked nose. He wore a plaid suit and was with a customer. Kaj looked at the jewelry in the cabinet and eyed the necklace by its distinct purple sapphire.

"Excuse me?" Kaj asked towards the shopkeeper.

The shopkeeper excused himself and then walked over to Kaj, standing on the opposite-side from him.

"What are you interested in?" the shopkeeper asked.

"How much for that necklace?" Kaj asked, pointing at his girlfriend's necklace.

The man opened the cabinet on the other side, pulled the tray out and then read the price tag. Kaj could see for himself what the price was and he frowned.

"Two-hundred and twenty dollars," the shopkeeper said. "It's good quality. Just received this one too. Eighteen karat – I verified it myself. Do you want it?"

"Two-hundred and twenty?" Kaj questioned. "I can't afford that… What about that bracelet?"

"The bracelet? That's three-hundred dollars."

"Okay… Thanks…"

Kaj left the pawn shop empty-handed. He looked around and then began to walk back down Walham Way so that he could return home. Kaj turned into the suburbs of North Harthdam at 16th Street and started to walk home. It was nearly six o'clock in the evening and the sun was still bright, but it was not too warm nor too cold. Kaj walked down 16th Street on the sidewalk, while at the same time, approaching 16th Street from Oben Avenue, I had just left Riley's house with her as we went for a walk through the suburbs.

"I can't believe they can be such brats," Riley remarked in reference to the siblings of some schoolmates. "They constantly bickered with each other, and the girl, Aggie, was such a deceptive liar. Tate was kept stealing from her, and it was hard to know if she was lying or not sometimes because of the fact that I simply didn't trust her."

"Yeah…"

"Anyways, I'm never going back to that house – it's not worth the ten dollars."

"At least you get paid with your work…"

"That's the benefit of running your own business," Riley said with a smile. "Vicky Babysitting is a success – I get to choose who I see, set my own hours, and make enough money so that I can buy what I want and save money for college."

"Yeah…"

"Speaking of such, I just bought this book that I've been reading and been obsessed with," Riley remarked. "You should definitely read it when you get a chance…"

"As long as it's not *Negro*, I might just have to."

"No, it's not. My dad recommended it to me – it's called *Nineteen Eighty-four* by George Orwell, and it's about this backwards dystopian totalitarian society where nobody is free and every part of everyday life is controlled by the government. It's awful – the setting that is, the book has been very eye-opening and well-written. It really makes you appreciate living in a place like ours – I could never see something like that happening here, at least. I hope that nothing like that ever happens here."

"Yeah…"

"Anyways, how was your date with Jamie?"

My ears flicked and jaw tensed. I looked at her with a frown.

"It wasn't a date," I corrected, "and it was awful."

I told Riley a brief summary of what had happened last night with the stakeout, my sighting of the thief, and then Jamie's blunder that caused the thief to leave. However, I did mention that I managed to locate where the person lives and wanted to return to investigate further.

"How are you going to investigate further?" Riley questioned. "Are you going to break into their apartment?"

"No…"

Riley laughed.

"Anyways, the gist of my experience was that I don't think I actually like Jamie as much as I thought that I did. He's kind of… absent-minded and has little common sense. I mean, who does that? Who shines a bright light when someone is trying to sneak and spy on someone?"

"Yeah, that was kind of dumb of him," Riley remarked. "I'm sorry that didn't go as you had hoped."

"It's okay… I realized a lot, and I'm relieved that I never have to do that again. I feel a lot better about being around Jamie now that this idea of us being together is gone."

"Yeah, that's good."

I looked forward and saw someone approaching us. Riley saw too.

"Is that Kaj?" I questioned.

"Yeah, he lives near me, remember?"

Kaj approached us and when we were closer together, Riley waved and Kaj timidly waved back. We passed each other, but Riley stopped and turned around.

"Hey stranger," Riley said, "not going to say hello?"

Kaj turned around, faced us, and replied, "Sorry, hello."

"What're you up to?" Riley asked.

"I'm just coming back from work," Kaj replied with a sigh. "What about you?"

"We're just going for a walk – how has your search for Kate and Meg's jewelry been going?" Riley then asked.

"Not bad," Kaj responded. "I managed to locate them both at Goldman's Pawn Shop down on Walham Way, but they're over-priced and too expensive to buy back. I'm going to let Kate know to tell Meghan so that maybe Elias can buy Meghan's bracelet in the least before someone else buys it."

"Don't you think that you should report that to the police?" Riley questioned.

"Why? The police didn't do much when Kate's dad told them about what happened to his daughter, so why would they do something now? I mean, I'll tell Kate and she can tell her dad, but I'm not going to phone the police."

"What are you going to do then?"

Kaj shrugged and replied, "I want to investigate this scam a bit more, but I don't see much point since they're leaving town after tomorrow. Even if I had evidence to give to the police, they'd just leave before they even do anything. Besides, I know where Kate's necklace is now so that as much as been solved and I'm content with that."

"You don't sound content – how about we help you?"

I looked at Riley as she suggested that idea.

"Help me?"

"Is there nothing that we can both do to help you out?"

"I mean, you could come with me back to the fairground and pretend to be vulnerable targets for this scam – if we could… I don't know, document that, then the police should do something about it, right?"

"Sounds like a good idea," Riley encouraged, "but in return, you have to help Emma with her project."

"Oh yeah? What's she been doing again? Something to do with books?"

"Missing books," Riley corrected.

Riley explained what I had produced from her research and investigation up to now, leaving out the details of how I felt towards

Jamie, but making note of his blunder last night. Riley proposed that I needed someone to take me to Declan Walham University so that I could look into the place that the thief lived at.

"Yeah, I can drive you if you want," Kaj replied. "I'm not doing anything else – are you going to be with Riley for a while?"

"Yeah," I sheepishly responded.

"I'm just going to go home and have dinner, let my mom know, and then come around to pick you up in about an hour. How about that?" Kaj offered.

"Sounds great!" Riley replied with a smile. "We're going to finish our walk and then go back to my place. See you in a bit!"

I looked at Riley with an annoyed glance. We continued to walk as we separated from Kaj, and he went home as he had said he would.

"Why would you do that?" I questioned.

"Why?"

"I don't need Kaj's help," I replied.

"Oh shush, yes you do. He's smart and he can be useful – he's definitely got a lot more common sense than Jamie Donovan does."

I couldn't argue with that point – I knew that Kaj had common sense and I was in fact impressed with the fact that he had come to the conclusion of his mystery regarding the necklaces.

"Besides, you seem so apprehensive around Kaj?"

"I'm apprehensive around a lot of people."

"You seem more so with Kaj," Riley pointed out.

"Kaj has a girlfriend, and I have no attraction of any kind towards him."

"If you say so," Riley said without desire to push the subject. "I believe you."

I sighed as we continued to walk together. We reached Rostill Avenue, turned left, and walked eastbound until we reached 14th Street. We looped around, returning to Oben Avenue, and then returned to Riley's house where I ate with her family. Riley lived in a larger home compared to the rest of the ones in the area – it was also a larger property near Harthdam Way, stuck in the midst of some forest. The house was two-stories and was designed like a farmhouse with a front porch, large barn-like shed in the back, and plenty of room. I liked her house since it was very cozy. I also liked her cat, a domestic short-hair named Ollie. At a quarter past six o'clock, Kaj arrived in his mother's Hiawatha Huron and he pulled up to the end of the gravel driveway. I sighed as I saw him, told Riley, and then left the house so that I could join Kaj for this venture to the university.

I was supposed to stay at Riley's house for a sleepover tonight. A part of me had grown tired with the investigation and didn't expect much to come out of our search around the residence that the thief went to. In the least, I felt a lot more comfortable around Kaj than I did with Jamie. I entered into the Huron and Kaj then backed up, turned around, and drove off towards Oben Avenue.

Kaj drove down 15th Street and came onto Walham Way, turning left and going straight towards Boundary Drive. From Boundary Drive, he went to the very end and turned left once more onto Bering Street. He then continued northbound until we reached Jarsdel Park, going around the roundabout, and then onto Shai Street just as the thief had driven off yesterday. Once at Riverside Drive, Kaj turned right and then left onto University Hill Drive, and from there, I directed him to break the silence between us. Kaj drove to the residence without issue and parked the car in front of the dormitory complex.

I got a better look at the dormitories, which appeared to be newly built and made of pure concrete from the outside façade. They had an appearance similar to a motel, where each residence had a door, window, and then it went to the next unit. Once Kaj turned off the car, he looked ahead and looked at me. I looked forward to the residence that I saw the thief enter yesterday, Unit #9.

"So, what now?" Kaj questioned.

"I… I suppose I'll go and knock to see if he's home," I replied, looking around the parking lot and not seeing the Hiawatha Seneca.
I stepped out of the car and approached Unit #9. Kaj joined me and stood with me as I knocked on the door, but no answer came as I expected. As much as I appreciated Kaj willing to take me here, I was okay with this result that we'd attempt to see if the thief was home and

then simply leave. I stepped back while Kaj stepped forward, not taking no for an answer, and knocked hard on the door.

"I don't think he's home…" I remarked to him, looking around the parking lot again. "His car isn't here either."

I turned back to face Kaj as he said, "So, what are you going to do?"

"Well, I'm not going to break into his apartment just so I can look around for some books," I replied, walking over to the window to peek inside. "Besides, I don't even think he has them here."

Kaj put a hand on the knob and tried to open the door. The door was locked. Kaj stepped back and I watched as he suddenly raised his foot and kicked the door open. Kaj looked around to ensure that nobody saw before he then entered into the apartment. I was stunned. Kaj put a hand on the knob to stop it from swinging back into him before he looked at me.

"Are you coming?" Kaj questioned.

I walked over and joined him inside but I didn't reply as I was still too stunned to speak. Kaj closed the door behind him. The force of the kick had blown the lock right through the flimsy wall it was locked into rendering it useless. Kaj looked around the apartment, which prompted me to do the same as I looked away from the lock. The dormitory was small and just as it appeared outside, the inside was like a motel room too with a bed on the left, desk and dresser on the right, and at the end, a small corridor where there was a closet, a sink at the end, and then a bathroom on the right. I walked over to the desk and looked at the top of the desk where there weren't any of the missing books, but instead some textbooks for classes having to do with political science, literary studies, and pedagogy.

Kaj began to look through the rest of the apartment to ensure they were definitely alone. He checked the bathroom and the closet, and he didn't see anyone else. The closet didn't contain any obvious sight or even container with books inside. Kaj returned to me as I sifted through all the stuff on the desk, opening the drawers to look inside and see if there was something to give a hint on where the books were. Kaj began to look around the dresser as I continued to search the desk.

I opened the wide drawer in the desk and found a travel map, similar to the one that I used to keep track of all the locations on Jarsdel Island that had been swiped by the thief, but this one was a different make but same concept. I opened the map and laid it on the table, and sure enough, this map contained all the locations of the secondary schools, marked with tick marks. Likewise, there were markings on King Island and Cliffe Island, possibly at the secondary schools there, but there weren't any other markings other than a circle. It was unclear if the thief intended to raid these schools as well. I closed the map, but left it on the desk. I then continued to search through while Kaj came to join me. I opened the other drawers and didn't find anything of interest.

"What do you have?" Kaj asked.

"A map that has the locations of all the schools that he's visited," I replied.

"Anything with his name?" Kaj questioned.

"No, only these post cards on his desk," I remarked, picking up the post cards underneath the textbooks. "Looks like they're from a lot of different places out East."

I handed the postcards to Kaj who looked at them. Two of them were from Burma; one from Mandalay and another from Rangoon, and one from Colombo in Sri Lanka. Kaj looked at the intricate designs that noted each culture and then turned around to look at the back of them, which read short messages addressed to a 'B. Ericson' at this residence in University Hill. I took the postcards back, looked at the name again, and then put them back down onto the desk.

"I don't see any sign of the books here," Kaj stated. "Want to look around some more?"

"No," I replied, "I think this map should be enough. I'm going to go and call the police, and then I think we should leave so that we don't get in trouble."

"Okay," Kaj responded, stepping over to leave.

Suddenly, however, before we could leave, the door opened and the thief entered and looked towards us.

"Who are you and what are you doing in my room?" the thief remarked.

I looked at the thief and he was surely young, approximately two or three years older than both Kaj and me. He had fair skin and was shaven. He didn't wear the flat cap this time, which displayed his fluffy dark brown hair that was cut short on the sides. He wore a grey plaid jacket this time with a dark green collared shirt underneath and plaid trousers. He also wore dark leather shoes. Kaj looked at him too, standing between me and the thief.

Kaj approached him as he raised a pair of fists towards Kaj, challenging him. Kaj raised his fists up too in order to defend himself. The thief drove a fist towards Kaj, missing him as he backed away and then returned a fist towards his cheeks. I understood that Kaj was not much of a fighter – his specialty in terms of sports was in swimming, lacrosse, and track and field. The most education that he would have in any sort of fighting would have been when the boys had wrestling practice in gym class. Once the fists went flying, all hell broke loose as the two scrambled towards each other. Kaj tackled the thief and brought him against the wall next to the door where he punched him in the face. The thief attempted to push him back. I stayed back to avoid the messy fight and I couldn't move around the side to leave so that I could call the police.

The thief swung a sharp punch towards Kaj's jaw, hitting him, and causing him to hit back with anger. Kaj attempted to control the arms as he pushed him against the perpendicular wall, next to the bed and then swung another punch back at the thief as he attempted to control him. Kaj pressed the thief against the wall hard to gain the upper hand. The door was now clear, but I didn't have the resolve to abandon Kaj in the mess that I had brought him into. Kaj hit the thief against the head again. The thief's movements became slowed down as he attempted to fight back. The thief swung another punch at Kaj as he broke free, but Kaj easily moved out of the way and swung a sharp punch back, knocking the thief out.

"Quickly, get me something to tie him up," Kaj said to me.

I went to the desk and fetched some duct tape that I had found as well as a pair of scissors. Kaj took the pair of scissors and began to tie the thief up while I stood back. Once I was sure that Kaj was safe, I moved towards the door so that I could leave and call the police. I looked down and saw a set of keys on the floor that had fallen. I picked them up and looked at them – it was a house key and a car key. I went to Kaj with them and showed him.

"Are these yours?" I asked Kaj.

"No," Kaj replied, "they must be his."

"I'm going to check the trunk of the car," I replied, "and after, I'll call the police. Are you going to be okay on your own?"

"Yeah, go and call the police," Kaj replied. "I'll keep the garbage in check."

I left the dorm and looked around for the Hiawatha Seneca. It was parked near Kaj's car. I walked over and brought the key into the trunk, opening it, and seeing the satchel that I had seen from yesterday as well as several boxes, some of them empty, and some of them carrying many copies of classic novels: Shakespeare, Victor Hugo, Charles Dickens, Jack London, and so many more famous authors from the past. I left the car with the trunk closed and looked around for a payphone.

I saw a payphone towards the opposite-end of the dormitory, so I quickly went over and picked up the phone. I dialed 911 and waited for a response. Suddenly, I felt myself grabbed backwards and away from the phone, causing it to drop and swing in place. A man put his hands over my mouth to keep me from screaming, pulling me back and into the parking lot where tape was put over my mouth. I attempted to struggle and break free, but it was useless. Instead, all I did was drop the car keys onto the floor in the hope that Kaj would find them. Once I was gagged, they pushed me into the trunk of a car and closed the top. The next thing I saw was nothing but pure darkness.

"She's called the police," someone said from outside. "We got to go."

I then heard a mumble.

"Forget him – let's get out of here!"

Next, I heard the start of the car engine and the motion of the car move. I understood at that moment, where I was being separated from Kaj, that I was being kidnapped and there was nothing that I could do about that.

Kaj waited for me to return, unaware that I was now gone, so in his wait, he decided to search the thief that he had apprehended and see if he could identify him. Kaj produced a wallet from the plaid jacket and opened it to find a driver's license that had the name of the thief, Blair Ericson, and his date of birth. He was born in 1949 and presently three years older than Kaj who was, like me, still only fifteen years old. Kaj saw that there was nothing else of use in the wallet, so he returned it to Blair's person. Kaj continued to wait from me, and before he could leave, Blair woke up, arms tied to his torso and legs tied together by duct tape. He immediately began to wiggle around on his bed like a worm. Kaj threw Blair onto the floor so that he could stop making noise by the springs on the bed. He waited another couple of minutes and then went over to close the door and lowered the blinds to give them a bit of privacy.

I didn't return of course, and Kaj grew worried and looked out the window for me.

"Where did she go..." Kaj questioned.

Blair began to mumble, but he couldn't speak since his mouth was covered in duct tape like mine was at this moment.

Kaj looked out the window again and saw the Hiawatha Seneca. He looked side to side, but didn't see me in sight. He finally decided to open the door and see if he could see anything noteworthy around. He looked down the pathway and to the end where the payphone was. I wasn't there, but the phone handle was still dangling from the chord. Kaj looked over to Blair who squirmed on the floor.

Suddenly, Kaj ran off and went over to the Hiawatha Seneca, looking at the car and then around again to see if he could see me somewhere around. Kaj couldn't. He began to walk towards the payphone when he saw something shiny on the floor. He walked over and picked up the key to the Seneca. He looked around once more and then went over to the car. He opened the trunk and saw the books inside. Kaj kept the trunk open and then turned around. Kaj's eyes glanced over to the skid marks on the asphalt from my kidnapper's getaway.

"Emma!" Kaj shouted as he looked around.

No response came. Kaj, more frightful than before, began to look around the immediate area until he came to the telephone. He picked it up and placed it to his ear to listen and hear if someone was on the line, but instead there was the sound of the dial tone. He put the phone back onto the rack. Kaj quickly came back to the dorm where Blair was attempting to stand up. Kaj went over to him and threw him back onto the ground with anger. He then approached, ungagged him, and pressed down onto him as he took physical control of him with both arms and legs.

"You weren't alone, were you?" Kaj remarked. "Who were you with?"

"Let go of me!" the boy responded.

"Answer me!"

"I'm not answering any of your questions…"

"Where did they take my friend?"

"I don't know who you are, or what you're talking about."

"My friend, the girl with red-hair, she's gone now. Where did they take her," Kaj enunciated for the book thief to understand. "She went to call the police, but the phone is dangling as if she was yanked away just as she was about to make the phone call. She's only fifteen-years old – what are they going to do with her? She doesn't deserve any of this…"

"Maybe you both shouldn't have meddled in our business…"

Kaj punched the thief across the face.

"You have nothing over me…"

"Yeah?" Kaj questioned. "Right now, maybe so… so maybe we'll just have to wait until the police arrive? Wait until I tell them that you know where a fifteen-year old girl was kidnapped to, and that she's in grave danger…"

"Yeah, what about you? You broke into my dorm," Blair remarked. "I'm going to press charges against you for sure."

"Go ahead, so we both go down. I'm good with that…"

"Yeah? I still won't tell them anything, and by the time that they even finish their investigation, my friends will be long gone before they can do anything about them."

Kaj frowned at the thief. He let go of him and stood up. He then picked him up and had him sit down.

"Alright, you've made your point," Kaj said, "but hear me out… the cops are going to be here at any moment. If they get here, you're going to go to prison, so let's make a deal – I bet you want to walk out of here free, while I want my friend back. If you tell me where she is, I'll cut you free."

"Bullshit," Blair replied. "You won't cut me free. If I tell you, you'll just gag me again and leave me for the cops, asshole."

Kaj couldn't refute that possibility. Instead, he started to pace around as he thought for a moment.

"What do you want to make this work then?" Kaj questioned.

"Cut me free, and I'll tell you where she is," Blair insisted.

"No way, you'll just leave before you tell me."

"Seems like we're at an impasse then."

"The question is, who has more to lose here," Kaj bluffed, "your freedom, or my friend."

"That would depend on you, partner."

Kaj eyed him and the two waited for a moment to see if either would cave to the pressure.

"I think you have more to lose here," Kaj insisted.

"I don't think so, because here's what I'm going to tell the police when they arrive. I'm going to tell them that I was on my way to my apartment when I had this chump stalking me on my way here. He then kidnapped me and held me hostage like a maniac – how does that sound for you?"

"They'll never believe you."

Both Kaj and Blair heard the sound of sirens from the distance.

"We'll just have to wait and see," Blair asserted. "Either way, I think you have more to lose here than me."

Kaj hesitated for a moment and then caved to the pressure.

"Fine," Kaj replied, "but I'm not going to free you just yet. What if you direct me to where they took my friend?"

"What?"

"Come with me and give me directions to where you think they've taken her, and in return, I'll let you go."

Blair hesitated for a moment before he responded.

"How do I know you won't just keep me tied and call the police then? What assurance do I have that you'll keep your part of the bargain?"

"What do you want for me to prove you?"

"Untie my hands," Blair reasoned.

"No."

"Untie my legs then."

Kaj hesitated for a moment before he responded.

"Okay," Kaj replied, "but once we're in my car. Otherwise, I'm not going to compromise with you anymore."

"Fine, but we need to hurry, because it sounds like those coppers are on their way here sooner than you think."

"Let's go then."

Kaj took ahold of Blair's arms and escorted him out of the apartment. He directed him into the passenger seat at the front of his car and sat him down.

"Close my apartment door and car trunk door," Blair requested.

"Why?"

"If you don't, we have no deal. Nobody can know that I was involved in any of this…"

Kaj glared at him for a split second and then complied. He went and closed the door to the apartment; at least, he shut the door seeing that he had destroyed the lock. He then went over to the car, shut the trunk, but left the keys atop. Kaj then went back to the car, entered, and sat down.

"Now, release my legs," Blair requested.

Kaj looked at him, locked the side door, and then began to untie the mess of tape around Blair's legs to let him free. Kaj started the car, pulled out, and then started to make his way out of the immediate area and back towards University Hill Drive. Kaj looked forward with concentrated eyes, occasionally glancing towards his hostage who sat uncomfortably with his hands tied behind him.

"Where am I going?" Kaj questioned as he drove onto University Hill Drive.

"Go into Lincoln, around Jarsdel Park, and go towards Northton. I'll tell you more once we're there."

"Okay…"

Kaj drove down University Hill Drive. He eyed a police car pass them as they went downhill and into Lincoln. Kaj went his own way, away from the help of the police to instead come and rescue me.

Part 3 – Chapter 27
Unknown Location
Northton, Jarsdel Island
September 1968 – 19:00 hours

I wasn't sure how much time passed between when I was forced into the back of my kidnapper's car, to when I arrived at the unknown location I was at now. All that I could recall were the sounds and feelings that I held from the moment that the trunk opened and they placed a sac over my head. They pulled me out of the trunk and I placed my feet onto the hard ground. They then led me away from the car and steered me for several minutes, moving from a rough hard surface to a smoother one. I was led to a metal stairwell where I was raised up each step with care, and then I was brought to the end where I was forced to sit down. I felt some adjustments made on my ties as they were planted together with the chair, and likewise around my feet. I was then left there for an uncertain amount of time as I heard the footsteps of my kidnappers disappear. Wherever I was, it was cold and quiet. My hands trembled in fear over the thoughts of what could happen to me, because I surely thought that this was my mind. All my curiosity had led to this, and I was shocked at the result of all my research to cause the end of me. I wasn't entirely sure though that this was my end.

I began to hear some voices from nearby as I sat on the chair and felt time pass by. I couldn't hear entirely what was being said, so I attempted to concentrate on key words that were mentioned, such as 'police' and 'escape.' I thought for a moment that they were talking about what led them to flee from the university, since I had heard them state that they needed to leave since they assumed that I had phoned the police, when in fact, I had only dialed 911 and then dropped the phone. I supposed though that a dropped 911 call would still be taken seriously by the emergency responders. As I thought about that conversation, my mind then thought about Kaj since I had forgotten about him in my panic. I had dragged him into something so serious and possibly put him in danger. I had left him with the book thief in his residence that we had broken into, and he may get in trouble for that, but I felt a degree of confidence that he would surely figure out that I had been kidnapped, if not by my sudden disappearance, then possibly by the fact that I had dropped the keys to the Seneca onto the floor. I knew that Kaj was intelligent. I began to hear some voices again as I thought about him.

"… leave by early Monday morning," a voice stated.

"Why not sooner?"

I didn't hear the response.

"How greedy can… be? What does Mammon…"

I heard a whisper in response.

"A week? What about the hostage we've taken. Shouldn't that escalate our concern?"

"There's no… We've done as much as we can here, and the rest is…"

I didn't hear the rest of the response.

"What are we going to do with her then?"

"I… I don't know who she is, but… We can't let her go."

My stomach sank as they talked about me. I missed a part of the conversation.

"Go…"

A pause came afterwards, and a minute passed by until I heard the sound of the metal floor echo, similarly to when the kidnappers had left. The footsteps grew louder and louder until suddenly, the sac over my head was lifted and I caught a glimpse at my surroundings and at least one of my kidnappers. I was in some sort of warehouse, and it appeared that I was on a catwalk at the back of the warehouse. The area looked abandoned, and the ceiling looked like it had caved in slightly and become exposed towards a corner where I saw moonlight pour in from outside. I didn't get a chance to look at the rest of my surroundings, because the one that pulled the sac from over my head looked directly at me as he crouched in front of me. He wore dark clothes and had unkempt brown hair. His skin was fair, and he had a tall nose, skinny cheeks, and a slender body. He also appeared to be young, possibly as old if not a year or two older than the book thief,

Blair. Half of his face was covered by a black bandana. He wore leather gloves that covered his hands. All I could see was his dark eyes and the saggy bags underneath. He looked malnourished. A pause came after he pulled the bag from over my head, and he looked at me with his eyes.

I was uncomfortable with him as he looked at me, so I attempted to look away and then he brought a gloved hand to my face. He placed it on my cheek and then motioned it down to the tip of the piece of tape around my mouth. I was annoyed at the sudden jerk of the tape from my mouth, but I didn't say a word and instead continued to avoid eye contact with the creeping eyes of the boy in front of me.

"You're very beautiful," the boy stated. "I've never seen someone as beautiful as you before…"

I didn't respond and instead looked away from him.

"I don't mean to be a creep," the boy remarked. "Honestly… I'll stop talking about it… What's your name?"

I didn't respond and continued to look away.

"You don't want to talk to me? I understand that… not a lot of people want to talk to me around here either. A lot of them don't like me, and a lot of them also mistreat me, but I'll make them pay. You weren't supposed to get involved with all of us though, and I'm sorry that you did, but I've been told that we can't risk our escape from the city by letting you just go free. We're leaving on Monday morning, but I don't want this next day and a bit to be too hard on you, so I want to make it up to you as much as I can. Can I get you something? Water? Food?"

I shook my head and then continued to look away from him.

"Why won't you look at me? You don't like looking at me?"

I didn't respond. The boy sighed. He stood up and stepped aside.

"What were you doing at the university? Why did you call the police? It doesn't make any sense – how did you come into all of this?"

I was just as confused as he was, except that I wasn't quite sure what I had stepped into.

"Will you at least answer that question for me?" the boy asked as he stepped over.

I didn't respond.

"You probably don't know anything then," the boy replied. "You're probably just a passerby that got scared at what she had seen, and we kidnapped you by mistake. I hate that. I'm sorry that the people who kidnapped you were such fools. I guess… we're both victims of their idiocy. I hate them. Stupid people… Am I right?"

I looked down and avoided eye contact with him again.

"You're awfully quiet," the boy acknowledged. "I don't understand why. Could you just tell me? Explain to me?"

I didn't respond. The boy turned around and walked back over to me.

"Please, at least tell me your name…" the boy asked as he crouched down in front of me.

I looked at him and the unpleasant look on his impish face. He reminded me a bit of Glenn, as if they were brothers, but this boy was shorter and older. There were minor details in their appearance that could distinguish them, but I didn't want to look at him anymore, so I averted my eyes. I looked aside, but could still feel the glare of his eyes on me.

I sighed and finally replied, "Catherine… my name is Catherine…"

"Catherine…" the boy acknowledged as he stood up and went back to the railing as he said my name once more. "Catherine…"

The boy took in a deep breath and then walked back over to me.

"I'll tell you what, Catherine, I'm going to get you out of here eventually, but not now. I can't let you go now because it's not safe. You have no business with us, and I'm sorry that you've been dragged into all of this," the boy said before he stood up and walked aside. "An innocent girl like you… a better world awaits…"

The boy grew silent for a moment, which caused me to think and compose myself. If I wanted to get more information from him, now was my chance.

"Who are you?" I asked.

The boy turned around and walked over to me.

"I can't tell you my real name," the boy stated. "All of us though are fighters though, fighting to free humanity from the tyranny of mankind, of the so-called authority that dictates our lives. Wouldn't you agree that the world would be a better place if there weren't any constraints upon any of us? Nothing to keep us down? Free to make our own choices?

I didn't respond.

"As a woman, don't you feel the constraints of society? The exercise of illegitimate power that hinders your choices?"

I didn't respond. All I felt was that I was being constrained by this person and whoever he was associated with. I still wasn't entirely sure who they were, but I felt motivated to ask.

"Where am I?"

"I suppose I can answer that question... you're in the abandoned remains of an amusement park," the boy answered. "I know, it looks like a warehouse, but that's because we're in the storage facility for the aquarium that was a part of that amusement park. I believe that the park used to be called *Joyland* or something like that – a capitalist project intended to stupefy the masses and fill the pockets of the greedy."

The boy turned around and walked over to me.

"You seem more willing to talk," the boy stated. "Will you tell me what you were doing at the university? You were looking into a car for some reason – what was that reason?"

"The books..." I confessed, "I wanted to know about the books that were stolen."

The boy looked at me and didn't respond. He walked over to the railing and then looked down. He shook his head.

"The power of the state is exercised through literature that teaches us subjects that are meant to shape and mold us in a certain way," the boy stated, "and these ideas that they present disable us from our potential in other fields, inhibiting our choice in other domains. All they seek is to force us into the same bricks that hold up their society together; the family, a mother and a father, and the aims of a nine to five o'clock job that provides us with sustenance and returns a share to the illegitimate state. What a world... does that sound like freedom to you?"

I didn't respond. The boy continued to speak.

"All of those books force onto teenagers archaic ideas that the state approves, but we wanted to change that. We stole them all. That was our part, so that the books could be changed for ideas that liberate the mind and encourage others to think about the dangers of the state through the consequences of their power, the enslavement of entire races, cultures, even our women, to the massacre of certain ethnic groups and those that oppose them when they are threatened. Make no mistake, but our society is a sociopathic and despotic one."

The boy grew silent for a moment.

"All of those books are going to be destroyed and replaced," the boy confessed. "I'm impressed that you were able to catch onto our runner for those books, but I suppose he's lost. I'm not worried about what he could tell those fascists in the police station, because we'll be gone before they can discover us. Is that all you were interested in? The books?"

"Yes," I quietly responded.

"I suppose you were curious," the boy answered. "I suppose that you liked the books too, at least so much as to wonder where they had gone... Dickens, Austen... I'll admit, some of those stories are beautiful, but within context. All information requires context when presented, but that's something that's outside of our control at this moment. The ability to provide context is within the power of the state, and until such time that this power is within our control, all we can do is manipulate information provided to avoid any multiplication of any bad ideas. Bad ideas cost lives, you know. Just look at Germany thirty years ago..."

I didn't respond.

"I'm glad that you brought that up, because it's been my interest to provide context to information, because information, especially in this day and age, is interesting. Bad ideas deserve to be destroyed and refuted, while good ideas need to be promoted and explained to the masses so that they can understand as I understand... All of this requires information to be controlled."

The boy grew silent again. He turned around and looked at me.

"I'm sorry, but the books will need to be destroyed," the boy admitted, "but don't you worry. My friends and I are only destroying copies of the book – the works will continue to exist as an idea, just as we exist as an idea. Do you know who we are?"

I didn't respond.

"If you only knew the truth, you could join us, but it doesn't seem like you're interested in our anarchic ideas. I… I want to keep talking to you, but I have to go now. I'll be back when you get hungry in the morning…"

I watched as the boy left and went down the stairs. He left me without the sac on my head, which I appreciated since I got to get a better look of my surroundings. I was in a warehouse for sure, atop a catwalk, and below me there were some empty boxes and ahead of me some empty shelves. The various shelves weren't organized into aisles, but instead were pulled over and piled atop of each other on one side of the room, while on the other side, there was an empty space with various boxes piled up nearby. In the corner of the room, there was a burnt-out pyre. The entire room couldn't have been larger than the gym at St. Augustine of Hippo Secondary. There was a small group of people in dark clothes and bandanas similar to the boy that had just spoken to me. I watched as they shuffled around with the boxes and then saw one of them set the pyre aflame.

I was horrified with what I saw next. The boy joined them and together, they started to take the books from the boxes and throw them into the pyre, adding fuel to the flame, and destroying the classic work in its entirety. I had no doubt that the books were the ones that had been stolen from all the schools on the island, and if I was to assume that this operation was wider than just Jarsdel Island, then it could include books from Cliffe Island, King Island, and even New Harlech and Lennox too. All of them were being thrown into the bonfire and reduced to ashes. I was sickened.

I averted my eyes as I thought about the copies of *Hamlet* meeting their end, unable for me to stop them, and how many more for all of their cultural significance, the stories that they tell and the message behind them. All of them were being blatantly ignored for this stupid idea that they were some sort of mechanism to control people, when they weren't. From what he had suggested, that was his assumption and his aim with the new literature that was provided. What significance did *Hamlet* play in civilization, as if civilization relied on the messages of action over inaction, reality over appearance; these ideas weren't mediated upon by everyday people to push them into a certain lifestyle. Likewise, the same could be said for the rest of them, because these were stories enjoyed and appreciated by a few, such as myself, who had worked so hard to get where I was now. I averted the thought that this was my end.

I started to struggle in the ties, but they were all tied very tightly around my wrists and the frame of the chair. Luckily though, my hands were slim and small, so I attempted to squeeze my hands through. I concentrated hard and closed my eyes as I pulled and pulled. I felt as if my wrists would detach from my hand. I stopped for a moment as I felt as if my efforts had made the rope tighter, cutting off circulation to my hands. I began to feel around for an alternate strategy with my finger, to attempt to loosen the rope my pocking and prodding at the other bits around me. I managed to make the ties a little looser so that I could return feeling to my hands, and with a bit effort, I started to pull out again and break free.

Once I was free, I took care to ensure that I was still quiet as to not make any noise or alert the anarchists below that I was now free. I quietly leaned over and started to untie the rope from around my feet and then I thought for a moment while I continued to stay seated. I looked down and saw that near where the anarchists were destroying books, there was an exit, but I had no chance to evade them and push through. Instead, I had to develop a different route – the boy told me that I was in the wreck of Joyland in Northton, which meant that there could be a limited amount of exits from a condemned site. I decided my best option was to find a way outside and attempt to find an exit from there. I took quiet steps and started to make my way to the end of the catwalk and look across to where my alternate exit was.

I hid behind a crate and looked over as they continued to destroy the copies of so many works of literature. I didn't understand their misguided motives, but I wasn't here to understand their motives or empathize with them. I wasn't even here by choice, ironically, but my objectives were to investigate the disappearance of the copies of *Hamlet*, which I had now discovered to be by these groups of people. With this information in my mind, I now had to safely escort myself out of the abandoned amusement park. I quickly moved forward, kept low, and stuck to the shadows. I hid behind another crate ahead and then continued forward until I reached the exit and stepped out onto the rest of the abandoned theme park.

Kaj drove the Hiawatha Huron through Lincoln as Blair Ericson directed him to, came around Jarsdel Park, and then went into Northton and came around onto Riverside Drive. I assume that at the back of Kaj's mind as he drove on Riverside Drive and came increasingly closer to where Joyland and Neumann Fairgrounds was located, that he believed that he would end up there. The situation with Eldon Hearne and his girlfriend was surely still on his mind, even if it was not at the front of it as he now staged an attempt to rescue me, unknown that I was already on my way out now, but nonetheless, it was on his mind. Just before they arrived at the amusement park, Blair told Kaj to take a right turn onto Reeth Street. Kaj drove onto Reeth without too much concern, but when he pulled into the large parking lot immediately afterwards, the suspicions set in his face.

"What are we doing here?" Kaj questioned. "This is an abandoned amusement park – you expect me to believe that my friend was kidnapped and taken to an abandoned amusement park?"

"Where else? I'm not lying to you," Blair replied. "I swear, this is where she'll have been taken. This is where we've been hiding out…"

"Okay…" Kaj responded, opening the car door.

"So, now that I've taken you here, you're going to let me go, right?" Blair questioned. "I can't be with you when you enter."

"I don't even know how to enter, or where I'm entering into. It's an abandoned amusement park – where are they supposed to be hiding in?"

"In the old aquarium. The entire place is rundown and we've been using it as our stronghold. You can get in through an alleyway on Bering Street between Cascadia Coliseum and the Bering Raceway. She's probably kept in a back room."

"Yeah? Right through the encampment set up by Neumann Fairground? Don't lie to me – I know where you're trying to send me.

I'm going to need an alternative route to get in before I even think about letting you go."

Blair was caught off-guard by Kaj's knowledge of the amusement park. He hesitated to respond for a moment.

"Fine," Blair replied, "there's a way in through the side, but it's only a way in and not a way out. If you go around the alleyway here with Bering Raceway, you should see a dumpster. If you climb up, you should be able to climb through one of the overtop windows and drop in."

"Let's go then," Kaj responded.

"What? I'm not going with you. Do you know what they'll do to me if they find out that I betrayed them?"

"No. If I remember, you refused to disclose who you were working with."

"They're not people that you want to mess with," Blair warned. "I refuse to join you."

"Then I'll lock you in my car until I return. How about that?" Kaj threatened. "You either join me, or this deal is off. I don't trust you, no less now that you tried to lead me into a gang of crooked carnies."

"Who are you and what's your stake in all of this?" Blair questioned. "You can't be with the police... You can't be RCMP either..."

"No, I'm not," Kaj responded, "but if you keep lying to me or don't do what I ask, I'll make sure that you do get to meet the police."

"Hmph," Blair responded, "I see. You're nothing more than a bourgeoise kid."

Kaj ignored him, stepped out and closed the door behind him. He went around and took Blair out from the passenger seat. There was a smoky scent in the air. Kaj observed the façade of the aquarium, which was blocked off by tall fence. The entire structure was made out of concrete and the front consisted of pillars with various double doors that led inside behind. The roof of the aquarium was low sloped, slanted, and made of concrete too. The two started to walk towards the end of the parking lot, passed the condemned entrance way to the aquarium that sat behind them, blocked off by the tall chain-link fence with barbed wire. They approached the entryway into the short alleyway, but the fence extended towards the entryway, which proved an obstacle. Kaj stepped onto the driveway and looked ahead before looking towards Blair.

"How are we supposed to get past the fence?" Kaj asked.

"There's a cut-through around the corner here," Blair explained.

Kaj went to the right and found the incision that was cut for them to enter into the pen that was the alleyway. The fence around the façade of the petting zoo was too tight against the wall for them to walk around. The alleyway was on a downhill slope. At the bottom of the hill, there was a back entrance into Joyland that was blocked off by fence. However, there was a dumpster nearby that did provide enough ground for them to possibly climb through an overtop window. Kaj went forward as he took Blair with him.

"Alright, climb up," Kaj said to Blair.

"How am I supposed to do that? My hands are tied."

Kaj took his hands to the tape and ripped it apart, piece by piece, freeing Blair's arms. He then grabbed him and began to struggle with Kaj. Kaj pinned him against the wall and towards the corner of the dumpster. Blair was stunned at Kaj's sudden anger. Kaj took hold of him by the coat and pressed hard against him.

"Don't mess with me," Kaj threatened. "If you try to run, I'll make sure that the police hunt you down and that you're included with whatever deviance is going on behind these walls."

"You have no idea, do you…" Blair responded. "Who we are? What we do?"

"You never told me," Kaj replied, letting go. "but if you betray me, I *will* tell your friends that you're the reason the police know about them too."

Blair frowned at Kaj. He stopped resisting and so Kaj released him. Blair stepped onto the dumpster and looked up.

"I'll give you a boost," Blair stated, offering his hands.

"I think I'll give you the boost," Kaj responded, offering his hands.

Blair frowned at Kaj again, but took the offer. He stepped his slimy boots onto Kaj's hands and he pushed him up and gave him leverage to climb through the broken window. Blair looked down at Kaj from atop. Kaj frowned at him as he raised his hand up for Blair to grab.

"You can tell my friends whatever you want about me," Blair reckoned, "but they're not my friends, and soon, they'll know about the threat that you and your friend pose on them. You should run while you have the chance."

Blair hopped down from the other side. Kaj brought both fists down onto the wall with an angry look on his face. He then took a step back on the dumpster and attempted to look around for another entrance. Kaj jumped and attempted to grab onto the ledge of the window to pull himself up, but he was short a couple of inches. Kaj looked for something to aid him, but there was nothing else in the alleyway for him to use aside from some palettes on the floor. Kaj hopped down and went to grab them, pulling them onto the top of the dumpster to provide increased elevation.

Kaj jumped back onto the top of the dumpster and carefully climbed onto the top of the two palettes that he had brought up. He then jumped once more, bringing an arm around the ledge of the window and hoisting himself up. Kaj looked onto the other side to see that the window entered into an abandoned exhibit room with empty tanks. He couldn't see Blair around. Kaj jumped down and then got a better look at the inside of the abandoned aquarium.

Kaj looked around and saw the various tanks around, including a cylindrical one in the center, with decorative walls that resembled a cavern. On the furthest wall there were larger encased tanks that had graffiti atop of them. In the middle of the room, there were lower tanks with exposed tops with signs that encouraged tourists to touch the animals and feel the animals inside, notably starfish and stingrays. All of the tanks were empty and there was no sign of sea life even with the décor that accompanied the display room. What remained were panels in front of each tank with descriptions of the sea animals that used to be inside. The large tank for example used to display a Giant Pacific octopus and below it displayed a useless fact regarding octopi possessing beaks. In the far left corner of the room on the wall parallel to where Kaj had entered there was a door that said, 'authorized personnel only.' Nearby, exiting into the alleyway that Kaj and Blair entered from, there was an emergency exit. On the wall to the right, there were two sets of double doors that led into the rest of the aquarium. Kaj looked around at his options and then went to the authorized personnel only, but it was locked.

Kaj went to the double doors and pushed through, entering into a larger display room with more tanks on the inner wall, while there was a larger tank with an arctic design that advertised the display of penguins. In the midst of the room, which stretched around in an arch shape, there were more display tanks that were low enough to display sea life that could be touched. The large penguin display only stretched on the curve of the right-side of the arch, while on the remaining side there was an abandoned café and entry way into an arena. In front of the café, there were some tables and chairs. Between the penguin display and the café there was another door that said, 'authorized personnel only.' The room was lit only by the natural light that seeped in through short wide windows at the very top of the rooms. Kaj went and hid behind a display case in the midst of the main area as he noted a group of suspicious people in front of the authorized personnel doorway.

Kaj observed the group and saw that they wore dark clothes and carried a variety of makeshift weapons on them. Some carried baseball bats, while others carried a crowbar or even a plank of wood with a nail on it. All of them had their faces covered by various means, either a bandana or a balaclava that covered their face. Kaj observed the four of them as they discussed in private.

"… got to be somewhere around here…" one of them said. "Let's split up and find 'em."

Kaj remained crouched and hidden as they split up. He assumed that they were talking about him, so he stayed put and prepared to navigate around them so that he could exit out of the attraction-side of the aquarium and locate Emma. Kaj remained where he was to wait for a bandit to pass and then he went around to another display case to make his way towards the other side of the aquarium.

Kaj saw that on the other side next to the café there was an entryway into a spectator's arena for a sealion show. A bandit went into the arena, while another one went down the rest of the main area towards the main entrance. Kaj followed from behind and hid behind the pillars on approach. He kept to the periphery while the bandit went down to the end through the main space. Kaj saw the bandit go into a set of doors at the left-side from the main entrance and disappear from his sight.

Kaj looked around and saw that the main entrance was blocked by the fence, so he came into the cashier desk and hid behind the counters as he went to yet another door that read 'authorized personnel only' only to discover that it was locked. He then remained hidden as the bandit emerged from the other side of the room and then went back down the corridor towards the café. Kaj came around the desk, went to the side room, and entered through. Kaj looked around and saw that he was in a barn-like petting zoo with fences and pens where animals would have been held in.

Kaj saw another 'authorized personnel only' door at the far right corner so he walked over, hopped over the fence, and then attempted to enter through. This door was locked too. Kaj came back around and returned to the main entrance of the aquarium. He hid behind a pillar, looked down, and then continued to go from pillar to pillar towards the café. Kaj saw three of the anarchists meet up with each other in front of the authorized personnel door that he knew was accessible.

"I don't see anyone," a bandit remarked. "Maybe she's not here."

"She...?" Kaj whispered to himself.

"She's got to be in the amusement park somewhere then. Keep searching."

"Hm..." Kaj said to himself.

"Hey, who are you?!" a bandit next to Kaj questioned.

Kaj turned and faced the bandit that emerged from the arena. He took a step back as the bandit took a swing at him with the bat. Kaj ducked around, went around the pillar, ran into the arena to escape the anarchists. Kaj turned around the entry corridor, and then came onto the top of steps that looked down to a large pool of murky water. The indoor arena seats was a semi-circle around the pool. At the back of the pool there was a platform with a door that led out of the habitat. At the front row there was tall barrier that marked the depth of the water and provided an underwater view. The water was approximately ten feet deep in total. Around the sides, there were taller seats that overlooked the pool. Much like the rest of the aquarium, the arena and seats were constructed out of concrete. Kaj turned behind him as he sensed the anarchists approaching him, so he started to go down the steps and towards the aisle at the bottom.

"Spread out! Corner him!" a bandit shouted.

Kaj saw the anarchists spread out and begin to enclose on him. He ran to the end of the aisle and then started to come up and around towards an exit that he spotted at the top, but as he brought his hands to the door, he realized that it was locked. A bandit swung the plank of wood towards him, missing and hitting the wall behind him. Kaj ducked back and went towards the elevated seats. Kaj saw two anarchists close in on him and corner him.

"Give it up, kid," a bandit taunted.

Kaj turned around and looked down at the drop to the water. He then looked over to the platform and decided to hop over the barrier and stand on the other side. The anarchists homed in on him, triggering him to push himself off and jump into the pool of water. Kaj closed his eyes as he swam through the water and then came up to the top. He began to swim towards the platform on the other side, pulling himself out of the water and removing his jacket as he was now drenched in murky water. He put his coat back on and began to shiver in place. Kaj turned to face the anarchists as they dispersed to pursue him through an alternate route.

Kaj went towards the door that he saw, opened it, and then continued into the depths of the service tunnel. He arrived into a tall shaft and looked up to see the door open and the anarchists come down from the main area. Kaj escaped through a door across from him and entered into the back warehouse. He looked over to the bonfire in the corner of the room and then up to the catwalk. He saw a door at the other side of the room that read 'emergency exit' on the front. Kaj went to a crate nearby and pushed it to block the door.

Kaj took a step back as he waited for the anarchists to attempt to push through. They struggled to break-in, which gave Kaj a chance to investigate the warehouse as he looked for me. Kaj caught a view of the open floor and then over to the pile of shelves on the other side. He climbed up to the top of the catwalk and then went down to the chair where I had left my ties. The scene was obvious. Kaj had confirmed that I had already made my escape, which meant that I was either somewhere in the park, or long gone. Kaj took a step to a door behind the catwalk that read 'authorized personnel only,' but it was locked.

Suddenly, a large bang on the door caused the crate to shift and for the anarchists to pour in. They proceeded to come towards him, which caused Kaj to take an alternate route on a perpendicular catwalk that went over the mound of shelves. Kaj looked down to the peak of the pile and decided to hop down, climb all the way down, and then escape through the emergency exit as he entered the park in search of me.

From the emergency exit in the warehouse, I made my way out into the abandoned amusement park and was near the back entrance that led into the alleyway that connected with Reeth Street. The back entrance was closed off by the tall fence, which meant that my only option was to find an alternate exit through the park. I looked ahead and saw the rundown wooden rollercoaster ahead at the far right corner of the park, covered with scaffolding around the side. There were various other abandoned attractions around. There was a deep fog throughout the park that made it difficult to see everything around me. I made my way through the abandoned park, seeing the other attractions such as a haunted house, a carousel, and some closed off fun games and concession stands as I got closer.

I stopped in the middle of the park as I looked around to reassess my directions. I also heard a sharp whistle sound from afar. I heard a rushed movement from nearby, unsure as to whether all these sounds were from nearby or coming from the fairgrounds next door. I looked over and saw a group of individuals appear – they didn't seem like the anarchists that I had seen in the warehouse since they didn't dress like them, but instead, as if I was hallucinating a fever dream where I was stuck in this abandoned theme park, they had the appearance of carnival freaks. I stopped and hid behind a concession stand to get a look at them.

There were seven of them, a tall, extremely muscular male with a bald head, thick eyebrow, and in a leotard suit; a slender female in a one-piece black-white leotard suit with black hair tied in a bun; a very short male with a ginger beard and balding head in overalls; a large, butch female with a tall beard growing off her chin; a strange, pale albino male with no hair, pointy ears and deep red lips that made him seem like a vampire-type creature in a black cloak; a pair of Siamese twins in a dress; and lastly, the most-normal of them, a tall man with a thick moustache like tusks of a boar, hooked nose, dark hair and a top hat. He appeared to be the leader of the pack as he talked. I observed that he wore a red coat, white trousers and held a whip in his hands, but most noticeably of all, there was a smile on his face; proof that one can smile and smile and be a villain perhaps.

"I've been told that the prisoner that was taken at the university has escaped," the man in the red coat said. "She can't get far and she cannot be allowed to escape. Find her by any means."

"Any means?" the strongman asked.

"Any means," the ringleader reiterated. "I have to return to the show. I want to hear good news when I return."

The ringleader left the freaks on their own.

"You heard the boss," the strongman positioned. "Everyone split up and find this girl."

The six freaks split up into pairs and went their separate ways. I thought about where I wanted to go and who I may have to run into. The strongman and the bearded-lady made their approach in the direction that I wanted to go towards, while the others, the dwarf and the twins, and the demon and the contortionist went elsewhere. I waited for a moment and then continued to go south in the direction that I was going, coming around to the rollercoaster where I didn't see the freaks nearby.

I went around the queue and came to the platform where the rollercoaster cart was. I looked at the path ahead of me and also the scaffolding nearby. I had heard from Riley who had heard from Zach that there was a way into this part of the amusement park via the scaffolding, so my aim was to walk on the tracks and find that exit. I started to walk along the tracks with slight paranoia, keeping my eyes down to take careful steps. The tracks led into the center of the coliseum-like shape, straight and easy with a slight curve down ahead. I went around the bend and came to another curve down then up then down.

Suddenly, I heard an alarm go off with a ferocious ding. I couldn't see to the control room, but I suspected that I was in immediate danger. I saw some scaffolding ahead and started to run. I heard the rollercoaster cart make its approach when I grabbed the scaffold beam and swung myself out of the way. I looked around to see if I could find out who was after me, but there was no one to be seen. I immediately set off back onto the tracks as I entered into short lands that curved around and met with some more scaffolding for me to come around to. The coaster came back around as I took refuge. I heard a whack from below and the snap of wood.

"Ho, ho, ho!" the strongman laughed from below. "Come down, little girl. Let us help you find your parents!"

The strongman had found a mallet and smashed a beam of the scaffolding, causing it to start to collapse. I carried onto the tracks and saw the cart pause at the gateway. I also saw the bearded-lady in the control room. I continued to run down the tracks now that it was my chance so that I could find the scaffolding, most likely the one closest to the active fairground, which was a part of the rollercoaster I was now coming back around to. The strongman jumped down ahead of me and blocked the path.

I heard the sound of the alarm go off again while the strongman made his approach towards me. The cart started to make its run. I took careful steps back. I was at a low point on the tracks, but waited as I took steps back to get lower and lower. The strongman beat his hammer into the tracks to make it difficult for me to continue forward. Once the cart came towards us, I jumped onto the ground and allowed it to run towards the strongman, but he evaded it as he grabbed onto the struts of the tracks next to him and hid. Next, I heard a whack of his hammer onto the ground nearby as I made my run.

I reached another set of scaffolds, but these weren't the ones that I wanted. I climbed up regardless and found myself on the peak of the tracks. The cart made its pass and I stayed here for a moment as I eyed the scaffold up ahead at the curve, going down into a space where I could possibly find my exit. I started to make my way down, but as I reached the bottom, I met with the strongman again who held the mallet in his hand like a hammer. I didn't have enough time to get past him and to the scaffold, so I jumped down again and made my way across to the other side of the rollercoaster. I reached some scaffolding on the opposite-side, climbed up, and then jumped over to another layer of the tracks to go north and then reach a set of scaffold that went to the second highest peak.

I met with the bearded-lady at the end where she stopped in front of me. I was at a decent height that was too dangerous to simply jump off. The cart had stopped running, which meant that I was in no hurry to leave, but as I started to back away, I saw the strongman at the top and on his approach, so I had no choice but to face the woman. I made my way towards her. She took a swipe at me, and I backed up, keeping my balance on the rails. I found that she was large and burlesque, which made it harder for her to keep her balance. I evaded her again and pushed her into a pool of water below, causing a large splash. I met the start of the attraction, which was not what I needed since I wanted to escape.

I continued forward and went back the way that I was going when I heard the sound of the ringing again. I suspected that the strongman had started the attraction again. I took cover in some scaffolding as the train passed by, and then I carried onwards as I aimed to reach that set of scaffolding. However, as I was about to come around, the strongman jumped down and met with me again. He swung his hammer towards me, hitting some of the struts of the rollercoaster and causing structural damage that made me anxious. I decided to jump down onto the ground and then continue towards the scaffolding that I had reached previously that went to the top of the ride. I continued down from there and reached the scaffolding that I wanted to go to, but not before him.

The strongman looked towards me and smashed his hammer into the scaffolding, causing them to collapse and fall over. He then proceeded to come towards me with the hammer, which triggered me to take steps back before I jumped down onto the ground again. The strongman jumped after me and I evaded him as I snuck through the struts and came to the other side. I now had to get away from this rollercoaster because it was pointless to escape from here. I reached the scaffolding that went up to the outer layer of the rollercoaster when I noticed that the strongman was no longer nearby. I continued forward once the cart made its pass and then went down towards the bottom, near where the lady had fallen. I noticed that she was nowhere to be seen, which meant that she probably climbed out and fled. However, as I looked down, I noticed that ahead, the strongman came around to face me. The strongman held the mallet in his hands and faced me around the other side.

"Come on, little girl. Play nice," the strongman threatened.

I looked at my options, and it was either the pond or an optimistic jump into a tent nearby. I waited for a moment as I went over my options. The strongman closed in on me, and from behind, the rollercoaster cart made its approach. I waited for the right time to jump off so that the cart hit into the strongman, throwing him off the ride and into some tents nearby. I landed in the tent that I aimed for and landed softly into its cover, sliding down and off so that I could continue my escape.

"There she is!" a freak shouted.

I ran back towards the amusement park and took refuge in the haunted house attraction. At the entrance to the attraction there was a sign that cautioned not to harm actors as you entered. The inside of the attraction was dark. I followed a black and white-tiled pathway that led to a larger foyer. Light poured in through windows in the ceiling, which provided enough light to see. Ahead of me was a staircase, but the attraction blocked it off and encouraged me to step to the right into a living room where there were loads of furniture piled around. I then reached a dining room with a long table in the middle. A portrait at the end of the corridor contained eyes that followed the looker. Without actors, the haunted house wasn't in the least scary. From the dining room, I was given two options to choose from. I paused for a moment as I looked both ways – I had no interest in getting lost in the haunted house since I only needed to hide for a moment before I went back out to find an exit. I turned around and jumped as I was met with the demon-looking freak who stepped towards me in a calm manner with his hands behind his back. I ran away and went to the left, entering into a kitchen where racks of plastic meat hung from the ceiling. I ran into a parlor where there was lone rocking chair in the corner, and then came around to a room with a casket that led to a corridor where at the turn at the end there was a figure of a person hanging from the ceiling.

Suddenly, I turned around and looked up above to the ceiling, which consisted of a framework with broken lights pointed down and holes that provided natural light. I thought I caught a glimpse of something moving along the ceilings. I continued forward and passed through a curtain that brought me back to the foyer. I was about to exit, but suddenly the contortionist pulled herself down and blocked my path.

"Don't leave yet, we're just about to have some fun," she said in her foreign accent.

I turned around again and saw the demon-like man arrive with a candelabra in hand.

"We have you surrounded. Give in."

I hopped over the fence to the staircase that went upwards and resisted them. From where I was, the ceiling was very low, but I could see the mess of beams that composed the ceiling alongside catwalks that I could possibly crawl along to navigate the top of the haunted house. The demon poured a liquid onto the floor and then tossed the candelabra down while the contortionist climbed upwards and proceeded to chase me. I went ahead and towards a catwalk. I hopped up and started to crawl through the top of the haunted house.

The contortionist grabbed me by the ankle, so I kicked her in the face, which upset her. I continued through and went along into the dining room where I hopped down onto the table. I could smell the scent of smoke again, which told me that I had to find an exit immediately before I became entrapped down here. I went into the other side of the maze and entered into a corridor that went down with many doors on either side. At the end of the hallway on the left there was a double door that led into a bedroom. I entered through and met with the contortionist as she dropped down from the ceiling. The contortionist swung her body towards me as if to kick me, but I evaded and came around to a bathroom where there was a bathtub filled with fake blood in the center.

I exited out onto the hallway from before and met the demon who stood in the way of the exit. I attempted to open one of the doors in the hallway and surprisingly, it opened and led into a nursery. I looked at the various dolls in the room and carried on into a music room where there was a piano and an exit to the hallway. The contortionist blocked the exit, while the demon was right behind. I climbed the piano and climbed back into the ceiling, looking around for a way out. I could see the smoke from the foyer ahead as well as a catwalk for me to crawl upon nearby. I carefully climbed from strut to the strut, feeling the presence of the contortionist climbing up to join me from nearby. I climbed into the catwalk and started to crawl away, but she grabbed me by my ankle again, but I shook her off. I exited down the corridor and came into the dining room where the flames had caught up below.

At the intersection between catwalks, I climbed into the one that went into the other side of the haunted house, but not before stopping to see the contortionist behind me, crawling faster than me as she nipped at my ankles. I waited for her to reach the intersection and then I started to kick at her, causing the fragile poles that held up the catwalk to come loose with each vicious kick. I kicked her in the head and then hit the pole again, causing one to come loose and being enough to cause the entire cage to collapse downwards with her inside. I continued through and made it to the room with the rocking chair. I then came around and met a dead-end at the room with the casket. I climbed down and noticed the fire was spreading along the exit corridor as well, which meant that I was trapped.

I turned around at the entrance into the parlor and noticed that the demon was behind me. He stretched out his hands from behind his back as thought to grab me. I stepped back and towards the fire. He lurched towards me and so I ducked around and came around the other side of the casket. I stepped up onto a stool near the casket as the demon came around, jumped up and grabbed ahold of a strut above us to swing my feet and kick the demon in the head. He fell backwards into the fire, causing his robe to catch fire, which provided me with an opportunity to run into the parlor. The fire provided enough light for me to see that there was an emergency exit in the corner of the room, so I went towards it, pushed through, and exited out. I turned around to ensure that I was alone before I ran off and made my way back into the amusement park.

"There she is!" a freak shouted out.

I ran back into the amusement park and ran back towards the warehouse and near the large carnival tent where the ringleader had gone to. If the carnival tent was connected to the fairgrounds, then I hoped that this would be my exit out from the park. I spotted a payphone near the back entrance to the park and I was curious as to whether it still had any power or was connected to a telephone line. I hoped that I could call 911 on the phone, but as it was, the Siamese twin was nearby so I could risk the chance to approach the phone. I turned around and saw that the dwarf had been behind me. I ran back into the amusement park once more, this time with intent to shake these two off me.

I hopped over the fence of the carousel and then took refuge there. The dwarf came around the queue, too short to jump over the fence, and confronted me with a pickaxe in hand. Meanwhile, the Siamese twin went to the control shack and started to fiddle with the controls. The dwarf stepped onto the platform and faced me. I heard the sound of the alarm bells ring and the platform start to rotate as he began to chase me around the carousel. One the carousel picked up in speed, I used my acrobatic skills to grab ahold of a horse as it was moving and swing around to kick the dwarf off the ride as we reached a top speed. I hopped down as he flew off and hit the pavement.

I went and grabbed the pickaxe and held it as I looked over to where the Siamese twin was in control of the machine. I aimed the pickaxe and held it in my hands, aiming to shoot it off towards her and the motor with a single shot. The pickaxe flew towards the shack and ripped through the wood. The twin jumped out of the way as sparks flew from the circuit board and the machine slowly came to a halt. I took the chance to immediately get off the vehicle. I went to the payphone, picked it up, and then dialed 911 so that I could alert the police and then make my exeunt.

Once I had finished explaining the situation at the abandoned amusement park as much as I could, despite the objections and questions from the dispatcher which I neglected in my urgency, I dropped the phone down. Suddenly, I jumped as I was met with hands on my shoulder, but as I turned around, I was met with relief as I reunited with Kaj.

"Relax, it's me," Kaj remarked.

"Kaj, why are you all wet?" I questioned.

"Because I just went for a swim," Kaj responded. "You escaped though… I'm so relieved that you're okay."

"What happened to the book thief?"

"Unfortunately, he got away," Kaj explained, "but that's not important anymore. Come on, we have to get out of here. There are these freaks chasing me."

"You don't say," Emma responded, "what kind of freaks have been chasing you?"

"There they are!" a bandit remarked as they exited the warehouse.

"Those kind," Kaj replied, taking Emma's hand. "Come on!"

We ran off from the back entrance of the amusement park, but as Kaj led us towards the amusement park, the unpleasant sight of the strongman and dwarf caused us to back away.

"Come on, let's go into the tent – it's probably our only way out," I encouraged.

"Good idea," Kaj replied as we ran towards the carnival tent.

Kaj and I entered into the carnival tent and came around a long-curved corridor.

"Are you okay?" Kaj asked as we got a moment to breathe.

"Hardly," I responded, "but I have a suspicion that whoever the book thief was abetting, they're involved in some sort of anarchist underground."

"Really? I suppose that would make sense. Blair – your thief, did say that he was involved with some dangerous people. What bothers me though is that we're at Neumann Fairgrounds and I suspect that somehow, my thief may be associated with your thief."

"I didn't think about that," I honestly responded, "but you're right. Kaj, we have to be careful though – there's the carnival freaks ringleader still lingering around somewhere."

"Ringleader? I think his name is Hammond Neumann."

"Yes," I affirmed, "I suspect that he's behind all of this. From what I heard; it sounds like the carnival acts as a front for their activities. They were taking the books to have them replaced with content that could promote their ideas."

Kaj and I came around to an intersection. We peaked through the curtains on the left and saw that it led us to the main performance arena. The curtains on the right led into a sort of backstage of the performance arena. Inside, there were various crates with props, cages with live animals inside, and mirrored desks. Kaj and I looked around as we searched for an exit.

"If we can find a way out, I know an exit route," Kaj remarked.

"Over here," I pointed out, seeing a set of curtains where a cold breeze came out from.

We walked towards the curtains that would have led us out to the residences of the carnival folk, but as we made our approach, we were suddenly met with the burlesque figure of the ringleader who stepped towards us. We stepped back as he approached us, but it was impossible to escape now as the strongman and other carnival freaks arrived to block our exit.

"So, there are two of them," Hammond remarked, looking down as he stepped forward.

"I recognize that one," a person behind him stated.

Kaj and I looked as some anarchists arrived to join Hammond from behind, and among them was Kaj's thief, Eldon Hearne.

"He's the one that I told you was in my tent yesterday."

"He's working with the girl?"

"I don't know – I've never seen her before," Eldon stated, "I don't think that either of them are with the police."

"They're too young," the strongman pointed out.

"Then they can be both be killed," Hammond remarked. "If they know about what is going on here, then they are a threat to us. Take 'em to the arena."

Before Kaj and I could even attempt to evade them, the strongman grabbed hold of Kaj and the bearded-lady took control of me.

"We don't know what you're talking about," Kaj refuted.

"Hush, little one," Hammond replied. "Don't try and fool me. You both know about our games and because of that, I'm afraid this'll be your end."

"What games?" Kaj questioned.

"The books, the jewelry," Hammond pointed out. "She knows all about our activities in removing all of the school books so that new content could be put in, while you have been studying us more closely. You know about all of the jewelry we've stolen and sold to fund our operations here – a quick income, but subversive activities cost us."

"So, you are a bunch of anarchists," Kaj stated, "so what's your goal? To bring down the government?"

"In a certain sense, but not how you'd imagine. We're nothing more than a cog in a larger scheme, and my carnival operations across all of North America to coordinate with groups in order to carry out the intentions of our collective, larger vision. Our intentions are subversion and demoralization, to destabilize society and usher in a new rule, one that is based upon our power and authority."

"For a carnie, you're certainly well-worded," Emma pointed out.

"Much thanks, I received a higher level of education, but never privy to finish those studies as the Great Depression put an end to that dream. I had a family to take care of, and although my wife did not survive those times, I found myself in the entertainment industry and with a keen ambition to dismantle the capitalist machine that had brought myself and so many, so much loss and suffering. Enough about that though, the pair of you seem a like middle-class children – stubborn children at that. I will see your ends."

Kaj and I were taken out and to the main arena where the lights lit up and spotlights began to move around as if there were preparations for another show. The center of the carnival tent, the performance arena, was a dusty pit surrounded by barriers that protected elevated seats from where spectators would watch the carnival show. Kaj and I were brought to a set of pillars, each on other sides of the dust pit. These pillars rose were connected to another that created a stand atop from where there was an acrobatic swing. Around the pit there were also circular stands of different heights. The ringleader appeared and stood on his own stand near the viewing stands. The spectator stands were empty. Kaj and I were tied to the pillars and then the music began to signal the start of this morbid show.

"Ladies and gentlemen," Hammond greeted, "boys and girls. I present to you the show of a lifetime. The inevitable deaths of two pompous kids caught lurking through our home tonight."

I felt around the rope ties that had been put around our ankles and felt that they weren't very tight. I looked ahead and saw that there was a gate that blocked our escape back into the backstage, but I did see the swings and thought of a possible escape with them onto the viewing gallery. Kaj felt around his ties too, but it didn't appear like he could break loose.

"Now then, without further ado, bring out the hungry lions!" Hammond encouraged.

The backstage gates opened with the cages that held lions on the other side opening as well. A pair of anarchists opened the cages. The lions stepped out and I became increasingly nervous to escape these ties. The lions made their way towards Hammond, which gave us a chance to escape. I noticed that Kaj was attempting the brute force method to break off the rope, which seemed to be holding up, while I attempted to squirm out of mine again. Hammond took his whip and threw it at the lions, causing them to bow down in omission to him and his power. The audience, consisting of the freaks and anarchists, continued to clap and cheer.

Kaj pulled at his ties as he forced the knot loose, eventually causing it to come undone around the pole, but not his hands. I managed to squeeze out from the knot that was around my wrist, causing my hands to slip through them and break free. Once I was out, I immediately went over towards where Kaj was so that I could help him out. I untied one of the knots from around his wrists and together we immediately began to climb up the ladder and escape the lions. Kaj pulled the rest of the rope off from his other wrist once he was atop with me, but now we faced the awkward situation of the lions and the heartless ringleader.

"What do we do?" I asked, grabbing ahold of the swing at this side. "I thought I could swing into the spectator stands, but it'll be too much of a jump."

"We'll need to do something about Hammond, otherwise, we're sitting ducks."

"What if we just wait for the police to show up?"

"We don't have any guarantee that the police will look for us in this tent. They'll probably search the abandoned amusement park and then miss us."

"Right…"

"Okay, I have this rope," Kaj said as he started to tie a knot at one end. "If I can secure this to the framework above us, do you think you could swing towards Hammond?"

"I could try," I replied, "but then what?"

"We'll need his whip if we're going to do anything," Kaj explained. "If we can get his whip, we can clear a way past either the anarchists or the lions to get out of here."

"I choose the anarchists," I remarked, looking over to them in the spectator stands, arming the confetti cannons.

Kaj rolled the rope down and it produced a fair length. He rolled it up and then looked up.

"Hm, the swing won't be enough for you to get to him from here," Kaj said. "You'll have to secure around the beam on the other side and then go from there."

"Got it," I replied, taking the rope into my hands.

"Do you feel confident?"

"Of course," I responded as I carried the rope around my arms.

I took hold of the swing and then looked over to the other platform. I took in a deep breath and focused on where I wanted to go. I then dipped forward and swung across, landing onto the platform and then setting off to bring the rope upwards while Kaj dodged the shells of confetti that were being shot towards him. Kaj took hold of the swing as it came back and secured it for me. Meanwhile, I took the rope he had given me and threw it upwards towards the beam.

I looked over and saw Kaj get hit by a shell and nearly fall off the platform while I messed with the rope. He held on and climbed back up. I continued to work, dropped the rope, and then pulled back as I grabbed ahold. I aimed towards the ringleader and then set off, swinging forward like Tarzan from a vine, pointing my feet towards Hammond's head to hit him off his stand and into the dusty pit. I swung back and then came over to drop down, onto the top of the platform, and then look over to where the whip was. I dropped down, took hold of the whip, and then ran over to the pole so that I could climb back up to where I was. However, as I went up the ladder, I noticed the lions go towards Hammond and also a cannon hit Kaj, causing him to fall to the ground and pique the interest of one of the lions. I looked over as the anarchists attempted to fend off the lions from their ringleader with the cannons at the same, which encouraged the lion to go towards Kaj.

"Kaj, here's the whip!" I shouted, throwing it towards him.

Kaj eyed the whip in the sand, grabbed it and then stood up as a lion was about to run towards him. Kaj took the whip and cracked it towards the lion, causing it to back off for a moment. The recoil on the whip cut Kaj on the cheek. He continued to swing it towards the lion until it finally ran off. He then proceeded to climb up, stopping for a moment to crack the whip once more and then come all the way up. Kaj eyed me as he came to the top, but then his eyes went over to the cannon as one was shot towards him.

"Be careful Kaj!" I yelled.

I watched as he dodged the shell.

"I'll send you the swing back!" Kaj replied

I watched as Kaj held the whip in one hand and readied to send the swing back towards me so that I could catch. However, before he could push forward, another shell aimed towards him and hit the fragile pillar beneath him, causing it to come loose and Kaj to nearly fall off had he not held on with one hand. I watched as he held on, nearly averting my eyes as him nearly falling off, but he put the whip in his mouth so that he could use both hands to hang on.

"Kaj!" I shouted. "Swing, Kaj! It's like a playground swing! Use your core!"

Kaj listened and he raised his legs up and then brought them back down as he started to build momentum. Once he had enough, he jumped over to join me and then took the whip from his mouth

"Let's get out of here now," Kaj remarked. "Come on."

Kaj took the rope and we used it to jump into the spectator stands and then use the whip to beat back the anarchists who fled from the ferocious crack of the whip. We climbed up the steps and then came down a set of ladders to the curved corridor around that brought us to the main entrance tunnel into the carnival tent. Kaj and I both ran to the end, ditching the whip in the mud behind us, and then running across the middle aisle of Neumann Fairground to reach the exit gates of the amusement park. A ferocious rain fell. Kaj took his hand and positioned it for me to climb the fence, and then I did the same to boost him up and come down onto Riverside Drive.

"Free at last," Kaj remarked as he embraced me.

"Hey, you!" a voice shouted at us.

Kaj and I were surprised and looked over to a police constable with a cruiser parked at the curb of the sidewalk. We both ran towards him and immediately began to explain everything that happened, which resulted in the entire Jarsdel Division arriving with lights and sirens to break into the fairgrounds and promptly arrest everyone they could find in sight. Kaj and I were to brought to an ambulance where we were treated by paramedics for our shock and terror.

There, we met with a police detective. He spoke in a southeast Londoner accent. He was fairly young and had light brown hair with blue eyes. He dressed in a black suit with a black tie.

"Evening," the detective greeted. "Sergeant Kingston, senior detective with Administrative Vice. I have some questions if you'd care to answer, related to your acts tonight. I know you've both been through a lot, but we're interested in the sort of people that you've come across in relation to an ongoing investigation."

Kaj and I both spoke with the detective. He told him everything that he knew about Neumann Fairground, including the story of his girlfriend's stolen necklace and girlfriend's friend's stolen bracelet. He corroborated his story with the fact that they were now in Goldman's Pawns Shop and there were receipts for the transaction at Eldon Hearne's tent. The police seized the evidence, but were unable to capture Eldon or his mother who both escaped. Meanwhile, I told the detective about my story, the stolen books, how I had learned that they were stolen, how I learned that more were stolen and that there was a pattern in the thefts, how I had found Blair Ericson, and where the books were now. I provided my testimony into what the anarchists had told me and corroborated my part with the location of the books in the warehouse. The police found what remained of the books and were able to confirm that these were the same as some of the ones that had been reported to the police from the few schools that did choose to report their incidents to the police. At the end of my witness statement, Detective Kingston closed his notebook and looked at me with surprise.

"You're a very remarkable lass, you know that?" Detective Kingston acknowledged. "Honestly, between you and your friend, you've not only stumbled into an anarchist cell in the midst of Harlech and put yourselves in danger, but come through and given us enough evidence to put a wrap on these operations. We'll be working with the RCMP and municipalities in other jurisdictions to see what else we can connect this traveling circus to, but in the meant time, I believe you both deserve a well-needed rest. I'll also be speaking with your parents, to let them know what a good kid you are. Both you and your friend can expect accommodations from the police chief for this work. Well done."

Detective Kingston left and I met with Kaj again who smiled at me.

"Well, if isn't Harlech's 'problem-solver,' Kaj teased.

I blushed and replied, "You act as if you didn't do anything... to me, you're the problem-solver. I'm just Emma Monique."

"All I did was uncover the scam with a fortune teller and his son, while you uncovered the entire anarchist group."

"You saved me," I replied. "I wouldn't have survived on my own if you weren't there with me. Between the pair of us, we both did an exceptional job. This wasn't what I expected when I looked into the missing copies of *Hamlet*, but I'm not disappointed."

"Right... well, this'll certainly be quite the story to float around when we get back to school next week," Kaj replied, seeing the journalists with their cameras. "The police are going to give me a ride back home to my mom now. I'll see you on Monday, problem-solver."

"I'll see you on Monday too."

Kaj left and soon enough, my parents arrived to take me home too. I was astounded at what had occurred, a part of me was troubled at what I had seen, and another was relieved to be home with Marius and Yvette, and knowing what my efforts had produced and the impact my actions had made. Kaj left an impact too; we both worked exceedingly well together, and I knew at that moment that to solve mysteries were my passion.

This night wasn't the immediate end of the police investigation, and over the course of the next month, I'd be called in to speak with the detective and I'd learn from Kaj of the progression from his side as the assailants of Hammond Neumann were prosecuted. Unfortunately, Hammond did not survive his injuries, where he had been mauled by the lion during our escape. The rest of the assailants confessed to the crimes and received high charges of sedition and treason for their involvement in fifth column activities. From what I understood, however, Blair Ericson was never found after last night as he seemingly disappeared from the face of the Earth. Although I didn't get to put him behind bars or salvage the copies of *Hamlet*, I at least confirmed that the books were stolen and that created enough encouragement by Ms. Christopher to abandon our study of *Negro* and promise to give us some sort of Shakespeare study later in the year, but not *Hamlet*. I was pleased. Kaj on the hand, would receive his grandmother's necklace back, while Elias would receive the diamond bracelet once both were seized by the Harlech Police Department and then released to them once they weren't needed as evidence anymore. This night marked a monumental shift both for me, and for Kaj, as we found ourselves, just as we found each other, powerful partners when it came to problem-solving.

PART IV: SEPTEMBER 1983

Part 4 – Chapter 30
Bertrand Residence
Saffron, Jarsdel Island
September 1983 – 14:00 hours

"If we're going to solve who murdered Eldon Hearne, we're going to have to work together," I propositioned to Kaj as I looked at him.

Kaj continued to hold Glenn Bertrand down. He sighed.

"You and I both know that there's something more that's going on here – remnant from what happened fifteen years ago."

"Hammond is dead," Kaj pointed out.

"His spirit rages on," I replied. "The evil that men do lives after them."

"What do you know, Glenn?" Kaj questioned.

"I'm not saying anything more," Glenn refused. "Get me a lawyer."

Kaj shook his head and brought both of Glenn's hands behind his back.

"You're under arrest under suspicions of murdering Eldon Hearne," Kaj stated. "You have the right to receive legal counsel without delay. You also have the right to free and immediate legal advice – there's a toll-free number that I can provide that is available twenty-four hours and seven days of the week. Do you understand?"

"Affirmative."

"Do you wish to call a lawyer?"

"Affirmative."

"You also have the right to remain silent. Anything that you do say or do may be used as evidence against you. Do you understand?"

"Affirmative."

Once Kaj placed the handcuffs on Glenn Bertrand, he went downstairs with me, and we walked to his police car. He kept Glenn down against the car as he radioed for a paddy wagon to take the arrestee back to the station. Kaj and I spoke in that moment.

"What do you propose?" Kaj asked. "The scam with the computers seems eerily similar to the old trick that Eldon and his mom used to play. You provide a solution for a problem that they created, one that's of no particular threat at all, but costs you and you alone."

"It's not all the same," I remarked, "this time there are no copies of *Hamlet* to go chasing; just some data that I've been asked to return."

"You should tell Detective Pearson of the weasel I'm bringing him, and in the meantime, I'll think of something if you don't have anything."

"I will," I replied, crossing my arms, "and I'll let him know of what you have. If you have time, you should visit Paul. He works at Calypso Tower in the sublevel as a systems manager. He's been my contact in all this and has some good ideas. You should visit him."

"Maybe I will."

"I'm going to go phone the detective and then see if I can do some research on Neumann Corporation. If I had to guess, it's somehow related to Hammond Neumann, or in the least, a tribute to him."

"Sounds good. I'll see you later then."

"Call me," I encouraged, passing him a business card.

Kaj took a business card from his notebook and passed it to me. I left and didn't turn around as I felt relieved to come across with Kaj again, ready to solve this case with him.

The next day, Kaj sat alone in his squad's office at the police station during his lunch break. He looked out the window, towards Northton as he thought about what had happened yesterday and reflected on the events from fifteen years ago. He stood up, left the office, and went downstairs to the parking lot to approach the Crown Vic. He then entered, closed the door, ignited the engine, and went forward onto the streets. Kaj turned onto Slade Drive and drove a short distance from the intersection at Taghman Street to reach the intersection with Lincoln Drive. He then turned right, came around, and drove onto Urhan Street where Calypso Tower was located. Kaj pulled into an alleyway, parked the car, and then waited for a moment. Kaj sat in his car and wrote a few notes in his notebook and then he exited out.

Kaj walked down the alleyway onto the sidewalk at Urhan Street and then looked over to Calypso Tower. He noted the sign that advertised the offices for the Harlech Herald and Dornoch Chronicles, but continued through to enter into the lobby. Kaj walked over to the security guard at the desk.

"Hi, Constable Kejsaren here to meet with Paul Schmidt," Kaj stated.

"Feel free to take a seat as you wait," the security guard replied.

Kaj didn't go over and sit down. Instead, he walked over towards the elevator lobby and waited nearby. Kaj had never been to Paul's workplace before. In fact, even he didn't know who Paul's client was since all he knew was that he worked with computers. He waited several minutes until an elevator dinged and the doors opened. A woman and a child left the elevator. Kaj didn't take the elevator down to the sublevel and instead continued to wait a couple more minutes into his lunch break for Paul to either arrive or not.

At half past twelve o'clock, the elevator dinged again and the doors opened to reveal Paul. Paul was dressed in a similar manner to how he had been dressed when I had met him, other than the sweater that had changed. He walked over and shook hands with Kaj.

"Nice to see you and thanks for making the time for me," Kaj said.

"Not a problem," Paul responded. "Emma phoned me shortly after you called yesterday and told me about what happened, so now I have a better understanding. I thought I'd never see you two working together – from what Emma told me, this is apparently similar to something you were both dealing with when in high school?"

"Yeah," Kaj affirmed, "a little bit with some familiar faces."

"Let me take you to my lab and we can talk more," Paul responded, eyeing the lobby behind as if he was paranoid of eavesdroppers.

"So, how've you been?" Kaj asked as they entered the elevator together. "I think it's been a couple months since we last saw each other."

"Yes," Paul replied, "a few months, I think. I've been extremely busy implementing a new computer system and these troubles have not helped me."

"What about outside of work? How have you been otherwise?" Kaj remarked, disinterested for a moment to talk about each other's careers. "You still doing okay?"

Paul sighed for a moment and then replied, "I've been… making improvements to say the least. How about you?"

"I've been as steady as a rock," Kaj responded. "Sometimes work can slow me down, but I'm where I want to be right now and nowhere else. I think what's been going on with this investigation has been the most interest I've had out of work in a while."

"Yeah, you seem as tired as I am," Paul remarked as the elevator doors opened, "but I'm glad we're all finding something intriguing out of this puzzle. How's your wife?"

"Hannah is fine," Kaj replied as they started to walk. "We've been thinking about trying for a second child now that Elias is a little older."

"Another child could add a bit more interest in your life at home."

"Yeah, I really want to have a daughter."

"You shouldn't hope too much on the gender of your baby. Otherwise, you'll disappoint yourself and take that anguish out on your second-born son. I would know, being the second-born son... but my parents did get a daughter in the end, so hold tight."

"Yeah... you're right."

Kaj and Paul arrived at the lab and entered through. The lab was as quiet and dark as when I had visited. Paul took Kaj to his workstation and then brought out a stool for Kaj to sit down. Kaj observed that there was a long roll of paper piled atop of Paul's desk. Kaj and Paul sat down together and he started to show Kaj the roll of paper which contained codes that he did not understand or care to understand.

"Has Emma explained to you what I've been up to?" Paul asked.

"A bit..."

Paul quickly reiterated and summarized much of the information that he had passed on to me already from my initial visit, from the fact that a hacker had breached into the computer system, the puzzling nature of how the hacker had entered since he had patched up the 'backdoors,' and the fact that the entire computer system database was on lockdown and they now had a few days to capture the hacker or else he would be booted out.

"I've been keeping a tab on our hacker to see what he's been up to – he's still connecting to our computer system despite the fact that we've isolated all vital data that he could possibly want to steal. From what I've observed, and I should have known this before I sent Emma to wander into a stranger's home, but it seems like the hacker has been using multiple modems to bounce around and hide his tracks."

"You're going to have to explain that to me a bit clearer."

"Right, sorry..." Paul replied, clearing the paper to show a map of Harlech above his desk. "Look, our computers are all connected to each other by telephone lines. Each line in a home or business is connected to a modem that forms the connection endpoint from the telecom company and their hardware, whether that is Polaris, BC Tel, or Shaw. In other words, all internetwork connections overlap with the telephone networks, which allows us to dial in to computers from anywhere we have a computer and a telephone connection. Our hackers have been abusing this mechanic by using our phone numbers to dial in to our computers and then hacking through our login to access our data and information. In the case of my client, by accessing our computer, they've been able to access an intra-network of computers that store valuable and confidential data.

I mistook the hacker to be logging in from one computer somewhere within Harlech, because when I traced the connection, I got a phone number from within Harlech, and so I assumed that our hacker was simply dialing in from the location with that phone number to our computers here. However, that would have been the simple model to base that theory, but in fact, it can get more complex. While the hacker could dial-in directly from his computer to my computer, that would have exposed his phone number and we would have been able to easily track him. In order to avoid that, the hacker has dialed into the modem of another household, and then used that modem to dial out to another modem, and he can do this as many times as he likes at the risk of slowing down his connection, but effectively concealing his phone number by showing the phone number of the last modem he connected with. I realized this detail when Emma told me that the location she visited with the phone number we had was owned by a widow who complained to her about telephone overcharges. The widow was being overcharged because the hacker had been piggybacking off of her system to come into our system, and was still doing so."

"The piggybacking costs others? I suppose that makes sense if they're using your telephone line to dial out to other places."

"Exactly. Now, from what I've observed from the hacker, when he hacked into our computer system, he spent a fair amount of time searching for and then stealing confidential data. Once we caught on, we took measures to prevent any further theft, but that hasn't stopped our hacker from logging on, which we've allowed at this time so that we can observe him, and then used our connection to dial-in to other telephone lines across the country. Last night, I was able to take a closer observation at our hacker's activities and I found this," Paul said, showing a line of code. "Our hacker has been logging on to these phone numbers and running the same command, installing a virus out of a few simple lines of code, and then leaving. Once I had an idea about this virus, I searched our computer system to find it and then I ran through the code to see what this virus does. The virus copies passwords and handles, and then stores them in a data file that the hacker is able to collect – this is how he is able to login without being detected, by using handles that belong to trusted users. You see, when the hacker initially hacks in, he does so by creating his own handle, which he doesn't expect to last long since when we become alerted to that intrusion, we're prompted to delete it to prevent any further unauthorized entry. I don't know how he does it, but it seems to be somehow a 'backdoor' mechanism built into the computers. In the case of our computer system, we've allowed it so that we can track him, but seeing these activities has told me that the hacker didn't rely on us to allow him to stay since he would have had access to countless logins to get back in. In order to circumvent that, I'll have to have all handles change their password once we get rid of this hacker from our system, but in the meantime, we won't do anything yet.

Now, here's what the hacker does once he has these logins. He starts to search for data, and I've been interested in the words that he's been using to search, since they're not the words that you'd expect: security, security program, protection services, defense system, and so on. I thought at first that he was looking for possible defense mechanisms in his targets, but then he started to go through data that contained these keywords, and they were related to cyber security programs from a defense contractor in the United States."

"Strange," Kaj remarked.

"Yeah, I thought so too," Paul responded, "and although those were the most common keywords, he did at times search for other keywords. In short though, it seems like he's data mining and transferring that data back to his own computer, but I don't know why."

"How do we find him?"

"There's only one way, and that's to involve the telecom companies. I tried to do that already, but there's a legal issue. We need a court order."

"Okay, so we raise the issue to Crown to get a court order then," Kaj pointed out.

"If you get a court order, you'll have to hope that the hacker is within the province though," Paul replied. "Otherwise, you'll run into another problem…"

"I think I feel confident that he's in the province, even the city," Kaj replied. "Is that it?"

"No… there's another problem. The hacker spent a lot of time last night on our system, and he has been back, but only for short stays. In order to trace his connection, we'd have to keep him on our system for a prolonged period of time, and I'm worried that we won't have the means to do that. I ran that problem through with Emma, and we were both stumped on any possibility that we could get the hacker to stay on our system, because it seems like that he checks in once and a while to see if we've lowered our defenses and there's any data for him to access."

"What if we do that then?"

"I do not think that my client would approve that idea, because they're very protective of their data and wouldn't weigh the risk in case we were to fail. I'll see what can be done, but in the meantime, I think that'd it be best if you could help us with a court order."

"Yeah… come to think of it though, I don't think I can get a court order since there's no active police investigation into all of this… I want to help, really, but our interest is in the murder of someone, so it'd be a bit of a stretch to go from there to this hacker stuff, although I'm sure it is somehow related to the bigger picture. I'll have to see if I can consult some people back at the station, so in the meantime, we'll have to put a pin on the court order."

"We don't have much time if we were to wait… my client wants to rid the hacker from our system by the end of the week. Once I rid him, he won't be allowed back… the only stall I've been able to put in place is pretending to fix this 'backdoor' and arguing that it's taking more time than it actually is, but my client can be pretty impatient so there's only so long that I can keep that up before I have to cave."

"I'll see what I can do," Kaj responded, standing up.

"Wait, there's more," Paul said, taking a folder. "Emma already has a copy, but these are my notes on what I've observed so far – sorry for the technical terms, but I tried to be as clear as possible. Emma tells me that this hacker is apparently the leader of some anarchist group – 'V' did you know that?"

"No, I'll take a look at this when I get back to the station. I'll have to chat with Emma again when I have the chance. I'll keep in touch, Paul. Thanks for all your help."

"No problem. I'll say, between you and Emma, the pair of you should be able to connect the dots between a murder and a computer hacker. Good luck."

"Thanks."

Kaj's radio began to go off with a dispatch as he left the room. He came into the sublevel corridor on his way to the elevator when he heard his callsign.

"Hotel Two-Two-Three," Kaj replied.

"Hotel Two-Two-Three, return to station as soon as possible," Sergeant Allard requested.

"Ten-Four."

Kaj entered the elevator with a nervous expression. After all that happened yesterday, Kaj felt that some sort of consequences would result out of his actions, and a return to station usually involved a talk with high command. Kaj exited Calypso Tower, made his way to the alleyway where his car was, and then drove off to return to the station as soon as possible.

Since I had seen Kaj again, I had spent my time researching Hammond (Hamon) Neumann and the possible connection between him and Neumann Corporation. From what I had remembered from my experience at Neumann Fairground, and the near-death experience that Hammond had put Kaj and I through with the lions, he was mauled by his own lions and experienced serious injuries that he did not survive from. I learned that information because he never stood trial since he died from his injuries. From what I remember as well, there was press coverage of the incident at Neumann Fairgrounds – I was never interviewed, but I remembered that Kaj was interviewed by *The Jarsdel Journal* specifically. I had to rely on open-source intelligence to find out more about Hammond and Neumann Corporation, and the best place to do so would be at the Harlech Public Library.

I travelled to the library for a second time on the same day that Kaj went to meet Paul. Harlech Public Library was located in Central Harlech, also known as the downtown area, on King Island. The structure of the library was newly built, designed like a colosseum on the outside with over seven floors (plus two sublevels) of books and archives. The library was located on Campbell and Hound Street. I looked at the façade of the library and then walked through the main plaza to reach the main doors of the building as I observed the structure. The structure was constructed out of a smooth concrete and the outer walls were thick. The main plaza simply consisted of concrete tiles two-feet by two-feet and entered into the main entrance to set off to work. I entered into the building lobby, which consisted of a fifth of the colosseum with a glass wall looking into the library from the lobby, and small stores and coffee shops situated on the innermost wall. The lobby only consisted of five stories of the entire structure, cutting the overall structure short at this side of the structure.

The ceiling consisted of glass and looked out to the grey skies above. I travelled over to the main entrance of the library and entered inside.

The library main floor consisted of a check-out desk directly ahead with an information desk on the left, and open floor on the right. Next to the information desk there were a set of stairs that went down to the sublevel. Around the check-out desk there was a supporting wall with elevators, and in front of this wall there was also an escalator and set of stairs to the upper floors. Around the perimeter of the main floor there were some shelves with the kid's section. From the second floor to the fifth floor the non-fiction could be found, organized in accordance with the Dewey Decimal System. The fifth floor only consisted of half of the entire area of the structure since the other half was a rooftop garden. The sublevels consisted of archives, also known as the 'Special Collections' and contained a plethora of archived content from across the region going back to the 1800s. This collection included books, periodicals, newspapers, pamphlets, ephemera as well as legal documents, census documents, government transcripts and minutes, and other documents. The library would surely have everything that I would need to learn more about the Neumann connection.

I walked towards the stairs that went to the basement and then reached the check-in desk to enter into the archives. Special Collections was a restricted area with limited access, but I made an appointment to enter today at this hour, so I made my way to the receptionist to check-in. I put my purse down in a tray and they sent it through an x-ray machine to ensure that I did not have any items that could be hazardous to the collections. Meanwhile, I was asked if I had any other metallic objects and then I walked through the metal detector to the other side where I was returned my purse and allowed to continue through. I walked towards the newspaper section of the archives, and in a sense of nostalgia, began to look through the cabinets of microfilm so that I could locate newspapers from this moment of time. The majority of aisles in this part of the library consisted of these same cabinets with microfilms and a few shelves that contained reference books. On the floor below, the original documents were stored and there were individual rooms from where original artefacts could be viewed with requested permission. I had requested to view the death certificate of Hamon Neumann, so before I went to see it, I had to view the microfilms.

I looked through the archives and collected archived newspaper reels for *The Sentinel* and *The Colony*. I was also able to locate newspaper reels for *The Jarsdel Journal*, which I was surprised to have been archived here. All three newspaper brands were still in action and have kept similar since the last fifteen years. I collected reels for the week immediately after the incident and then took them with me to the microfilm machine. The incident at Neumann Fairground made the front cover of both the Monday copies of *The Sentinel* and *The Colony*, where it was told that the investigative work of 15-year-old Kaj Kejsaren and Emma Monique resulted in the unearthing of an anarchist cell in the midst of Harlech. The newspapers went into detail about how the anarchists were connected to a national student group known as the Students for a Democratic World, which in itself was connected to a far-left radical group known as The Subterranean Dwellers, or Dwellers for short, both of which were names I recognized from the court trials but paid little attention to. As I reviewed the newspaper, I reminisced over the events and how Kaj and I had opened a serious can of worms in the city. I looked through the rest of the newspapers and attempted to do a bit more research into these militant groups.

From the newspapers, I looked into depth into the court cases that occurred following the investigations, and overall, I didn't realize that in comparison to the rest of the trials, Kaj and I partook in barely a small percentage of the overall criminal trial. The trials took place a year after the events at Neumann Fairground, which in adolescent years was a lot of time since the initial events, and I remembered that I was not that invested in keeping up with the trial. As I reviewed the names of the defendants, I noticed that there was someone that shared the name as Hamon – Nahman Neumann, eighteen-years old at the time of the court trial and sentenced to ten years in prison. As I continued to review the court transcripts, I pondered for a moment – I didn't believe that this same Neumann could be the founder of Neumann Corporation if he had been in prison for ten years. I noticed another name that I was familiar with in the transcripts, but not associated with the kidnapping that took place – Sylvia Parker, who was a current councilwoman, holding the Lincoln seat with the Progressives & Labor Cooperation, a municipal political party in Harlech, and Felicia Brower, likewise, a member of the Progressive & Labor Cooperation who ran last election for the Attlewood councilmember seat, but lost. I was surprised to see both of them to have been involved in the trial, but it appeared that they were members of Students for a Democratic World and prosecuted for involvement with the Dwellers – both of them were sentenced for their roles in an attempted bombing at Harlech City Hall. Both of them were associated with the current mayor, Tom Manning, who himself was a member and leader of the Progressives & Labor Cooperation. I looked back into the relevant information for my current case as I became sidetracked, seeing that most of the carnival freaks that were directly involved in the incident at Neumann Fairground received sentences of up to ten years.

I was unsettled by the fact that these people could very well be out of prison by now more than I was by the fact that some of their associates were now in public office. I had a policy when it came to politics, and that was simply, out of past experience, to not get involved. I looked into a bit more detail into the criminal trial and noticed that Eldon Hearne was eventually arrested and sentenced to ten years in prison. There was no mention about his mother. I made a note of this detail for Kaj, as if he didn't already have access to more extensive details of Eldon's criminal records. Aside from legal documents and court transcripts, I didn't have any access to criminal records or police incident reports, and I there was no ability to get these other than a Freedom of Information request that could take months to process, so I made a note of all the associates to Hamon Neumann so that I could pass on to Kaj to see if he could get access to that information through him sooner. Once I had put together all this other relevant information, I was finished with the microfilm, and it was nearly six o'clock in the evening.

I went downstairs to the viewing room where I met with staff and security. I was required to surrender my purse and be searched for any items that could damage the archived content, and then escorted to a private room with a tray that contained the document I requested to see in a leather pouch. Once I was alone, I opened the pouch and touched the document with latex gloves on. The death certificate, or more accurately, the registration of death signed off by the physician that was responsible for Hamon Neumann at Harlech General, was simple and straightforward. The cause of death on Hamon's certificate was cardiac failure due to (or as a consequence of) bodily injuries that resulted from arrest by police, which was coincidentally tied to bodily injuries that resulted from being attacked by a lion. A note was written below that stated that a significant condition tied to and could have attributed to the cause of the death was diabetes. I had no idea that the physician had ruled injuries sustained by being apprehended by the police as more significant than those received by the lions. In fairness, I had never actually seen what happened to Hamon after I kicked and receive the whip from him, nor did I ever see him again once Kaj and I ran to the police. However, what I had been told was that the lions had killed him. Regardless, I never felt guilty over my ties to his death since he had literally attempted to sacrifice us to the lions, and Kaj and I were forced to escape from that madman, and any connection I had to him being attacked by the lions I attributed to self-defense, but this news still came as a shock. I put the document back into the pouch and put the pouch back into the tray. I went back to the front desk and then went upstairs so that I could research Neumann Corporation with the time that I had left.

I went upstairs and decided that the only way I would find any books, magazines or periodicals related to Neumann Corporation would be through the card catalogs. The card catalogs were a series of cards kept in cabinets on the main floor which listed every book, magazine, or periodical that was available and categorized them based on key words related to the content. I went through more than hundred cards to put together a short list of books that I would look at. Based on my review of the card catalog, the books and magazines that would be beneficial for my investigation could be found in the social science section under the economics class. As I put together my list, I stopped as I suddenly felt as though I was being watched. I turned around briefly to catch a glimpse, but didn't see anyone nearby that was looking at me. I felt uneasy and so I quickly finished my list. I went upstairs to the three-hundred section and found the thirtieth class of that section to start to find books related to Neumann Corporation.

I picked up several books and then went upstairs to the sixth floor where the eight-hundred section for history was located and stopped at the twentieth class of that section for biographies to pick up, *The Story of a Neumann*, which I believed would shed some light on the founder of Neumann Corporation. I read the back of the biography and unsurprisingly, the novel was about a man named Nathan Neumann, co-founder of Neumann Corporation. I didn't know what I had expected, but the ties between Neumann Corporation and Neumann Fairground were nonetheless clearer to me. Although I had yet to read the book, which I now decided to check out, I suspected that Nathan was none other than Nahman, much like his father who was referred to as Hammond Neumann when his name was in fact Hamon Neumann. I picked up the book, but as I was about to leave, suddenly, I was met with a click noise and noticed the shelves began to close in.

I hurried to the end, slipping through before the shelves could smother me or trap me in place, and before I took a moment to recover, I hurried to the other shelf to see if I could catch the suspect that attempted to hurt me. I put the book about Nathan Neumann in my purse and carried the other hardcover books with me in my hand. I ran quickly down to the end of the corridor and caught a glimpse of a figure, fleeing from the incident, so I went after them. The library was quiet at this hour and there was barely anyone around. I went to the opposite-side of the floor and went down the corridor as I saw the suspect flee and come down and aisle. I followed on a parallel aisle nearby and then caught sight of them going up to the seventh floor. I hurried up the escalator and arrived at the top floor, looking around at the many tables and desks that were around in this area, and then looked out towards the patio garden.

I put my books down on a table so that I could maneuver better, and then I started to walk around and get a look for whoever had been after me. Half of the seventh floor consisted of the patio garden, and I couldn't see anyone around in the open floor space who wore dark clothes like the perpetrator, so I came out onto the patio and looked around. I went up to the perimeter arcade that overlooked the downtown area and looked around the aisle to see if I could see anyone, but I was alone outside. I stepped back and went back indoors, but as I went to fetch my books, they were gone. I tensed my face as I was frustrated at my source of information being taken from me. I looked back around at the crowd to see if anything had changed or anyone had moved, suspecting that the perpetrator was in plain sight, but I couldn't spot a difference. I put the book about Nathan Neumann back into my hands and went downstairs so that I could check it out.

I caught a taxi outside of the library and went home with a slight degree of paranoia at what had just occurred. I didn't understand entirely why someone would have been sent to me, but I didn't believe it was entirely to simply observe me. In my field, I had received requests to observe people, surveillance tasks, and when it came to that craft, you never allowed yourself to be seen or caught by your target. This person made themselves known and failed to hurt me. Whoever had sent that person, they had sent them to hurt me and throw me off my investigation. I was too disturbed at the events at the library to begin to read the book about Nathan Neumann, and even when I returned home, I locked the door and retired to my bedroom. Once I settled in, I began to go through the book and skim it for important information. I caught a sense for how this person could have both been an anarchist and son of Hamon Neumann, and it all made sense now.

In the biography, the author does not make any reference to Nathan's anarchist past, but instead says that he was born in Seattle, Washington in 1950 where he was involved in his father's circus business and spent a lot of time travelling across the continent. The book did not speak much about Hamon or his wife, and I thought that it was curious that he was born in 1950 when I remembered that Hamon had made a reference to losing his wife during the Great Depression – although it was possible that he had remarried. The only mention about Nathan's mother was that she died in the late fifties due to an unfortunate acrobatics accident during a show at Hurricane, Utah. Otherwise, the books alleged that Nathan had a typical childhood for an introverted teen who always had an interest in computing. When it came to the incident in 1968, the novel alleged that Nathan had been arrested for involvement in left-wing civil rights activism that resulted in him being incarcerated for ten years, but that he was released early in 1974 on condition. Nathan stayed in Harlech and went to school at Declan Walham University where he dropped out later on and invented the Neumann Machine with his friend, Steven Garrett, at Garett's parents' home in New Harlech. The invention of the Neumann Machine and his talents in computer science resulted in a lot of prestige – I skimmed the rest of the novel to see where Nathan Neumann was now, and it said that his friend, Garett, took on the business role of Neumann Corporation, ironically, while Nathan spent most of him teaching at the Declan Walham University where he accepted a teaching position as an associate professor and team lead for a brand new computer laboratory that he funded and was named after his father. I finished looking through the biography and took notes of all the important details I thought relevant to the current case.

Once I had finished taking notes, I lay back in bed and thought about the day and all the information that I had collected. I looked over to the answering machine and noticed that I had a voice message. I sat up and then stood up so that I could play the unheard message.

"Hi Emma, it's me, Paul. I spoke with Kaj earlier today and went over some of my latest findings…"

Paul went over the same information that he had gone over with Kaj and presented the same problem to me. He kept tabs on the hacker throughout the day today, and was most likely still at the laboratory at Calypso Tower. Paul said that the hacker had signed-in in the evening, but logged out soon after. The length of the stay was less than two minutes. Paul told me that Kaj had spoken to someone at the police department to get them a search warrant, but beforehand, he would need us to develop a plan to trace the hacker in order to present his proposal to Crown. Paul went over the needs of the plan, which basically required us to keep the hacker online for ten to fifteen minutes, long enough for the trace to be completed with Polaris.

I sat at my bed as I thought for a moment. I looked at my notes and then stood up to sit down next to my cat. I stroked him and thought about everything that I knew now about the hacker, and my suspicions that this hacker was none other than Nathan Neumann, the vengeful entity, Piato, seeking to continue his father's aims. Paul said that the hacker had spent a lot of time yesterday searching through databases elsewhere, looking for keywords to extract information, but now he's not using the connection at Calypso Tower to do that, but he's still searching through the database there in hopes that he'll find some sort of relevant information that he can download. I stood up and went over to my office so that I could pick up the phone as I thought about an idea.

I waited for Paul to answer the phone and he soon picked up.

"Hey, it's me," I greeted, "I listened to your message and I think I have an idea on how we can keep the hacker on the line over at the tower."

"How?"

"You said that he's looking for information, so let's give him some information."

"I can't expose information related to the client to this hacker – that's be shot down when I present it…"

"No, we don't give them real information, but fake information. We'll create a date file with information that this hacker is looking for, make it long enough to take ten to fifteen minutes to go through, and then we'll leave it in the open for him to come across. If he takes the bait, we'll be able to complete the trace."

"A honeypot…"

"Exactly."

Part 4 – Chapter 33
Harlech Police Department – Jarsdel Division
Northton, Jarsdel Island
September 1983 – 13:00 hours

Kaj drove back to the Jarsdel Division headquarters in Northton with a tight anxiety in his stomach. He dreaded to know what consequences would result from his interference in the investigation of Eldon Hearne's death, but he knew that it would come sooner or later. Kaj parked the car and opened the folder that Paul had given him so that he could review the notes, but the anxiety must have been too much for him to concentrate, so he took the folder with him and went across the parking lot. Kaj drove himself into the lobby, walked to the elevators, and went upstairs to the Harthdam Beat office where he met with Sergeant Allard at her cubicle.

"Hey," Kaj greeted, "you wanted to see me?"

"Not me," Sergeant Allard replied. "Rosztóczy asked for me to get you to come back to the station."

Kaj nodded and stepped back. Staff Sergeant Rosztóczy had his own office to the side. Kaj walked over and knocked on his door. The office wasn't the most private office, nor the nicest one in the building. The only window that the office had looked in from the rest of the office space and consisted mainly of a desk in the corner, a computer, a locker in the other corner, and a corkboard in front of the computer with the team schedule. Staff Sergeant Rosztóczy stood up and opened the door. He invited Kaj into his office and offered for him to sit down in the chair next to his desk. Kaj nodded and stepped in

"Kaj, what did you get yourself into?" Staff Sergeant Rosztóczy questioned with a smirk on his face. "Do you know why I've asked you to come and meet with me?"

"Because of the murder case from yesterday?"

"Yes," Staff Sergeant Rosztóczy replied, "it sounds like you did a bit sleuthing of your own yesterday and found some interesting details that the detective overlooked. I've also been told that some information you've contributed has possibly connected the murder to a gang-related incident. I heard all of this from Captain Kingston, the commanding officer of Administrative Vice, who was in my office this morning. He wanted to meet with you and I told him that you were on shift at the moment. He's upstairs, in Captain Benavidez' office right now. I suggest you go and speak with him so that you don't keep him waiting."

"Yes, sir."

Kaj stood up and exited from Staff Sergeant Rosztóczy's office. I should note a quick rundown of the Harlech Police Department; like many metropolitan municipal police departments, Harlech Police Department consists of three major departments: Operations, Investigations, and Administration, each of which was led by a Deputy Commissioner who report to the Commissioner. Operations divided into three divisions: King Division, Jarsdel Division, and Cliffe Division, each led by a Commander, and their respective jurisdiction was within their respective islands. Each division was further divided into Patrol Districts, and each island contains two districts each. Each district was led by a Captain, and within each district there were beats, which were led by Staff Sergeants. These beats were divided into squads, which were each supervised by a Sergeant. Kaj worked in Operations, Jarsdel Division, Patrol District Four, and within the Harthdam Beat under Staff Sergeant Rosztóczy. Captain Benavidez was in charge of Patrol District Four. The gap between Staff Sergeant and Captain was a long distance, where Staff Sergeant was the upmost rank that had any sort of engagement in the field; the role was also administrative, they were the team lead for a beat, and they were also a sort of field manager that operated within their beat and sometimes would attend calls. Staff Sergeant Rosztóczy was typically so overwhelmed with administrative work that he would seldom leave the office to join the rest of the team. The rank of Captain was purely an administrative and managerial role. There was a rank between Staff Sergeant and Captain; Lieutenant, but this was a support role in Operations as each Captain, or Patrol District, had three lieutenants assigned to a Captain, and in total, six lieutenants in a division, and these rotated as the Watch Commander who was responsible for supervising all operations on the island during a shift. This organization was at least how it was run in Operations, where Investigations and Administration each had their own organization and division. In Investigations, there were two sub-departments: Investigation Services and Investigative Support Services, each led by a Commander. Investigation Services was divided into four sections: General Investigations, Major Crimes, Administrative Vice, and Traffic Investigations. Each section was led by a Captain and divided into units, which were each led by a Lieutenant. Every unit consisted of a mixture of senior detectives (sergeants) and junior detectives (constables). For example, Captain Kingston led the Administrative Vice section and Kaj's partner's older brother, Lieutenant Russell Steele, led the Homicide Unit, which was within Major Crimes. To say that Captain Kingston wanted to speak with Kaj was a big deal, because he was more than a senior detective and contained a lot of influence within the police department. Secondly, Captain Kingston was not just any officer, but the very same detective that had taken charge of the investigation at Neumann Fairground fifteen years ago. Kaj surely stood in the elevator with this note in mind, because Kaj never forgot about the charismatic detective who interviewed him and inspired him for years to come.

Kaj arrived at the top floor of the police station and stepped down the corridor and around to Captain Benavidez' office. Kaj knocked on the door and waited for a voice on the other side, not Kingston's voice, but the firm voice of Captain Benavidez to welcome him in. Kaj opened the door and stepped inside. Captain Benavidez had a nice office with a view towards Harthdam from the back window. The desk was centered at the back of the room and in front of it were two chairs, one of which was occupied by an older gentleman, Captain Kingston. Captain Benavidez was a Southeast Asian male with brown skin, dark eyes, and black hair. At the top of his lips, he had a thin moustache. The distinction between staff sergeant and captain/lieutenant was also in their uniform, where a staff sergeant wore the dark blue shirts like Kaj, but had blue epaulettes to mark their rank, a lieutenant and captain wore clean, pristine white shirts with black ties and black epaulettes.

They also wore jet black dress pants instead of dark blue cargo pants. Captain Benavidez wore the white shirt and black trousers, but Captain Kingston did not wear the uniform, like most detectives, and instead wore a plain brown suit with a tie and dress shirt. He wore suspenders and held his handgun in a holster underneath his jacket. Kingston had grown a lot older since they had seen each other last and his hair was now a medium grey and face wrinkled. Kaj arrived into the office, which prompted Captain Kingston to stand as a sign of respect, while Captain Benavidez remained in his seat.

Kaj had never met Captain Benavidez personally, since he did not typically come to their beat office and usually only met with the staff sergeant weekly. Nonetheless, Captain Benavidez looked at him as if he was familiar to him and smiled confidently. Kaj had met Captain Kingston, but he did not walk towards him as Kingston offered his hand for a handshake with the assumption that Captain Kingston remembered him, and instead, assumed that he had been forgotten in the last fifteen years.

"Ah, you must be Constable Kejsaren," Captain Kingston greeted in his elegant accent, "the man of the hour, so to speak. The name is Captain Kingston, Administrative Vice – a pleasure to meet you."

"Nice to meet you too, sir," Kaj replied in a nervous tone.

"Please have a seat, Constable Kejsaren," Captain Benavidez remarked, standing up as Kaj sat down. "I'll leave you two to discuss. I have a meeting with Commander Walden in the board room in a couple minutes."

"If you wouldn't mind," Captain Kingston replied. "I don't want to bore you with the details of my investigation again. I tend to drone on and on as you know, so a moment to chat with the lad heart to heart is all I ask."

"Very well," Captain Benavidez responded, leaving.

Captain Kingston waited for Captain Benavidez to leave, and then he stood up and walked towards the window as he put his hands behind his back.

"I'm sure your staff sergeant has already informed you of why I wanted to meet with you, my dear boy."

"Staff Sergeant Rosztóczy told me that you were impressed with my contributions to the murder of Eldon Hearne since it opened the possibility of it being gang-related."

"Yes, in a nutshell," Captain Kingston replied, "as you may know, Administrative Vice concerns itself with a variety of crimes from narcotics and sex crimes to the broader criminal organizations from gangs and extremist political groups. A cusp of crime that we focus on are radical extremists, but in recent years, the extent of organized crime has grown so exponentially in Harlech that we haven't been able to focus on radical groups with the same level of effort. Eldon Hearne was known to us for his involvement in a scam fifteen years ago that was used to fund the activities of an anarchist group known as the Dwellers, who were disbanded nearly ten years ago at the conclusion of an investigation that I participated in. Over the last decade, a multitude of these extremists had been released from prison by the current government for reasons not known to us, but in our expertise, believed these people to still be a threat and kept tabs on them. Although we haven't been able to put the same effort, some friends of mine in the RCMP Security Service have had more time than me to keep an eye on some of these released inmates. Eldon Hearne was someone that we had kept an eye on, but didn't believe to be involved with any nefarious groups, that is, until his body turned up this week.

"Detective Pearson tells me that you've done some investigative work and that you were able to find a connection between Mr. Hearne and Neumann Corporation. He also tells me that you believe that there could be a connection between Mr. Hearne, Neumann Corporation, and a hacker that my section has been investigating known as Piato. Now, I'm not too familiar with computer systems, and neither is our detective who has focused on Piato, Detective Pomphrey, but he's been tasked with investigating both far-left and far-right activities on the Internet, and reporting back to me. Currently, there is no legislation to punish hackers, but from what Detective Pomphrey has deduced, there seems to be a group of hackers within the city that have taken it upon themselves to steal personal information for their own personal use. Amongst this personal information has been credit card information. Tell me, because I'm curious to know exactly what it is that you believe is going on as it was not apparently clear to me when Detective Pearson spoke to me."

"Well…"

Kaj explained to Captain Kingston as much as he could from his own investigation yesterday, how he visited Eldon's place of work, discovered that he had a license from Neumann Corporation to repair Neumann Machines and that there were also a lot of broken Neumann Machines. He then explained how he knew that Eldon's previous scam had involved him and his mother scamming their targets by stating that a personal item was cursed and that in order to release the curse, they would need to pay or give up that item. Likewise, the computer viruses were seemingly a replacement for this curse, which forced owners of Neumann Machines to pay to have their computer's repaired by Eldon's technicians who could seemingly release the curse for a fee. Kaj explained how he was able to pin a connection between Eldon with a person known to him from high school, Glenn Bertrand, who had designed a machine that Eldon and his mother used at Neumann Fairground and likewise had been a chief engineer in the design of the Neumann Machine, which made Kaj believe that the faults with the Neumann Machines were deliberate. Kaj then explained how the connection to the anarchists came about when he spoke to a friend of his, a software engineer and system manager, who had trouble with a hacker known as Piato, explain to him that there were sometimes measures put in place to computers by the designers know as 'backdoors' that hackers would exploit. In a similar manner, Kaj believed that a 'backdoor' could also be placed in Neumann Machines to provide an entryway for the hacker in addition to the fault that would require owners to visit a licensed repair shop such as the one owned by Eldon. Kaj explained that his friend had no idea how a hacker like Piato could have entered into their computer system, which runs on Neumann Machines, since he had ensured that the standard backdoors were patched up, but that there was still a gap in which the hacker had entered which must have been known by the hacker who must have been an associate or involved in the design of the Neumann

Machine. Lastly, Kaj explained that Neumann Corporation, which shared similarities in its name to Neumann Fairground, must therefore have some sort of tie to Piato, and by extension, the anarchist underground that they were investigating; if they capture Piato, they could close in on the anarchists.

"Brilliant," Captain Kingston stated, "but there remains the means in which we would locate this hacker…"

"There is a way," Kaj proposed, "but it would require a court order…"

Kaj explained to Captain Kingston what Paul had explained to him, where the computer network across the city was run by telecom companies such as Polaris and BC Tel, and that in order for them to track the hacker, they would need to force these companies to comply with the search. Additionally, they would also need the hacker to stay connected for at most twenty minutes, but his friend was seeing about a means to have that happen. Kaj then explained to Captain Kingston the sort of things that Piato was doing in his activities, which peaked his interest.

"Interesting…" Captain Kingston responded as he looked at Kaj, "very well, I would like to sponsor your attempt to locate this hacker, but in order to do so, we'll have to provide a proposal to Crown so that a judge can provide us with a court order to force these telecommunication companies to comply with us. Meanwhile, I will also work with a proposal to present to the commander and deputy commissioner for an operation to arrest this hacker. If there is some sort of association between this hacker, the anarchists, and Neumann Corporation, we will need permission to proceed as the backlash if we're wrong would be significant. Rest assured, we will find this scum, this weasel, Piato, and put him to trial, and hopefully with him, the rest of these dreads of society.

Captain Kingston came around to Kaj and offered his hand. Kaj stood up and shook it.

"Constable Kejsaren, it's a pleasure to have gotten this chance to speak," Captain Kingston said. "Are you on the day shift tomorrow?"

"No, I start my night shifts tomorrow," Kaj replied as the two started to walk out of Captain Benavidez' office.

"What a shame... have you ever written a proposal for a search warrant before?"

"I have, sir," Kaj replied.

"Good," Captain Kingston replied, "have a draft copy written and prepared for my desk by the day after tomorrow if you can come up with an idea to entrap this hacker and trace his location. I'd like to read through it before we send it to a good judge I know who I believe would share our conviction. In the meantime, hopefully you think of a good idea to put in that proposal – this investigation relies on it, son."

"Yes, sir," Kaj responded. "I will, sir."

"Very good. Now, back to your duties. A beat like Harthdam knows no better constable to have on their team."

"Thank you, sir."

Kaj left the office, hiding a smirk across his serious face until he reached the elevator. He revealed his wide smile as the doors closed and returned to the office to immediately telephone Paul and let him know the good news, that he had a green light to retrieve a search warrant provided that they developed a reasonable plan that included how they would keep the hacker connected to the computer system so that a telephone trace could be completed by the telecom company. Once Kaj had finishes speaking to Paul, he left the office with the same smile, thinking of possibilities as he returned to his regular duties for the rest of the shift, and even afterwards as he drove home and returned to his family.

Part 4 – Chapter 34
Calypso Tower
Lincoln, Jarsdel Island
September 1983 – 18:00 hours

A day passed, Kaj wrote his draft request for a search warrant during his night shift, and it was reviewed by Captain Kingston on the following morning. The day afterwards, on Kaj's day off, he received a phone call from Captain Kingston that the request had been forwarded to Crown, reviewed by a judge, and that they had been granted their search warrant to have Polaris and BC Tel comply with a telephone trace for the hacker connecting to Calypso Tower. The search warrant had been faxed to both companies, and now it was up to Kaj to coordinate the telephone trace with them. Kaj spoke with Paul, and Paul spoke with me earlier in the day to let us know of the good news. However, we still needed to prepare the data file, and so I made my way to Calypso Tower to give Paul a hand before Piato visited Calypso Tower to do his daily check and then log off. I wrote a share of the data file with Paul in the laboratory, and I also reviewed his share to ensure that it was juicy enough for the hacker to be enticed to stay online, but also believable enough to not be obvious for what it really was.

I worked from a computer near the front of the lab. Ever since the incident at the library, I had attempted to keep a low profile and keep my office locked to the public. I stayed in my bedroom and attempted to write a draft of my report for the client since I knew that it would be a long report once we completed this case. I received a phone call from Mr. Harrington earlier and he wanted to receive an update on the investigation, and so I told him that we were in the process of attempting to locate the hacker. Mr. Harrington asked a lot of questions, including whether the police were involved, and without the gut to lie to my client, I confessed that they were, but not for the purposes of the data but only in the hacker. Mr. Harrington asked me to keep him updated and wished me luck on my attempt to locate the hacker, but also to ensure that police kept away from their data. I thought this request was strange given that Mr. Harrington had said that they had initially attempted to go to the police but were denied assistance. However, it wasn't my place to question the client, although I held my suspicions. I attempted to keep these details in mind as I drafted the data file, which was difficult to do when I didn't know who this client was yet, but had to somehow compose information that was valuable, but at the same time, didn't compromise the identity of the client. Paul told me that we could make it work if we made the info be related to his computer laboratory and the implementation of a new cyber security system to counter a supposed hacker that had infiltrated their database. I liked the idea since it seemed to coax the ego of the hacker to take in bait that mentioned him by name. I worked on this data file for a couple hours into the evening – it felt nice to work with someone, no less, a friend from high school.

Suddenly, I heard an alarm go off from Paul's workstation, so I looked up and over as there was no noise except the beeping of the alarm from his computer. Paul then reared his head out from behind all of the machinery and looked over to me.

"We just had the hacker come in," Paul stated, "he's seen our data file."

"Oh no…" I remarked as we had yet to finish putting together all of the info. "It's too early…"

I ran over to Paul's workstation and joined him.

"He's logged in. Right now, he's listing users," Paul remarked as he looked at his computer screen. "Can you phone the detective?"

"Sure thing," I replied, picking up the telephone and dialing the telephone number for Detective Pomphrey.

Kaj had sent us contact information for a detective, Detective Pomphrey, who I remembered from the police reports that Detective Pearson had given me. Kaj said that Detective Pomphrey would connect us with a senior technician at Polaris who was known to the Harlech Police Department, specifically the Administrative Vice section since he had been involved in numerous telephone traces for vice cases.

"Detective Pomphrey."

"Hello, this is Emma Monique. I was given your contact information by Constable Kaj Kejsaren. He told me to contact you for a telephone trace that would need to completed at Calypso Tower."

"Oh, sure. Just a minute…"

I waited as the detective included someone else in the telephone call.

"Hey Jarrett, it's Gerard. How are you?"

I rolled my eyes as the detective decided to make small talk with the technician.

"I'm good. What's up?"

"Just related to that phone trace that I was talking to you about earlier. I have Emma Monique with the computer lab at Calypso Tower. We have the hacker connected to them, so we need to trace the incoming call."

"Sure thing. Hi, Emma," Jarett greeted, "can I get the phone number associated with the modem that the hacker has connected to?"

"He's left," Paul noted, "I don't understand…"

"What do you mean?" I whispered to Paul.

"Sorry?" Jarett replied.

"Sorry, I was talking to my colleague. It looks like the hacker just left…"

"That's a shame," Jarett responded.

"What's going on?" Detective Pomphrey asked.

"The hacker left before we could even start the trace," Jarett clarified.

"Bad luck," Detective Pomphrey replied, "well, we'll try again some time. Emma, Constable Kejsaren told me that you and your colleagues would have some sort of method to trap the hacker when he showed."

"We do, but it's reliant on him coming across that information," I replied. "It looks like he left before he could even search through the databases as he usually does."

"Alright, well, let's try our luck for next time then," Detective Pomphrey replied. "Jarett, I'll call you back when we have a secure line again."

"Sounds good," Jarett responded, "but just so we're all on the same page, my shift ends at midnight today and there are no other technicians on tonight who are familiar with traces."

"Understood," Detective Pomphrey remarked, "I don't intend to stick it through the night either. If you guys catch this guy before midnight, we'll do the trace. Otherwise, we'll have to wait for some other time."

"Okay…" I replied, slightly annoyed, "thank you."

Both the detective and technician hung up. I put the phone down and then looked at the computer screen. There were currently several users logged in, including Paul, 'PSchmidt,' who was listed at the top of the screen. I took a moment to view the hackers actions once he logged on and then left. All he did was type out the command to list all active users and then leave. I put a hand on Paul's shoulder to comfort him as it seemed as if we had been defeated tonight.

"Maybe he'll show up again later tonight…" I suggested.

"Maybe," Paul replied, "but two days ago he did the same and left. Yesterday however, while I was typing out a fake email on another account, he listed all the users and then began to go through the emails. Since the client's restricted email communications at the moment, he didn't stay more than four minutes."

"Hm…" I thought about what Paul had said for a moment. "What time does he usually come around?"

"Anywhere from now to late at night," Paul replied. "He does seem to visit at least twice an evening if he doesn't do much the first time, so maybe he'll come back. Last night he only made one visit while two days ago, he visited twice. Although, that time, he did the same when he came back and just left. I don't understand what he does sometimes…"

"Were you logged in two days ago when he visited?"

"Of course."

"What about yesterday? You said that you used a different account to type the bait?"

"Yes. Do you think there's a pattern? When he infiltrated a bunch of networks, I wasn't logged on and I was only monitoring the printout."

"Maybe he knows that you're the system manager," I suggested. "If he sees you logged in, that might scare him and cause him to back out. Why else would he list all active users when he logs in and then just leave?"

"I suppose that makes some sense," Paul replied.

"In a way, it's probably good that you scared him off now," I said. "We're not ready for him yet. If he does visit again, how long do you think we have to put together the rest of the bait?"

"I'd say four or six hours…"

I looked at the time as it was just a couple minutes past six o'clock in the evening.

"Okay, we should have it done by then, I think. Also, Paul, the technician asked me for the telephone associated with the modem. Do we have that information on hand?"

"I believe it's been the same one all this time, but there are several telephone lines and modems, so I'd have to quickly check to be certain. Luckily, I know the node and port by now."

"Do you have to be logged in to check?"

"No, there's a separate terminal that I can check."

"Okay, then this'll be our plan: when we're ready, you'll log out and we'll wait for the hacker to come in. When that happens, you'll check which modem he's connected to while I'll phone the detective and telecom company to get the trace started. Hopefully, everything will be smooth sailings."

"Alright, sounds like a plan," Paul affirmed.

I returned to my computer station and continued to work on fake emails. I had a lot of fun with the emails, and after the near-miss that we had just now, we set to implement our plan with determination that we'd be able to capture this hacker's location once and for all. We completed the email chain within three hours, rife with keywords such as 'security' and 'defense' to lure the hacker, and then buzz words like 'revolutionary' and 'life-changing' to keep the hacker in. Once I sent the last email, I stayed logged in, using an account that Paul had created for me with a pseudonymous handle, 'CBard,' while Paul logged off. Paul had set up a program that would alert us when the hacker logged in by phoning a pager that he had. Meanwhile, I had brought some files and notes for me to review, put together, and prepare to include in my final report to Mr. Harrington. I returned to highlighting my preliminary notes, summarizing ideas, and drafting my report as we waited.

At eleven o'clock in the evening, I became doubtful that we'd have our second chance, and if he did decide to show, it would be in vain to our hard work this evening. Paul and I discussed our options half past an hour in case he didn't connect before midnight.

"I suppose I could stay logged on," Paul proposed, "and that way, if he really is scared of me, he shouldn't look at the emails."

"What if he isn't scared of you? What if he doesn't see the risk-cost the same and goes ahead to read the emails anyways?"

"If that happens, then we'll just have to start over," Paul remarked with a sigh.

Paul and I waited around for another fifteen minutes, and still there was no sign of Piato. I realized that there was an unlikely chance he'd show in the next fifteen minutes, so I contemplated phoning a taxi. Paul lived nearby and easily walked to work from his apartment, but I had a fair distance to travel. Paul and I continued to wait in silence until ten minutes to the end of the hour, at which point, Paul stood up from his desk.

"Well, we'll try again tomorrow. Perhaps Kaj can join us too. In the least, we have an idea of what to do when he does come around, so it should be a smooth operation to trace him."

Paul's pager on his belt began to set off. He looked at it and I stood up with anticipation that it was him.

"Call the detective," Paul exclaimed, going over to the terminal. "I'm going to check which modem he's connected to."

I quickly stood up and went over to a telephone across the room. I dialed the phone number of Detective Pomphrey and waited nearly a whole minute for him to answer.

"Detective Pomphrey, Ad Vice," the detective greeted in a tired voice.

"Hi, Detective Pomphrey, it's Emma Monique again. We have the hacker connected to our modem again. Could you call Polaris?"

"Sure... one second," Detective Pomphrey dialed to connect Polaris in the telephone conversation. "Hey, Jarett, sorry to bug you before you left work, but we've got that hacker again. I have Emma Monique on the line.

"No problem," Jarett responded, "what's the telephone line, Emma?"

I looked over to Paul as he looked at me. Paul told me the telephone number, which I repeated to Jarett. I could hear him typing on the other side in silence. Once I gave him the number, Paul went over to his workstation, presumably to see if the hacker took the bait.

"Hold on for a moment," Jarett said, "I've got the active line... I'm sending a tech to check that line right now."

I waited for a minute, then two minutes, both of which felt like eternities in themselves.

"Looks like the line is connecting through with a BC Tel line. I've got to get ahold of them," Jarett said. "Standby."

I waited for another couple of minutes. I hadn't heard from Paul, but I could hear the printer shooting off a long sheet of paper, which meant that the hacker must have taken the bait. After five minutes, nearly ten minutes in total, Jarett came back to the call.

"Alright, gents, we've got him," Jarett remarked. "The end of the line is a local number – Gerard, I'll send you the details via fax."

"Good work," Detective Pomphrey remarked, "what's the location?"

"It appears to be a telephone number coming from University Hill, either the residences or the university itself. I'll have to cross-reference the telephone number with our database, but I'll include that with the report I'll send you. I should have that sent to you sometime tomorrow."

"Alright, thanks for your help, Jarett. Take care."

Jarett hung up and it was just me and the detective.

"So?" I questioned.

"Well, you heard him – the hacker is coming from University Hill. Most likely a university student, so we'll have to wait for an address and go from there. I appreciate your assistance with our investigation – we'll be in touch."

Detective Pomphrey hung up. I slowly lowered the phone, and despite the fact that we had traced the hacker, and even the fact that we had done a fair share of the work, I was annoyed at the way the police shunned us now that they had their information. Regardless, I knew more than them – this was Nathan Neumann for sure, and he was connecting through from Declan Walham University, most likely his computer laboratory, and so now I had to take the next step for my own interest; the interest of my client, to retrieve that data and that was it. Paul joined me in the main hub of the computer lab. I slowly looked over to him.

"He's read through all the emails and downloaded them. So, what do we have?"

"They've narrowed it down to University Hill – I knew it. Piato is Nathan Neumann."

"What are you going to do now?"

"I don't know what I'll do specifically, but I'll have to update Mr. Harrington tomorrow morning with this information. I'll most likely have to infiltrate the university to get ahold of that information."

"Okay, that's great," Paul said with a smile. "Well, we did it, didn't we?"

"Yeah, I guess with did," I replied, raising a smile. "I didn't think it'd be a possible, but we did do it."

"I know how I'm going to celebrate," Paul remarked, "I'm going to go straight home. The client should be relieved that we can kick out the hacker now and can open our network."

I was relieved for Paul's progression, but I wasn't done quite like him. We walked together to the main floor, and then once on the street, we split ways as I went to the taxi cab I had called. I lowered my smile once I was alone, plotting the way I would infiltrate the university, because although Paul had finished his tasks, I had yet to finish mine. I was going to get that data no matter the cost.

The next morning, I woke up to get ready for the day ahead. The new day provided me with a fresh perspective on the situation. I intended to visit Declan Walham University before the Harlech Police Department as it seemed that our partnership had been cut off at this point. I wasn't even sure if Kaj would partake in what was to come, or if his own organization would cut him off too and go ahead with what they had received from us. I had no intent to join them. I had my directive, and my intentions were solely in the wishes of my client. I was so close to completing this case and receiving my generous payment that could finance me for the rest of the year. I woke up Bill as I hurried around the apartment, leaving to visit the fitness center nearby where I started my day out with a jog and then a shower before I returned home to have something to eat.

At half past noon, I sat down at my desk and wrote down notes of what the operation last night had unturned. Once I had composed my notes and organized the current situation, I picked up the phone so that I could speak to Mr. Harrington. I dialed his phone number and then waited for a response.

"Hello, this is Patrick Harrington," he greeted.

"Hi, Mr. Harrington, it's Emma."

"Ah, Emma, good afternoon," Mr. Harrington remarked. "How's the investigation? I heard from our system manager that they'll be able to re-open our database and expel the hacker now that you've located this miscreant."

"Yes."

I explained to Mr. Harrington the trace that had been completed and that the hacker had been located to be operating from University Hill. I then told him that I believed that the hacker was an associate professor out of my research of local anarchist groups and the fact that Nathan Neumann had a history of anarchist activities. I stated that I intended to recover the data by going to the university to infiltrate the laboratory there.

"What about the police?" Mr. Harrington asked. "What is their take on the situation?"

"I'm not entirely sure," I replied, "it seems that they won't be working with us anymore and I'm not sure what direction they'll take with the information they have. From what I understand, it could take some time before they act since they have a lot of legal hoops and formalities to tie up."

"Good, then it's important that we retrieve that vital data before they can get a glimpse at it," Mr. Harrington stated, "but Emma, there's going to a change of plan. Your task will still be to recover this data, but I'm going to ask that you work with Mr. Schmidt to do so given that it's come to our attention that the data in question could be fragile. In order to recover the client's data, you'll need to provide access for Mr. Schmidt to hack into the computer used by the hacker so that he can recover the data and delete whatever exists on the hacker's computer."

"Understandable," I replied.

"And if that proves to fail, or should the plans change," Mr. Harrington explained, "there will be a contingency in place where Mr. Schmidt will provide you with the means to destroy that data entirely so that nobody can read it. I believe he said that he would develop something for you this morning, so if you could see him before you head to the university and also speak with him to organize your cooperation in this matter, you should be set to complete your primary objective."

"Yes, sir."

"And lastly, Emma, should the police get involved while you're off, I have another request from our client," Mr. Harrington remarked. "The client has requested that you assist the police, specifically Constable Kejsaren, in any way possible as you proceed."

"Okay…"

"It's important that we assist law enforcement as we move forward, treating them as our allies rather than foes, despite this unwillingness to cooperate with each other. Constable Kejsaren had demonstrated to be a valuable ally and he could be of use in endeavors in the future."

"Yes, sir."

"Very well, I won't hold you much longer. All the best, and I look forward to hearing from you when the deed is done."

"Yes, sir. Thank you, sir."

Mr. Harrington hung up and I brought the phone down as I sighed. I stood up and went back into the bedroom to get ready to leave, picking up my hat and purse, and then returning to my office to put together my papers. I put my purse down on the couch as I grabbed my coat, put it on, and then turned around as I heard a knock on the door. I hesitated for a moment given my recent paranoia in regard to visitors, but as the person knocked again, I stepped over and looked into the peephole in case it could be another client, or worse, another assassin.

On the other side, I saw Kaj dressed in a suit, waiting for me to open the door. I didn't hesitate for another moment to remove the chain lock, turn the deadbolt, and then open the door to look at him on the other side.

"Hi," I greeted, "what's up?"

Kaj looked into my office and then back at me.

"Can I come in?" he asked.

"Yeah, sure," I replied, stepping back to allow him into my home and office.

Kaj stepped in and I closed the door behind him. I picked up my purse and then came back around to the back of my desk as I looked over to him.

"Sorry, were you about to leave?" Kaj asked.

"Yes, but don't worry about that. What brings you over here?"

"I just wanted to ask about what happened last evening," Kaj said as he continued to look around my office. Kaj was very perceptive. "I heard that you and Paul had a successful trace."

Kaj finally looked back at me as he finished looking at my stuff.

"Yes," I replied, "we thought for a moment that we wouldn't get him to take the bait, but at the last minute, he showed and took the bait, so we phoned Detective Pomphrey, and he phoned Polaris to run the trace. You wouldn't believe it, but the original source of the call came from University Hill. Polaris wouldn't tell us exactly where on University Hill but told the detective that he'd include it in his report once he finished checking the owner of the telephone number, and it didn't seem like the detective would share that info with us."

"Yeah, I can believe that," Kaj replied.

"Do you know who the owner of the telephone number is?"

"No," Kaj denied, "I just had a phone call from Captain Kingston this morning and he told me to come to the precinct on King Island for a presentation. I don't know what for, but if I had to guess, it would be for some sort of operation to raid the university."

"Interesting, when do you think that would happen?"

"I don't know," Kaj responded, "it could be anywhere from tonight to next week, to next month. I'd assume the department would act fast in case Piato attempts to skip town."

"Do they have the slightest idea of who Piato is?" I asked.

"I told them that whoever he is, he'd most likely be an important person with Neumann Corporation just to give them a sense to tread carefully, which is what we're doing. If it wasn't for the potential ramifications, I think we would have gone and busted the place last night."

"Do you have an idea of who Piato is?"

"No," Kaj replied, "but I'd have to assume that whoever they are, they were with us that night at Neumann Fairground."

"You'd most likely be right," I responded. "Kaj, Hamon Neumann had a son – Nathan Neumann, the co-founder of Neumann Corporation."

"Really?"

"Yes," I replied, "and Nathan Neumann is an associate professor now at Declan Walham University where he funded a state of the art computer laboratory. When you get to the presentation, don't be surprised if the telephone number is tied to the university – it could also be a reason why you'll have to be careful since this could develop into a significant public event if police decide to raid a public university."

"I suppose we've really come up with another major story then," Kaj remarked, oblivious to the consequences I just suggested to him. "We really have a habit for that, don't we?"

"Let's not aim for another," I remarked with a frown.

Kaj looked at me for a moment with a serious glance. I knew what he was doing.

"Were you going to the university just now?" Kaj questioned.

"No," I answered, "I was going to go and see Paul."

"But you were going to go to the university eventually, weren't you?"

I looked aside and then back to him as I replied, "Of course, I have a job to complete."

"Don't you think that it would be kind of dangerous to go all alone."

"I can take care of myself," I replied. "I'm not sixteen-years old anymore. Between all we've been through, and the many more adventures I had after we split paths, I can handle myself, Kaj. I'm not the same person you once knew."

Kaj didn't respond to that.

"I'm not going to get myself into trouble. I'm just going to do what I have to do – anything that you and the rest of the police have to do, go ahead and do it. I have no interest in Nathan, the anarchists, or whatever it is that they're up to. I'm going in for my client's data and that's it."

"Okay..." Kaj replied.

We both looked at each other for a minute.

"Well, I better go then," Kaj remarked. "I don't want to be late. Let's keep in touch."

"Certainly," I responded, "keep me updated."

Kaj stepped back and opened the door to leave.

"And Kaj," I suddenly said before he left.

Kaj looked at me.

"Stay safe too."

Kaj nodded and then left. I half-expected him to crack a joke, but he was a lot more serious and mature than I remembered him, so likewise, he was not the same sixteen-year old that I remembered, if the sixteen-year old I remembered was even that same boy. Kaj left my office and went downstairs to his Ford Bronco. He drove from Saffron to Bromley in King Island where he parked in the large parking lot at the main police headquarters. The facility was newly built to replace an earlier building that was located closer to Keswick. Kaj quickly made his way to the main floor and then into a conference room where there were various tables that faced a small, low stage with a podium and projector screen next to it. The projector displayed the logo of the Harlech Police Department. The tables were positioned to face the stage, but they were all lined up in a U-shape to create a space in the middle that didn't obstruct the view of anyone. At the back of the room there were some additional chairs. There were seldom people sat down at the tables as most of them were stood up, conversing with each other. Kaj saw a lot of high-ranking officers: captains, commanders, and deputy commissioners. Aside from Captain Benavidez, Kaj didn't know any of them. Kaj caught sight of Captain Kingston who was dressed in his uniform and approached the podium with a folder in hand. Captain Kingston looked to Kaj as he took his seat and gave a nod to him. Kaj nodded back at the captain to acknowledge him and then listened as the presentation began.

"Good afternoon," Captain Kingston greeted, "I've gathered you all here today to propose a special operation in regard to an ongoing investigation that takes place in both our physical world, and also the cyber world. Ten years ago, Declan Walham University was the site of a student organization known as Students for a Democratic World, which was connected to a radical group known as The Subterranean, and whose followers were known as 'Dwellers.' In an investigation that I had taken part in at that time, a majority of the group members were arrested, and both the student organization and radical group were dismantled by 1974. The extent of these anarchist activities was in the near bombing of our very own city hall, but thanks to the work of the team in that time, was prevented beforehand. Today, the threat of anarchists has arisen once again, as history repeats itself, but in a different manner. Today, anarchists have taken refuge in the cyber world to plot their activities under the guise of pseudonyms, and are able to act in such anonymity that has created a difficult task for our investigators to get to the bottom of these miscreants.

"In the last year, my section has tracked the activities of an anarchist group that associated themselves under the simple consonant of 'V.' These perpetrators that have baited, scammed, and stolen personal information off of civilians in the Greater Harlech area, including credit card information, security information, and other personal information. The extent of this group's reach has proven to be any personal computer designed by Neumann Corporation, as in recent months, the number of Neumann Machines that have reported a fault or computer virus has been higher than past years and been the target of hackers. My section has produced evidence that suggests that these machines were designed with intent to be easily hackable. This week, my section arrested and interrogated Mr. Glenn Stephen Bertrand, a computer developer that assisted with the design of the latest Neumann Machine and who confessed to a 'backdoor' mechanism that was intended to allow for easy access to any who know the gate and key. Mr. Bertrand is also a suspect in a homicide case led by Detective Eric Pearson with the Homicide Unit as earlier this week, the manager and owner of a used computer shop, had been murdered in South Harthdam. In addition to selling used computers, Mr. Hearne's shop was also licensed by Neumann Corporation to repair these computers, and further investigation of the computer shop has produced disks with copies of personal information extracted from personal computers that have been brought to the repair shop. The investigation at the shop has shown ties between Mr. Hearne and Mr. Bertrand, and the current homicide investigation is ongoing, but the evidence suggests that the murder was targeted and in relation to the widespread scam at hand.

"Now, although the 'backdoor' mechanism of these computers has been confirmed by our suspect in custody, the objective of the operation that I propose is not to go against Neumann Corporation, but to apprehend a suspect with knowledge of this 'backdoor' mechanism and who has used this mechanism in practice to various hacker activities under the pseudonym of 'Piato.' In the past year, 'Piato' has acted as a leader amongst the anarchist groups, promoting and encouraging his followers to steal bank information and credit information in order to 'take from the bourgeoise.' In the past year, the Harlech Police Department has received a large volume of calls through our non-emergency line from callers that have claimed misplay with their bank accounts and credit card accounts, in which sums of money close to two-hundred thousand dollars in total have been reported to have been stolen to each claimant, totaling more than a hundred-thousand to a million across the board. Additionally, documented activities of Piato has shown intent to rob classified information from governmental websites as he searches for keywords and inserts himself into closed government networks. Although the potential that Piato is an operative with either the Soviet Union or People's Republic of China is low, as per our colleagues in the RCMP Security Services, the risk remains that any classified information could be exposed and rushed to the wrong hands. The actions of Piato and his followers have demonstrated an apparent issue of public safety concern, and the use of these funds could be used to support the activities of these anarchists, which relate to 'revolutionary' and anti-governmental rhetoric that is also of public safety concern.

"This week, my section underwent an operation to trace the location of the hacker, Piato, and has produced his location to be at Declan Walham University campus. This morning, we have confirmed that the telephone number associated to the university has originated from the Hamon Neumann Memorial Laboratory, a computer lab that consists of various computers and databases that are open to the students at the campus, which suggests that the hacker is either a faculty member or a student. In order to arrest the hacker, I propose an evening raid of the campus to seize all equipment, which could contain stolen information that has been seized by Piato. The seizure of this equipment, which has already been denied to us by the university officials, could hold a tremendous amount of data valuable to the continuation of this investigation, but is sure to meet resistance from the students at the campus and would require assistance from Operational Planning Support. It is vital that this equipment is seized as soon as possible, and if possible, to detain or arrest the hacker at once in order to learn more about the anarchist underground that poses a threat to public safety in the city."

Kaj listened as Captain Kingston went through the plan for the special operation, and at the end, he took questions from the rest of the police management before it was decided that the operation would go ahead with approval. At the end of the presentation, Captain Kingston shook hands with some of the management, chatted, and then made his way over to Kaj before he left. Captain Kingston shook his hand and patted him on the shoulder.

"Congratulations on the approval," Kaj said to him.

"Ah, I knew they'd come around. Sometimes they can't say no."

"When do you think this'll happen?"

"Operational Planning Support will have to raise a team to assist, but I intend to have this done tonight before any vital information can be deleted. Time is of the essence. I've had a word with Captain Benavidez and would like you to join us if you will. I wouldn't want you to miss this momentous occasion.

"Thanks, sir. I appreciate it. I will certainly be here."

"Good," Captain Kingston remarked. "Why don't you come to my office, and we can discuss a bit more."

"Sure," Kaj agreed.

Captain Kingston and Kaj left the meeting room and went upstairs to Captain Kingston's office. They stepped in and came into a personal office similar in size to Captain Benavidez at Jarsdel Division, but with a view of the river and marina. The windows were also taller and wider, which provided more light. The furniture appeared to be newer too. At the corner of the office, there was a bird cage with a parrot inside. Captain Kingston and Kaj stepped in, and at once the parrot squawked at him.

"Don't worry about him," Captain Kingston remarked. "He's an old bird."

"Brawk, old bird," the parrot replied.

"Come, sit down," Captain Kingston said. "Can I offer you a drink?"

"No, thanks," Kaj responded as he went to sit down in front of the desk.

"Not even a glass of water?"

"I'm good, thanks."

Captain Kingston came around to his desk and asked, "Do you fancy the view?"

"It's nice."

"Yes, I wouldn't ask for any other office than this one, that's for sure."

"I didn't realize pets were allowed," Kaj remarked.

"Oh, well, he's a party-piece, that one," Captain Kingston replied. "He's fancied by a lot of the team and management. How do you like animals?"

"I don't mind them."

"Do you have any at home?"

"No, sir."

"Right. Personally, I adore them – just about all of them for their own beauty…" Captain Kingston remarked as he sat back. "At any rate, I wanted to have word with you."

"Yes, sir?"

"Tell me, how long have you been with the Harlech Police Department?"

"Almost six years," Kaj answered.

"Really? Interesting that it's taken this long for me to notice you," Captain Kingston replied, looking at Kaj closer. "You do remember me, don't you?"

"I do, sir."

"I should have expected that someday, that young boy from the fairground should happen to join the HPD, but I would have expected that same boy would have shown himself by now."

"I've tried to stay in my lane," Kaj replied, "if anything, this has all been by chance."

"Do you really think so?" Captain Kingston questioned. "You've got a keen, observant eye, my dear boy. An eye like yours is wasted on the streets and should be properly used. You remind me a lot of myself when I was younger... but I suppose we've had a different life. You're married, aren't you? Do you have any children?"

"I do, sir. A son."

"I don't," Captain Kingston remarked, "but I am married. The appeal to have children has never been within me..." he said with a sigh, looking aside. "Not that I want to drag you down with me, but hopefully (or rather hopefully not) you'll might see that our heirs aren't always set to be as we are, to live as we are, and in part that's our fault, but on another hand, it's completely out of our control. Nonetheless, from father to son, there are certain constants that continue... I digress..."

Captain Kingston stood up and walked over to his window as he looked out. He grew silent. Suddenly, he then turned around and motioned Kaj to stand up.

"Run along now," Captain Kingston said, "and enjoy the rest of the afternoon. I'll be in touch for you to join the briefing later this evening. Should all go well, I'll be sure to put in a good word for you to Commander Peterson to have you out of that uniform and into the ranks of some real men of the force. In mean time, run along to that wife and son of yours."

"Thank you, sir."

Part 4 – Chapter 36
Harlech Police Department – King Division
Bromley, King Island
September 1983 – 15:00 hours

Kaj left Captain Kingston's office, returned home and spent time with his wife and son. At five o'clock in the evening, Captain Kingston phoned Kaj to have him join Operational Planning Support at their office at Jarsdel Division so that the details of the plan could be gone over. At a quarter past five o'clock in the evening, Kaj left his family home and drove to Jarsdel Division.

Kaj wore the same suit that he had worn at the presentation at King Division to Jarsdel Division, but took his uniform with him in his duffel bag so that he could change into the dark blue uniform for the raid. Once he was dressed, he went to the second floor where the Operational Planning Support unit had their office. Each division had specialized units located at the station. Jarsdel Division had Operational Planning Support, which was a specialized unit that handled riots, civil unrest, protests, and large-scale events that could lead to protest and civil unrest, such as the operation at the university. The unit consisted of thirty constables, some of whom were part-time members, and they were led by three sergeants and a police captain. Captain Dylan Simpson was a bitter and jaded man, more-so than any officer that Kaj had met in the entire police force. Jarsdel Division was also home to the specialized Mounted Unit, which handles crowd control, but would not be involved in this operation. In addition to Operational Planning Support, some extra members from the Lincoln Beat were brought in. Kaj met with Captain Simpson and Captain Kingston at the front of the room as he arrived to join the support unit. Captain Kingston wore a regular suit as opposed to his uniform, while Captain Simpson wore a tactical police uniform like the majority of his unit.

"Ah, this is Constable Kejsaren," Captain Kingston introduced. "He's the constable that I told you about earlier."

"Nice to meet you," Captain Simpson remarked, looking at him.

"Constable Kejsaren is a patrolman with the Harthdam Beat – isn't your son in that same beat?" Captain Kingston asked.

"My son is with Patrol District Six, Attlewood Beat," Captain Simpson clarified.

"Ah, right," Captain replied, slightly embarrassed turning to Kaj. "My dear boy, why don't I take you over to the unit that you'll be with."

Kaj and Captain Kingston walked away from Captain Simpson.

"Nevermind him," Captain Kingston whispered to Kaj, "he's never been the same since the police board denied his promotion to commissioner in favor of Commissioner Sullivan."

Kaj was seated with the members of the Lincoln squad and then Captain Kingston returned to the front of the room so that the briefing could begin. Among this group was also several detectives, two males and a female, who Kaj presumed to be with Ad Vice, Gang Unit.

"Good evening, ladies and gentlemen," Captain Kingston greeted from a podium next to a projector screen that listed the operation, 'Operation Deviant Weasel' at the front. "In less than two hours to sundown, at nineteen-hundred hours, we are about to proceed with one of the most high-profile operations in HPD history since the riots in 1971. Now, our objective is not to agitate the public at University Hill, but your involvement in this operation comes out of a forecast of probable demonstrations amongst a saturated anti-police and anti-authority population. Our objective is primarily to apprehend all evidence that could benefit the investigation of anarchist activities within the city in the form of computer data held in computer machines located at the Hamon Neumann Memorial laboratory at the Declan Walham University campus. In the way of that seizure of evidence, there is sure to be resistance amongst the student and faculty members, especially within the laboratory, and in response to that probability, the authority to detain any who interfere in the police operation is permitted. Anybody who is apprehended is to be taken to the paddy wagons and brought back to the precinct on King Island and will be dealt with at a later time. At the commencement of the operation, Foxtrot-One-Ten will provide presence at the exterior of the laboratory while Tango-Twenty and Tango-Thirty with Traffic Support will install checkpoints at both exit points to screen all personnel attempting to leave the university."

"My units, X-Ray One-hundred, Two-hundred, and Three-hundred will take position around the exterior areas around the campus, especially the main plaza where One-hundred will provide presence and where any sort of demonstration is sure to take place in solidarity with the staff and students. Our hopes is that we can keep the activities within the laboratory so quiet as to avoid any immediate demonstration, but the chances are there nonetheless," Captain Simpson explained. "No communications have been made with the administration at the university at this time, so our arrival is one-hundred percent a surprise to them."

"Yes, "Captain Kingston confirmed, "our last communication with the faculty was when we had requested that they willingly provide us with access to the data bases at the laboratory, which they denied, and so we will have to take these items by force. Tango-Ten will cordon off the street immediately in front of the laboratory and this area will be restricted to our members and paddy wagons. Some reconnaissance provided from my section has suggested that his street is optimal for the wagons in case any detentions are needed to be brought out of the building to avoid exposure to the public. Now, the computer data files will be kept in tape reels that should be located in the laboratory. The search warrant authorized by Crown permits us to seize any and all tape reels and cartridges at this location to assist in our investigation as well as any hard-drives or other items that could provide useful in the investigation. All of these reels will be seized and taken back to King Division. A separate wagon for these reels will be provided in addition to boxes to store them. To the extent of the seizures, escorted by Foxtrot-One-Ten, my team will seize the reels and ensure their safe transport back to our office. Ideally, this should all be done in a few hours, but if a disturbance arises, we will handle them as they come. Are there any questions so far?"

Captain Kingston and Captain Simpson answered some questions and went through the rest of the briefing with the entire group. At the end of the briefing, there was still some time left to sundown, which allowed the teams to organize and then prepare for deployment. Kaj split up from the rest of Operational Planning Support, most of whom would ride in the paddy wagons to University Hill, while Foxtrot-One-Ten would drive in their cars to the university. Half of the entire squad was with this operation, while the rest was responsible for the Lincoln Beat with assistance from Northton Beat. Kaj received a radio from their office and was told to use his same callsign, Hotel-Two-Twenty-three. Once with the appropriate gear, Kaj and the rest of Foxtrot-One-Ten stepped down to the parking lot where the Crown Vics waited for them. The twilight was quiet, and the skies were partly cloudy, which was an improvement from earlier when it had been entirely cloudy. Captain Kingston and Captain Simpson separated to monitor and lead their own sides of the operation, where Captain Kingston and Simpson would join the team on the field while the lieutenant second to Kingston was positioned at the dispatch office in Northton to monitor calls from University Hill related to police presence and act as a liaison with Operational Planning Support.

Kaj rode with Constable Bateman from the police station and into Lincoln with the rest of the police vehicles. Kaj looked ahead at the intersection with Riverside Drive and University Hill Drive as Traffic Support established their checkpoint and allowed them to pass through. The road was then closed off except to local traffic. The siren lights were flashing at the intersection, but they weren't howling. Constable Bateman drove up into University Hill and proceeded to the location of the laboratory in the midst of the campus. Kaj rode into the obscure road in front of the campus where there were plenty of trees on the sidewalk on both sides, obscuring the concrete, modernist façade of the laboratories.

Hamon Neumann Memorial Computer Laboratories was similar to the rest of the buildings on this campus as they had that minimalist construction habit that was popular in the last two decades despite being a newer building. The front of the building contained stairs that went up to the front of the building. The windows that lined the second floor of the building were narrow and tinted so nobody could see inside. Constable Bateman drove past the building and brought the car around to block the other side of the road and create a blockade. The rest of the police cars arrived, and the lights caught the attention of students nearby. Kaj stepped out of the vehicle and looked around and then made his way towards the front of the building where Captain Kingston was directing some of the officers from X-Ray Three-hundred to take position around the perimeter in order to protect the perimeter of the building. Meanwhile, Foxtrot-One-Ten met up with the detectives and Captain Kingston so that they could proceed into the building.

Kaj walked with the detectives into the building and they made their way downstairs to where the computer laboratories were located. The detectives and police units followed a corridor that resembled a high school with lockers at the sides of the walls and students nearby with backpacks, not much older than high school students, observing the sudden police presence with intrigue, and some with fear. They walked around and came to the main laboratory in the basement where a set of double doors with a pin-code lock prevented them from entering. Nonetheless, an officer with a battering ram came over and prepared to burst the door open. With a careful calculation of the ram, the doors swung open, and they barged in, presented their warrant, and asserted themselves to the students bent over and enslaved to their computers. Kaj looked at the room and saw that it was enormous, much larger than the laboratory that Paul had in the basement of Calypso Tower, but similar in design. There were lots of machines that Kaj did not understand what they were for, but added to the aesthetic of a computer lab. The machines had bright lights, there were wires that ran above the ceiling on racks, and there were also machines as Captain Kingston described to the left of the room with reels that rolled on.

"Harlech Police Department, Investigative Services – nobody leave the room, this is a police search. Everybody stay where you are while we complete our duties!" Captain Kingston announced.

"What the hell are you doing?!" a man questioned from a machine in the center of the room. "What is this? You're not going to find anything here!"

"There they are," Captain Kingston remarked, pointing at the machines with the reels. "I want all of them."

The officers went ahead and walked over to the machines that ran the reels.

"Hey!" some students cried out as they went to the machine.

"We'll have to turn the machines off," Captain Kingston remarked.

"Are you nuts? If you turn that off, thousands of researchers will be cut off from their data. This is a university, you one-eyed brute."

"Enough from you," Captain Kingston beckoned. "We're here to seize evidence related to a police matter. Either turn off the machine, or we'll force it off ourselves."

The man grunted. Another, older gentleman appeared from a side office.

"What's going on?" the gentleman questioned.

"Harlech Police Department," Captain Kingston stated. "We're here to seize important evidence in a police investigation, and this warrant signed by a magistrate of the Crown has authorized us to seize evidence believed to be stored on these tapes."

The gentleman looked at the warrant, adjusting his glasses and then looking back at Captain Kingston.

"There's more than a terabyte of data on all those reels combined," the gentleman stated, "if you take those reels, we'll all be left without any data on any of our computers. The entire lifeline of this laboratory is on those tapes… Why don't you just tell us what you want and we'll comply."

"I'm afraid those are details that I'm not able to disclose with you," Captain Kingston remarked. "An attempt was made earlier to assist the investigation, but that time has passed. I'm afraid that in order to ensure the accurate information is brought to us, we're going to have to take all of these and assess the data ourselves."

The gentleman didn't look too pleased. He looked to his colleague behind him, the rude man, and then back to Captain Kingston.

"Preston, why don't you take the system down – one-by-one, and we'll give them what they want," the gentleman stated. "I don't want any trouble."

Preston appeared conflicted. He took in a deep breath and then went to the machines that held the rotors. Before he could turn the machines off, a student stood up from his computer and pushed Preston back to prevent him from turning the machine off.

"Don't do it, man!" the student protested.

"Hey!" Constable Bateman remarked, going around to break him off.

Before the constable could come around, another student stood up and pushed Constable Bateman back and into another tall machine behind, which prompted Kaj to step in and take him down onto floor.

"Hands behind your back!" Kaj shouted. "You're under arrest!"

The words 'under arrest' prompted the rest of the staff to protest within the own laboratory, resulting in a scuffle. Kaj kept the kid down as his peers took down the rest of the students in the room, putting the handcuffs on the student before he brought him to his feet. Kaj looked over to Captain Kingston as he brought the student down onto the table to control him.

"Hey, I'm cooperating, man! Why do you have to be so harsh!" the student complained to Kaj. "Fucking Nazi!"

The boy was not cooperating as he kicked his feet back at Kaj's legs.

"Tell your men to let my boys go," the gentleman argued to Captain Kingston. "Please. They didn't do anything wrong."

Captain Kingston was unmoved by his pleas as he crossed his arms.

"Get these miscreants out of here!" Captain Kingston shouted, waving his hand.

"With pleasure," Kaj remarked, pulling the student back and preparing to escort him out of the room.

Suddenly, the student dropped weight, which prompted a detective to come around and assist Kaj. They lifted the student up and brought him back to his feet so that they could escort him out and bring him to the paddy wagon outside.

"I bet you fucking enjoy being a hero, huh? Fucking fascist fuck!" the student shouted as he was brought over to the paddy wagon. "Let me go! Help! The police are abducting me! Help!"

"Shut it," the detective remarked in a stern voice.

"Fuck you."

Kaj pinned the student againt the side of the truck and then looked down at his trousers. The detective that assisted Kaj stood back and crossed his own arms.

"Do you have any weapons or anything that I should be worried about on your person?" Kaj questioned.

"What the fuck? Who do I look like to you?"

"Answer the question, kid," the detective barked back.

"No, I don't have any weapons, you stupid fucks!"

Kaj padded the side of the trousers to search him, and once he decided there was nothing in his pockets. He read him his rights, brought him around and then loaded him onto the truck. Kaj stepped back and saw some students looked on from behind the police line. The sun had set and it was significantly darker than when they had entered. Kaj stepped back onto the sidewalk and looked over to the detective.

"You alright?" the detective asked.

"Of course."

Kaj looked at the detective. He had medium length chestnut-colored hair and fair skin. He was the same detective that Kaj had to speak to over the phone to brief in regard to police trace and speaking with either Emma or Paul. His name was Detective Gerard Pomphrey.

"Come on, let's get back in there," Detective Pomphrey remarked.

Kaj and Detective Pomphrey returned to the computer laboratory, which was significantly a lot quieter. Two constables positioned themselves at the front door to provide access into the labs. Kaj and Detective Pomphrey entered to join Captain Kingston and another detective, the female with dark hair, Detective Mitchell, as the gentleman turned off the machines himself and they started to unload the reels and put them on tables to be packaged and secured.

I didn't get a chance to go directly to Declan Walham University since Mr. Harrington wanted me to visit Paul one more time to discuss a plan of action for retrieving the data now that we had the probable location where it could be. Due to anonymity of the client, if I were to recover the files, I would inevitably come across the name of the client as well as confidential information not intended for me. In order to avoid that issue, the client had spoken with Paul to have him recover the data instead. Paul argued that he would be unable to do so without knowing exactly where the data was within all of the databases at the university, and furthermore, would somehow need physical access to the computer system in order to pull that data since if he were to log in remotely, it would leave behind a trace to Calypso Tower, the client, and himself. Paul had an idea that he could transfer the data back to the client and then delete it from the servers through me, but the client wasn't pleased with solely that idea because of the probability that it could fail, no less with police on the hunt behind us. The client was adamant that the police could not collect that data. The client directed Paul to somehow develop a means by which the data could be quickly deleted if something were to go wrong, so he developed a computer virus that could do that exact thing and put it on a floppy disk. The plan that Paul and I developed over the afternoon was as such: I would travel to the university and infiltrate the office that Nathan Neumann works from. With all the data that Paul had collected about Piato, he was sure he had a couple guesses to what the password could be, so he gave me a list of handles and passwords to try out. I would have to find the computer terminal that Nathan Neumann works from in order to log in as him. Once in, I would search for the data with the help of Paul and collect the data on a separate floppy disk that I would then deliver to him. This virus was our contingency – before I left Calypso Tower, he gave me the floppy disk and all I had to do was insert the virus into any terminal to set it loose on the database and destroy the data that the client was worried about. I wasn't satisfied with the plan, but it was a plan that worked with the client and would ensure that I was paid. Despite the fact that we had to minimize a trace back to us, I wasn't a computer wizard with the operating system I would encounter, so I would need guidance. Paul and I decided that he could help me if I phoned him from Neumann's office, but that left a trace back to Calypso Tower if the police or university ever decided to check outgoing calls to Calypso Tower. A workaround was established, something that I had picked up from a previous case I had once worked on. Paul and I decided that the only manner to avoid a trace back to the client would be if I phoned Paul at a payphone in a quiet area from where he could guide me from. I chose the only one that I was familiar with, a payphone at La Galleria shopping center nearby. I didn't see any problems with the plan once we had that workaround, so at a quarter to seven o'clock in the evening, I left Calypso Tower and took a taxi to University Hill.

Luckily, I had an extensive knowledge of the campus as an alumni there, so I had the taxi driver take me to twelve-story administrative tower at the edge of campus. The computer laboratory in itself was on the other side of the campus, but I didn't need to go there since the applied science faculty had their office on the ninth floor of the administration tower. The taxi pulled up at the end of a cul-de-sac closest to the plaza in front of the tower. I looked at the tower and saw its horrendous design, a complete twelve-story tower whose structure was composed entirely out of concrete. The windows from the second floor and upwards were square-shaped and tinted. The main floor of the tower had tall rectangular windows on the wider sides. The tower was rectangular shaped with a wider side that faced north and south. I paid the taxi driver and then made my way towards the entrance of the tower before it closed. At this time, most faculty would have gone home while the tower would still be open until eight o'clock in the evening. I entered into the main floor and approached a board that listed all of the departments and their offices that faced the elevators in the corridor ahead. Not much had changed in the last ten years. As

I suspected, Nathan Neumann had an office on the ninth floor, Room 919. I entered the elevator and then rode up to the ninth floor. If Nathan was the type of person to spend late nights in his office, hacking into all sorts of computers, then I had to be cautious that he could either be in his office, or arrive at any point. Additionally, as I rode up the elevator, a thought passed through by brain that he may recognize me if we were to run into each other – I was obviously someone of interest to him given that ever since Glenn had been arrested, I had a run-in with a stranger at the Harlech Public Library. I also couldn't forget the role that I had at Neumann Fairground where he could not have been too far behind. He may have witnessed the incident in the carnival tent where I had kicked his father and taken his whip, leaving him to the mercy of the lions. Although, the attending physician at Harlech General didn't believe the lions and injuries sustained to have been his end. I didn't even witness the lions attacking him. The police were said to have been the end of him. If Nathan had any sort of common sense, he'd realize that, and I believe that to a certain extent, he did realize that since up to now, I had never had any issues or been the victim of any sort of plot of revenge. Neither had Kaj, at least that I knew of. If there was anyone that Nathan had opposed, it was the so-called 'capitalist system,' or in other words, everyday people like Ms. Swanson, who were victims of the senseless attacks by Neumann's followers. I had a moment of silence in my mind as the elevator took me to the ninth floor and then opened its doors.

I stepped into the lobby and looked left and right. Ahead of me was a concrete wall with a corkboard that listed various flyers for the applied science department. The floor at my feet was thin and colored in terracotta red. I proceeded to the right and started to look for Room 919. I heard the sound of a vacuum cleaner nearby as custodial staff cleaned the offices at the end of the day. A majority of the doors around were closed. I arrived finally at Room 919 which was also closed. I took a bobby pin from my hair and produced a screwdriver from my purse. Although it wasn't anything like kicking a door down, over the years, I had learned my own set of skills when it came to picking a lock, as well as my own comfort when it came to breaking the law to get a job done, albeit, with hesitancy and as a last resort. I unlocked the door and then slipped behind before the custodian could come around with the vacuum. I turned around and looked around the dark room. The sunset had dimmed and there was barely enough light in the room to see around since the office looked to the east. I stepped forward as I looked around the office.

I looked around and observed that it was a standard office with bookshelves on the left and right-side, a desk in the center, and a computer atop of the desk. Behind there was a table in front of the window with various papers and folders. I kept the lights off as I came to the bookshelves where there were various books, mostly technical books that had to do with computer science, programming, and such. I walked closer towards the desk and came around to the table near the window. There were various picture frames atop of the table with black and white photos, including a photo of the Neumann travelling circus group with all the carnival freaks and the Hamon Neumann. I picked up another photo next to it which had two boys, one that appeared older while the other appeared younger, side-by-side together in an office with various folder boxes and at least five different variations of a computer model. The male that looked older was dressed in a grey suit with a black tie. He had fair skin, a thick dark brown beard with similar medium-length dark brown hair. He had a thick pair of glasses in front of his eyes. The boy next to him had slightly longer, lighter hair that came down over his forehead. He also had a slim figure and bony face with a pointed jawline. His nose was pointed and he had a clownish grin on his face. He was dressed in a white shirt and light grey pants. He was sat atop of a table while the older male was dressed on a chair next to him. They appeared as if they could be father and son. I looked at the younger male since I thought I recognized him slightly, but I wasn't certain. I wasn't sure which one of these two men were Nathan Neumann, but I assumed that one was Nathan while the other was his business partner, Steven Garrett. There was no chance that the older male was Hamon Neumann and the younger male as Nathan since Hamon had a distinct moustache. I looked at the next picture and saw that it was of one of a female that appeared to be from either the twenties or thirties. I presumed that this female was Nathan's mother. She had similar hair to the boy in the second picture in the same light brown shade, and even their jawline was similar although she had a hooked nose. Once I was done looking at the pictures, I came around and looked at the computer terminal – it was still turned on, but not logged in.

I brought my gloved hand to the mouse to confirm that I was not logged in as Neumann already, and so before I called Paul, I fiddled around with the suggested handles and passwords. The handles were creatively put together by Paul based on common handles that users in his system used, while the passwords were put together from one's used by Piato. I typed out the initial handle, 'NNeumann' and then typed in the first suggested password 'Tapeworm' and then hit enter. It didn't work. I entered 'NNeumann' again and then typed the second suggested password, 'Vendetta' and then hit enter. The password didn't work. I typed the last suggested password, 'Bakunin' and then hit enter, but still it didn't work. I started again with a different handle, this time trying 'Neumann' and going through the passwords, but it didn't work. Lastly, I tried 'NathanN' as well as 'NahmanN,' but neither worked. I was at a loss. I looked at three suggested passwords that had been previously used by Piato, and saw a pattern. Each of the passwords held some significance to Nathan, where Tapeworm was the software he used to transfer data, Vendetta was what he seemingly desired, and Bakunin must have been the anarchist philosopher he idolized. I thought for a moment, looking around the room as I noticed the presence of some of these keywords, such as a book on Tapeworm and a book by Mikhail Bakunin. I looked behind and at the picture of Nathan's father, so I attempted that as a personal password for his account at the university. I tried all three handles and the simple password of 'Hammond' and 'Hamon,' but both failed. I didn't suppose that he'd use his own surname as a password, so I looked at the picture of his mother who he had lost earlier in his life. I attempted to remember what his mother's name was from the biographical novel that I had skimmed. I was at a loss for a brief moment. Suddenly, it came back to me. I typed out 'NNeumann as a username and then 'Melinda' as his password, and it worked. I was in.

I picked up the phone next to me and started to dial the phone number for the phone booth at La Galleria shopping center, and then I waited for Paul to answer. I looked at the time on my watch and saw that it was twenty minutes past seven o'clock in the evening. I had to speed up the process to avoid running into Neumann. I waited for Paul to answer. Paul picked up the phone after a brief minute.

"Hey," I greeted, "it's me. I'm in."

"You were able to log in?" Paul asked.

"Yeah, but not with the passwords you gave me. I had a get a little creative, but now I'm in his account. What do I do now?"

"I wonder if he's a super-user..." Paul questioned.

"How can I check?"

"Nevermind that for now," Paul replied, "it's probable that he's not since it's he's just an employee. Okay, here's what you have to do. First, you're going to need to see what drives are available for you to connect into from the computer. You know that command, right?"

"Yes," I replied, typing to list available drives.

"We've got three drives to choose from. E-drive. C-drive. A-drive."

"I'd start with E-drive. It could be most foreign one."

"Okay," I replied, typing the command to list directories. "Looks like this directory connects to a lot of administrative sub-directories. I'll check the local drive."

I switched to C-drive. A-drive was likely to be the floppy disk directory.

A lot of different file names started to display on the screen, rolling down and down. On the bright side, the operating system restricted file names to twelve characters, including the period and extension (i.e. .doc) which account for a third of the character limit, so in reality, it was eight character names.

"Paul..." I remarked, "it's a lot of files... Do we have to go through each of these?"

"No," Paul denied, "there's a shortcut for us. NDOS is designed to narrow down searches for us. The data that was stolen was written on text files."

NDOS was an abbreviation for Neumann Disk Operating System, which was the operating system that all Neumann Machines used. Paul explained the shortcut for me, and I waited for the list of files in the directory to come to an end. I then narrowed down the search to text files and it brought the list down to ninety-six total files in the local drive.

"Okay, so what are some keywords that these text files might be listed under?"

"Either the hacker kept the original names, or he named them himself. A keyword would be 'Harlech' or anything with 'PG' at the start."

I searched through the ninety-six files. Thankfully, they were in alphabetical order. I went through the files that started with the letter 'H' and there was nothing that started with 'Harlech.' I went through the files that started with 'PG' and there was nothing there that started with 'PG.'

"Nope," I denied, "it's not here."

"Okay… try the digits of the telephone number for my laboratory," Paul suggested. "That's seven-digits."

"Okay," I replied, "looking down at files named by number. "No."

"Damn… alright," Paul replied, "then the files aren't on the local drive. We'll have to try the network drive that this computer connects to."

I typed the command to switch to the E-drive and looked at all the sub-directories. The sub-directories were named after local departments. I suspected that these would be associated with a network at the administrative tower as opposed to the entire campus. I opened 'Applied Science' and then opened the sub-directory for 'Neumann,' but there wasn't much inside. Only a measly twenty-two files, and a lot of them had to do with computer science.

"Paul, I don't think that this computer is it," I stated. "In fairness, Neumann wouldn't use this computer when he hacks. He uses the one at the computer science laboratory since you could probably dial-up there. I can't dial-up here. This is his work computer. Should I sneak into the computer lab?"

"If he's not here, then he's probably there right now," Paul warned. "Hm, I seem to remember before I left Declan Walham that there used to be a central network room somewhere in the main building of the university. All computers connected to that room, and you could access any computer from that terminal. A safer option would be to make your way to that room and then dial-in to the laboratory…"

"We don't have that telephone number, remember?" I replied.

"No, but there should be a text file somewhere that provides all of those numbers to assist the faculty with connecting to each department. If you go to the mainframe, you could possibly find that…"

The line cut out.

"Paul? Hello?" I questioned, but there was no response.

I thought for a moment that Paul had run out of time on the payphone, so I put the phone down and attempted to dial him.

"I'm sorry, but the number that you are trying to reach is unavailable. Please hang up or press pound for more options."

I put the phone down. I still had a telephone connection, but I couldn't dial him. I looked at the computer screen and decided to log out so that I could make my way to this central computer room in the main building. I approached the door out of the office and slipped through to the other side. I entered into the corridor and noticed that the hallway was dark with only a flood light at the end of the corridor that provided light. I wasn't sure if the custodian was still around since I couldn't hear the vacuum cleaner anymore. I travelled to the end of the corridor and came around to the elevators where there were some more floodlights that provided light. I clicked a button to call an elevator, but the button didn't light up as I pressed it. I waited for a moment, but no elevator showed up. At this point, I believed that the power had gone out for some reason. I was deeply suspicious of the circumstances, but there was backup power, but inevitably, I deduced that the telephone connection out of the campus must have been down, which was why Paul had cut out. I looked around for a moment and then decided to step towards the fire exit so that I could go down the staircase. I put my purse on my other shoulder and crossed it across my jacket as I went down the flight of stairs with urgency – I had to get to the central computer room at once.

Kaj crossed his arms as the last of the reels were packed into cardboard boxes and hauled out by a member from the Lincoln Beat and a detective. He held a dissatisfied look on his face, eyes looking around the laboratory as if something was bothering him. In the last half hour, the radio channel had received a few calls from dispatch of a potential anti-police student demonstration in the plaza as a student had appeared with a sign that said, 'Pigs Should Go Home' and a lot of people had started to join that student. From one person to another, word had started to disseminate amongst the student and faculty population, and a protest was inevitable, but up to X-Ray to contain. Still, despite all that had occurred up to this point, and more to come, Kaj held his tongue as the last box was taken and it was now time for them to leave.

"I hope you're satisfied," the older gentleman remarked. "You won't find anything in those reels other than data from this laboratory and a slew of programs that the likes of your minds couldn't even comprehend."

"I hope for your sake that's true, otherwise we will be back," Captain Kingston remarked, turning to Kaj and Pomphrey. "I believe that it's time that we leave, gents."

Pomphrey uncrossed his arms and nodded.

"Wait," Kaj finally said, uncrossing his arms, "Captain, are we sure that this is it?"

"Of course, it's it. It's all of our life's work," the gentleman barked back. "What more do you want?"

"What are you on about, lad?" Captain Kingston questioned Kaj.

Captain Kingston and Detective Pomphrey both looked to him.

"If this is the data that we're hoping for, don't you think that it's been a little too easy and too accessible for us. All it took was to break down the door, and a brawl with a couple of students. As much as I'd like to believe the Person of Interest we've been after never expected for us to catch up to him, I hardly believe he wouldn't be paranoid to put up a bigger barrier in the way, no less, keep data like the type that he was collecting away from other students."

Captain Kingston looked at Kaj and then back to the gentleman.

"Is this the only room with reels like these?" Captain Kingston asked him.

"Well, I mean," the gentleman remarked, "I don't know exactly what you're looking for since you've been so secretive..."

"Answer the question," Pomphrey snapped.

"Every department has their own computer lab for their own network," the gentleman answered, "and this lab takes care of this department. Every lab has their own storage system. I don't know what it is you want, but believe me, only our department research is on the reels that you've grabbed."

"So, out of interest of not accidentally losing all of your precious data when it gets to our boys, who by the way, can be a bit clumsy, why don't you spit it out and tell us where the rest of the databases here can be found," Pomphrey threatened.

The gentleman held his head and didn't immediately respond.

"The databases at each department only store what is needed, while the rest is taken to a facility nearby that stores all of that data as a type of archive. All of the data is still accessible technically, but only if you dial in."

"Can you show us where this facility is located? Would you be able to identify reels that belong to your department?"

"I could... but I don't have access inside. Access is restricted only to those that work within that department, and all of that is maintained by Information Management & Information Technology Services. I can't get you into the department."

"That's okay, we have our ways of getting into places," Detective Pomphrey replied. "I'll go with him since I'll detract attention."

"Very good," Captain Kingston responded, "I'll see what the status is with the protest so we can transport those reels."

Detective Pomphrey and the gentleman left the room. Kaj stayed with Captain Kingston.

"I noticed that something was bothering you," Captain Kingston remarked once they were alone. "I appreciate that you spoke your mind, because even I had a discomfort with the whole situation. Hopefully we can find what we need in those archives..."

Kaj looked around the laboratory to ensure they were properly alone. His eyes were looking for someone, and I was sure that at this time, his eyes were looking for Nathan. He wasn't here however, just as at this time, he was neither at his office. Suddenly, the lights went out as the blackout affected them too. Kaj and Captain Kingston were both stunned at the sudden power failure, but the emergency floodlights turned on and gave them a bit of light. Kaj looked around as if someone was with them.

"What the hell's happened?" Captain Kingston questioned. "Let's leave and join the others upstairs."

"Command-One," Captain Kingston said over the radio.

"Go ahead for Command-One," Captain Simpson replied.

"Command-One, this is Delta-Thirty. We've just been hit with a power outage at the laboratories. What's the status on the demonstration at the main plaza?"

Captain Kingston's request was met with a pause.

"Delta-Thirty, the number of students at the protest is quickly gathering support from other students. We're estimating at least forty to fifty people right now, but the protest at this time is peaceful."

"Ten-Four, we've cleared from the laboratory, but have received word of additional storage at an area within campus."

"Ten-Four."

Kaj and Captain Kingston came out to the street by the entrance into the laboratory. At either side of the street, behind the police cars, there were rowdy groups of students who were kept back by members from X-Ray Three-hundred. The paddy wagon with the arrested students had already left, but the wagon with the boxes for transport remained on standby. Captain Kingston went over to coordinate a place to bring the truck and relocate X-Ray Three-hundred. Kaj remained on standby nearby as he waited for updated orders. Suddenly, the radio was met with the sound of furious students in the background as Detective Pomphrey attempted to communicate with them.

"Delta-Thirty," Detective Pomphrey spoke over the radio.

"Delta-Thirty," Captain Kingston repeated.

"Delta-Thirty, I'm near the main plaza on my way to Information Management, but I've run into some protesters who're heckling my escort. I'm behind the lines of the protest and I'm going to need some backup."

Captain Kingston immediately looked over to Kaj.

"Go to him," Captain Kingston said to Kaj before bringing his radio up, "Ten-Four, Delta-Three-Twenty-five. Hotel-Two-Twenty-three copies and is enroute."

Kaj immediately left and went down the street, reaching an intersection and continuing forward to go through an alleyway behind the science building. The end of the alleyway led to a main road that went up to the plaza. Kaj hurried through and saw X-Ray One-hundred ahead, maintaining the peace as the noisy crowd protested from the plaza with their vile signs that swore damnation against the police. The police stayed at the end of the cul-de-sac and kept their distance from the protesters who lingered on the other side of the plaza. Kaj looked ahead, but couldn't see Detective Pomphrey nearby, so he went ahead towards the left-side of the protesters, and around a corner underneath a shelter of the concrete building nearby. There, Kaj saw Detective Pomphrey in an argument with some students as he attempted to get by, but they blocked the main doors into the building. Kaj immediately ran forward to support him.

"Get out of the way," Kaj demanded.

"Blow me," the protester replied.

"Dammit, Kaj, just arrest these losers."

Kaj didn't wait for another second to argue. He grabbed the student in the center that had just cursed at him and took him down to the ground.

"You're under arrest," Kaj stated before taking his radio, "Hotel-Two-Two-Three."

"Hotel-Two-Two-Three," dispatch replied.

"I've got a Ten-Thirty-one at the Howard Center east entrance at DWU; going to need a wagon."

"Ten-Four."

"Hey, let go of him!" a student cried out.

"Cram it, tough guy," Pomphrey replied, "just back off."

"You back off, you fucking pig."

The student spat at Detective Pomphrey, which resulted in him immediately apprehending him. Kaj pushed back at the other student as he attempted to get him off of his friend who Kaj was now atop of. The students at the protest noticed and started to gather around them. Their shouts were loud, calling for Kaj and Pomphrey to let go of the students that the captured. Kaj picked up the student and pinned him against the door.

"Kaj, call for more backup," Pomphrey recommended.

"Hotel Two-Two-Three."

"Hotel Two-Two-Three," dispatch replied.

"Ten-Thirty-three at the Howard Centre, east entrance at Declan Walham University. I repeat, Ten-Thirty-three at the Howard Centre east entrance at DWU. Need X-Ray One-hundred to assist."

"Ten-Four."

Kaj took out his baton, extended it, and swung it at a student as he attempted to get in close.

"Back off!" Detective Pomphrey shouted. "Get back!"

Kaj looked to the side as he saw the gentleman that they had been escorting was still nearby, sat down as if he had fallen and on the ground.

X-Ray One-hundred arrived and began to get into a fight with the students as they surrounded Kaj and Pomphrey, which stirred their attention towards them and got them to back off. Some members came around to support Kaj and Pomphrey as they held their arrests. A few students continued to confront them and shout vile words at them. The members that came to support Kaj and Pomphrey formed a line between them and started to get them to back off. Kaj could see the fight that ensued behind the line as others challenged the police. X-Ray One-hundred held on while X-Ray Two-hundred came around to assist.

"Dammit, we're going to need this entire plaza clear if we're going to get the wagon in. No way with all these idiots out of here," Detective Pomphrey remarked.

A couple of regular members from the Lincoln Beat arrived to assist Kaj and Pomphrey with their arrests.

"Pass me some cuffs," Pomphrey remarked.

A member passed him some cuffs.

"You're under arrest for assault against a peace officer," Pomphrey stated before he went through his rights. "Do you understand?"

"Fuck you," the student replied.

"Get this piece of shit out of here," Pomphrey remarked, passing him off to a constable. "You two, get that other piece of shit off Constable Kejsaren and get him out of here too."

"Yes, sir," Constable Bateman replied, taking the student away.

"Are you alright, Kaj?" Pomphrey asked.

"I should be asking you that," Kaj responded.

"Dammit, where'd that guy go?" Pomphrey questioned, looking around. "Whatever, he said that this is the building and IMITS are located in the basement. "We're going to need this area clear though."

"Delta-Thirty," Pomphrey radioed as he switched back to their channel.

"Delta-Thirty," Captain Kingston remarked.

"We're at the building, but this protest is turning into a riot. We're going to need it clear before we get the wagon over here."

"Ten-Four," Captain Kingston replied. "See if you and Hotel-Two-Twenty-three can find another way in. I'll inform X-Ray of the need to clear the area."

"Copy that."

"I'll go around and find another way in since I'm in plain clothes," Detective Pomphrey stated. "You stay here."

Kaj stayed put as he looked around. His eyes wandered at the continued fight between some students and some members of X-Ray, but his eyes roamed as if he was looking for someone in particular. I wasn't sure if Kaj knew what Nathan Neumann looked like since I had forgotten what he had looked like, but there was a chance that he remembered from the trial, even though he didn't even recall that Hammond Neumann had a son. On the other hand, perhaps an image existed in Kaj's mind of what this perpetrator must have looked like, or maybe, Kaj was familiar with the computer mogul. Kaj stayed where he was until he couldn't anymore and had to go in to defend a constable that was having trouble with a student.

The protest had turned into an intense brawl between students and police. A facilities car that had been parked nearby had been set aflame. A lot more students seemed to have joined as even as the fight went on, it surely did much to flare out. Kaj recovered from an arrest and then noticed the arrival of a van and several wagons to haul the arrestees back to the station. The protest had met its crescendo.

"Attention," a loud P.A. announced from the van, "this is the Harlech Police Department. This gathering has been declared an unlawful assembly and you are now ordered to disperse and leave the area in ten minutes, or you will be suffered to immediate arrest. Failure to disperse will be determined an unlawful act and will be dealt with the appropriate level of force as authorized by the Criminal Code of Canada. Please follow the directions of the officers who will assist those that are willing to leave in a peaceful manner. Do not return to this area."

The audio repeated itself. X-Ray Three-hundred came around to join the fight and slowly but surely the fight started to calm down as students grouped together and were backed off. The plaza was cleared, and the paddy wagon was brought around to load arrestees. Captain Kingston came around to meet with Kaj.

"Where's Detective Pomphrey?" Kingston questioned.

"He went to find another entrance," Kaj replied.

"Nevermind that, this'll do now that the protest is under control," Kingston responded. "I just had a word with the university president, and he has me informed that the cause of the power failure is unknown. He also mentioned that the university facilities had detected an unwanted person in their computer system and suspect that he had caused the power failure – the subject, none other than Piato. He's here and we must find him at once."

Detective Pomphrey arrived to join up with them.

"What's going on?" Detective Pomphrey questioned.

Kingston repeated what he had said and then added, "I want this hacker found. I've asked the president to have his team cooperate with us for this search. He's put me in contact with the supervisor and I've been given the telephone number associated with the breach. It's said to be coming from the Howard Centre, or that immediate area. Gerard, I want you to continue with your maneuver to the database – I've asked the supervisor for support in that field and he's given me the pin-code. Kaj, I want you to assist Gerard in that field while we get a perimeter on the building. Whoever this hacker is, he isn't far. Am I understood?"

"Yes, sir."

"What about the others?" Pomphrey asked.

"I have them on other duties at the moment," Kingston responded, "we're spread a bit thin here, lads. You're my two best men on the job right now. Don't let me down."

"We won't, sir," Pomphrey responded, looking to Kaj. "Come on, we've got this."

"We're on it," Kaj encouraged before he left.

"Good luck, lads."

From the ninth floor of the administration tower, I came down to the ground floor only to stop as I approached the exit as I noticed the stack of smoke in the distance and march of students on the road ahead, going towards the art building nearby. There were also flocks of them in groups, discussing amongst each other with signs as if they were preparing for something. I wasn't sure what was going on at this moment, but with the sound of police sirens, I could be sure that whatever it was, it was not good. I stayed in the lobby and decided to return to the elevator so that I could travel into the basement level. I came into the underground that stretched the entire campus so that students could travel from building to building without having to step outdoors.

The sublevel of the administration tower was a small lobby with study spaces around and a corridor that led westward to the sublevel of the art building. The walls of this underground consisted of concrete, while the floors were small terracotta tiles. The area was darker than usual, but lit by the same floodlights kept on by auxiliary power. I walked down the short corridor and entered into the wider corridor that consisted of the art building. The art building was square-shaped with the perimeter in the sublevel being the corridors and the centre on the surface being an open courtyard. On the surface, the perimeter consisted of wide pillars through which staircase ran up to the second floor. On the second floor, there were narrower corridors and also classrooms that looked into the courtyard. In the underground, the centre consisted of lecture halls, washrooms, and other separate rooms. There were also some coffee shops and restaurants on occasion as this area was like a shopping centre almost. I came into the corridor and was near the northeast corner on my right that connected and led to the archeology and ethnology department. I began to remember the layout of the underground on the northwest corner, my faculty building branched off. I wasn't going to go in that direction as I instead went left and towards the southeast that connected to the applied science building. I needed to travel to the centre of the university where facilities maintenance and information management (IMITS) were located on the lower levels.

I moved down the corridor, going south towards applied science, and it was quiet as most students had evacuated since the power outage, while few, still confused, remained. After a hundred-meters, I arrived at the corner that connected to applied science where there were lots of tables and chairs around. I continued westward and went towards the corner that connected with the centre block and also the science building. Likewise, the corridor was only one-hundred meters and consisted of the same mix of lockers, exits through staircases to the aboveground, and lecture halls and other spaces. I arrived at the end and travelled through to the center of the school, which was the Howard Centre. The Howard Centre went deeper into the earth than the art building tunnels, going down to a total of seven floors below where there was the steam plant that kept the lights on. From sublevel one, I could look down behind the railings to the pit beneath. Above on the main floor, the Howard Centre connected with the main plaza where at this time, although unknown to me, the riot was breaking out. If I were to continue forward, I would arrive at the athletics department and business centre. However, I was right where I wanted to be, going down into the depths to access IMITS. Since the elevators were down, I moved to the staircase and started to go down floor by floor, reaching the bottom where there was a student space and also a set of stairs that were restricted by a door handle that required either a pin code or a key. Since I had neither, I picked the lock to get through into some more concrete tunnels, but these less decorated, as I was now in the maintenance depths.

I had never been here before, so I was now in unfamiliar territory, but luckily there were signs that pointed right for the steam plant, while right for maintenance. I didn't want to go to the steam plant, so I figured that IMITS would be with maintenance. I went left and went around the curved corridor, one of which went to a key shop, some workshops, and a paint room before finally the door to IMITS. I picked the lock and entered into an office space with a door behind that led into the laboratory with rows upon rows of database machines all connected to a terminal in the corner. I walked towards the terminal and signed in with Neumann's account, and then I took the floppy disk and inserted it into the drive. I booted up the disk, copied its contents, and then clicked the executable file and typed the command to run. I stayed put for a moment to ensure that the command ran as I expected, and without having to much else, the screen pulled down lines and lines, each of which were moving too fast for me to read as I assumed that it searched for the files that belonged to my client. I had never seen a program run so quickly, but at the same time, I had never seen a computer like this one that was connected to so many other machines.

At the end of the code, I read that the program was unsuccessful. I moved the program to a different drive and then executed it, but before I could hit run, the program was missing, almost as if it had been deleted, or moved elsewhere. I attempted to re-copy the program from the floppy disk, but as I attempted to type, I couldn't type anymore. Then, the terminal began to type itself and present a message. I read and my eyes widened with fright as if the computer spoke to me, but it wasn't the computer – it was Nathan.

'Hello Catherine,' the terminal read, 'or should I call you, 'Emma' instead?'

I froze as I finally recalled who Nathan was, that boy that had talked to me in the warehouse at the aquarium where I was kept tied to the chair – that was Nathan.

The terminal allowed me to type, and I typed out, 'Who is this?'

'You don't know who I am? Did you really come this far to not find out my name?'

"I know exactly who you are," I replied in person, and then I typed, 'Nahman.'

'I do not use that name.' Nathan replied.

I quickly typed, 'Why are you doing this? You created an empire, and now you've taken to petty crime?'

A brief moment passed and Nathan replied, 'At a certain point, wealth loses its worth to a person. I suppose I never had an affinity for the material. There is not much to me that money can buy me that I desire. I cannot even be proud that this wealth was my own considering I had ridden on the success of others and by chance and opportunity find myself here.'

'What do you mean?' I replied.

'The operating system that I had designed was a project between myself and my partner at the time. Luckily, we both had the right connections that funded our project and allowed our project to eventually reach the market to a point now where 30% of computers run our software, while 15% of all computers use our hardware worldwide. By my calculations, these percentages are larger in Harlech where more than half of all computers run our software and nearly half of them use our hardware. It was never my own work, or my own efforts that landed me where I am now, but unlike my partner, business had never been my pleasure.'

'What is your pleasure?'

'You know what that is,' Nathan replied, 'and that is why you are here, isn't it? To put an end to my pleasures, as your meddling had put an end to my father?'

'I did not kill your father.'

'I know,' Nathan replied, 'and it has been these last fifteen years that I've tried to understand what had happened all those years ago, where my father went wrong, and what I could do better to improve upon and achieve what he did not achieve. I did not need a circus or railroads to reach the entirety of North America as I am now privileged to access computers and telephone networks that stretch the entire continent and beyond to access whatever database I wish without so much as leaving the city. With all the resources at my disposal, I could now avenge my father and punish those that had punished me, taken my father from me, taken my friends and my life from me, while also doing better than him to achieve our mutual goals.'

'What are your goals?'

'Do you not remember my father's goals? I will explain them to you again… My father aimed to create chaos within the city, cooperating with anarchists from city to city, which was our own network. The goal was never to overthrow the authority, but to take control by other means: subversion. The reason why my father and I had our connections with students was because these were the minds of the future, easily malleable and easily manipulated when presented the injustices of society. For that reason, our followings were in the school systems, and for that reason, I have made Declan Walham University the place that I reside at because I am at home here. Although a minority of us had been arrested, the criminal justice system could only keep us for so long, and with changing opinions, we have easily been reintegrated into society with the majority that had not been arrested where we can continue our previous work with each other. Fifteen years later, an entire generation has now found itself in a position able to take control of the system that had once punished us, whether that is as politicians, administrators, teachers at your local school, or a professor at your local college. We are now everywhere, and I am here where I have grown my own cult out of my own students, as well as those that I know across the world from the United States to Europe.'

I looked around as I waited for Nathan to continue with his confession, and I eyed a printer nearby that could print this out. I turned back to the screen to watch him continue, but he had stopped.

'So, you intend to educate an entire generation again? Is that it?'

'No,' Nathan responded, 'that is the cusp of my intentions. My father intended to use his followers to sow chaos through public disobedience and defiance to demoralize society. I intend the same as well, but through covert means that could not expose us. The glory of computers and the interconnectedness allows us to reach each other and act by pseudonymous means. With a computer in every home, I have expanded my operations with the changing times and unleashed my followers to steal from the rich and sow chaos through the web.'

'So, you're a bunch of hooligans then,' I responded, 'I thought more of you, Piato.'

'Do not be so insolent,' Nathan responded, 'I am not finished yet. I have had the privilege to have many resources at my disposal, and my computers in itself were one of them. As I said, there is at least one in every other home in Harlech, and with that much access, I've taken it upon myself to ensure that I have a key to every other home. In the room you are in now, there are terabytes upon terabytes of data related to everyday people, collected for research purposes so that I could better understand people, and with that data, better subvert them. This project has been my own, because in truth, I do not understand people, but by analyzing their habits, I hope that I can effectively subvert and if possible, convert them.'

I thought for a moment, and then I understood, so I typed, 'Is that what Eldon was doing then? He was collecting data?'

'Eldon was a piece of that machine and there are many like him, although none as greedy.'

'Did you kill him?'

'I did not, but I will tell you that his unwillingness to back down on his desire for more resulted in his end. Although he was my friend, he would have seen my end too, just as your friend had seen to my father too through him. At that time, however, we did not have the resources that I have and that was our lesson. I have been able to self-fund my operations, and my followers too as I have instructed them in the art to steal from creditors and stab those financiers in the back that had stabbed us too.'

I didn't understand much in that last sentence, but the rest of this confession had made sense to me and answered the questions I had. Although I could have supposed that Nathan had just confessed his plot to me by his own ego, I noticed that there was a trickle of code behind this dialogue. I didn't realize, but he had not confessed for the sake of confession, but to stall me from realizing that he had been running a program.

'What are you doing?' I typed out, attempting to execute a stop command, but I couldn't since I was not a super-user. 'Stop this.'

'I'm afraid I cannot,' Nathan responded, 'with the police on my tail, I'm afraid that I have to commandeer this program that you've sought to bring into the system for my own purposes: to rapidly delete all of this data that could criminalize me. The police will leave emptyhanded, and even if you are left behind, they'll never believe the words of one person. You can never prove who I am, as I am just Piato.'

I quickly hit the print command to cause our conversation to print out.

'What are you doing?' Nathan questioned. 'I saw that – do not think that any of this can incriminate me. You are powerless to stop me and by the time the police arrive, I will be gone.'

'We shall see,' I responded, but to no reply.

I started to panic. Although I could be certain that my client's data would be deleted, I was woeful at the fact that all of the data would now be deleted, including that data which would incriminate Nathan and the downfall of his plot. I supposed that it was none of my business since I wasn't a police investigator, but the police were here, and if I left now, I could be held responsible for obstruction of justice since this was my computer virus that I had brought with me. I took the floppy disk out from the disk drive and then hesitated to act. I started to debate whether I should stay or leave.

Kaj and Detective Pomphrey entered into the Howard Centre and walked down the short corridor to reach the top of the overview that looked down to the sublevel. They stood near the bookstore that was closed and various other shops in the immediate area.

"Come on," Pomphrey said as he passed the elevator, "the old man said that the control room should be on the lowest floor."

Kaj and Detective Pomphrey made their way through the building and followed the exit signs that led to the staircase that went down to the bottom. Kaj noticed that Pomphrey was walking with a slight limp, which told him that he was slightly injured from the scuffle above. Once at the bottom, they went to the same double set of doors that I had entered through, but used the code to get through. They then entered into the curved corridor, went down the maintenance end, and reached the IMITS office space where they kicked down the door and then went through to the database room with guns drawn. Kaj and Detective Pomphrey took cover at the door just beforehand to prepare to breach. They nodded to each other and then Pomphrey opened the door, walking through and bringing his gun towards the computer terminal ahead. Kaj entered through and raised his gun towards the same direction, but there was nobody at the computer.

I took cover behind a database as I heard them come through, but as I looked from around the dark corner, I recognized Kaj and the police detective. I held the papers that had printed in my hand and continued to hesitate if I should go around them, or present myself with the possibility to assist. I didn't recognize Detective Pomphrey since I had never met him, and I wasn't sure if he would be a friend or a foe. I decided I would go around them as they approached the terminal, coming up from behind and looking towards the door from where my freedom was guaranteed. I quickly went across, but before I left, I paused for a moment and turned around. I took cover behind the door, looking around the corner to see what they would do with the problem I had created for them.

Kaj and Detective Pomphrey put their guns away and looked at the terminal.

"What the hell is going on?" Detective Pomphrey remarked at the line of code that ran across the screen. "Do you know what this is?"

"No," Kaj denied, "I'm not familiar with junk like this, but if I had to guess, something is certainly going on."

"I'm seeing 'delete' come across the screen over and over again," Pomphrey remarked. "You don't think our hacker is attempting to delete the data? How do we stop him?"

"I don't know," Kaj complained. "I'd have to call someone."

"Fat chance with the phones down," Pomphrey remarked, "I'll radio the captain to let him know."

I sighed, turned around, and before I decided to help them, I stepped around and decided that I would help them after all. Kaj turned his neck to me as he saw me appear, while Pomphrey quickly pulled his handgun out and raised it towards me, but Kaj quickly stopped him from aiming it at me as he pushed it away.

"Stop," Kaj remarked, "she's harmless, at least to us. What are you doing here?"

"I told you that I had unfinished business," I remarked, holding the papers in my hand, "but I see that there's a problem."

"Who is she, Kaj?" Pomphrey questioned.

"Her name is Emma Monique," Kaj responded, "she's the one that helped you yesterday with the trace. She's a private investigator whose helped us get to where we are."

"Oh…" Detective Pomphrey responded, "so what's she doing here?"

"Emma is here on personal business for a client who had data stolen by the hacker," Kaj responded. "Emma, do you know what's going on?"

I stepped closer as Detective Pomphrey put his handgun away.

"Looks like all of the data is being deleted," I remarked, "if I had to guess, the hacker – I mean, Piato, is erasing his tracks."

"So, that son of a bitch came here and is deleting our evidence," Pomphrey remarked with a disgruntled tone. "Can you stop it?"

"Let me try," I replied, putting the papers into my purse and then reaching over to the console.

I sensed Kaj looking into my purse at the papers I had just hid. I put my hand on the keyboard and entered the commands to terminate the program, which I had already tried, but to no avail.

"I can't," I concluded to them, "if I had to suspect, I'm not a super-user, which means that I cannot override this command that was issued by someone who is a super-user, notably our hacker."

"You mean he's not logged in as a super-user?" Kaj questioned. "Who is he logged in as?"

I entered the command to show the login for NNeumann.

"NNeumann?" Pomphrey questioned. "Strange… isn't that the founder of Neumann?"

"Yeah," Kaj dismissed, "but he's logged in as that, so what's going on?"

"Looks like whoever executed this command didn't use this terminal, but did so from somewhere else," I replied, looking at Kaj.

"Can you trace him? Paul was able to trace the hacker, so maybe he's not got this intricate tail behind him and we can directly trace him."

I paused for a moment and then attempted to remember the command that Paul had used when he initially traced the hacker to Ms. Swanson's house. I remembered and typed it out for user Piato, and it showed a telephone number.

"Yeah, he's connecting from somewhere," I replied, thinking for a moment, "and since the power is down, that must mean that telephone lines out of the campus are down too."

"So?" Detective Pomphrey questioned.

I looked at him and replied, "If the phone lines are down, then the only lines that are available are local connections within the campus. The hacker, or at least, the terminal that he's using to execute this command must be from somewhere on campus. If you want to salvage whatever data that remains, you'll need to find that terminal and stop it."

"Okay, so we just find out where he's connecting from," Pomphrey concluded. "Let's run that telephone number by dispatch to get the location. Come on, Kaj."

"Wait," Kaj responded, "how do we stop the program? I'm not really familiar with this system."

"You just have to enter the 'stop' command," I replied.

"Okay…" Kaj responded, "I'll go and find this terminal."

"Alone?" Pomphrey questioned.

"You've done enough walking and if we get into another fight, such as with this hacker, you might not be in a state to safely continue. Besides, I need someone to stay with Emma and communicate with me in case I need help."

Detective Pomphrey hesitated to agree, but then said, "Fine, I'll stay here and talk to you, but if you need help, make sure to call for it."

"I will," Kaj responded, "alright, let's run this number with dispatch."

"Delta Three-Twenty-five," Detective Pomphrey communicated once he changed channels on his radio.

"Delta Three-Twenty-five," dispatch replied.

Detective Pomphrey gave them the telephone number and they waited for a moment to reply. The telephone number originated from the business centre nearby.

I gave Kaj a quick rundown on how to get there without going outside and then said, "Be careful, Kaj. He could be out there. I suspect that he's connecting through the departmental computer lab, so you should make your way there."

"Alright," Kaj affirmed, "I will. Wish me luck."

Kaj left and began to go back upstairs, but stopping at sublevel one as I had directed him so that he could follow the underground tunnels and evade the plaza. Kaj ran with his gun drawn, checking his corners and ensuring his own safety as he made his way from the Howard Centre and down the corridor that went to the business centre. Once

Kaj left, I started to check how many files there were and at what pace the deletion was occurring, and in total, by my estimate, we had less than forty-five minutes left to stop the process before every file in the databases were deleted.

Kaj entered the business centre and looked around. The centre was three-stories tall with an open space in the centre and corridors left and right with railings that looked down the centre from the second and third floor. Kaj assumed that he would find the computer laboratory on the ground floor, so he stayed put and began to check the rooms around until he found a tunnel at the back that went around the perimeter of the building. He went around and found a door that read 'Computer Lab' and kicked the door down, entering through, and finding a terminal that was turned on. Kaj checked the room to ensure that he was alone and then went to the terminal.

"Delta Three-Twenty-five," Kaj spoke over the radio.

"Delta Three-Twenty-five," Pomphrey replied.

"Delta Three-Twenty-five, I've found the room, but no sight of the target. I'll try and terminate the program."

Kaj typed the command, but he was unable to stop the process.

"Delta Three-Twenty-five, I'm unable to stop the program."

"Why can't he stop it?" Pomphrey asked me.

I thought for a moment then looked back at him as I replied, "He's not there. He's covered his tracks again. He's using the terminal at the business centre to mask his true location, delaying us from finding him. Tell Kaj to trace Piato."

"You better explain to him," Pomphrey responded, passing me the radio.

I explained the command to trace the user connected to the system. Kaj carefully typed the command and then waited for a phone number to appear. He repeated that phone number back to us and then I wrote it down on a piece of paper.

"Hotel Two-Twenty-three," Kaj stated over the radio.

"Hotel Two-Twenty-three," dispatch responded.

Kaj gave them the phone number and waited for their reply. The connection was from the Science Department.

"Ten Four," Kaj responded over the radio before he changed channels, "Delta Three-Twenty-five, the connection is from the Science Department. I'm making my way over there."

"Copy that," Pomphrey responded.

"Hotel Two-Twenty-three," I stated as I grabbed the radio, "be advised, the current process is estimated to be complete in thirty minutes. I repeat, estimated completion in thirty minutes."

"Ten-Four," Kaj replied before he left and returned back through the business centre.

Both Pomphrey and I turned around as we met with Captain Kingston (who I barely recognized fifteen years later).

"What's going on?" Captain Kingston questioned. "You – I've seen you before, but where?"

"This is Emma Monique, sir," Detective Pomphrey replied, "we've run into a bit of an issue and Ms. Monique is assisting us troubleshoot this problem while at the same time, we have a chance that we could apprehend the hacker."

"You'll have to explain to me in detail, detective," Kingston responded as he looked at the computer screen.

Detective Pomphrey began to explain what was occurring while I continued to hold my breath as Kaj made his way to the Science Building. He returned to the Howard Centre on sublevel one and then went through the tunnel that came to the sublevel of the Art Building. He then went directly towards the Science Building, which brought him through a narrower corridor that replaced the tiled terracotta floor with terracotta-colored linoleum floor. Kaj searched around the narrow corridors, seeing lots of signs for different types of biological and chemical laboratories until he finally found a room in the corner that led into a computer lab. By that time, Detective Pomphrey finished explaining the situation to Captain Kingston who stayed with us as we waited to hear from Kaj.

Kaj entered the lab and came across two males huddled at the terminal. Both of them wore dark clothes with sweater hoodies that had the black hoods pulled over. They also wore bandanas around their face. Kaj aimed his handgun towards them as he stopped.

"Harlech Police," Kaj shouted, "put your hands up!"

Kaj looked at the students and didn't see either of them as Nathan. A student held a baseball bat in his hand.

"Go ahead, shoot us," the student remarked, "you're not getting to this computer."

Kaj tensed his finger on the body of the handgun and stepped closer to them. He then put his handgun away and took out his pepper spray to mace them with the solution and cause them to reach for their eyes. Kaj kept his eyes averted as the flow of the spray came towards him, but once clear, he pulled them onto the floor and then came to the computer. Kaj tensed his finger over the keyboard and attempted to terminate the computer with twenty minutes left to completion, but the command didn't work again.

"Dammit!" Kaj shouted, banging his fist on the table and then reaching for his mic. "Delta Three-Twenty-five."

"Delta Three-Twenty-five," Pomphrey responded.

"Delta Three-Twenty-five, I'm at the Science Building, but the command isn't working again. He's not here."

Kaj ran the trace command and saw the phone number come up.

"Keep trying to trace the source," Detective Pomphrey encouraged, "you've got less than twenty mikes left."

"Ten-Four..." Kaj responded, changing channels, "Hotel Two-Twenty-three..."

"Hotel Two-Twenty-three," dispatch responded.

Kaj read out the number for them to give the location and then waited. They responded with the telephone number being associated with the university library.

"Ten-Four," Kaj responded, "please send units to the computer lab in the basement of the Science Building to apprehend two assailants in an investigation."

"Copy that," dispatch replied.

Kaj began to exit the room while I reached for the radio to talk to him.

"Hotel Two-Twenty-three," I remarked, "you won't be able to access the library from the tunnels. The only way in is through the main plaza on the surface."

"Copy that, Echo Mike," Kaj replied as he made his way to the art building tunnels.

"The protesters have set up their demonstration in that area, right in front of the library," Captain Kingston remarked. "He won't be able to get through. I'll contact Command-One to clear the area for him."

"That'll be messy," Pomphrey commented. "I'll head up…"

"No, stay here," Captain Kingston replied. "I'll go, but you stay with Ms. Monique in case she needs assistance."

"Okay…"

Kaj came up a staircase and exited out near the art building courtyard that overlooked the plaza where the initial riot had occurred. He went down, came to the steps that looked towards the main plaza behind where the protesters remained in front of a four-story concrete building on the right. The noise from the automated voice that told the protesters to disband continued to cry out and Operational Planning Support took position in front of the protesters as they kept them back from the Howard Centre.

"Command-One," Captain Kingston remarked over the radio.

"Command-One," Captain Simpson replied.

"Command-One, we're in the process of tracing the hacker on campus, but our officer on scene needs access to the library building. Have your team create a way through for Hotel Two-Two-Three."

"Ten-Four."

Kaj stepped down and made his way over as Operational Planning Support began to close in on the protesters to get them to clear out. Some cannisters were shot from the police side that created a barrier of smoke, which triggered some of the protesters to haul Molotov cocktails at the police, which triggered a fight between the two sides. Kaj made this way through with his baton drawn to clear the way as he came to the shattered glass doors of the library. He went through the vestibule and entered into the lobby. Kaj stepped down some steps and came onto the terracotta carpet of the main floor of the library where there were some protesters who were grouped together and noticed Kaj enter.

"Beat the fascists!" an anarchist cried out, causing the other two to ensue on him with their makeshift weapons.

Kaj stepped back as an anarchist hurled a baseball bat at him and took his pepper spray to mace them. Another anarchist attempted to whack Kaj with a shovel, causing him to drop his pepper spray. Kaj stepped away as the anarchist kicked it out of the room, leaving him with his baton only. The other anarchist held a broken bottle in his hand. Kaj swerved out of the way of the shovel while the anarchist with the bottle hid behind him and the anarchist with the bat continued to cry out. Kaj stepped back and then took advantage of the weight of the shovel as it came down to step down on it to disarm the anarchist.

Kaj swung his baton at the anarchist with the bottle and hit him in the arm, causing him to instantly drop the bottle on the floor and cry out in pain. Kaj then struck him in the leg and threw him onto the floor while the last anarchist ran off. Once Kaj had subdued the anarchists, he looked around the darkened library to see where the computer laboratory could be if there was no sublevel. Kaj came around and entered a study space near the check-out desk where he saw various computers at the back. He couldn't see any of the computers to be on, so he looked around the rest of the floor until he found a closed door behind the library administrator space behind the check-out desk. Kaj swung the door open as he kicked through and entered into a database room.

Kaj drew his handgun before he entered the dark room and as he went through, a figure around the corner swung a chair at him, knocking back and onto the floor. The person, who Kaj saw to have worn a regular sweater and trousers, but with a bandana around his mouth, swung the chair down towards Kaj, which caused him to take his handgun, aim it back at him, and fire towards him. The person crouched in fear, allowing Kaj to stand up and take his baton out while word on the radio expressed the concern of shots fired from somewhere. Kaj put his handgun away and carried his baton as he looked at the person ahead of him, seeing through to him that it was Nathan, Kaj eyed him as he held the chair in his hands.

"I won't let you stop me," Nathan expressed, "you're out of time."

Kaj looked at his watch and noticed that he had less than ten minutes left.

"It's over, Neumann," Kaj replied. "You're going to jail."

"Wealth can buy a lot of things, I'm told. I won't be going anywhere, surely."

Kaj took the opportunity to rush towards Nathan and take control of the chair with one hand while he swung at him at his hip with the baton. Nathan relinquished control of the chair, allowing Kaj to pull it off and throw it aside before Nathan started to run off. Kaj quickly chased him down and tackled him onto the floor before he could turn the corner.

Nathan struggled, but Kaj gained control of him and put the handcuffs on him. Kaj then took him with him into the control room where he threw him onto the floor.

"You're too late," Nathan cried out, "all of the data is almost gone. There's nothing left."

"Shut up!" Kaj shouted as he went to the terminal and typed out the command.

I watched from the other side as I saw the scroll of text suddenly stop and let out a deep exhale as it was over.

"Did he do it?" Pomphrey questioned.

"Yeah, he did it," I replied, "it's done."

"Delta Three-Zero," Kaj remarked on his mic as he went back over to Nathan.

"Delta Three-Zero," Captain Kingston replied.

"Delta Three-Zero, I've stopped the program and salvaged whatever data remains. I've also apprehended our suspect in the investigation. I've got him Ten-Thirty-one ready for transport."

"Ten four, Hotel-Two-Two-Three. I'll send a car to pick up the suspect."

Kaj picked up Nathan and brought him onto his feet, saying to him, "Come on, you piece of shit."

"This isn't the end," Nathan remarked, "you think this is victory, but it's not…"

"If I were you, I'd shut the hell up," Kaj barked at him. "You're worse of a loud mouth than him, so use your right to remain silent and shut it."

Nathan begrudgingly kept quiet as Kaj brought him out of the library and towards a paddy wagon that had been brought over now that the protesters were cleared. He loaded him into the back and then met with Captain Kingston. Nathan would keep quiet and not even speak once to the police through the rest of their investigation, but it didn't matter since the deletion provided enough evidence to advance charges in what would make the headlines tomorrow as a shocking reveal that the co-founder of Neumann Corporation had been arrested on allegations of organized crime.

Meanwhile, while Kaj received his congratulations from Captain Kingston, I quickly deleted the conversation between me and Neumann, and decided that I wouldn't pass on the confession to them. I believed that they had enough evidence to proceed with charges and I had no place in their investigation other than where I already was. After Detective Pomphrey had thanked me, he turned his back to contact the captain to have detectives come down to haul the reels out of the room. I took that chance to insert the virus once more to finish my task and ensure that my client's secrets, whatever they may have been, were safe. I then decided that it was time for me to leave, which took the detective by surprise.

"I'm not sure if I can let you leave," Detective Pomphrey remarked, "are you sure you can't stay for a bit?"

"The job is done," I replied, "I helped you and there's nothing more for me here. I'd rather just go home."

Detective Pomphrey hesitated for a moment and then replied, "Alright, fine, I suppose that's true. You did us a great favor just now, and I guess that's twice now. You've got a real knack for this sort of thing – you should have joined the police department and been an investigator."

"I am an investigator," I replied, "just not for the police."

Detective Pomphrey didn't reply and I walked past him and simply left. I wouldn't say that I had stayed out of guilt that I had compromised their investigation nor the promise to Mr. Harrington, and I wasn't even sure if there would be enough data behind or know exactly what was deleted, but the virus worked to delete the client's files, so I assumed that the rogue virus may have missed the data entirely if not in portion. All in all, I had stayed because I had owed it to Kaj not to double-cross him – this was his investigation, and I would never do anything to rub against another investigator in his or her work. Detective Pomphrey didn't suspect that I had any foul play in the matter, and so I left, with the confession in my purse to burn when I got home, and so I began to walk away from the campus towards the west side where it was quieter.

I passed the residence that Blair Ericson had stayed in as I walked off, and I thought back to him who had escaped fifteen years ago. From what I had heard, Blair had disappeared from the face of the Earth, while at the same time, I had also heard that he was still alive, but taken on a new life as a Catholic and a new persona as a teacher at St. Augustine of Hippo. I never took the time to validate those facts. It was not mine to pursue him. I was not the police. It was not up to me to enforce the laws of the land, but only to provide a service to my customers, which I had completed. My allegiance was to nobody, and in my opinion, even someone like Blair deserved a second chance at life, so I was at peace to know that he was doing no harm, provided he wasn't teaching kids about *Negro* or other deposed novels with a crooked and subversive agenda in mind. I passed through the campus and walked downhill through the park peripheral to the campus and snuck back into Lincoln where I went to meet with Paul to debrief with him.

Once home, I retreated to my bedroom and sat down, looking at the confession in my purse which I would reference for my report to the client. I looked around and sighed as Bill jumped onto my bed and sniffed me. I put a hand on his head and gave a soft smile at him, but then lowered it as I sighed. There was much that was rotten about Harlech, and the years that had passed, I had stopped celebrating triumphs in major cases that were little less than assurance that I could eat and sleep in this shelter I called home. I couldn't help but feel the same, even since I had assisted the police and Kaj with an even larger case, because that was not my interest. I knew that Kaj would celebrate tonight with Captain Kingston and Detective Pomphrey, but I wouldn't, even alone. Yes, we had unraveled the son of Hamon Neumann just as fifteen years ago we had done the same with him, but that didn't change the fact of what Neumann had said in which many alike him were all around the city, partaking in the act of subversion and engaging in the process of demoralization of the public to see through their wishes. In other words, the battle had been won, but it seemed to me as if the war was far from being won, and this war was not one that I fancied to fight in, but I knew would be the one Kaj would pursue – his game, and for that reason, I frowned out of fright for him and would continue to keep myself to myself, even if he would expand and take on the world as they would surely promote him.

This conclusion was what I took from this case, where fifteen years ago, I celebrated with Kaj, I now feared for him in my home at the end of a similar incident. All I could was hope that in the last fifteen years, he had truly changed and not allow for the mistakes of the past to repeat itself, or for vices of old to resurface, but to allow the virtue of his and his deep love for others, to help others, and be a knight that protects others in this hellish city that he was all too familiar to. Yes, the battle had been won, but this victory would be the first of many to come for Kaj as he presented himself on the battlefield and demonstrated himself capable to Harlech Police Department, whose own core, rotted from the inside and was not a safe haven, because malice was everywhere, and just as it can take hold of a police department, so can it take hold of even him as he had now risen up to the challenge, inserted himself into the game, and positioned himself to the wit of the demons for a fall if he didn't keep himself in check at these times. To him, at this time, I recall that I all I could wish to say was simply, 'Best of luck to you, Kaj.'

www.ingramcontent.com/pod-product-compliance
Lightning Source LLC
Chambersburg PA
CBHW070634180626
46817CB00006B/2122